OTHER BOOKS BY
RACHEL ANN NUNES

HUNTINGTON FAMILY
Winter Fire
No Longer Strangers
Chasing Yesterday
By Morning Light

ARIANA SERIES
Ariana: The Making of a Queen
Ariana: A Gift Most Precious
Ariana: A New Beginning
Ariana: A Glimpse of Eternity
This Time Forever
Ties That Bind
Twice in a Lifetime

ROMANTIC SUSPENSE
A Bid for Love
(originally entitled *Love to the Highest Bidder*)
Framed for Love
Love on the Run

OTHER NOVELS
A Greater Love
To Love and to Promise
Tomorrow and Always
Bridge to Forever
This Very Moment
A Heartbeat Away
Where I Belong
In Your Place
The Independence Club

PICTURE BOOKS
Daughter of a King
The Secret of the King

FLYING HOME

RACHEL ANN NUNES

SHADOW
MOUNTAIN

This is a work of fiction. Characters and events in this book are products of the author's imagination or are represented fictitiously.

Library of Congress Cataloging-in-Publication Data
Nunes, Rachel Ann, 1966-
  Flying home / Rachel Ann Nunes.
    p. cm.
  ISBN 978-1-59038-798-6 (pbk.)
  1. Orphans—Fiction. 2. Adult children—Fiction. 3. India—Fiction.
4. Identity (Philosophical concept)—Fiction. I. Title.
  PS3564.U468F59 2007
  813'.54—dc22   2007025621

Printed in the United States of America
Publishers Printing, Salt Lake City, UT

10   9   8   7   6   5   4   3   2   1

To my sister Mary Liechty,
who is always there when I really need her—
just like a sister should be. I love you!

ACKNOWLEDGMENTS

Thanks to Jana Erickson for the suggestions that made this book better and to Suzanne Brady for her editing. This novel wouldn't be what it is without the help of these two talented women. I also acknowledge all the others at Shadow Mountain for the efforts they have made in typesetting, design, and promotion. You are a great team, and I enjoy working with you.

Additional appreciation goes to Tami Bradley for showing me Nevada. Your generosity and kindness knows no bound. I'm further indebted to Kellie and Brad Nielson for sharing their experiences in Ukraine. Finally, thanks to my husband, TJ, whose love and support makes it possible for me to follow my dream.

PROLOGUE

Saturday, August 29, 1981

Unalterable and unforgiving as a gaping hole in a cemetery, the event would forever after stand out in memory. There was nothing out of the ordinary to signal its coming. The pans sat on the immaculate stove as they always did each afternoon in preparation for dinner, their empty interiors open, ready, beckoning. Sounds from the television floated in from the adjoining family room. Somewhere outside a dog barked, and a horn honked as a car passed the house.

Clarissa Winn set out the vegetables. Steamed broccoli florets with sliced carrots would go nicely with the meatballs and spaghetti. She picked up a knife.

The shrill of the kitchen phone broke through the sounds of the television. Clarissa looked up from the broccoli and reluctantly reached for the phone, hoping it wasn't someone from the PTA asking her to take on another project, or the pastor needing a pianist for services the next day.

"Hello?" she asked, tucking the phone between her ear and neck. If it was one of her friends, she'd get a start on cutting the vegetables while they talked.

"Is this Mrs. Clarissa Winn?" a man asked, his rich, melodic voice boasting a distinct British accent that made her think of exotic places to which she had never traveled.

"Yes, I'm Clarissa Winn."

"My name is Dr. Mehul Raji. I am calling from Calcutta, India, from Charity Medical Hospital. It is about your sister."

"My sister?" Clarissa's grip tightened on the knife in her hand. *Sister.* She hadn't heard the word in relation to herself for far too long. "You mean Karyn?"

"Yes, Karyn Olsen Schrader."

"Has something happened?" The words hurt Clarissa's throat.

"Indeed. It is with great regret that I must inform you of the death of your sister and that of her husband, Dr. Guenter Schrader. They were killed in a plane accident last Saturday as they traveled to give medical care to the inhabitants of several remote villages here in India." The words were measured and exact, but now the doctor's British English was heavily accented with whatever language he called his own. "Please accept my heartfelt condolences. Both Karyn and Guenter were valuable members of our staff and will be deeply missed."

Clarissa's eyes filled with tears. *My sister is dead.*

The hand with the knife shook. Her reflection in the shiny surface of her four-quart saucepan was distorted—as distorted as her soul.

The television blared. Outside came the happy ringing of the ice-cream truck. Life as usual.

"I would have called you sooner," Dr. Raji continued, "but

only today did we find your number in a box of Karyn's belongings. I am happy to be able to reach you."

Clarissa barely heard his voice. *Karyn is dead.* The words came with a furious pounding of her heart. Still, she gripped the knife, poised over the broccoli, her hand turning white.

"I wish to know what instructions you have for me regarding their four-year-old daughter, as you appear to be her only living relative."

Suddenly Clarissa was listening again. So Karyn had given birth to the daughter she'd longed for. "Is she okay?"

"She is unhurt, but there is concern. She has not spoken to anyone since the accident. At the moment, she is in the care of a woman in whose house Dr. and Mrs. Schrader were living, but we expect that you will want her sent to America. Is this not correct?"

Sobs pierced Clarissa's awareness—bitter cries that hurt her to hear. She tried to answer the doctor, but words refused to come.

Karyn is dead.

Her husband's arms came from behind, wrapping around her body. "What's wrong, honey?"

Only then did she realize that the bitter crying was coming from her own throat. She swallowed her sobs with an agony that threatened suffocation. The knife moved in her hand.

Travis reached for it, rubbing the flesh and loosening her grip before taking the knife. "Give me the phone," he said softly.

Clarissa watched as he talked with the doctor from India, her own disbelief and shock mirrored in his dark eyes. Finding a pen in the drawer, he wrote down a number. Then he set the phone on the cradle.

"It's my fault," Clarissa moaned. And it was—as surely as if she had forced Karyn onto the plane that would eventually crash.

"No, it's not. It's not anyone's fault."

"It is."

He sighed. "If it's yours, then it's mine, too."

She shook her head. "No, no. Mine. I'm her sister." *Was,* her mind corrected. *She* was *my sister.*

Travis put his arms around her. She gazed up at his familiar, dearly loved features, stared into the eyes she would never have known had it not been for Karyn, the sister she had betrayed. *Oh, dear God—how did I let this happen?* There was no chance for making amends now.

"Her daughter," she said aloud. "What about that poor little girl?"

"She'll come here, of course."

She nodded. "We'll raise her as our own."

An unexpected—unwanted—surge of joy welled within Clarissa's breast. Only fleetingly did she consider that someday they would have to tell Karyn's daughter the truth.

CHAPTER

1

L iana Winn's fingers flew over her calculator, making
long tallies of numbers that spewed onto a long curl of
white paper. She hated working on this account for
more reasons than one. Wealthy Jim Forrester, the obscenely
young owner of a computer consulting firm, didn't exactly
cheat on his taxes, but there were many points she felt
stretched the realm of belief: vacations in Hawaii, elaborate gifts
for clients, deluxe hotel rooms with heart-shaped bathtubs.

After two years of doing Forrester's taxes and avoiding his
blatant advances, Liana had tried to refuse being assigned to his
case. But he was Klassy Accounting's most important client,
and when he had requested her personally, her boss made it
clear she had no choice but to accept.

"You about done with the Forrester case, Liana?"

Liana's fingers stiffened over her calculator as she looked
up into the small watery eyes of Larry Koplin, her boss. He was
a tall, balding, barrel-chested man who wore tailored suits and

who might have been commanding if not for his swollen cheeks, thin shoulders, and scrawny limbs.

"Nearly, Mr. Koplin," she said, keeping her voice calm. "I'm just finishing a few numbers. Once I put them into the computer, I'll be finished."

Koplin's pale face darkened with a brief frown, which Liana knew was because he had invited her time and time again to call him Larry instead of Mr. Koplin. Liana had tried, briefly, half-heartedly, but the time when he had inspired friendship was long past.

"Good." He twisted his thin, too-long fingers, as though washing them. "I knew you'd be done soon. I told him to come over in an hour. He'd like to take you to lunch."

Distaste rolled through Liana, but she was careful not to show it. "Thank you, Mr. Koplin, but I won't be able to go. I need to finish at least two more accounts before I leave tonight."

Koplin's smile did not reach his watery eyes. "Nonsense, a girl has to eat."

Liana stifled a sharp retort that would have detailed her *womanly* capability of buying her own meal. She had learned to do at least that in her nearly thirty years of life, thank you very much. Instead, she said, "I think we promised Jones and Dean that their accounts would be finished by morning, didn't we? Lunch with Forrester could take hours."

She watched contrasting emotions battle in Larry Koplin's puffy face as he pitted the money he would receive from those accounts against the points he would earn if he could coerce her to have lunch with Forrester. Liana remembered a time when she had believed in him—a time when his smile and a promise of a bright future had drawn her away from her previous job. It was an offer he still touted, but Liana had discovered that his "bright future" meant this minuscule office and nothing more.

Koplin's greed for money won out. "I'll tell Mr. Forrester you can't possibly get away now. Just see that you finish those accounts."

Liana felt the sudden urge to quit right that instant, to turn her back and walk out, just to see him scramble for a replacement. Maybe then he would recognize the four years of hard work that had earned her this pitiful closet she called an office—an office she now despised. But she had bills to pay, which her monthly paycheck barely covered, so she had no choice but to swallow her anger. "I will, Mr. Koplin."

He nodded sharply, causing the loose skin under his chin to wobble, and turned on feet that seemed small for his towering height and protruding chest. As he walked down the aisle between the gray cubicles, he was followed by surreptitious stares from his employees. One of the nearest women, a new employee named Jocelyn, cast Liana a sympathetic glance through the door, and Liana smiled politely before returning to her work. The anger gradually faded as she put the incident aside. She would not allow anything to affect her work or her state of mind. She was in control. Anything else was unacceptable.

When the phone rang, she reached for it, eyes glued to her computer screen. "Liana Winn," she said. Tilting her head to support the phone, she continued entering numbers. Earlier in the day, she'd hoped to finished work early, but that hope was fading fast.

"Hi, it's me."

She smiled despite her dark mood. Her brother's voice was always a welcome sound. "Hi, Christian. What's up?"

"Actually, I need a favor."

"Ha, what else is new?" She rolled her eyes. He was forty, and she was still bailing him out of one thing or another.

"Well, a friend of mine has to get a bit of tax work done—pronto."

"Sorry." The phone pressed hard between her ear and shoulder, and already her neck was beginning to ache from the awkward position. "I'd like to help your friend, but I can't. Maybe next month, after the fifteenth."

Her brother wasn't having any of it. His voice took on a pleading note, one she always found difficult to ignore. "Oh, Liana, come on. The company he works for is a client of mine. If I lose that account, my boss will *kill* me."

Through the open door of her tiny office Liana could see a buzz of activity in the cubicles where she had worked until her promotion a few months earlier. Fingers typed at keyboards, creating an unlikely symphony that hummed evenly on the air. There were voices, too, but lower, almost covered by the incessant tapping. Ringing phones added shrillness to the din. March was one of the accounting firm's busiest times of the year, surpassed only by the madness that consumed the first half of April.

She willed herself to be strong. "If this guy changes advertising firms because I can't work him in, then he's no friend of yours."

"It's his company I need to impress, not him, and that means if they need a favor, I deliver. This accounting thing really isn't even Austin's department. He got stuck with it because of me."

Not again! She stifled a sigh. "And how on earth did *that* happen?"

"Well, I was in this meeting yesterday, and they were

discussing my new advertising design—which they seemed to like, by the way."

"Christian," she groaned.

"Okay, okay. So they started in about how their financial manager had run off on them and how the new one—the owner's nephew or something—can't start until he finishes college next month. Bottom line, they're in a big bind and need help quick if they want to avoid paying more penalties. Next thing I know, my mouth opens all on its own, and I'm telling them I know someone."

"Know someone? Who do you think you are—the Mafia?"

He gave a short laugh. "Come on, will you just meet with him? If it's too much work maybe you could file another extension. Pleeeeease? His office is just outside Vegas, only a couple of miles away from yours. It's a quarterly thing, I think, so it can't be too big, can it?"

Liana sighed. Christian had no idea how difficult quarterly filings could be. He was a genius at dreaming up creative advertisements, but numbers escaped him completely. "Depends on the size of the company. Can't your friend come in and meet with my boss? Maybe someone else could work him in here."

"Can't see that happening. Austin would never trust a company with a corny name like Klassy Accounting." Christian's voice rose in mimic of the commercials that were being run on the radio. "Klassy Accounting—no job too big or too small." He snorted. "No offense, but it's true. Please, Liana Banana? What do you say? Do it for me?"

The use of her childhood nickname made it more difficult to deny his request. "Let me think a moment," she said, raking her hand through the long strands of her dark hair. If she skipped her twenty-minute lunch down at the corner deli—

again—and didn't take her afternoon break, she might be able to finish work by seven or so, and that would leave enough time to see Christian's friend. Even as she thought this, the strong aroma of a TV dinner, coming from the small alcove that lamely served as an employee break room, wended its way into her office, making her stomach ache with emptiness.

"Okay, okay," she agreed with resignation. "I'll take a look. But you'll have to pick me up and stop at McDonald's or somewhere on the way so I can eat as you drive. I'm famished."

"Deal. You won't regret this, Banana. I love you."

"Hmm." She hung up the phone.

Daylight was already beginning to fade as Liana exited the front door of her building. Outside, she found Christian parked in a no-parking fire zone, lounging against his green BMW, a car he was still paying for and would be for at least another three years. He greeted her with a wave and a grin that always made people feel he shared their secrets. "I got you Chinese," he said as he opened the passenger side door for her. "I know how you love it."

"I *enjoy* it." She slid into the car.

Christian rolled his eyes. "Oh yeah, I forgot. You don't love anything . . . or anyone, right? Except for me." Grinning, he placed his hands on his khaki dress pants and leaned down until his eyes were even with hers. "Come on, tell me you love me. Tell me I'm your favorite brother. Why don't you ever say it?" They both knew he was teasing, and yet there was an undercurrent of sincerity to his plea. To him things like saying "I love you" made a difference, but Liana knew that saying so only set a person up for loss.

She snorted in annoyance and pulled her door shut. Her brother barely had time to jump out of the way. "Hey!" He slapped the side of the car, but lightly so there was no chance of damaging the finish.

She watched him saunter around to the driver's side. Handsome by any standard, Christian had dark, laughing eyes and longish brown hair combed back from his square face. He was fun-loving, adventuresome, generous—and completely irresponsible. Though Liana was more than ten years his junior, she often lent him money, patted his back when his relationships didn't work out, and handled all his finances. He joked that he'd never marry until he found someone just like her. What he didn't seem to realize was that someone like her was unable to maintain a stable romantic relationship.

"Be careful of the seats," Christian warned, sliding behind the wheel. "Leather and Chinese don't mix."

"I know, I know."

As Christian drove through Las Vegas, Liana ate her Chinese food with the plastic fork provided. He'd bought her favorite, curry chicken, but had ordered fried rice instead of regular white. She closed the rice carton with distaste and opened the chicken, careful not to spill it on her black suit or Christian's precious leather seats. Her stomach rumbled in anticipation, even as the spicy flavors brought her mouth to life.

Weaving through the post rush-hour traffic, Christian babbled about his job, a girl at work that he was thinking about asking out, and how much it had cost to repair a scratch in the paint on his car. There was no pattern to his speech, and he punctuated his stories with unexpected exclamations. His voice was a welcome relief from the monotonous sounds at the office.

Sometimes the continuous tapping at work was more than

Liana could endure, and she had to envision herself elsewhere to survive the day. When she'd first started in the cubicles, her daydream had been a quiet beach with nothing but the occasional cry of the seagulls to interrupt her peace. Then two summers earlier she had taken a vacation to Catalina Island in California, where the beaches had been filled with boisterous people and the constant roar of the waves hurling themselves up the beach. After a while, the rise and fall of the white-crested waves had been as bad for her as the tapping on the keyboards—too much rush and hurry. She'd gone home disappointed and had begun to dream of a remote cabin in the mountains.

Last summer she had stayed in her brother Bret's cozy new cabin in the mountains of Utah. She wanted to hike over the soft, fragrant layers of pine needles and escape Nevada's penetrating heat. It had been wonderful—at first. Then at night the wind singing through the trees became a constant sound, somehow hauntingly familiar, as though someone had only muffled the tapping from the keyboards. After three sleepless nights, she went home early, resigning herself to never escaping the cacophony of the accounting office. From that time on, she'd hated her job.

"Here we are," Christian said, all too soon.

Swallowing a bite of chicken, Liana gazed at the new three-story building liberally dotted with impressive windows. Large gold lettering on the front window next to the double glass doors spelled out *Goodman Electronics*. "What did you say the company does?"

"They sell televisions, DVD players, that sort of thing. Austin also runs a charity organization to help orphans in Ukraine. His grandmother started it. But that doesn't have anything to do with his job here."

"Well, I hope they're not too big." The larger the company, the more work she would be in for.

Setting aside the remains of her chicken, Liana grabbed her black briefcase, climbed from the car, and walked with Christian to the doors. Almost immediately, a buzzer sounded and they were let inside.

Behind the wide, room-length reception desk sat a lean man dressed in a dark business suit. He was tilted back in the chair with his hands behind his head and his feet on the desk. His eyes were fixed on the monitor in front of him, as if nothing could tear him away. Black hair covered his head, the corners arching high in the front—a sign of intelligence, her father used to say—and the tanned, chiseled face already sported a five o'clock shadow.

He moved as they approached, languidly pulling down his arms and coming to his feet. He was tall—at least a head taller than Liana. His eyes stayed on the screen a few seconds longer, and Liana wished she could catch a glimpse of what so fascinated him. Then his face turned in their direction, his welcoming smile echoed by a friendly gleam in his black eyes.

Individually, his features weren't anything to speak of—his nose was too large, his chin too wide, the forehead too high—but taken all together he was positively the most arresting man she had ever seen. Liana didn't know if it was because his eyes were the color of midnight or if it was the way he looked at her. Certainly he wasn't the most handsome man she'd met. Take Jim Forrester, for example. That man had the blond good looks of a surfing king, though his merits were decidedly spoiled by his certainty of his beauty—not to mention the existence of a Mrs. Forrester. Liana never allowed good looks to impress her.

"Austin, this is my sister, Liana Winn," Christian said. "Liana, this is Austin Walker."

He walked around the desk, offering his hand. She looked up into his face and murmured something, schooling herself to show nothing of her momentary admiration.

Austin's eyes didn't leave hers. "Are you the wonder woman who's going to free me from this accounting mess?" His voice was low and rich, with a hint of familiarity that made her uncomfortable.

"That depends." She averted her eyes from his stare. "Where are the papers so I can get started?"

The smile on Austin's face faltered but steadied almost immediately. "Right this way." He took an ID card hanging from his waist on a thin retractable elastic cord and swiped it through a metal reader near the door next to the reception desk. "Through here." He held the door open for them.

As Liana passed, she caught a whiff of Austin's cologne, or perhaps it was only fabric softener someone had used on his white button-down shirt. The scent reminded her of hiking outside Bret's cabin—a slight fragrance of pine mixed with the freshness of a mountain breeze. The scent was gone almost before she could identify it. She slipped past, felt his gaze boring into her back, and wondered why he so disturbed her.

It's not just him, came an unbidden thought. She remembered Jim Forrester and Mr. Koplin. They were only a few in a long line of men that made her feel uncomfortable. Truth be told, the only men who didn't make her nervous were her brothers, Christian and Bret. Liana forced the thoughts away and continued down the hall. Men were irrelevant. She didn't need anyone. No, not even Christian, who had called her Liana from her first day in America—instead of Lara, the legal name she detested. Not even Christian, who had held her shaking body while she sobbed for her mother during those first weeks and months after the plane accident, and who had eased her hunger with ice cream stolen from the freezer in the middle of the night when she had been too upset to eat her dinner. Not even Christian, who had promised never to leave her—a promise she couldn't bear to elicit from his parents, the aunt and uncle who had adopted her. If she kept telling herself she didn't need him—or any of them—it might become true.

"It's that one over there." Austin slipped around them and opened another door with a swipe of his card.

The accountant's office was dim, lit only by the darkening light coming through the wide, unshuttered windows. Austin flipped on the overhead lights, and the room sprang from the shadows. To one side sat a nice oak desk, and beyond the desk, tall oak filing cabinets lined one wall. A high oak bookcase bordered the opposite wall, and a narrow table held a vase of flowers. But the most obvious piece of furniture was a small round plastic table in the middle of the room, standing awkwardly alone, unattached to any chair and of notably different quality from the rest of the furniture.

"Everything should be here on the table," Austin said. "I had a secretary make hard copies of everything and do the best she could to organize it."

Liana grimaced at the mounds of papers and files lying on the small table. Though neatly organized, the stacks were also thick and numerous. Generally, she preferred to leave everything on the computer until the final go-through. Everything except her tallies of numbers. Those she liked to have on tangible paper—either on her adding machine or, in the old-fashioned way, with pencil and pad.

"I know it looks like a lot," Austin said. "But I can help. I'm good with numbers. I'm just not sure what to file or when."

Carefully, Liana set her briefcase on top of one of the stacks.

She looked around the room and spotted a chair behind the desk. Thankfully, it was padded.

"There's a chair." Austin started for it at the same time she did.

"I can do it."

Their hands touched on the back of the chair, and Liana pulled away hard. The chair shot from the horseshoe desk toward the table, banging into it. "Wheels. What a nice invention," she said, not meeting Austin's gaze. She felt like an idiot.

Ignoring the men's polite chuckling, she sat down to work. After a while Christian and Austin started whispering, breaking her concentration. "Isn't there somewhere you two can go for about forty minutes?" she asked.

"Uh, yeah." Austin motioned Christian to the door. "We have an employee lounge where we can catch a little TV. And I should check my e-mail. Are you sure you'll be okay?"

"Don't worry about me. I'm only stealing your company secrets." Her eyes returned to the papers.

Austin hesitated, but Christian pulled him away. "She's joking."

"Of course she is."

Liana didn't look up until they left. Though she was alone in the room, she still felt Austin's midnight eyes upon her.

Austin led Christian once more down the deserted hallway. "You didn't tell me your sister was so . . ." Austin hesitated, searching for words that wouldn't offend his friend.

"Beautiful?" Christian supplied.

"Well, she is attractive." When Austin had first caught sight of her in the surveillance monitor, he was stunned at her appearance. She was a slender woman who walked with an undeniable assurance, a woman confident in her own skin. Her medium brown hair should have been ordinary, but it was thick and wavy, nearly long enough for her to sit on. Her face was gently heart-shaped, with prominent cheek bones and smooth, soft-looking skin. The formfitting black suit she wore emphasized slender curves and contrasted with her large eyes, the color of a clear morning sky.

He had been reluctant to look away from the monitor to greet them, knowing that surely the reality would never live up to the image on his screen. The perfect woman. Such a woman might make the perfect American family a believable concept. And he didn't believe.

In person she was exactly like the image on the monitor—except that as she greeted him, her face became hard, all traces of warmth locked away from view. She was still beautiful but in a cold, corpse-like way that Austin associated with old movie actresses who had already lived out their youth and now waited only to die.

He was accustomed to admiring glances from women, or at the very least, offers of friendship, but not even a glimmer of interest sparked in Liana Winn's eyes. From her first glance she made it clear that she did not care about him as a person; she was here only as a favor to her brother. Under her cool stare and crisp acknowledgment, Austin knew an awkwardness that had not been his since junior high school.

"Ah, here we are," Austin said. They had arrived at the employee lounge. The room featured three beige leather couches grouped in front of a huge plasma screen, the company's latest best-seller of which Austin was particularly proud.

Christian made an exclamation of approval and immediately sank into one of the couches, remote in hand. But he didn't turn on the television. "About my sister . . ."

Austin sat on the other end of the couch and waited. He realized he'd been quiet far too long in the hall and that Christian had correctly interpreted his silence. "It was good of her to come."

Christian seemed to be struggling with what he wanted—or didn't want—to say. He shook his head. "Truthfully, she didn't want to, but I'm her favorite brother." He grinned.

"Hey, I'm my sister's *only* brother," Austin said. "At least your sister has a choice."

Christian's grin faded. "Actually, a lot of her choices were forced on her. She's had a hard life. That's why she can sometimes be . . . rather distant. But I promise you, she's as good with numbers as I am with designs."

A silence fell between them, and Austin figured Christian was as much at a loss for words as he was. But Austin was also curious. During the five months they'd known each other, Christian hadn't talked much about his family, and now after meeting Liana . . . well, she was a mystery that intrigued him.

"That reminds me," Austin said into the awkwardness. "The board approved your designs for our magazine campaign this morning."

Christian propped his foot on the wide coffee table. "I knew they were good." In another man Austin might have considered this response arrogant, but Christian was simply Christian. He was as willing to admit when his ideas stank as when they were brilliant.

Christian pointed the remote at the television, and the screen flared to life. For a long while they watched in silence, but Austin couldn't focus on the lawyer show that played out before them. His thoughts were on the woman sitting alone in another room at a round plastic table filled with papers.

"So what happened?" he asked finally, unable to stop the words that insisted on tumbling from his mouth. "Did she break up with her boyfriend? Lose her job?"

Christian pulled his gaze from the television. "I think she was a policeman once and—"

"No, not the show. I mean your sister. You said she had a hard life."

Christian's expression became pained. With a flick of his wrist, he muted the sound. "I was afraid this would happen.

Austin, I consider you a friend, and I love my sister, but believe me, you don't want to get involved."

"I'm not involved. I'm just curious."

Christian sighed. "Well, I guess it won't hurt to tell you a little. She does hate her job—her boss is a real jerk—but that's not what makes her. . . ." He shook his head. "Anyway, what I meant by a hard life is that her parents died when she was only four."

"Parents?" Austin was mortified at his own ignorance. "We've played racquetball every week for four months. You never said your parents were—hey, wait a minute, didn't you mention having dinner with your parents this Sunday? For your mother's birthday, I think it was."

"That's *my* mother. Liana's real parents were my aunt and uncle. Lived in India, of all places. I never even met them. Apparently, there was some bad blood between my mother and my aunt—they didn't talk for years—but we adopted Liana when they died. It was really hard on her. She didn't talk for almost a whole year after she came to us, except to tell us to call her Liana." Christian's unfocused eyes stared into the air near Austin's right ear. He was obviously reliving the past. "Wasn't even her name," he added softly, shaking his head. "Just a nickname she'd picked up. It was really sad."

Austin felt terrible. He had pried where he shouldn't have pried. Sorrow welled up inside him as it always did lately when he heard about someone dying. His grandmother's death last year had left a wound that still felt fresh, but he couldn't begin to imagine the sorrow Liana had experienced at such a young age.

"Sorry," he muttered, staring at the muted television set.

"It's okay. Really. I'm glad she came to live with us. I don't know what I'd do without her. She's always stepping in to help me. I just wish I could do more for her."

Austin nodded but remained silent—though a dozen more questions sprang to his mind. He was relieved when Christian turned up the volume of the TV, making it impossible for them to talk comfortably.

After a few more minutes, Austin stood and removed a couple of sodas from the corner refrigerator. He tossed one to Christian. "Uh, if you don't mind," he said, raising his voice so it could be heard over the television, "I'll run up to my office and check my e-mail there. Won't be but a few minutes." He thumbed over his shoulder at the door.

"Sure. I'm comfortable here." Christian unscrewed the cap on his bottle.

"Should I look in on your sister, do you think?"

Christian checked his watch. "It's only been fifteen minutes. She'd just be annoyed."

"Okay. I'll be back in a few."

"Take your time." Christian's eyes had already returned to the television, his drink halfway to his mouth.

Austin went up to his third-story office that smelled of furniture polish and air freshener. Obviously the cleaning crew had hit his office while he'd been out. He entered the space between his double-sided oak desk and sat in the black leather chair. A few clicks of his computer brought up his e-mail. The third message was from his charity's main employee in Ukraine, and he read it while another fifty messages were downloading.

Dear Mr. Walker:

I'm e-mailing you to confirm that we did receive the ship-ment you sent. I went myself to assure that it was dispersed to the orphanages. Much thanks was given to me, and this I now pass on to you.

I also want to give you thanks for letting me work for you. The directors are most helpful to my dilemma now, and I hope to be finding documents about my sister soon. Even if it was not to one of these orphanages that she went, other orphanages will now treat me with respect because of the incentives I can give them. You have been very generous with me.

It is my deepest hope that my sister was adopted by a nice Ukrainian family, since foreign adoptions were not allowed at that time. I pray she is still alive. Although my little Sveta was healthy when we left her at the baby orphanage, I cannot be sure that she did not become ill later or develop a disease. Perhaps that is why she was transferred to a different facility. I wish I was knowing exactly when it was that we left her at the orphanage. I think I was fourteen or fifteen, but it may have been earlier or later. I remember only that it was very cold and snowy outside. I remember how she clung to my neck and how my tears fell onto her cheeks.

I am sorry to burden you with these concerns. However, you have been so helpful and kind, I feel you will not mind. I am hoping my English is improving enough with the tapes you gave to me last year so when you come again to visit, we can converse more better. I will take you to see more of my country.

Sincerely yours,
Olya Kovalevsky

Austin could almost see her in his mind as he read her e-mail. Short Olya, with her close-cropped brown hair, light blue eyes, pinched face, and too-thin body. Every time he had seen her during his last visit to Ukraine, she had worn bright lipstick and eyeshadow, as if to hide the sharp curves of nose, cheek, and chin.

During their hours working together Austin had learned about Olya's missing sister, and the story had interested him deeply. Olya had been a young girl when her mother had given birth to a baby. Eventually, the burden became too much for the family, and they were forced to give the child to an orphanage. When Olya returned years later to find her sister, she learned the baby had been transferred to another orphanage, which had burned to the ground. Most of the records were lost. Olya had not yet determined where her sister had been sent after that, but she still clung to the hope of finding her.

"I have to know what happened," she had said simply, her eyes speaking volumes of hurt that she would not voice—maybe could not voice.

He had questioned her no further, not wishing to add to her wounds. But he wondered why she felt such a strong drive to find her sister when she had not been responsible for the decision to leave her. He also wondered how it had happened that Olya herself had not been given to an orphanage but stayed with her mother long enough to know and love a little sister. How had it felt to watch her sister go into the arms of a stranger? How had it felt for her to know that if the ages had been reversed, she would have been the one cast aside? These were questions he dared not ask. Perhaps they were ones no one ever asked but kept in silence, as though doing so would stave off the pain.

Austin knew pain. He knew the rejection of a father who drowned his failures in a bottle and rained his frustration down on his only son. Words had become swords, piercing the fragile shell of his young self, a shell that had necessarily grown tougher over the years. Sometimes he would still lie awake in the night and wonder why his mother had not defended him or at least whispered positive words to him about his worth. Why had she stayed with his father? Why had she allowed him to treat her and their children that way?

These were also questions he could not ask—then or now. Instead, he had asked others: Why was the sky blue? Why did dew wet the grass each morning? Why did babies spit up so much? Why did they hiccup? Why was the mail sometimes late? What made it snow? His mother, too exhausted for life itself, had been unable to respond.

On the surface they were the poster family for the American dream. A sizable Wyoming farm, a small home, a car, two children, a dog—what more could a man want? Yet Austin's father wanted more—a lot more—and having repeatedly failed, he could not find the courage to adjust his dreams or learn to make happiness in whatever circumstances he found himself. He had failed to see the important things, like a son who yearned for his approval, a daughter who planned to escape his abuse by leaving the farm she loved, or a wife who trembled at his every mood shift. No, he had seen none of it, not even when it was far too late.

Austin's grandmother, his mother's mother, had been his salvation. She had encouraged his insatiable curiosity, valued his opinions, and in the end had given him the confidence he needed to break free of the emotional death grip his father had on him. One thing she had not been able to do, however, was to rid him of the guilt he felt about his mother; just as his mother had not been capable of protecting him, he had not been able to save her.

Pulling his mind from these troublesome thoughts, Austin

read a few more e-mails and shot off responses to the most urgent. Then he retraced his steps to the employee lounge. The show was just ending.

Christian stretched and stifled a yawn. "If we had a place like this at work, I might never actually work again." He winked to show he was kidding.

Arriving at the office where they'd left Liana, they found her bent over the round table, her long hair spilling over her shoulders and fanning out on the back of the chair. She didn't look up as they entered but remained concentrated on the documents before her. One hand made furious notes with a pencil, while the other was fisted in her hair, gripping the strands near the scalp. Her high heels were off, a foot tucked up under her lithe body.

"How's it going?" Christian asked.

She started slightly and then looked up at her brother and smiled, all the earlier hardness gone. Austin's heart fell to his stomach.

Her gaze moved to Austin. "It's doable in my time off work—barely," she said, rising to her feet. "But only if you're as handy with numbers as you claim. It would be a lot easier if you had a decent accounting program instead of the one you use." She waved at the papers. "Most of this could be automated better. Your company's far too large to use your current system."

Austin was impressed with her assessment. "That's exactly what the owner's nephew said. He plans to reorganize everything when he starts working here."

"It'll take a lot of time, but it'll be worth it. Meanwhile, there are still some records I'll need—two to begin with: a list of nonretail sales, if you had any, and a verification of monies paid out in employee salaries, bonuses, and so forth. I'll let you

25

know if there's anything else." She handed him several papers. "You can start with these. Of course, if they're already on your computer system, they'll be easier to calculate."

"You want to start now?" For the past thirty minutes, the sides of Austin's stomach had been glued together with hunger. He hadn't imagined they would begin the project tonight, only to assess it.

She shrugged. "We should get started if you want to avoid some pretty hefty fines."

"Okay. I just need to make a quick phone call." He picked up the phone on the desk and punched in the number for Chinese delivery.

Christian raised his hands to chest level as he backed toward the door. "Well, if you two have it under control, I guess I'll take off. Austin, walk me out?"

"Go," Liana said, making a shooing motion. "But you owe me."

Austin held the phone to his ear. "No, *I* owe you. We'll pay you whatever you ask, of course."

A wry smile twisted her lips. "Don't worry. You'll get a bill." For an instant their eyes met and held. Austin found himself trying to remember what he had been doing.

"Lee's Chinese," chimed a melodic voice in his ear.

"Oh," he said. "I'll have an order of cashew chicken with rice. Plain, not fried." He shot a questioning glance at Liana, covering the receiver. "Want anything? It's on me." She shook her head. Shrugging, he gave the man on the phone the address and promised to be waiting at the front door.

When he hung up the phone, he found Liana watching him. "Plain rice, huh?" she asked. There was a flicker of something in her eyes, something Austin couldn't interpret. But just as suddenly it was gone.

"Come on." He motioned to Christian. "I'll let you out of the building."

With a wave at his sister, Christian followed him from the room. "That reminds me," Christian said in the hall, "Liana will need a ride back to her office for her car."

"Not a problem."

"Don't keep her too late. During this season, she goes to work like at five or earlier."

Austin grimaced; few conditions could get him up at five. He definitely was not a morning person. Not since he'd left the farm. "Okay. I'll try. And thanks, Christian."

"You're welcome." Christian paused at the entrance, looking uncharacteristically nervous. He ran a hand through his hair. "Hey, don't mention to Liana what I told you, huh? About her parents. She's a very private person."

Austin slapped him on the back. "I certainly won't bring it up, if she doesn't."

Yet even as he watched Christian drive away, he wished he knew more. Why hadn't Christian's and Liana's mothers been close? Why had Liana insisted on a name change at the tender age of four? How had it felt going to live with complete strangers? These were, he knew, more questions that might not have answers—or at least answers anyone would care to share.

Maybe his mother had been right after all; he did ask too many questions. Still, it was too bad there wasn't someone who knew the whole story. If he were in Liana's shoes, it would drive him crazy not knowing. Maybe once he knew her better—if she let such a thing happen—he'd ask her how she felt about it.

He waited at the front door until his food arrived, feeling guilty about leaving Liana to work alone. As he walked back to the accounting office, he wondered if she liked plain white rice.

CHAPTER
3

Diary of Karyn Olsen
Monday, January 7, 1966

I met a guy today, a really gorgeous guy—in the campus cafeteria of all places. And on my twentieth birthday of all days! It must be fate. His name is Travis Winn. I would have missed him completely if my biology teacher hadn't let us go early. Angie and I walked into the cafeteria and there he was, sitting with Angie's cousin! We walked up to them and started talking. Well, Angie did. I just stood there with my mouth feeling like it had glue in it. I was afraid I'd say something stupid. He is so gorgeous. I mean, REALLY. He's tall and built like a football player—not the really big ones, but nice and strong. Just the perfect size for me. His face is squarish but very nice, and his eyes are pools of dark chocolate (imagine me, boring old Karyn, writing that!). His hair is even darker than his eyes. Tall, dark, and handsome—that describes him exactly. He has a smile that melted my heart. By the time I finally found my tongue, he and

Angie's cousin were finished eating. We hadn't even gotten our food yet.

Angie teased me all the way back to our apartment. She could see I was gone on him. (Boy, am I ever!) I told her she had to help me find out more about him. I felt something in my heart when we met, and I'm not going to let it go without trying. Be still, my heart. How will I ever make it through the rest of this day without seeing him?

After Christian and Austin left her the second time, Liana removed her laptop from her padded briefcase. It was thin and the best her boss could afford. Too often she had to go to a client's office or finish up something at home after work hours, and the extra money she earned for the company had paid for the laptop a hundred times over. It would cut down her work on this case immensely.

She looked up as Austin returned with his Chinese food. He smiled. "I got you a fortune cookie."

"They're not real fortunes." She remembered the first time she had opened one when she was six. It had read, "You will bring your parents much happiness." She had thrown both the cookie and the fortune away.

"You afraid? Go ahead, open it." His black eyes echoed his verbal challenge.

"Okay." She cracked the cookie, drew out the small paper, and read it aloud. "For good fortune, buy more of Lee's cookies." She looked up at him and smirked. "I'm sorry. I was wrong. That is a real fortune if I ever heard one—a real fortune for Lee."

He threw back his head and laughed with an abandon she envied. "You got that right. Next time I see the old man, though, I'm going to tell him he owes me a cookie."

Liana pondered for a moment that there actually was a Chinese man named Lee and that Austin knew him well enough to demand another cookie. If she didn't like something about a restaurant, she simply moved her business elsewhere. Getting to know the owner would mean she'd owe him something, if only her patronage. Better to keep at a distance.

"Here," she said, handing him some papers. "These have to be tallied first. You'll need a chair."

"There's one in the next office."

Silence reigned as they worked. Liana sneaked a glance over the desk at Austin, who was eating his Chinese food with chopsticks in his left hand and punching numbers on his keyboard with his right. *He's left-handed,* she thought. To her embarrassment, he looked up and caught her gaze. She raised her eyes slightly and pretended to be deep in thought. He darted a glance at the ceiling behind him where she stared but thankfully didn't interrupt her. Liana went back to work, her concentration broken.

After a few moments of silence, he finished his food and spoke. "So I heard it's your . . . ah, mother's birthday this Sunday."

Her hands dropped from her keyboard into her lap. "Yes." Her response was clipped as she wondered why he'd hesitated over the word *mother.* Had Christian talked to him about her? She'd *kill* him if he had. He had no right dredging up the past like that, especially with someone who was a total stranger to her. *She* had put it behind her. Why couldn't Christian?

As a child, the mystery surrounding the estrangement between Karyn, her birth mother, and Clarissa, her aunt, had consumed Liana's every waking moment. But she no longer cared what had caused the rift. Except for the occasional flash of memory that caused her to jerk awake, sweating with longing in the night, Clarissa Winn was the only mother Liana knew. Now she wanted only to forget there was another woman who had loved her, forget the anguish that clutched at her heart whenever she remembered her birth mother's face. She wanted to rid herself of the terrible aching pain of loss that refused to allow her to love Clarissa as deeply as a daughter should. Though neither had ever given voice to the reality, the gulf between them was almost as deep and wide as the ocean that had once separated Clarissa and Karyn.

Liana felt Austin's eyes on her, and she refused to meet his gaze; instead, she stared down at the screen of her laptop. "Do you have the totals?"

He gave them to her without comment, but when she accidentally met his eyes, she saw pity in them. Or was it compassion? She felt bitterness in her gut, though she refused to let the emotion show in her face. How dare he feel *anything* for her when she had not invited him to do so or allowed him into her confidence! She made up her mind then and there that she didn't like Austin Walker. She didn't like him at all, and it would be none too soon to wrap up this project and get out of here.

———•—•———

Austin was relieved when at last Liana pushed back her chair and stood, stretching her arms out in front of her. "That's it," she said. "Before we can go on, I'll need you to find everything I wrote on this list. Also, is there a computer I can use that has all this information? I'd like to have it on my laptop, too."

"Sure," Austin said. "This one has everything on it. Do you want to copy it over now?"

"No." She placed one last file folder on a pile. "Let's call it a night. How about tomorrow? I can come again after work, but it might be late."

"Sure." Tomorrow was Friday, and Austin had a date with a woman named Sonja, but he could break it. The most important thing right now was seeing this work finished in time. Sonja wouldn't like it, though.

"You won't have to be here," Liana told him, as though reading his thoughts. "From here on out, I just need our computers." Her voice left him no doubt that she would prefer to be alone. And maybe he should let her. He would much rather go out with Sonja than add numbers with an ice princess.

"Not a chance," he surprised himself by saying. "You told me you were out for company secrets, so I'll have to be here to protect them."

Her sudden smile delighted him. "Okay, then, tomorrow it is." With a move made deft through practice, she slipped her laptop into the briefcase and clicked it shut. "I'm ready."

He walked her out the back way where his full-sized white pickup truck waited, gleaming in the moonlight. Two years ago he'd bought the vehicle, and he still felt a rush of pleasure whenever he saw it.

"A truck?" she asked, arching a brow. "I didn't figure you for a truck."

He opened the door for her and helped her climb inside. "What did you figure?"

"Hmm, let's see. You're the sales manager of a midsized chain of electronic stores. Not a Jag. Hmm. Nor a Lexus. Maybe a Mercedes? A red one?"

He laughed. "Oh, no. I'm a Ford man myself, although I do have a sister named Mercedes. Besides, red is a little too noticeable. I hear that people who drive red cars get more traffic tickets."

Her smile was back, and in the moonlight she looked beautiful. Austin had to remind himself twice that they were not on a date and that no goodnight kiss would be awaiting the end of their evening.

She gave him directions, and silence came once more between them. Austin flipped on the radio to his favorite country station. He looked to see if she approved, but her profile was expressionless. He wished there was more light.

"Here," she said as they came to her building. "Turn here. My car's in the back."

Her car turned out to be a sleek green or black—it was difficult to tell in the dark—Chevy Cavalier convertible. Austin was surprised; she seemed more conservative than the car hinted. "I never pictured you for a convertible," he said, coming to a stop.

She shrugged. "I like to feel the wind on my face."

Austin thought he might like it, too. If she'd been any other woman, he might have asked for a ride.

There was only one other car in the lot. Austin wasn't sure because of the distance, but he thought it was a red Mercedes. She reached for the door. "Looks like just about everyone's gone home. That's surprising; it's only ten."

Austin smiled. "Do you often work late?"

"Only during March and April."

"Ah, tax season."

"Yep." Her voice suddenly sounded so weary that he felt guilty for adding to her workload. She should have been home resting or out with friends.

"Liana," he said, "I'm really grateful to you for helping me out. I didn't know what to do when I got stuck with this job.

It's hard to find someone at such short notice—especially someone you can trust."

"We'll get it done," she replied lightly, pushing her door open. "See you tomorrow."

"I'll wait until you get your car started."

She opened her mouth as though to speak but slipped down to the blacktop without uttering a word. After only a few steps she stiffened and came to a stop. Austin followed her gaze to a man who had emerged from the building and was now striding in their direction. The weak lights in the parking lot didn't reveal much about the man's appearance, but he walked with enough purpose to cause Austin alarm. Opening his door, he went around the truck and joined Liana.

"Who's he?" Austin could see now that the newcomer was about his height but weighed at least sixty pounds more—most of which was gathered in his chest and stomach. "Looks like Dracula with a belly."

She gave him an amused glance. "My boss."

"Oh, sorry."

"It's okay."

She didn't look okay. If Austin thought her face closed before, it now became a veritable fortress.

"Liana." The man's voice showed superiority even in that single word.

"Yes, Mr. Koplin?"

"I thought you went home."

"No, I just left work. I've come back to get my car."

Koplin's gaze shifted over Austin. "Oh, a date."

"A favor for my brother." There was the slightest trace of annoyance in her voice. Austin imagined that she would much rather tell him where to go than to give him the satisfaction of an explanation. He found himself silently cheering her spunk.

34

"Oh, nice to meet you." Koplin held out a hand to Austin. "I didn't know Liana had a brother."

"Well, actually, I'm not her brother," Austin said, his nose tingling at the strong smell of soap and disinfectant that radiated from Koplin. "We just met today. I'm Austin Walker, sales manager of Goodman Electronics."

Koplin's brows shot up. "Goodman's?"

"My brother does advertising for them," Liana said.

Austin nodded. "Our accountant quit, and we have some reports due, so when her brother said he knew someone who could help . . . well, that's how Liana got involved."

Liana cast Austin a look that told him she wished he had kept his mouth shut.

Koplin's eyes narrowed as he pointed to the briefcase Liana carried, wringing his long fingers. "Did you use your laptop?"

"Yes."

"I'm sure you know that company equipment is limited only to company business. We'll have to talk about this tomorrow."

Austin had to stop himself from challenging the man's cold, arrogant words, but Liana nodded, her expression devoid of reaction. "Now if you will excuse me. Goodnight, Mr. Koplin." She turned to Austin. "Goodnight, Austin."

Austin watched her walk away, back rigid and head held high. She showed no sign of concern, and he marveled at her calmness. That was one woman who would not allow anyone to push her around.

Larry Koplin nodded at him and took a step away. Hesitating, he asked, "You really just met her today?"

"Yes." *If it's any of your business,* Austin added silently.

Koplin's hand reached up to smooth his tie over his chest and belly. "I just wondered, since she called you by your first name. The way she addressed you—I thought you might be friends. Never mind. It was nice to meet you. Goodnight." He turned and hurried across the parking lot to the red Mercedes.

Austin felt compelled to go after Liana, and he reached her as she was about to slip into the convertible. *Green, it's dark green,* his mind noted. The top was up tonight, though the Nevada weather was warm enough for it to be down.

"Wait," he said. When she hesitated, he continued. "Look, I didn't get you into trouble, did I? I could talk to him, if you want."

Her eyes appeared dark blue in the night, as fathomless as the evening sky on the farm where he grew up. "Everything is fine, Aust—Mr. Walker." Her voice wasn't raised or angry, but each word came with deliberate precision, as though etched in stone. "But you aren't my knight in shining armor—I don't need one. I fight my own battles, and Mr. Koplin doesn't frighten me. Now, will you please let go of my door? I'm tired and I'd like to go home."

He stepped back and let her drive away. If that was the way she wanted it, so be it. She was no concern of his. "A witch," he muttered. "The face of an angel, a heart of ice." He shook his head and snorted. "Knight in shining armor. Well, excuse me for trying to be nice."

Pushing all thoughts of Liana from his mind, he strode back to his truck and revved the engine to life. He'd better call Sonja tonight if he was ever going to be forgiven for breaking their date.

———

Liana was furious, and now that no one was around, she allowed herself the weakness of showing anger. *How dare Mr.*

*Koplin question where I've been or with whom! He had no right. He's
my boss, not my father or my husband. He had absolutely no right!*

She hated the way he'd made her feel—as if she were a
child who had to account for her time, as though she weren't
capable of taking care of herself. Like a child who had begged
to go on a plane with her parents to a remote village in India
and had been refused.

She didn't really know if she had begged to go. The memories of that time were all but gone, but as a child she had imagined asking to go with her parents on their last flight. She
understood why now: the belief stoked her feelings of abandonment, which in turn caused anger, and the anger obliter-
ated the guilt of not going, of surviving without them.
Understanding this now did not change the facts or her
feelings.

After a few moments of raging at the absent Koplin, a sliver
of fear wove its way into her thoughts. She hadn't thought he
might be annoyed that she had used the laptop for outside
work. She'd heard others at Klassy Accounting (no job too big
or too small) talking about the extra money they made outside
work hours using the laptops they'd been given. Everyone did
it. As long as doing so did not infringe upon their work for
Koplin, what did it matter? She hadn't stolen a client or used
something that was consumable. She'd been doing a favor for
someone—and not for the first time. There wasn't even a company policy about the matter. What was Mr. Koplin's problem?

Then she knew. She'd upset his plans for lunch with Jim
Forrester, and he was trying to teach her a lesson. He might
even threaten to fire her, but he wouldn't dare follow through
until tax season was over. Even then, he would hesitate,
wouldn't he? She was good at what she did.

Before pulling onto the freeway, heading toward Henderson

where she lived, she stopped and put down the top of her convertible. Then she pulled her long hair into the thick elastic band that she always kept on the dash. Accelerating quickly, she reveled in the cool breeze slapping against her face and sliding over the top of her hair like a gentle touch. Almost it felt as though she were flying. Flying like the eagle on the picture in her tiny rat hole of an office. There was no tapping of keyboards in the breeze at this speed, only white noise that soothed and calmed.

When she eased the Cavalier into place outside her small condominium, her anger had died, taking with it the fear. Whatever Mr. Koplin said tomorrow, she would deal with it as she dealt with everything—by herself with her head held high.

Inside, her condo was utterly quiet, without even the muffled hum of the air conditioner, which frequently drove her mad during the summer. Setting her briefcase on the floor, she turned on the light in the narrow entryway. The stairs leading up to her room beckoned, but she ignored them and stumbled to the small kitchen. There, she downed three aspirin tablets with a meal shake from a can. Most people used these to lose weight; she used them to fill her stomach when there wasn't time or energy for a proper meal. Sometimes the shakes and nutrition bars were the only things she ate all day, though often they didn't do much for her gnawing hunger.

Her eyes burned and her head pounded. Willing the aspirin to start working, she wandered into the living room, the only other room on the first floor besides a bathroom and a laundry closet. This was her favorite room and the largest in the two bedroom condo. It featured a gas fireplace which she rarely used, a sliding glass door that led to the tiny patio out back, and built-in shelves with room for a large TV but which she used only for her extensive collection of books. She read avidly, everything from fantasy intended for children to non-fiction books on political science. The only books she didn't read were the romance novels that made no sense to her. How could there really be a happily ever after? There was always the next morning and a new set of problems. Her favorite books were the Anne Perry mysteries, because in the end they were logical, believable, perhaps even predictable. She liked that.

Scattered appealingly here and there and on the walls were knickknacks, pictures, and other decorations. These were mostly of her adoptive mother's choosing, some coming from her childhood home. Clarissa had wanted her daughter to feel comfortable and loved when she moved into the condo. Tears came to Liana's eyes at the memory. Strangely enough, those pictures and knickknacks did more for her than she was ever able to let on.

Avoiding the flowery Victorian couch that was great for looks but lacked everything in comfort, she headed to her sloppy green easy chair, another cast-off from her parents' home, to wait until the throbbing in her head abated enough for her to attempt the stairs. Her eyes drooped.

She didn't know this place or these people. A lady wept in front of a child who stared with wide, frightened eyes, her face slick with tears. Another woman tried to comfort the first, who refused to be comforted. Still another woman reached for the child, who stared and stared without speaking, more tears sliding down her cheek. As the people began to fade—growing smaller and smaller, grayer and grayer, until it was all black—a high, terrified scream pierced the darkness.

Liana awoke, breathing in short, violent gasps. Her hand went instinctively to her heart, which now pounded with more intensity than her head had earlier. With a moan, she came to her feet, glad for the light she had left burning. She stumbled through the room, tripping once or twice over her own feet, which felt encased in lead. Using the thick wooden banister, she pulled herself up the stairs to her room. She sat on her queen-sized bed in the dark, breathing deeply to calm the terror that remained from the dream. Long ago this nightmare had come often, but now it was much more rare. She supposed it derived from an early memory in India, of her mother's friends after her death. The silently weeping child must be herself.

Fumbling in her nightstand, her hand closed over the small faded snapshot she had once carried everywhere. By the dim light that filtered in the door from the first floor, she could see the happy blond couple smiling out at her. Between them was a thin, brown-haired child, who despite her somber eyes looked content. Below the picture on the white border was a name, printed neatly in Christian's fourteen-year-old hand:

Liana with her parents Guenter and Karyn Schrader

She no longer remembered why she had insisted on the name or where she had gotten it. Christian believed it was a nickname that meant something in Romanian, the first language of her birth father. She had never dared to check.

"Write Liana," *she said tearfully, shoving the bent photograph toward him.* "I know how to spell it. Mamata taught me. L-I-A-N-A."

"Who is Mamata?" *Christian asked.*

Liana knew Mamata was the lady who had watched her when her parents were at the hospital, but she couldn't—wouldn't!—use so many words to tell him this. "Write Liana," *she repeated.*

"But you're Lara," *he said.* "Lara Clari Schrader. I mean, Lara Clari Winn, now that you're adopted. That's what we went to the judge for today. You're Lara now. Lara. I know we've been calling you Liana like you wanted, and I'll still call you that if you want, but Mom thinks you'll be happy to have your real name when you *grow up. Aunt Karyn, your real mother, gave you that name. You should use it."*

More tears stung her eyes. "No, no—Liana." Even if she had been willing to talk more, she found it impossible to explain how desperately she needed to be called Liana. Again she shoved the photograph at him.

He stared at her. "Okay. Don't cry. I'll do it. It's okay. Shush now." Taking a pen from his pocket, he slowly printed the words. "There you go. For what good it'll do."

The memory faded. Liana clutched the photo to her chest and lay on her bed in the dark. Her face was wet with tears.

CHAPTER
4

Diary of Karyn Olsen
Friday, January 11, 1966

*I know I didn't want to go to college so close to home, but now
I'm grateful. I love this school. Go Cal Poly! If I hadn't been here, I'd
never have met Travis.*

*Today I skipped biology (Angie took notes for me) and went to
the cafeteria early again. My heart was banging around like crazy in
my chest for fear that Travis wouldn't be there. But he was. Angie's
cousin was not (yay!). I took a deep breath and went up to him.
Gosh, I'm always shy and nervous around guys, but this is so much
worse! When I'm around him I feel as if I'm looking over the edge of
a cliff. My breath whooshes out of me, and I can barely speak.*

*Then he invited me to sit with him! I couldn't believe it. I raced
to get my food, afraid he would change his mind, but he was still
there waiting for me when I got back. I think he really likes me. (Oh,
please, God, let him like me!) I never worried much about the way I
look. I mean, I don't look too bad or anything, but I never really*

cared before I met Travis. Just two days ago I only wanted to rush through college and finish my degree so that I could be a nurse and help people. But meeting Travis . . . I don't know. Things seem different now.

Liana awoke at 5:29 A.M., her body anticipating her alarm clock by one minute. She was accustomed to waking early and normally it was her best time. Not so this morning. Her head felt full of sludge, and her neck ached from sleeping on the pillow wrong. *Great way to start a morning,* she thought.

In the darkness, she pushed herself from bed and into the connecting bathroom. There, she downed two aspirin, shed her clothes, and stumbled into the shower. She turned the water first too hot and then too cold, letting it sluice over her. Immediately her body came alive. Out of the shower, she slathered herself with one of the many tubes of lotion she had in her cupboard next to the large array of bath salts, bubbles, and candles. If there was one room that was her, it was the bathroom. Soaking in the bath after a hot day was her favorite luxury.

Her hair took a very long time to dry, and most days she let it remain slightly damp. But today she wanted to look her best when she faced Mr. Koplin. After blow-drying her hair, she added a few hot rollers to enhance her natural curl. As she waited for the curlers to cool, she meticulously applied her makeup, using waterproof mascara so that it wouldn't run from the heat that steadily increased as summer approached. It wasn't in case she cried, she assured herself. Mr. Koplin wasn't important enough to cry over.

How things had changed from when she had first met Larry Koplin at a local charity fund-raiser she had attended. He had seemed so kind, so utterly concerned with providing help for abused women, impressing her with not only his generous contribution but with his nice suit and confident manner. She had also been eager to escape the awkward situation of a romance gone wrong at her previous job—the failure had been hers, of course; she simply couldn't commit.

Only much later did she realize that for Koplin business came before any other consideration. But at the expense of what? Employees who constantly feared for their jobs, employees who often worked overtime but who had little hope of bettering their situations? It was no wonder Liana's two best friends at work—her only friends there—had quit the year before, Merriam to raise a family and Franz to accept a better job at another company.

And yet the women's shelter was flourishing for the first time in years. Koplin had likely saved lives.

Was that why she stayed? Liana wished now that she had left Klassy with Merriam and Franz. Life there had been difficult without them, but she had been afraid. Afraid, yet also hopeful for the office and raise Koplin kept hanging in front of her like a tasty carrot. When it finally came, she understood it hadn't been worth the wait; she had sold her soul for a silver-plated dime.

From her walk-in closet, Liana chose a maroon suit dress that had always made her feel feminine and confident. She told herself she made the choice because of her pending interview with her boss; it had nothing to do with the later appointment at Goodman Electronics. Nothing at all.

Her cupboard was bare of even her customary English muffins, so she made a mental note to stop at McDonald's on her way to work. Fortunately, her headache had abated, though the pain in her neck persisted. She rubbed it with an impatient hand as she ran to her car.

Thirty minutes later, Mr. Koplin's executive secretary looked up from her desk as Liana entered Klassy Accounting. "Mr. Koplin asked me to tell you he's waiting in his office," she said.

"Thank you, Marla," Liana replied, ignoring the hint at her supposed tardiness. So what if she was usually here at six-thirty or seven? Official working hours didn't begin until eight, and that meant she was a half hour early.

She felt the glances of her coworkers as she walked purposefully toward Mr. Koplin's office. Though she'd worked with them for years, she didn't know any of them well and suspected they were all secretly hoping she'd be fired. She'd overheard a man once at the coffee machine saying something about an ice maiden. The conversation died when they noticed her, leaving no doubt as to who was the topic of conversation. That day she wished she'd tried to make new friends after Merriam and Franz left. Instead, she had drawn further into her shell, telling herself that was what manager material did. Back then she had believed Mr. Koplin's promises.

I don't need them, she thought, squaring her shoulders and lifting her chin. *And I can handle Mr. Koplin.* She tried to recapture some of the indignation she had felt the night before, but her heart fluttered in her chest.

Mr. Koplin waited for her behind his long mahogany desk, his door open so that she had no chance to collect herself while she knocked. "Come in," he called, glancing at his watch purposefully.

Liana stood before the desk, keeping her face stoic. "You wanted to see me, Mr. Koplin?"

A muscle twitched in his fleshy cheek. "Yes. Thank you. Please shut the door and have a seat."

Liana was tempted to request that the door remain ajar, or

that Marla come in to witness the conversation, but she was too proud to suggest either. She could handle this alone.

She sat on the padded chair in front of his desk, her laptop on her knees. Mr. Koplin's office was full of expensive-looking furniture, paintings, and knickknacks, none of which showed any taste. While some pieces would have been nice alone or with something else, the crowded, careless way they had been arranged screamed of trying to impress—and failing miserably.

Mr. Koplin folded his hands together on the desk, looking grave. "I am very concerned with your personal use of company equipment—especially during this busy season."

"I'm sorry. I didn't realize that was company policy. It won't happen again." She wouldn't grovel, but she would apologize.

"Well, the problem is that you used it for accounting purposes, which is not the same as, say, keeping a diary." Mr. Koplin smiled, apparently finding himself amusing. Liana didn't react, though she really wanted to let loose a good sneer. "Basically," he continued more soberly, "by using the equipment to do taxes, you've taken potential business away from this company. That is what disturbs me. It makes me question your loyalty."

"I've worked here for four years. I've been loyal."

He stared at her, and she felt as though he were trying to peer into her heart. "Are you planning on staying with this company?"

"Yes." Or she had been—until now.

"Good." Koplin stood and walked over to his window, one of the few in the building, and pulled up the shutters. "Now let's see what we can do to rectify this situation. I believe you intend to be loyal to this company, but I will expect you to prove it to me as I have proven my appreciation to you by moving you from the cubicles. You have the ability to go far with us here at Klassy Accounting."

At one time Liana would have believed him, but in the past few months the realization had hit that there was only one way she could advance: changing her parenthood. At this branch of Klassy Accounting two managers divvied up the workload. One was Mr. Koplin's daughter, and the other was a cousin. The second branch was managed by Mr. Koplin's brother and his son-in-law. The advertising president, payroll supervisor, and executive secretary were all equally related in some way. For all his promises, there simply wasn't room for Liana in managing: She didn't have the right blood.

Koplin stared out the window. "Of course," he said casually, "if Goodman Electronics needs help, we can set them up here." He turned to her. "Yes, I think that would be a good idea. That way we help both Mr. Walker and our company."

Now Liana understood. After finding out that Austin was the sales manager of Goodman's he wanted their account permanently. He was envisioning quarterly reports, employee withholdings, and tax documents galore. Dollar signs shone from his watery eyes as he imagined larger and larger companies flocking to him for help. More wealthy men like Jim Forrester. She almost laughed aloud. Instead, she said, "He didn't want to go to our company—to any company."

"But he knows you now. He'll come."

She clenched her jaw. "I did that work in my *free* time."

"With *my* equipment."

"I'll have to be paid for my time."

"You're on salary." Mr. Koplin's eyes glittered. "But perhaps a bonus is in order for finding a new client. However, if they choose not to go with us, we'll have to rethink your position here."

Liana knew what that meant. If she didn't obtain a contract with Goodman's, he wouldn't fire her—yet—but he would make her life miserable. The bonuses she earned for completing important assignments would be lowered, the worst cases would come her way, she would lose her tiny excuse of an office. In short, he would make her working life unbearable. It was as if a veil had been taken from her eyes and she could finally see him for who he really was. Not a community-driven man who did good for the sake of doing right but a man who was active in the community for the appearance of goodness, for what it could do for him. Yes, Larry Koplin was a man who valued control more than kindness and money more than morality. Employees were simply the means to an end.

Liana would not give in to the immediate satisfaction of telling him that Austin already had a replacement accountant. Let Mr. Koplin dream over the stacks of hefty bills he would send to them, of the vacations he would take to Tahiti. Not telling him would buy her a few hours of peace as she decided what to do. "I'll talk to him," she said.

"Very well." Smiling, Mr. Koplin wrung his hands like a dishcloth. "You may go then. And try to be a little earlier tomorrow, would you?"

She hesitated at the door. "Tomorrow's Saturday."

"Didn't you see the memo this morning? We need everyone to come in a half day to make sure we beat the deadlines."

You mean to line your pockets, she thought. But it was standard procedure during tax season, and to be fair they would be given monetary compensation in the form of bonuses. Liana forced a smile and left the room.

Near lunchtime Mr. Koplin came into her office, making it seem more confining than usual. The smell of bitter coffee coming from the break room was overpowering, and as she looked up from her computer screen, Liana's empty stomach felt nauseated.

Koplin frowned disapprovingly at the eagle in her picture, making his thinning eyebrows resemble sickly caterpillars. "Have you talked with Mr. Walker?" he asked. "I could squeeze him in about four to discuss his account, if he can make it."

Liana looked up from her computer. "He's already hired a new accountant, so he doesn't need us."

"What?" Mr. Koplin's face reddened. His hands alternately twisted and clenched the other.

"It's Mr. Goodman's nephew."

"Oh." His mouth worked, but nothing further came out.

Liana watched him without expression. He released his hands and brought one to his round chest. "You—you knew this," he accused.

"I would never steal business from this company," she said. "I was only helping my brother." For a moment, she hoped he would show reason, that he would see the situation as she did. He had helped the women's shelter, and he served on the local school board as well. Maybe she was wrong about him. Maybe she had somehow misunderstood his threats. If she could only clear it up . . .

He abruptly turned and left the office. Even without his disquieting presence, Liana didn't feel better. Perhaps she should have told him right away about Goodman's nephew instead of letting the pot simmer. She had just been so angry, and yes, hurt.

She was about to go out for a late lunch when Mr. Koplin returned with several thick files. He had Jim Forrester in tow. "I need these two accounts finished before you go home tonight, Liana."

Inwardly, she sighed. From the looks of the files, she'd be

here until eight—if she hurried. The payback for the incident with Goodman Electronics had begun.

"Oh, and Mr. Forrester wanted to ask you a few questions about the figures you calculated yesterday," Koplin said.

This was getting worse by the minute. "Okay," she agreed, though she knew there was nothing she had missed, nothing he could question.

Mr. Koplin wasn't finished—something she should have been prepared for, given the malicious gleam in his eyes. He smiled as he said, "I told him you could take a long lunch."

Behind him, Jim Forrester winked, and Liana felt her already taut nerves stretch to the breaking point. She would talk to Forrester about his account, but not in a hundred years would it be over lunch. Taking a deep breath, she said, "I'm sorry, but this is simply not a good time." She motioned to the files he had just given her. "I'll be here until eight as it is."

"All the more reason to take a nice break now." Mr. Koplin's sugar sweet voice held an undertone that Liana recognized as threatening.

"I'll be happy to go over his account here," Liana countered.

"Will you excuse us for a minute?" Mr. Koplin said to Forrester with an air of tortured patience.

"Sure." The surfing king look-alike winked again at Liana, showing no sign of discomfort at the scene. She watched him with growing anger as he wandered away from her door to talk with one of the other employees.

"Look," Mr. Koplin said in a low voice that bordered on ugliness. "Jim Forrester is one of our largest accounts. We can't afford to lose him. I strongly suggest going with him. It's just a lunch—nothing more."

Liana matched his serious tone—without the ugly

undertone. "Not only do I not have time but I don't feel comfortable with him. I do not want to be in a social setting with him, especially not alone. There's no need for me to leave the office to discuss his file."

"It's just work."

"Is it?" Liana held his eyes. He looked away, obviously uncomfortable, and she felt a sliver of victory. There was some conscience left in the man.

"It's a question of loyalty, Liana," he said more normally. "I'm not asking you to do anything but eat lunch. Smile and do a little hand-holding. We all have to do our share of that."

"We can talk here."

"He wants to eat lunch."

"No."

"Your job is on the line."

She was stunned into silence. How could this be happening? She felt numb. More than numb. Frozen. Taking her lack of a response as acquiescence, Koplin motioned Forrester over. With her boss's tall frame taking up much of the free space in her office, and Forrester blocking the door, Liana felt suddenly claustrophobic.

"We've worked it out," Koplin said. "Liana will be able to get away for lunch after all. Won't you, Liana?"

That last patronizing question was all Liana could take. Slowly, she took her purse from the desk drawer, pausing to shove her stash of meal bars inside. Then she stood and reached for the eagle painting on the wall.

"Liana, what—"

"I'm leaving, Mr. Koplin."

"What?"

"I quit."

"You can't quit!" Red seeped into his face. "We've got too much work to do."

She smiled coldly, allowing triumph to show in her eyes. "Maybe you should have thought of that before." Shoving past them, she emerged from the tiny office, feeling suddenly as light and free as the eagle who had inspired the picture she carried. Was this how Merriam and Franz had felt when they left for the last time? If only she hadn't valued the financial security—however slim it was—more than her self-esteem. She would have already been free of Mr. Koplin and this dead-end job.

"What about my account?" Forrester asked, his good-looking face creasing with concern.

Liana paused. "I've documented everything. Anyone here can help you. Perhaps Mr. Koplin will make the time." She smiled. "I'm sure he's free for lunch. I'll bet you could even get him to pay."

Without another word or glance at the two men, Liana started down the space between the rows of cubicles. Their last exchanges had attracted attention, and for the last time Liana felt her coworkers eyes fixed on her as she marched out of the room and to the elevator. It felt good leaving, knowing she'd never have to see her boss or any of them again.

"Wait! Liana!"

She turned to see Jocelyn, the only person who still made friendly overtures toward her. Jocelyn was young, blonde, and very smart, though Liana doubted that many of their coworkers made it far enough past her good looks to learn that about her. Not participating in office friendships had left Liana with plenty of moments to observe their interactions and to evaluate their work.

"I heard what happened—or much of it," Jocelyn said.

"Don't quit! You should stay and fight. It's sexual harassment, that's what it is. Koplin knows that guy's a leach. He had no right to try to make you go with him. You could win. I know it! My boyfriend's sister is an attorney, and I've talked to her plenty about it."

Liana felt an unexpected rush of emotion at her sympathy. She clenched her lips tightly for a moment until it passed. "I don't want to work here, that's all." The words came out more coldly than she intended.

Jocelyn's youthful features drooped. "I know it's none of my business. I'm sorry." She turned to leave.

Without thinking, Liana reached for her shoulder. "No, thanks. Really. It's nice of you to care. But I—it's just not worth it. I'm going nowhere here."

Jocelyn smiled. "I know what you mean. I've only been here two months, and I'm ready to quit. I mean, I'm not related to the right people to qualify for advancement."

"At least it only took you two months to figure it out," Liana said dryly. "It took me four years."

Jocelyn raised both brows. "That's a long time."

"Too long." Liana was relieved that the elevator chose that moment to arrive. "Well, good luck."

"You, too."

Once in her car, the adrenaline pumping through her veins abated, and Liana shook her head with amazement at her own audacity. How was she going to pay the mortgage on her condo? Buy food? Her savings would tide her over for a while but not for long. She began to feel distinctly sorry for herself. Maybe she should have gone to lunch with Forrester. Handling him wouldn't have been too difficult. That way she could have at least found another job before she quit. Tears stung her eyes, but she didn't allow them to fall.

Shoving her car into gear, she pulled from her parking place. Manually, she shifted gears several times as the car sprang forward into the weak traffic. The movement, the power, somehow comforted her. The pushing on the clutch, the shifting of gears, was something she could easily control—enjoyed controlling. Once on the freeway she drove as fast as she dared, letting the wind rip through her hair, tangling it, until the painting on the passenger seat threatened to blow out. She leaned over and carefully set it onto the floor.

Seeing the eagle reminded her of her freedom, and she told herself that leaving her job was not a setback but an opportunity. While she finished the job for Goodman Electronics, she would advertise for freelance work; it wasn't too late to take advantage of the tax season. Somehow she would make ends meet. No, she'd do more than that: she would fly high. She was still in control.

CHAPTER

5

Diary of Karyn Olsen
Thursday, January 17, 1966

The past days have rushed by. I changed my biology class to later in the day so I could "accidentally" meet Travis more often. Turns out he's there only three days a week at that time. The other two days (Tuesday and Thursday) he has an engineering class. Angie told me that. She asked her cousin all about him. Turns out they went to high school together and just happened to run into each other in the cafeteria that day. (Angie says it's coincidence. I say it's fate!) Now they're keeping in touch. Anyway, Travis is a senior (!) and is going to be a civil engineer. Isn't that brilliant?

He hasn't exactly asked me out yet, but Angie and I arranged to run into him outside his math class today, and she told him about the welcome dance they're having tomorrow. She convinced him to come with us. I'm so excited I could scream. I called Clarissa right away, and she promised to do my hair. I have to be beautiful. I will just die if he doesn't ask me out soon.

Liana arrived at Goodman Electronics at three o'clock, locking her eagle painting in the trunk of the car before going inside. There were two receptionists behind the long desk, and she waited while the younger of the two called Mr. Walker's office to tell him of her arrival.

"He'll be right down to escort you inside," she told Liana. Her bright hazel eyes ran over Liana's hair, and belatedly Liana wondered if her wild drive had made her unpresentable. Turning from the desk, she surreptitiously combed her fingers through her hair, smoothing it.

Within minutes Austin came through the door with his hand outstretched. "Liana," he said, "thank you for coming. I didn't expect you so early, though. I thought I wouldn't see you until seven or eight."

"I was able to get away." His touch was warm on her hand, and Liana thought his smile was genuine, though she wasn't sure why he wasted it on her. She certainly hadn't encouraged him.

"I've got everything ready that you requested," he said as he led her down the hallway. "I've even arranged a computer for you, but I'll need to stop at my office for that on our way. Sorry about what happened last night. Hope you didn't get into trouble."

Liana shrugged. "Well, I'm not going to be using my laptop." In fact, she'd left it back at the office when she'd quit. "But this afternoon I copied everything I'd need from it—I even have the forms I'll need." She had thought herself paranoid while she had done it after her first discussion with Koplin, but her instincts had been proven correct.

"That's good." He pushed the button for the elevator.

His third-floor office was as large and spacious as her office at Klassy Accounting had been small and cramped. *The difference of being well employed,* she thought. Perhaps that was what was wrong with her life. She was talented and hardworking—maybe she should start her own business. The idea was not new, but always before she had been scared to try. Now she had nothing to lose.

Not only was Austin's office large but the U-shaped oak desk, leather chair, and leather couches under the long windows radiated an understated opulence. Many of the tasteful accessories obviously had stories behind them: a signed baseball with a glass covering, a polished star-shaped rock being used as a paperweight, and two framed pictures on the wall— one of a boy leaning against a black-and-white cow that towered over him, and another of an older girl and that same boy feeding a small spotted calf. The front half of the desk was littered with papers, atop which sat a thin notebook computer; the far side held a regular computer with a flat screen, a printer, a fax machine, and an electric pencil sharpener. It was a setup that invited hard work with convenience.

Austin picked up the laptop. "I think it's basically the same kind as you were using last night. Perhaps a later model. Thinner."

Liana told herself not to get choked up about his noticing what type of laptop she used. *Of course he'd noticed. He's in the business, and it's a brand he sells.*

"I had one of the guys pull it out of the warehouse in case you wanted to work on our account at home," he continued. "I didn't know what software you needed, though. I had them install everything we have a license for."

Liana thought of her accounting programs on both her work laptop and her desk computer there. Those were some things she hadn't been able to copy. But his programs would be just as good. "That's perfect," she said.

57

They left his office and went to the room they'd been in the night before, now awash in natural light streaming in from the windows. "I had a better chair brought in," Austin said, setting the laptop down on the round table. "The other was a little stiff."

Drawing a flash drive from her purse, she connected it to the computer. "Maybe that was why your accountant quit."

Austin looked at her for a second, brows high, and then he laughed. "Hey, that was a joke. Good one."

"I do know how to joke." For some reason his surprise made her defensive.

He nodded. "I'll stay until you get started, but I have a conference call I have to make in fifteen minutes."

"Just show me how to access the necessary files. Do I need a password?"

———————

After his conference call with managers in three different states, another call came through on Austin's cell phone. His sister in Wyoming barely waited for him to answer before she began to speak.

"You'll never guess what happened, Austin. Old Whittaker died, and Grandma must have gotten through to him because he left his whole estate to HeartReach! I just got off the phone with his lawyer. It's not as much as one might have thought, given how much land he owned, because apparently some of it was used as collateral for his cousin's children's educational loans, which were never paid back. But it's upwards of four hundred thousand, and that's twice what we raised for HeartReach last quarter. The cousins are a little disgruntled—or rather the children of the cousins are—because they thought they'd inherit."

"Don't know why—they never even visited." Austin leaned back in his chair and stretched his feet out under the desk. "I'm sorry the old guy's gone. He was. . . ." He stopped. Memories of the past rushed into his mind, of the days when he had been on the brink of adolescence and had still hoped to gain, if not his father's love, then his respect.

"You ain't no good—you never been no good. How many times I got to tell you to clean out them stalls right?"

Austin's heart sank. He'd been cleaning the stalls all morning, his sweat caking the dust on his face, until the straw and hay penetrated his clothing and made his whole body itch. Until the ripe smell of manure no longer registered on his senses. He'd done a good job— better than his father usually did—and all as a surprise. But his father had come back from a trip to town full of drink and meanness.

"The cows just mucked them up a bit when I let them in." Austin tried not to cry; he'd learned that only made his father angrier.

"Do it again. I swear, I thought havin' a boy might make life easier someday, but you're just a lazy brat. Stop starin' at me, and clean that stall again. I'm goin' to kick you if you don't git goin' right now."

Old Whittaker—old even then—poked his head in the door, just in time to witness this latest declaration of love. He cleared his throat. "Walker, I come to see that cow you're selling."

His father's countenance changed immediately, and he hurried over to shake Old Whittaker's hand. Austin watched as they haggled over the cow, glad at least it wasn't Patches, his favorite milk cow. He felt dizzy from a day of hard work with nothing since breakfast but a drink of well water from the pump to sustain him. When his dad went up to the house to arrange a bill of sale, Old Whittaker turned to him.

"Don't pay him no mind, boy. Your grandmother tells me you

might be the president of the United States one of these days, if you set your mind to it." He took out a dark bottle from the inside of his jacket, took a swig, and then offered it to Austin.

Weak from lack of food, Austin reached for it, but Old Whittaker snatched back his hand. "No. Better not. Your father's got the sickness. You might have it, too. I seen it time and time again. These things run in a family. You want to be president, you got to stay away from firewater."

"Firewater?" asked Austin.

Old Whittaker nodded, staring at him with his small, close-set eyes and bulbous nose. "It's what the Indians a long time ago called alcohol. Mark my words, boy. If you don't want to be like your father, stay away from this." He waved the bottle. "It's like a drug to folks like you."

Austin believed him. Austin looked like his dad, walked like his dad, and to his grandmother's dismay, even talked like his dad. "I'd kill myself before I became a drunk," he vowed.

Looking back, Austin believed that resolution in the barn, with Old Whittaker looking on, was a big part of why he didn't join many of his peers in throwing away their lives on the bottle.

"Austin. Austin! Are you there?"

"Yeah, sorry. I was thinking about Old Whittaker."

"Isn't it wonderful? That money will buy a lot of supplies for those orphans."

"And it means we can get it to them sooner. Do you think you could look into flight arrangements?"

"Not a chance in the next week or so. We're swamped here. Wayne'll be out planting, and Buttercup's due soon and I'm worried about her. It's twins at least, and she's pretty small. Plus all three of the boys have been sick with something that's been going around the school. I'm sorry, but you'll have to do it all yourself this time. That reminds me. Where do you want the money? In the same account, or do you have another you'd rather use that gets better interest?"

"Just use the same one until I figure it out." He blew out a long sigh. While he was grateful for the windfall, being the president and chief bottle washer for HeartReach was a lot of work, and he wasn't willing to quit his job to run the charity full time. Taking a salary from the charity would mean fewer orphans they could help, not to mention a severe cut in pay for him.

He hung up the phone and went to check on Liana. She was busy at work, her dark head bent over the keyboard, brows drawn together in concentration—or was it irritation? Whatever it was, she had worn that look during most of the time they had spent together. She was either perpetually thinking or perpetually angry. Her long hair had a windblown look that was oddly appealing, and he noticed for the first time that her mouth was slightly too wide for the proportions of her face. It was a mouth for smiling and laughing—for kissing.

"Need anything?" he asked.

She shook her head.

"You aren't hungry? We could take a break and go out for a bite."

"No," she said, coming to her feet. "I think I'd rather just go home, if you don't mind. I can work better there."

"You mean without me interrupting?"

Her unexpected smile warmed him. "Actually, that's not what I meant. It's just that I'm used to working at home. The sounds are different here. Takes more concentration."

"Well, call me if you need me." He jotted a number down on a business card he pulled from his suit pocket and handed it to her. "I've added my home number."

61

"Thanks." She closed the laptop and tucked it under her arm.

"About last night," he said as he walked her to the front desk. "I really am sorry if I got you in trouble." He thought he detected a flash of emotion in her face as he had when he mentioned it earlier.

"It's fine. Don't worry about it." She adjusted the laptop under her arm. "I'll be in touch when I'm finished, unless I need more information. No news is good news in this case."

"Thanks." He watched her walk out the door.

CHAPTER

6

Diary of Karyn Olsen
Monday, February 14, 1966

 I'm about to get ready for the Valentine's Dance. Now I know why Clari always spends so much time in front of the mirror. She's already beautiful, but she wants to look her best for her dates. I wonder if she has ever liked someone as much as I like Travis. He is so gorgeous! I can't believe he finally asked me out! It's been over a month since we met, and we've eaten lunch together exactly twelve times. When he couldn't make it last Wednesday, he even let me know so I wouldn't expect him. We laugh and joke like crazy when we're together. He's really fun. (And did I mention gorgeous? ☺) I think he hasn't been able to ask me out before because it is his last semester and he's terribly busy with school. A good thing, too. I'm finding it hard to concentrate in class since I met him. I even got a B on a test in biology—my first B in my whole life. Now I'll have to work extra hard to pull an A in the class. I'm not going to think about that now—I'm going out with my Prince Charming. I wonder if I'll get my first kiss tonight? (I don't count Jeremy in high school. I only let him kiss me because he was moving to Georgia and I felt sorry for him.) Is it too early, I wonder, to think about someday bearing Travis's children?

On Sunday evening Liana drove up to her adoptive parents' street in Paradise. With a cursory glance at the wide, squat house and yard, which featured elaborate desert plants and decorative rocks separated by small patches of grass, she saw that her siblings had already arrived for the birthday fest. Christian's BMW was in the cobbled drive, and Bret's more conservative blue Honda Accord was in front. Liana parked behind him.

She walked up to the house with familiar reluctance. She had grown up here but still felt she didn't belong. Yet if she didn't belong here, where did she belong? Certainly not in India without her parents. She didn't remember anyone else from that time except, vaguely, a woman named Mamata, who had taken care of her while her parents worked. Even her parents were only shadows in her memory. It might have helped if she had more photographs and memorabilia from her life in India, but she had arrived at the airport with nothing more than a birth certificate, her passport, and the single family picture. She remembered vividly feeling lost without her mother to hold her hand or her favorite doll in her arms. Her mother was buried with her father in India, but where was the doll now?

Liana stopped to watch the colors splayed across the wispy clouds in the western sky above the house, a myriad of oranges, yellows, and reds. These same colors made up the stucco and rock work of her adoptive parents' house, as though the bucket of the sky had spilled the colors down upon the house. She had always loved the sunset; it stirred something deep inside, making her somehow want to both cry and laugh.

"Oh, you're finally here," Christian said, meeting her at the door. He had a small piece of meat in his hands, which he popped into his mouth, wiping his fingers on his jeans. Opening his arms, he pulled her into a hug, which she enjoyed but did not return.

"No thanks to you. I worked all day on your friend's account. What a messed-up piece of work! I'll be glad to wash my hands of it."

He swallowed his mouthful and grimaced. "Sorry. I honestly had no idea it would be such a problem."

"Just don't be surprised if he pulls the plug on your advertising campaign when he gets my bill."

"Too late. It's already been approved. Oh, yeah. Uh-huh. I am the man." Christian strutted around, making strongman poses until she laughed.

"Stop that!"

Smiling, he drew her down the short entryway, past the small kitchen and into the family room where everyone had gathered on couches that were situated around a brick fireplace.

Bret saw her first and stood up to greet her, dressed as usual in tan pleated slacks and a matching button-down shirt. Serious and thoughtful to a fault, he was Christian's complete opposite. His blond hair, blue eyes, oval face, and lighter build were echoes of his mother. Neither startlingly handsome or overtly gregarious, he was good-looking and friendly enough to be popular. He always had sweet girlfriends who had so far waited in vain for a marriage proposal. Liana had never felt as close to Bret as she had to Christian, though he was nearer in age, being only five years older, but she trusted him as she trusted no one else. If he said something, he meant it. Christian might forget, but Bret would not.

"Liana," he said, smiling. Like Christian, he hugged her, but the contact was brief, more deliberate than spontaneous.

Travis and Clarissa Winn were close behind him, offering their hugs. Travis's was bold, Clarissa's hesitant, and Liana returned them briefly. "Thank you for coming, Lara," Clarissa said.

Liana stiffened, though she had known it was coming. Her adoptive mother was the only person besides the teller at the bank who ever called her by her legal name, Lara Clari Winn. A name she had come to detest. A name that constantly reminded her that Christian and Bret were really her cousins, not her older brothers at all, and that her biological parents had died when she was only four.

"Happy birthday, Mother," Liana said, forcing herself to say the word that had always been awkward on her lips.

"Sixty-five." Travis grinned, a hand on his wife's shoulder. "But she doesn't look a day over fifty." He was a tall, large man who had gained too much weight in the past years, so much so that he now wore his dress pants well below his natural waist. His temperament was much like Bret's—serious, dependable, solid. His full head of hair was salt-and-pepper gray, and his white brows made a nearly solid line above his eyes. There were creases in his square, ruddy face, small rolls, actually, that would have looked more like wrinkles had he been a thinner man.

"Nonsense," Clarissa said, but she looked pleased. She stepped back to survey Liana. "How are you?" Worry creased her brow in fine lines that matched the tiny lines etched into her otherwise smooth skin around her eyes and mouth. Her blonde hair—she was still blonde, though whether the blonde now came from a bottle Liana didn't know—came to her shoulders, gently curling under. She was fairly trim from her daily stint at the local gym, and she generally wore clothing that would be more appropriate in a nice restaurant than in the high school classroom where she spent most of her time teaching calculus to teenagers. Today she wore a shiny brown skirt that swept the floor and an off-white blouse that glittered with gold embroidery.

"I'm fine," Liana said.

"You look a little tired."

"I've been up late."

"Oh?" Clarissa raised her eyebrows, plucked into a thin arch and accentuated by brown pencil. Liana knew what was behind the probe. Clarissa wanted grandchildren, and she hoped Liana's late-night adventures might somehow be related to dating.

"Just work."

"How's the accounting business, anyway?" Bret had resettled himself on the couch and was fingering something in his wallet.

Liana swallowed hard. "Fine. And how's the bridge building?" Bret had followed in his father's footsteps to become a civil engineer, something that had made Travis very happy.

"Stretching out," Christian answered for him. "Get it? Bridge building—stretching out. Oh, whatever. It's there. It's boring. Isn't there something else to talk about?"

Silence fell heavily over them. Liana was riveted to the scene, feeling as she so often had growing up that she was an understudy, watching the real actors play their parts.

"I've met a girl," Bret said into the awkward silence. "I'm getting married."

"You're what?" Travis and Clarissa said together.

"About time." Christian sat carelessly on the couch next to Bret. "You'll be thirty-five next month, won't you?"

"Look who's talking. Last I heard, you turned forty."

Christian flashed a wide grin. "Yeah, but I'm an artist. That excuses everything."

Bret rolled his eyes.

"Are you really getting married?" Clarissa's pale face flushed with eager excitement. "When do we get to meet her?"

"Well, she would have come today, but she had an out-of-town job. She's a model. Here, I have her picture." Bret removed a photograph from his wallet.

Liana had drawn off to the side to observe them, but now her curiosity propelled her forward with the rest of the family. She expected to see a young, sweet-faced girl in a snapshot, but instead a blonde vision of made-up perfection stared at her from a professional photograph. The youth was there, and the expression mimicked innocence, but wide brown eyes told a different story. This was a young woman who knew exactly what she wanted and would do anything to get it.

Christian whistled. "Now that's some woman. Congratulations, brother!" He slapped Bret heartily on the back.

"She is very pretty," Clarissa said. "What's her name?"

"Britanni. With an i on the end. Britanni Medford."

"Whatever happened to that other girl you were seeing?" Travis asked. "The one from Alabama. I liked her accent."

"Went back to Alabama, hopefully," Christian said. "Good thing, too. She'd have Bret married with a half dozen children by now if he'd let her."

Clarissa glared at him. "And what's wrong with that? I could use a few grandchildren."

"Don't get me wrong, Mom," Christian said hastily. "She was a cute little thing in her way, but this girl"—he pointed to the photograph—"is worthy of bearing the next generation of Winns."

"We'll look forward to meeting her," Clarissa said, placated. "Now I think it's about time to eat. Your dad and I have everything set up in the dining room. Lara, if you'll give me a hand with the vegetables and the potatoes while the men argue over who's going to cut the roast, we'll get this show on the road."

"I'll do it," Christian said. "Bret's having a hard time taking his eyes from his fiancée's face."

Clarissa leaned over and kissed Bret. "This is the best present you could give me," she said a little too loudly. "Now if only your brother and sister could follow your example. Come on, Lara." With her usual grace, she swept from the room.

The dinner went smoothly—Christian had obviously decided not to be overly annoying. Clarissa served the food, one plate at a time. So long had she done this that she could gauge their portions with uncanny accuracy. "Thanks, Mom," Christian and Bret said. Liana smiled her appreciation.

As the meal progressed, Liana watched them interact, almost a stranger amidst her own family, her feelings confused and varied. She loved Christian, she trusted Bret, and she was grateful to her aunt and uncle, the couple who had adopted her and raised her as their own. Gratitude was something she could freely give them—much better than love, she'd told herself throughout the years. She still believed that. Gratitude didn't make you shrivel up inside when someone died. Only love did that.

"So, Lara, you said you've been working," Clarissa prompted, smiling at her from the other side of the long table. "Sounds like that boss is a slave driver. Maybe you should look for another job. You certainly have the training for it."

Liana shifted on the padded wooden chair. She'd hated her

job and had no idea why she'd clung to it, but she didn't want to talk about how she'd walked out. After she made plans for the future, after she was sure she wouldn't become a burden, then she'd tell them.

"Actually, that was my fault." Christian finished pouring himself a second glass of wine and set the bottle down. "I asked her to do a favor for a friend of mine. Nice guy." He flashed Liana a smile. "He seemed to like you, by the way."

That was the last direction Liana wanted the conversation to head. She'd already been haunted by a dream last night in which Austin's midnight eyes had stared back at her from a wrecked plane. "Not my type," she said, and to Clarissa she added, "It's just this time of the year. Things'll slow down."

"Then who is your type?" Christian asked.

Liana kicked him under the table. "He drives a truck, for crying out loud. And listens to country music. I bet he even has cowboy boots."

"He did grow up on a farm."

"See?"

"What's wrong with a farm?"

"That's enough, Christian," Clarissa warned.

"I'm about finished." Travis set down his fork. "How about some birthday cake?"

"And presents," Bret added.

Clarissa smiled. "Oh, you guys didn't have to do that. What's one more birthday?"

"You love presents, and you know it," Travis teased, putting his hand over hers.

That much was true. Clarissa was a giver and always remembered everyone's birthday, including the paperboy, the neighbor, and the pastor at the church. But the flip side was that she expected everyone to remember her birthday each year. Fortunately, Travis was good at picking up on Clarissa's hints, Bret had an e-mail reminder system, and Christian had Bret. Liana didn't need an outside reminder; she had every important date written in the calendar of her planner, especially those she commemorated alone each year: the date of her parents' death, the day she had been ripped away from Mamata and sent to America, the day her aunt and uncle had adopted her.

"I left my present in the car," Christian said, standing.

Liana followed suit. "Me, too."

They walked out together, going first to his BMW. Liana lifted her face to the sky and took in a deep breath of cool night air. The sun was gone now, and the stars had begun to appear.

"What'd you get her?" Christian asked.

"I bought gift certificates for that day spa she was hinting about. Came with a special spa bathrobe."

Christian groaned. "I should have done that."

"What did you get?"

"Bret got her a lead crystal vase, so I ordered her a matching candy dish."

Liana shook her head. "Christian, she's a mature woman— she's had a lifetime to collect vases and dishes. What's she going to do with another one? Next time, get her a ticket to someplace."

"Isn't it the thought that counts?"

"Not when those vases will likely end up in my condo. Then again, at least I can use them." She patted his shoulder and started walking toward her convertible.

Christian grabbed a package from the passenger seat of his car and hurried to catch up to her. "If this is going to end up at your place, I guess I won't have to buy a present for your next birthday. Hey, why's that in there?"

Liana stared into the trunk of her car where she'd stashed her present. Next to the gold foil package lay the eagle painting. "I'm taking it home, that's all," she said, wishing the moon didn't cast so much light.

"But you told me once it was all that kept you going at work."

Liana grimaced at his memory of what had been a weak moment. "Now I want it home."

"But I painted it so that you . . ." He paused. "You always loved watching birds when you were little. I'd see you out in the back before they built all those houses, pretending you could fly. I think you were trying to go back to your nanny in India."

"I didn't know you saw me." Liana could barely get the words out. What would he have said if he had known she hadn't been pretending to fly to India but rather mentally following her parents' path, trying to relive their last moments on the plane, trying to somehow join them?

"You really hate it, don't you?" His voice took on a flippant note as he studied his painting, but Liana knew him too well to believe he didn't care. He had always been insecure about his talent, which was the reason he was working in advertising instead of making a living as an artist.

"I love it just as I've always loved it. Okay, look, the truth is I quit work."

"You quit?" He opened and shut his mouth in surprise.

"Yep, on Friday. I should have taken the picture inside already, but I've had a lot on my mind." Liana became aware of a numbness in her fingers where she had been clutching the edge of the trunk. She forced herself to relax.

"The old man let you quit? No way. He's too money hungry."

She gave him a twisted smile. "You always did see right through him. But he didn't have a choice in the matter. I left."

Christian folded his arms across his chest. "Why? You'd better tell me or I'm going in there to beat it out of him." His words were calmly stated, but his eyes held an unmistakably angry glint.

Liana sighed. "It's nothing, really. Mr. Koplin saw me with Austin and raked me over the coals for using company equipment to do outside work. Your friend has a big mouth or it wouldn't have happened at all. Not that it's really his fault. The next day Koplin tried to get me to get Austin to hire our company. When he found out there was no way Austin could do that, he made it clear he was going to make my life miserable . . . so I quit." She reached for her mother's package, willing the discussion to be over, but Christian's next words stopped her.

"What did Austin say about that?"

"Austin? You've got to be kidding. It's none of his business."

"But you said that if he hadn't opened his mou—"

"It's personal. Doesn't have anything to do with him." She waved toward the house, where her parents and Bret sat blissfully unaware of her problems. "And don't you go telling them, either. I'll be fine. I've been thinking about starting my own business anyway."

Christian shook his head. "I feel terrible. I mean, if it weren't for me, you'd still have a job."

"Yeah, and I'd still be using your painting as a way to get me to show up there."

He smiled and reached for her hands. "Liana, I'm glad you like my painting. I thought for a moment there that you really didn't, and you're the only who believes in me."

"You could be a real artist if you wanted," she said, returning the pressure on her hands.

73

He shook his head. "Naw, not really. I never had enough angst or enough drive. And I like the way I live too much. Artists don't always drive BMWs."

That much was true. Christian made good money in advertising, but it always slipped through his hands like air. If he made any less, he wouldn't be able to survive. Still, the neglect of his talent was painful to Liana, who could barely draw a straight line under duress. Perhaps, had he been raised differently, he would have followed another direction, but in a family of engineers and mathematicians, there was little room for his artistic growth. Although their parents had never shown disappointment in Christian's obsession with art, their obvious pleasure with Bret and Liana's choices spoke volumes.

"I'm fine, Liana," Christian said softly, more attuned to her thoughts than was comfortable for her. "I love my work, and I'm happy dabbling with painting on the side. Not everyone has to be a Rembrandt."

"Well, don't get too settled." She slammed the trunk shut. "I'm not settling for a secondhand crystal candy dish for my birthday. I want another painting."

CHAPTER
7

Diary of Karyn Olsen
Tuesday, February 15, 1966

It's after the dance now, but the next day, since it's already one o'clock. Travis didn't kiss me, except on the cheek at the door to our apartment. He didn't even hold my hand. I am so depressed. Is something wrong with me? Is it because I'm so big? But I'm not really fat, just tall and big boned, and he's tall, too, so it can't be that.

We did dance almost every dance, and he told me how nice I looked. He even bought me a box of candy and a card. I gave him a package of silver-wrapped Hershey Kisses in a heart-shaped box I found at the grocery store. It was a hint, but he didn't get it. Why didn't he get it? My Prince Charming should get it. But I'm not giving up. He is just too good to let go.

Austin was late getting to the office Monday morning. He'd been up early checking out flights to Ukraine, reading up on investment strategies, and calling Tammy, the woman in charge of purchasing for HeartReach. But Tammy was visiting her daughter and her newest grandchild. He hadn't even been able to reach Mabel, who was responsible for sending out quarterly solicitations to sponsors. After three hours he was disgusted to find he had accomplished absolutely nothing. That's what he got when he tried to wake up before any sane person. He should have stayed in bed.

"Good morning, Mr. Walker," chimed the receptionists at the front desk.

He had to stop himself from growling. "Good morning, Holly, Shannon. Hold my calls, will you? I have a meeting in a few minutes."

"Mr. Goodman's here," Shannon answered, "and we told him we'd direct you to the boardroom when you arrived."

"Thank you." Austin stifled a sigh. Mr. Goodman's presence at the meeting this morning likely meant an out-of-town trip in the immediate future for Austin. He might have to cancel his racquetball appointment with Christian, and, unless he could talk Mercedes into arranging a flight, sending an immediate shipment to Ukraine would have to wait. *Maybe I should talk to Mabel about a promotion,* he thought. But he'd tried promoting her before, and the mother of eight claimed to be happy licking stamps and mailing letters.

"Oh, Grandmother," he said with a sigh as he rode the elevator to his office. "Why did you choose me?" But the reality was that Austin loved his involvement with HeartReach. He just wished he was as good at managing the charity as he was at selling electronics.

The phone rang the minute he opened his office door, and Austin frowned at it in irritation. Why couldn't the receptionists do their job? He was tempted to let it ring and go to his meeting, but it might be important—maybe that's why they'd let it through. He sprinted across the room and dived for the phone. "Hello, Austin Walker."

"Finally," said a voice. "I thought for a minute that you weren't in."

"Who is this?" Austin demanded.

"Christian. And what's eating you? Sounds like you woke up on the wrong side of the bed."

"I've got a meeting. They weren't supposed to let any calls through."

"I know, I know. They told me. And I told them it was a matter of life and death."

About to sit down in his leather chair, Austin froze. "What's wrong? Is it Liana?" Why else would Christian be calling? His advertisements had been approved and their racquetball appointment was still days away, so there was nothing urgent they needed to discuss.

"No, Little Miss Muffet—of course it's Liana."

Austin sat abruptly, gripping the phone with an intensity that surprised him. "Is she okay? What happened?"

"That's what I want to know." Christian's voice was hard. "What'd you say to her boss? I got her to help you because you needed it. I didn't know it would cause her to lose her job."

"Her job?"

"Yeah, her job."

"So that's why she was acting odd on Friday—and why she came early."

"Odd? She was acting odd? How so?"

The challenging way Christian spoke irritated Austin. "Just odd, but I didn't think anything of it because she—" He stopped. Truth was, both times he'd seen her, Christian's sister had been acting a little odd.

"You should have kept your mouth shut when you ran across her boss."

"Whoa, Christian. I didn't know I'd done anything to get her fired. Come on. You've known me long enough to know I wouldn't purposely hurt someone."

There was a deep breath on the other side of the line. "Okay," Christian said with a sigh. "I appreciate that. But now what? I worry about her, you know."

Austin knew. If it had been Mercedes, he'd worry too. "I'll see what I can do."

"Thanks."

Austin hung up the phone. He rubbed his chin for a moment, thinking back to when his relationship with Christian had passed into friendship. Had it been when Christian had turned in his first designs last year? No, their bonding had taken place months later on the racquetball court when Christian had talked about his paintings, and they had fallen into a discussion about their pasts. Austin hadn't exactly told Christian about his father's abuse, but he'd seen understanding in Christian's eyes. Neither had Christian outlined his family's lack of encouragement, yet intuitively, Austin had known. Both understood what it was to be a disappointment to their fathers. Both knew what it took to forge a new life for themselves.

Austin felt more than a little guilty for his part in Liana's dilemma. If only he had kept his mouth shut when they had been talking to her boss. He had recognized trouble in the man's eyes from the minute they'd met—typical of small-minded men who enjoyed power. Well, he'd just see about that.

Picking up the phone, he dialed the receptionist. "Shannon, could you get me the number for"—what was the ridiculous name of the firm?—"um, I think it's Klassy

Accounting or something equally cutesy. Klassy with a K. Then put me through. Be sure you tell them who's calling. I need to talk to the owner, I believe. Can't for the life of me remember his name."

"That's a first," Shannon said dryly.

"Believe me, I was better off forgetting this time."

"You remember the meeting with Mr. Goodman?"

"Yeah, I remember. This'll just take a few seconds. Let me know when you have someone on the line."

Austin waited at the window with his hands behind his back. Down below, he could see cars zipping about as though they possessed minds of their own. None of them were convertibles. He wondered where Liana was at that moment. He tried to think of her alone, sad, or confused, but the image was difficult. His phone rang, and he sauntered toward it.

"Mr. Walker, I have Mr. Koplin's secretary on the line."

"Thanks, Shannon." Then to the other voice on the line Austin said, "I need to talk with—with . . ." What was the name Shannon had just said? Since Austin had a proclivity toward forgetting names during the first few encounters, he and Shannon had worked out a system in which she always mentioned the name shortly before Austin would need it.

"You need Mr. Koplin," the woman at Klassy Accounting said. "I'll connect you now."

After a few clicks and a brief wait, a voice answered. "Hello, Mr. Walker. Larry Koplin here. Good to hear from you. Can I take it that this call means you've reconsidered using Klassy Accounting as your permanent accounting firm?"

Austin could picture the man wringing his hands with delight. "No, that's not it at all. I'm calling about Liana Winn. What's going on?"

"If you mean Liana, this is her own doing." The kiss-up

79

tone had gone from Koplin's voice, though he was still painfully polite. "I asked her to make good and offer you a contract with us. I did everything I could to assure her place here."

"Is that why you fired her?"

"It was her choice. And to tell the truth, I think it's ungrateful of her. Sure, she has talent, but we gave her a chance. We made her who she is."

"So she owes you, is that it?" *More likely, you think you own her,* Austin thought.

"Well," Larry Koplin said, leaving no doubt as to his opinion, "everything we ask our employees to do here is for the good of the firm."

Something in the way he said the words told Austin he was lying. "I don't know exactly what happened," he said, "but you definitely need to reconsider Liana's employment." He thought about going further and saying that if he didn't, Austin would make certain Klassy Accounting never had any of Goodman's business or the business of any of their associates, but the point was moot. None of them would hire the firm anyway.

"I tell you it was her—"

"I'm late for a meeting with Mr. Goodman." Austin cut him off. A quick look at his watch assured him this was about to be true. "Good day, Mr. Koplin."

Austin grabbed a portfolio from his briefcase and ran from the room.

The street in Henderson was deserted, though a few small children were playing dodgeball in one of the front yards. Austin was amazed that they found room to play on the tiny patches of grass, bordered by decorative cacti. Coming from the lushness of his parents' Wyoming farm, the Nevada desert had been a shock for him at first, and every now and then it still surprised him as he recalled acres of wheat and alfalfa and lazy summer mornings on the grassy bank of the swimming hole. He'd learned that Nevada had its own beauty in the succulent limbs of the cacti and flowers they produced and in the stunning palm trees, but though the display was nice, sometimes even exceptional, it wasn't home. It wasn't where his mind went when he dreamed. Strange that his mind had room for good memories of the farm, when it was crammed with so many that brought heartache.

He climbed from his truck, smiling as a red ball bounced in his direction. With both hands he scooped up the ball and tossed it back to the waiting children. "Thanks, mister!" came a shout, and then they were back at play.

Liana's condominium looked like any other on the street, except there was a potted plant in a decorative vase on the narrow porch. The plant was dead and the soil dry. He checked the address he'd printed from the Internet one last time before ringing the bell.

She opened it after only a short delay, and the surprise in her blue eyes told him she had not used the peephole. "Uh, hello." She was dressed in baggy, blue plaid pants and a sky blue T-shirt that matched her eyes. What was she doing in pajamas at nearly two in the afternoon? He waited for her to open the door wider and to ask him in, but she remained clutching the door with one hand, blocking the space between the door and the frame with her body.

"How's the work coming?" he asked.

"Nearly done." Her brows drew tightly together, showing clear displeasure. "But I said I would call when I finished. Why are you here?"

"I heard about your job."

She grimaced. "Christian."

"He was worried. I'm glad he called. After all, it was my big mouth that got you into trouble."

Her arms folded across her chest, and Austin knew things weren't going well.

"I talked to your boss. I wouldn't be surprised if he called and offered you your job back."

"You called Mr. Koplin?" Her eyes opened wide with disbelief. "Just who do you think you are? I told you before, Mr. Walker, that you weren't my knight in shining armor. I can handle myself." She shook her head in disgust. "For your information, I wasn't fired. I quit. The man was an overbearing, male chauvinist jerk, and I was going nowhere fast in that company. It was way past time I found a new job."

"Well, I maybe could work something out at Goodman's. It wouldn't be accounting but—"

Her face flushed. "You don't get it, do you? I can handle it. I have a degree. I know what I'm doing. *I'll* work things out."

"Well, I . . . you see, . . ." What was it about her that made him feel so insecure? He was accustomed to solving problems; he was good at it.

"Look, come in, and if you'll wait a minute, I'll print you out your forms. Then you can send them off by express mail and forget any of this ever happened." She turned and stalked into her condo. He followed more slowly.

The narrow entryway led into a sizable living room that seemed to be full of books. She pointed to a Victorian couch covered in a pale, flowered print. "Sit there." She herself settled into a puke-green easy chair that looked more comfortable than any chair that ugly had a right to be. From a side table, she picked up the laptop he'd given her. "Just a few more things . . ." Her fingers flew over the keys.

After ten minutes, she left the room and returned with several sheets of paper. "There's more. It'll take time to print them all."

"I could do it at the office."

"I need to check over it all once more." She sat in her chair and focused on the papers in her hand.

Austin shifted his weight on the uncomfortable couch. "Look, I was just trying to help. I didn't mean to . . . you know."

To his relief her brows relaxed, and she smiled. He didn't like to admit it, but that smile did funny things to his insides. "I know," she said. "And I do appreciate the concern. But I really do know what I'm doing."

"So what exactly are your plans?"

She contemplated him for a few seconds without speaking. "Accounting, taxes. I'm going to start my own business. It might be a little rough at first, especially if I'm not able to pick up clients before the tax season is over, but I'll make it work."

For a fleeting second, he could see vulnerability in her eyes, but it lived so briefly that he wondered if she was even aware of it herself. A protective urge, one she most certainly wouldn't appreciate, came to the forefront of his emotions. He often had these feelings where other people, less fortunate than himself, were concerned. Mercedes said the urge grew out of the helplessness he'd felt as a child, the helplessness to change his own life and that of his sister and mother. She said he needed to prove he could change everything he perceived as unjust.

Maybe she was right.

"I'll be okay," Liana assured him. Or were the words for herself? He couldn't tell. Perhaps a little of both.

An idea came so swiftly that for a moment he didn't reply. "Well," he said, leaning forward to give himself a rest from the stiff back of the couch, "since you're basically starting your own company, I might have a job for you. That is, if you think you can handle it." Adding this last bit was pure genius, he told himself when he saw her chin go up at the challenge.

"What do you have in mind?" Stiffly, she laid her papers on the end table.

"Well, aside from my job as sales manager of Goodman Electronics, I'm also the president of a small charity."

She relaxed slightly. "Christian told me. Your grandmother used to oversee it?"

"Yes. She started out in Africa and India. Then in the early 1990s she began sending most of our aid to Ukraine. A few of our ancestors were Ukrainian, and she felt a connection to the country."

Austin had felt it, too. He'd been there a dozen times as his grandmother's emissary when she had become too feeble to travel, and he had been amazed at the architecture, especially the impressive churches and cathedrals, which for him typified the Ukrainian determination to live. Despite centuries of struggle for autonomy, including decades of Soviet oppression and brutality, both the churches and the Ukrainians had survived.

"Why did she only start sending aid to Ukraine in the nineties?"

"That's when Soviet rule ended and the country opened its door to international aid."

"Ah, that's right. I remember reading something about that."

"So just before my grandmother died, she made me the new president. It's not a big organization, but we manage to do quite a bit for our size. We have a buyer who purchases items to send to Ukraine, a lady who sends out donation requests, and we've been using the advertising firm your brother works for when we have events. There's even a toll-free number for people to call if they want to donate by credit card—we pay a service to take care of the calls. My sister usually arranges flights, and I do finances. In Ukraine we have a full-time worker and two part-timers. That's about it."

"Sounds like a lot of work."

He sighed. "It is."

"Why don't you quit your job and do it full time?"

"I think my grandmother intended for me to make the charity grow to the point where I could do that. And perhaps I could some day, though I really want the money to go to the children, instead of a large salary."

"Which you are accustomed to receiving." A faint smile played on her lips.

"I guess it sounds a bit selfish."

"Well, I understand your wanting to maintain your current lifestyle. But if you worked at it full time, you might be able to grow the charity to the point where you could help more children *and* get the salary you need."

"You're probably right. But truthfully, while I like to be involved, I don't think I could do it full time. At least not right now. I enjoy my job at Goodman's. I'm good at it."

"I'm sure you are." She propped an elbow on the worn arm of her chair, one finger on her chin. "So what's this job you had in mind?"

Austin thought her words sounded forced, as though she wished she didn't need to ask. He had to struggle to keep the grin from his face. "We could use some financial help—especially now. We've received a large donation from the estate of a man who knew my grandmother. I had them put it in the bank, but I need to see how that's going to affect the charity in tax terms."

"Shouldn't change too much. And you've been doing the accounts, so why pay someone else to do it?"

"I've only done the accounts since my grandmother died last year, and I'm finding they take much more time than I expected. Time I don't have, since I often have to go away on business." He paused a moment before adding, "So, will you do it?"

Her head leaned to the side to rest on her hand while she considered a moment. "Okay. I'll need all the current statements as well as access to past records, of course."

"They're in Wyoming." He'd forgotten that. "Or most of them. I often go to my sister's for the weekend, and since the rest of the charity employees are there, it seemed only logical to keep them there. I do have some current bank records at my house, though."

She shook her head. "I'll need more than that."

"Yeah, I know." Austin rubbed his chin, feeling the stubble that had already begun to appear. He contemplated his options and made a quick decision. "Well, how about taking a trip?"

"What?"

"I'm going to be visiting several states this week for business, and one of the places I'm headed is Wyoming. I was going to fly, but I could rearrange my schedule and drive instead, and then you could come with me. It wouldn't take more than thirteen hours, give or take an hour. Then while I go to Casper and Sheridan to take care of business, you could take a look, see what you need, and we'll bring it back." He could make up one of the days lost in traveling on Saturday.

"Wyoming?" she asked.

Austin didn't know her well, but he thought she looked stunned at his proposal. He liked the idea of being able to surprise her. "Yeah, Wyoming."

"Can't you just bring everything back with you?"

"Too many boxes, even for my truck."

"I don't know," she hedged.

"Come on. It'll be fun. A vacation of sorts." Austin suddenly found himself caring whether or not she accepted his offer. "You'll love seeing the farm where I grew up—belongs to my sister and her husband now. It's very green there, or will be soon. Spring is a wonderful time to visit. Everything is coming alive. A lot of baby animals are born; crops are put in and begin to sprout. Consider it a vacation. It'll only take, what, two or three days, tops. I'll do all the driving."

"Okay." Her response was so soft he almost didn't catch it.

"Okay?"

She nodded verification. "When do we leave?"

"In the morning. I'll pick you up at six."

She stood, signaling an end to their conversation. "I'll be ready. Your papers should be finished by now. I can check them fast." She left the room and returned with the printouts after several long minutes.

"Thank you," he said.

"Don't thank me yet. My bill is in there, too."

He grinned. "Good."

They stood at the door now, but Austin found himself reluctant to leave. "I'm glad it worked out—I mean for the charity."

"It hasn't yet." A smile softened her words.

Allowing her the parting shot, he strode down the sidewalk. He was tempted to look around and see if she was watching, but he controlled himself and made his way to his truck. He looked then, but he'd parked too far to the right to see into the covered porch. Shaking his head, he backed up and drove away.

CHAPTER 8

Diary of Karyn Olsen
Monday, February 28, 1966

I wish Clari could do my hair for my date with Travis, our first since Valentine's, but when I called her, she said she had a ton of calculus tests to correct by tomorrow. Whatever possessed her to teach math at a high school, I'll never know. At least she's always around to help me with math when I need her, although lately I've been asking Travis instead. He's so busy with classes that I hardly see him except when I need help. At least he's not dating anyone else. I had Angie ask her cousin. Her cousin thinks Angie likes Travis, but it's not true. She's seriously dating Craig.

Tonight we're going to a movie. I mentioned I was going at lunch, and Travis acted excited about going with me. We're still having lunch together at the cafeteria almost three times a week. Sometimes he talks about building bridges and stuff, and it bores me to tears. Compared to the excitement of a living cell, or the birth of a new baby, bridges are so . . . well, boring. But I do love him, so I try to listen, though some of the concepts escape me. He is so intelligent and bright! I hope our children (one girl and one boy, of course) take after him.

Liana awoke Tuesday morning feeling much more positive than she had in the past few days. The darkness seemed to exude a sense of expectancy, though she didn't think the feeling derived from the impending trip to Austin's childhood farm. The only memory she had of visiting a farm was on a first-grade field trip—and that hadn't been a pleasant experience.

"Come on, children," Miss Jones called. "It's time to ride the horse."

Liana felt her heart pound in her chest. What if she couldn't control the horse and she fell off? Even when she saw the horse's owner leading the children around on the horse with a rope, she couldn't bring herself to climb up onto its back. She didn't know the man—what if he let go?

"I don't want to ride," Liana told her teacher.

"She's a big baby," Jody said to Robby. A few of the children laughed.

Liana slunk away to the picnic table in shame and anger. While the others were riding, she hid Jody's sack lunch for revenge. It wasn't exactly her fault that the farm dog found the lunch before Jody did, but after returning to the school, the teacher sent her to the office for punishment. When her mother arrived, Liana clenched her jaw and told the principal, "She's not my mother. She's not!"

Clarissa's face flushed. "Come on, Lara," she said softly, blinking back tears.

It wasn't until she faced Christian at home that Liana began to feel bad. "She's your mother whether you like it or not," he scolded. "The only one you've got. And you'd better treat her better. She's my mother, too, and I don't want to ever see her cry again like she did today." Christian stared at Liana so sternly that she started crying.

"Okay," she whispered, silently, vowing never again to tell anyone that Clarissa and Travis were not her real parents. But the knowledge remained inside, alive and eating at the soft parts of her no one could see. Her real parents were dead, and that made her angry at everyone.

Liana showered and dressed before slipping downstairs to the kitchen for a quick bite to eat. Her small suitcase stood like a solitary sentinel by the front door, reminding her that she was traveling to another state with a man who was almost a complete stranger. She didn't quite understand her reasons for going, but Austin had come alive when talking about the farm, and she had felt compelled to accept. Still, she would never have agreed to go if she hadn't been desperate. Yesterday morning when she had been on her way to the grocery store, her Cavalier had thrown a rod and the man at the garage had quoted her thirteen hundred dollars for a repair. Thirteen hundred! She felt it was an outrageous price, though she had no choice but to pay. Buying another car wasn't an option. She'd looked far and long for a nice used convertible she could comfortably afford.

Over the weekend she'd spent several hours calling acquaintances, sending out e-mails, and putting advertisements in various newspapers, but so far she had received no response. Most people had already made their tax plans or would rely on a company with a solid reputation. She would be lucky to pick up a few jobs in the next two weeks. Though she was confident she would be able to build her business in the long term, for now she would have to live frugally to survive.

As much as she didn't want to admit it, Austin's offer was a godsend—even if it meant she had to endure his company for thirteen hours. But one thing she would not do was tolerate his music. No way, no how. She went into the living room to get the laptop Austin continued to lend her for this new job and to gather a few of her favorite CDs, including some that had been popular when Christian was a teen. As a child she'd spent a lot of time with him listening to his music, and it had found a permanent place in her collection.

Austin arrived promptly at six, before the sun had risen, though the sky to the east was alight, heralding the coming of day. He wore blue jeans, a white T-shirt, and sandals, all of which made him look leaner and taller than she remembered. His black hair was shorter today, combed back and slightly sticking up, clearly showing the high arches in his hairline. There was a scar she hadn't noticed before near the top left arch that disappeared into his hair.

"Got a haircut?" she asked.

He grinned. "Yeah. Going to see my sister and all."

"She lives on a farm—don't all farm boys have long hair?"

"Not my sister's boys. She trained to be a hair stylist once."

"I see."

Hefting her suitcase, he waited while she locked the door. "You really should do something with that plant."

She shrugged. "Looks fine to me."

"It's dead."

"What are you, a farm boy?" She thought it was amusing that a farm boy had worked his way up a corporate ladder to be the sales manager of a sizable firm. Though the store chain might be small potatoes when compared with the industry giants, it was still impressive.

"That's right. I'm a farm boy, through and through. You hungry?"

"No, I ate something."

"I'm stopping for a bite, if you don't mind. If I can find a place that's open for breakfast."

"I know a place."

He opened the door to his truck, and while she climbed in next to several plastic grocery bags filled with snacks, he set her suitcase in the truck bed next to his own. They drove to her favorite McDonald's and then on to the freeway. "Fastest way is through Utah. Ever been there?"

She nodded. "My brother—not Christian but Bret—has a cabin in the mountains there. Uses it to ski in the winter."

"Oh, where?"

"Near a place called Sundance. I only went there once. It's very beautiful."

"Still cold I bet, this time of year."

They fell into a surprisingly comfortable silence. Beyond the window the Nevada landscape flew by, buildings gradually falling away to long stretches of uninhabited land. The sun emerged from the east, crawling slowly up the cloudless blue sky. As Liana stared at it, a vision of another sun-washed landscape superimposed itself in her mind, one from before, when her parents had been alive. Along with it came an overwhelming sense of loss and anger. Tears stung her eyes like acid.

"Uh, Liana." Austin's voice shattered the unwelcome memory. "You're ringing. At least I think you are."

Shaking thoughts of the past from her head, she rummaged in her oversized black handbag for her cell phone. She smiled her thanks but didn't look at him directly, afraid he'd see the emotion in her face. "Hello?" she said into her phone. She glanced furtively at Austin and was relieved that he was concentrating on his driving and not on her.

"Hi, it's Christian. I got the message you left last night on my cell. What's this about going to Wyoming with Austin? I got the impression you didn't like the guy."

"It's business." She switched the phone to her other ear so there would be no chance for Austin to overhear Christian. "I've agreed to do some accounting work for his charity, and we're going to get the paperwork in Wyoming."

"You're driving? That doesn't make sense."

"Cheaper than flying. It's a charity, remember?" She felt more than saw Austin nod his head. "Besides, we have a load of paperwork to bring back."

"I guess. But all that time alone with Austin?" The amusement in his voice came through loud and clear.

"Gotta pay the bills."

"Oh, I see. Does this have anything to do with the car problem you mentioned? Do you need help? Look, I don't have a lot saved, but it's yours if you need it. Better yet, you could come and live with me."

"And get stuck cooking and doing your laundry? You're crazy."

"I mean it. If you need help—"

"Everything's fine," she assured him. "I'm a big girl, in case you hadn't noticed."

"Oh, yeah? I'm not too sure about that. Tell me, what do you have in the pocket of your blouse?"

Liana's hand went instinctively to the front jacket pocket of her brown stretch denim outfit where she carried the photograph of her parents. "I'm not wearing a blouse with a pocket." Underneath the jacket she wore a snug polyester T-shirt, but he was right at least about the photo. Though she no longer carried the picture around every day, there was no way she'd leave town without it.

"Whatever. I know you have it with you." His voice had

become gentle, bringing a lump to her throat that she could not swallow.

She was tempted to hang up on him. "Is that wrong?"

"No. But it tells me . . . forget it. Let me talk to Austin."

"I'll give him a message. Wouldn't want him to get into an accident or anything while he's driving." No way would she let them talk about her. "Well?"

"Never mind."

Just as she'd thought.

"Take care of yourself," he said. "And try to have a little fun, eh?" With that he ended the connection.

Liana returned the phone to her purse. "Big brother Christian," she said.

Austin laughed. "I hear you. Mercedes is just as bad."

"Thing is, I'm the one who keeps bailing him out." She leaned back more comfortably and adjusted her seatbelt. "Last year he invested in some multilevel scam. Then there were those people selling bogus stock. Before that it was a swimming pool he tried to put in the first floor of his rental house. The owners weren't too happy."

"*Inside* the house?"

"Yes, inside."

He laughed. "Sounds like Christian. Have to admit, Mercedes isn't anything like that. I never have to bail her out. But she does always try to use psychology on me to find out how I'm feeling. Kind of annoying."

Liana arched a brow. "I thought you said she studied hair dressing."

"Yep. And psychology, retail management, building contracting, and even animal medicine. She has a lot of interests."

"But she ended up back at your parents' farm."

"She loves it there." He glanced from the road to her and

back again. "Besides, there was no one to take over when my dad couldn't do it anymore. She married the hired man and settled down to raising grain, calves, and babies."

There was something he wasn't telling her, but Liana couldn't begin to fathom what. "So where's your father now?"

"In Rock Springs." His voice was clipped. "Now how about some good music?" He reached for the radio.

"Oh, no. I am not driving thirteen hours listening to that country twang you forced me to hear the other night. I brought some real music, the good old kind. Ever hear of Foreigner?" When he grimaced, she added. "Don't worry, I brought along Chicago and Cory Hart for a change of pace."

"Weren't those all before your time? I know they're before mine."

She shrugged. "I hung out a lot with Christian."

"That explains it." Then he asked hopefully, "Any Neil Diamond?"

"Not a chance. But I do have some Air Supply that you might—just might—be able to talk me into playing."

"Well, there's something." He put his hand over the CD player. "Tell you what. I'll listen to your music now if you promise to listen to mine later."

"I guess it's only fair," she conceded. "But don't expect me to sing along."

CHAPTER
9

Diary of Karyn Olsen
Thursday, March 7, 1966

Travis wouldn't come over, even when I told him about my dad being in the hospital, because he had a test to study for. He reminds me of Clari (she couldn't take me either because she had to teach), always so responsible. It makes me so sad to think of my father all alone in the hospital, not being able to speak because of the stroke. Of course Lydia is probably there, but that's not the same thing as your daughters. Don't Travis and Clari know that sometimes PEOPLE should come first? Yes, there are deadlines and tests and bridges to be built, but the most important bridges should be between people.

Thinking back, I've been much like Travis and Clari my whole life. I've always wanted to reach out, to do something incredibly important to help people, but what have I accomplished in the end? I've been too shy to do much of anything except study and get good grades. I wonder now if I've ever turned aside someone who needed *me. I must be more careful. That's partly why I chose to go into nursing. Deep inside, I hope nursing might help me do something that connects with people on a whole new level. Will it? I don't know. I only know that I love Travis. Maybe nothing else is important.*

"Are you sure Wyoming has any farm country?" Liana asked, doubtfully eyeing the passing terrain. "It looks more like desert to me. Not even weeds dare to grow."

Austin understood what she meant. During the past several hours of traveling, there had been miles and miles of nothing but flat gray sagebrush. "Once we get closer to the Wind River Valley, everything will change."

"I guess I'll take your word for it." She hefted a CD in her hand. "Kenny Rogers?"

He fought a smile. "Sure."

The hours had flown by more rapidly than Austin had thought possible. As the miles fell behind them, so had much of Liana's sternness. By the time they had reached Utah, she had agreed to listen to his CD of Kenny Rogers' greatest hits. And now she had requested it again. Her preferred song on the CD seemed to be "Lucille," a song he'd never cared for. On the other hand, she didn't like his favorite "Lady"—probably because of the bit about being a knight in shining armor— which made her roll her eyes. Austin was almost sorry they were making such good time. He'd always had a bit of a lead foot, and the short stops they'd made along the way for food and gas hadn't caused much delay. But there was always the drive back to Nevada.

The clock had ticked barely past seven-thirty when Austin pulled up to his sister's ranch-style house northeast of Riverton, Wyoming. The sun had set nearly an hour ago, but the western sky was still radiating light. Liana could now sing every word of Kenny Rogers' "Coward of the County."

The low-slung farmhouse was bordered by several tall shade trees. A small grove of fruit trees grew to the right of the house out past the garden, and beyond them sat another gathering of shade trees in the distance where the small family cemetery had stood for generations. For miles on either side of the house and trees stretched row after row of neatly plowed earth. And somewhere beyond the fields lay the large corral and the area Mercedes and Wayne had turned into grazing land to try their hands at raising a hundred head of cattle. Austin's eyes drank it in eagerly. There was something about this land that knew him, that somehow reconciled the confident, successful man he was now with the scared, frightened boy he had been. The free-roaming, laughing boy he'd been. The abused boy who had rebelled and run away to college and made good. Only here were they all present. Here was his heart—tucked safely away from his daily existence in Nevada.

He rounded the truck, but Liana had already opened the door and jumped down. Her eyes wandered over the house, the yard, and the fields. "Welcome to Walker Farm," he said, a little proudly. "Ah-oh. Here comes the welcome wagon." Their arrival had not gone unnoticed. Three red retrievers appeared from the side of the house, bounding toward them, barking at the top of their lungs.

Liana stepped back a little. "Don't worry. They won't hurt you." He went down on one knee in front of her to greet the dogs. "Hi, guys," he said. "And lady," he nodded at the smaller of the three. "Liana, this one is Di—named for Princess Diana. This big guy here is Thunder, and this last is their son, Jellybean." Austin made an apologetic face. "He had another name once, can't remember what, something more dignified, but he loves jellybeans—any sugar, really. As long as you have something to give him, he's your friend. Doesn't matter who you are. Yep, something of a disappointment to his noble parents."

"He's cute." Liana bent over, gingerly offering several fingers. Jellybean licked them eagerly before pushing his head into her hands. His parents were more reserved, regarding her with thinly veiled suspicion.

"They'll warm up to you," Austin said, rising. "So where are the others?"

Liana shrugged and then colored. "Oh, you're talking to the dogs. Austin, I hate to break it to you, but I don't think they'll talk back."

"Maybe not. But they can show us where to go. Obviously no one's at the house or they'd have seen us by now. Come on, Thunder, Di, find Mercedes." He took a step toward the side of the house.

As if understanding, the dogs bolted, only to come halfway back, bark enthusiastically, and run ahead again, encouraging the slower humans to follow. Ignoring the excitement of his parents, Jellybean stayed with Liana and Austin, sniffing their pant legs hopefully. Liana produced a chocolate-covered mint from her jacket pocket, which he downed with one gulp, wagging his tail for more. "Be careful," Austin warned. "You'll never get rid of him."

She smiled—a real smile that he had seen her use only with her brother. "Maybe that's not so bad."

Maybe it's not, he thought.

The dogs led them to the spacious backyard where a swing set made with huge logs graced a patch of scruffy grass. "That's the biggest swing set I ever saw," Liana said.

"We do things right on a farm. No wimpy stuff for us."

She shook her head. "I think all this fresh air is getting to you."

He laughed. "Good thing, too."

Beyond the swing set was a small barn and a connecting corral. To the right of the barn was the large garden where his sister grew vegetables to eat fresh or to can for later. Rows of peas that he had helped her plant weeks ago were already springing from the earth. He could almost taste them, could almost see a little boy filling his pockets with the fat pods and munching them as he sat on the wide branch in the old oak by the river.

"What kind of fruit do they grow?" Liana asked, motioning toward the small fruit orchard beyond the garden.

"Apples mostly. We also have some pears and cherries, but they have to be a rather hardy variety to grow here. The cherries are called North Star, or something like that. My sister planted an apricot, but it does poorly. They don't look like much now, but in a few weeks, they'll be completely green. As a boy, it was always such a miracle to me. One night I'd go to sleep and the leaf buds wouldn't have opened, and then the next morning, boom, they'd be out. I could never catch them at it."

She gave him another real smile for his efforts, and Austin began to feel a little lightheaded. *Because of the fresh air,* he told himself. *That's all.*

They could hear voices as they approached the barn, low but excited. "Now, Darrel," a woman said, "stop teasing your brothers. They're still feeling sick."

"Aw, Mom, they should be in bed if they're sick."

"And miss Buttercup's babies?"

"I don't care how sick I am, Darrel, I ain't gonna miss this."

"Me neither."

"Boys," warned the woman, and immediately there was

silence. Even the dogs, who had disappeared inside the barn became quiet.

Then the woman spoke. "Here it comes."

Without thinking, Austin reached for Liana's hand. "Hurry," he urged. They entered the barn, blinking as their eyes adjusted to the dimmer light inside. In the nearest stall they found Mercedes and her three sons kneeling around a small animal.

"It's a goat, isn't it?" Liana whispered to Austin as they stared over the gate into the stall.

He grinned. "Of course it's a goat."

She shrugged. "I never saw one before, except on TV."

"It's not just any goat. It's Mercedes' baby. Name's Buttercup."

Mercedes looked up and saw them. "Austin," she said, her voice glad but low. "You made it just in time."

"Hey, Uncle Austin," chimed his nephews together. Austin smiled and nodded at them, but they were too busy watching the goat to pay him much attention.

The brown-haired mother goat strained, bleating softly. With her gloved hands, Mercedes gently helped the new baby's head from the tight confines of his mother's narrow body. Austin heard Liana gasp softly beside him, and he tightened his hold on her hand to echo the feelings. He had seen animals born hundreds of times since his boyhood, but every time seemed new to him—what a miracle it was that something could grow and survive inside another living being and emerge healthy and unharmed.

The newcomer slipped his way completely free, falling into the fresh straw, supported by Mercedes' hands. She began to rub the dark gray coat with a blanket, but Buttercup turned quickly and began to lick her baby, stripping the remains of the sack that had protected it in the womb.

"Another girl," Mercedes said. Still on her knees, she felt Buttercup's sides. "Yep, that's it. It's all over, little mother. You did good. We just need the afterbirth now, and then you can rest." She looked up. "Austin, can you keep an eye on what she's doing with the baby while I take care of the placenta? She's a first-time mommy, and I want to make sure she knows what to do."

"Sure." Austin became aware that he was still holding Liana's hand. Letting it go, he pushed the dogs aside and let himself slowly into the stall. He squatted close to the baby goat.

"Sometimes it takes a while for the afterbirth," Mercedes said. "Darrel, you can let the other baby go now. Nursing will help it come."

Austin glanced at his oldest nephew, who was sitting importantly in the straw on the far side of the stall. In his lap was another tiny baby goat, her coat a shiny dark brown like her mother's, though it was streaked with gray near her tail. Darrel released his hold on the baby, who wobbled to her feet, bleating. Buttercup bleated back. In a matter of seconds the baby found her mother's teat and began nursing.

"Twins," breathed Liana. "They're so tiny."

"Goats often have twins and even triplets," Austin told her.

The second baby goat was on wobbly legs now, urged by her mother. Her gray face looked almost comical with its white and brown markings. Adding to the effect, the fine gray hair of her coat had already begun to dry in places, standing up on end. Austin felt an urge to pick up the baby, but he knew it was best to let the mother follow her instincts. At last Mercedes sat back on her heels. "Ah, there we go. We're really finished now."

She climbed to her feet and pulled off her gloves, tossing them into an old bucket. She was a thin, tall, strong-looking woman, whose dark hair was drawn back into a short braid.

102

Her skin was freckled and tanned with exposure to the sun, though she had few wrinkles. Her wide mouth seemed strained to Austin as she smiled, but the warmth in her black eyes was unmistakable. She checked her hands and then threw her arms around him. He hugged her back.

"I'm so glad you've come," she said. "We've missed you, haven't we, boys?" She drew back to let Darrel hug his uncle, but the other two boys remained sitting in the straw. "They're still sick," she explained.

"And I thought they just weren't excited to see me," Austin teased.

"Mom said we couldn't touch you," Joseph complained.

"Nonsense." Austin crossed the stall and gathered the skinny boy into his arms.

"Me, too! Me, too," shouted Scott.

"Boys, you're too old to be carried."

"But they're sick, Mercedes." Austin bent and picked up the other boy.

"Two at once!" Mercedes raised her eyes heavenward. "Well, it's your back. And your health if you catch something." Her eyes now fell on Liana. "I'm sorry about all this," she said, motioning to the goats. "But nature is one thing you can't ask to wait."

Liana shook her head. "It was wonderful."

"This is my sister, Mercedes," Austin said belatedly. "And these little scamps are Joseph and Scott. Joseph has the red hair like his daddy. They're eleven or twelve or something."

"I'm only eight," corrected Joseph with a big grin. "And Scott's seven."

"I'm eleven," said Darrel.

"Oh, yes." Austin turned toward his oldest nephew. "This is Darrel. He's the oldest and keeps everyone in line."

Mercedes rolled her eyes. "More like teases them to death."

"And this lady here is Liana Winn," Austin said, dipping his head toward Liana, who was leaning her elbows on the short gate of the stall. "She'll be working on the charity accounts for HeartReach."

"About time, too," Mercedes said, offering her hand. "I mean, it's about time he found someone to help out. Glad to meet you."

Liana, her eyes wide and face white, didn't respond to Mercedes' greeting. Austin stared at her, feeling puzzled and more than a little annoyed at her reaction.

Mercedes took back her hand. "My hands might be a little dirty," she said, examining them.

"It's not that." Liana made a face. "I'm really pleased to meet you, but something's eating my hair!" Sure enough, the horse from the next stall had his nose curved around the wall of the stall, stretching toward Liana.

The boys began hooting, and even Austin couldn't stop himself from smiling.

"Oh, that's old Setzer," Mercedes said. "Wouldn't hurt a flea. He just wants some attention." She came out of the stall and began scratching the bay's white-striped nose.

Hoisting her purse higher on her shoulder, Liana turned and gingerly reached out her hand to stroke the horse. "Hello, Mr. Setzer. Nice to meet you. But didn't anybody ever tell you that you shouldn't chew on a stranger's hair? You should only chew on the hair of people you know. It's more polite."

The boys laughed again, and Darrel went over to examine her hair. "Don't look chewed to me. Just a little wet. Next time, I think you should wear a braid like Momma."

Liana smiled at him. "I think I will."

Mercedes went back inside the stall to pick up the old

bucket that held her gloves. "Let's go on up to the house. We should leave Buttercup alone now. Come on. Darrel, leave on the lights. I'll need to get her something to eat, so I'll come back out after dinner. Hope you're all hungry." She waited until everyone left the stall and then shut the gate.

"Believe me, I'm hungry." Austin loved his sister's cooking. "If I could find a woman who could cook like you, I wouldn't be a bachelor."

Liana gave him a teasing glance. "I have a meal bar in my purse if you can't wait."

Mercedes laughed. "Oh, those things are awful. Wait till you taste my fried chicken and potatoes. You'll never eat another of those bars again." She linked her arm through Liana's and began to share her recipe.

Austin followed his sister and Liana up to the house, carefully balancing the weight of the two younger boys. "Hurry," urged Joseph. "You're letting them—" The rest of what he was going to say was choked off by a bout of coughing.

"You're letting them beat us," Scott finished for him.

"That's because you guys must have gained about fifty pounds since I saw you two weeks ago," Austin told them, pretending to stumble. Screaming and giggling, they clung to him.

Ahead, Mercedes and Liana had reached the covered back deck that Austin had helped them put in when Scott was born. Mercedes had wanted to sit in comfort with the new baby and watch the other boys play on the swings or in the yard while Wayne was working in the fields. Mercedes was still chatting away as Liana listened politely, looking as if she were enjoying herself.

Coming here was a good idea, Austin thought, remembering the feel of her soft hand in his. *A very good idea.*

CHAPTER

10

Diary of Karyn Olsen
Wednesday, March 30, 1966

My father died yesterday. He's really and truly dead. Dead. I never noticed before what a terrible-sounding word that is. I wonder how it feels to be dead and what he might be doing now. I feel really odd about him dying—not like I want to die myself, but really, really sad. There was so much we missed. After he left Mom for Lydia, I never saw him that much. I remember that time he didn't come to my fifth grade play, and I was mad at him and wouldn't visit him and Lydia for a whole year. Then when I was a teenager I was too busy for him. Now I regret that. Still, he didn't try hard, either. Mom says he was the same kind of father that he was a husband— a careless one. But he did pay for college. He left me money for the rest of my education in a trust fund. Good thing, too, because Mom couldn't help, and I didn't think I would get good enough grades if I had to work. Besides, if Travis and I get married right away, we'll have to live frugally for a while.

Travis has been very nice these past weeks. He took me to see Dad practically every day at lunch, and he helped me study for my tests last week, too. I don't know what I'd do without him. Mom and Clari have their own grief to deal with (believe it or not, Mom still loves him after all these years). Travis says he'll go with me to the funeral on Saturday. I really love him. He makes me feel as if everything is going to be okay. I can't believe that three months ago I didn't even know him. My whole life has changed.

For Liana, dinner at Walker Farm was a strange sort of organized confusion. After a heartfelt prayer of thanks, offered by the oldest boy, Darrel, the food was served in the pans it was cooked in, set in the middle of the sturdy wood table. Everyone helped themselves, including the younger boys, who had begged to stay at the table for dinner with Uncle Austin even though they were sick. The older dogs sat beneath the table, watching eagerly for bits of food to drop. Jellybean stood, walking from one person to the next, his mournful whimpers occasionally gaining him a surreptitious morsel from one of the boys. Jellybean didn't leave Liana out of his begging, though she had already given him the rest of her mints while Mercedes was setting up dinner.

The conversation had not stopped for an instant. Liana had never been one for making small talk, but Mercedes didn't seem to notice. She included Liana in her dialogue as though they had known each other for years. The boys were also vocal, especially Darrel, who had appointed himself spokesman for his sick brothers. Growing up, Liana and her brothers had not been encouraged to speak at the dinner table unless spoken to. Not so Mercedes' boys. They inundated Liana with questions. "Where are you from? Do you live on a farm? What's a CPA? How did you meet? What is your favorite food?" Austin fired questions right back about every aspect of their lives, including whether or not they'd been up at the swimming hole yet this year (no, their mother hadn't let them). Try as she might, even Liana couldn't sit back and observe. She found herself answering questions and even asking a few herself.

After dinner, she and Austin volunteered to wash up while Mercedes put the younger boys to bed. "Can't we sleep with you, Momma?" asked Scott as they stood up from the table.

"No, your dad'll be home tonight after finishing in the north field. In fact, he should be here any minute now. But I'll set up a cot for me in your room in case you need me during the night. Your cheeks are too rosy—I think your fever might be coming back." She sighed. "Too much excitement for sick boys."

"It's just a cold, Momma," Joseph said. "We'll be better in no time."

"Thank the Lord for that."

The voices faded, leaving Austin and Liana alone. "So are we staying here?" she asked. Though they hadn't discussed their sleeping arrangements, she had assumed they'd use a hotel, or perhaps stay in his grandmother's vacant house.

"Is that a problem?"

"No, I just assumed your grandmother's place was empty." She picked up several plates, scraping the remains into the dogs' dish as Austin was doing.

"Finally rented it last month. To a nice couple. She lived about seven miles south of here." He shook his head, a hint of a smile on his mouth. "I can't believe I used to walk out to her place a couple times a week when my dad was using the horses. It was worth it, though. She was some lady. My mother never had half her drive for life."

"I never knew either of my grandmothers. They both died before I was born."

He made a sympathetic noise in his throat. "I assume one of your grandmothers was American, but if you lived in India, was your other grandmother from there?"

She wondered how he knew all that. "Christian must have told you about India."

"A little. But he'll shoot me if he knows that you know that I know." He grimaced. "Or something like that. I promised not to bring it up."

She snorted. "You didn't; I did. Don't worry. I'll take care of Christian." She put the dishes into the sink of soapy water he'd prepared.

He washed a plate and handed it to her for rinsing. "You were going to tell me about your non-American grandmother?"

She ran the dish under the tap, smiling slightly. "I wasn't, but I guess I will now. She was Romanian. She married a German soldier, and they had my father—my real father. I mean, birth father. There's not much other information about her. My dad grew up in Romania but was educated in Germany. He became a doctor and went to work in a charity hospital in India. Several years later that's where he met my mom, when she went to India. She was a nurse who delivered babies. They died in a plane crash on their way to help poor people in a village. That's all I know."

"I'm sorry, Liana. I really am."

She looked over and found him watching her. "Thank you."

They washed the dishes in silence for a moment, and then he said, "You were lucky to have a father who dedicated his life to helping others. My father dedicated his life to becoming rich, and when that didn't happen, he dedicated the rest of his life to making others—well, never mind. It's enough to say that he was a disappointed old man."

"And your mother?"

"She dedicated her life to him. He threw it away." He stared down into the soapy water without further explanation, washing dishes quickly, the muscles in his jaw clenching and unclenching. Liana was curious about what might have happened, but she couldn't bring herself to ask. *Let him keep his secrets,* she thought. She wanted to keep hers.

"At least you know who they are. Or were," she said, not knowing if his mother was still alive. She had stopped rinsing, and his washed dishes were piled up in the sink under her still fingers. "I have to admit that not knowing more about my family makes me feel that something's missing, something that might make a difference in my life. Yet at the same time I find I don't really want to know it at all. Knowing more might make losing them more difficult."

"Maybe it wouldn't." His eyes bore into hers once more, and she found she couldn't look away. "Maybe knowing more would help."

Liana stared at him. Why had she opened her big mouth? She had never confessed her curiosity about her birth parents to anyone since the horse incident in the first grade. She had even stopped wondering about them privately—or had she? Maybe burying thoughts of them had only been a matter of survival.

With effort, she dragged her eyes from his and began rinsing dishes again. "Well, real parents are those who raise you," she said, forcing her voice to be light. "That's what's important."

"Yes, but in a case like yours . . ." He sighed loudly. "Don't mind me. I'm too curious for my own good. My mother always used to tell me that."

Liana detected a trace of bitterness in his words, but she pretended not to notice. There had been too much confession as far as she was concerned. She was relieved when Mercedes returned to the kitchen, her step slower than before but still energetic.

"Goodness, you're all but finished," she said. "That's just great. I really appreciate your cleaning up." She grinned at her brother. "What, no complaints about not having a dishwasher, Austin? You must be coming down with something. You'll be running a fever before long. And don't say I didn't warn you about getting too close to the boys." She took out a dish towel and rapidly began to dry and put away the dishes Liana had set in the dish rack. "Now, about sleeping arrangements. Liana, you'll have Austin's room. He comes to visit so often that we keep it clear for him. Of course, it's not the one he used as a child. Once he got old enough to leave Momma's bed, he slept in here by the old wood stove. Long gone now, thank heaven. I do like *some* modernization." She grinned at Austin pointedly.

"If I'm sleeping in Austin's room, where will he sleep?" Liana asked.

"Why, in the barn." Mercedes laughed when she saw Liana's expression. "Don't worry, there's actually a bunkhouse connected to the barn. Small but useful for our seasonal help. I keep the place up."

"I'll go get our suitcases." Austin let the water out of the sink and dried his hands.

"Good. I'll set out the apple pie. I didn't mention dessert before because that's the last thing the boys need right now, getting over this bug. I made the pies this morning so Wayne could take one with his lunch." Mercedes set out three small plates and from a cupboard took out a pie covered with a white cloth. "Liana, why don't I show you to your room while we wait for the suitcases?"

Austin's room, Liana corrected silently. So strange that he had a room here and a house or apartment back in Nevada. Was there a room in India that she would recognize as once having belonged to her?

"The kitchen, this alcove here where I used to sleep as a child—you can see I use it for my sewing now—and my Darrel's bedroom is what used to be the old house," Mercedes was saying. "In the early seventies, Dad finally built an indoor toilet and an additional room. The little boys sleep there now. Over the years Wayne and I've added two more bedrooms and a living room."

Liana looked around as Mercedes talked. She could see that each addition had been created in the design of the times, making a mishmash style overall but one that was comfortable and welcoming. One that didn't mind if children talked without first being addressed and where dogs ran free, begging for scraps under the table.

"Here's Austin's room." Mercedes swung open a door. "I opened the window this morning for a few hours and gave it a dusting, so it should be okay. There are fresh sheets on the bed. The bathroom's right down the hall." She pointed.

"Thank you. It's great." Here and there, Liana could see snatches of Austin—both the boy and the man, though he reportedly hadn't used this room as a child. Mercedes must have saved some of his things and put them here. There were old posters of country singers, photographs, a rusty piggy bank, a rock collection, books, a tape recorder with a stack of country music tapes, and a computer. Liana could see Austin in almost every item, as though his permanent mark was on the room. She wondered idly if she had left any permanent mark in India, or if the graves of her parents were all that remained.

"In here are most of the records from the charity." Mercedes opened the closet door to reveal three tall stacks of boxes, one topped with a brown cowboy hat. "I didn't know what to throw away when I moved it from my grandmother's last month, so I kept it all. There's more in the hall closet. Austin'll know about the current records. He was talking about putting it all on computer. Grandma didn't use computers."

Liana raked her hand through her hair. Organizing the documents would be a big job, but then she needed a job—any job. Maybe she should volunteer to do more than just the accounting. She was good at organizing. Yes, she'd volunteer to computerize the records—but for a paycheck, of course. After all, she had to get her car fixed and pay the mortgage.

Mercedes laughed. "No need to look so enthused," she said with a laugh. "I know it's a disheartening mess."

Liana took her hand from her hair. "Actually, it looks interesting. I like working on accounts. They're so . . ." Liana didn't finish. Accounts were predictable, and numbers never lied. They didn't expect things from you. They didn't die and leave you alone. But she wasn't about to share *that* with Mercedes. "Hey, I've been wondering—how'd you get your name?"

"Oh, that." Mercedes laughed again. "My father had big dreams when I was born. He wanted to drive a Mercedes."

"Oh, I see."

"Yeah, and he also wanted to move to Austin, Texas, and become a cattle rancher," Austin said from the doorway. "He was sure he could find his dream there. It certainly wasn't in Wyoming."

Mercedes' laughter died at the resentment in her brother's voice. "You should go see him," she said.

"No." Austin turned to Liana. "I see Mercedes has shown you our infamous charity records."

"Not much of a filing system."

"I haven't had time to do anything with it. Grandmother used to have everything organized, but in the past ten years or so, it's gotten out of hand. She never liked computers much."

Liana took a deep breath. "I could get it organized and on computer as part of the job you're hiring me for. I mean, if you're interested."

Austin smiled. "I'm definitely interested. Your last bill was quite reasonable, and we might as well work this job in now since we have a little cash flow with the Whittaker donation I told you about. Truthfully, it might take organizing everything to update the finances anyway. I don't know how Grandmother got along."

"She didn't bother much about papers—she just wanted to help those poor children." Mercedes moved past Liana toward the door. "Come along, now. There's pie to be eaten."

"Do you still have that videotape I made of the orphanages in Ukraine last year?" Austin asked on their way down the hall. "I'd like to show it to Liana."

Mercedes nodded. "I have it. But after the pie, okay? I want her to at least taste it before you drop the weight of the world on her shoulders." Austin snorted, but he acquiesced to her request.

The slice of apple pie, topped with a generous dollop of freshly whipped cream from Mercedes' prized milk cow, was the best Liana had ever tasted. Mercedes certainly had a way with food.

"She's the granddaughter of Patches," Mercedes explained, giving them each another spoonful. "That's the cow Austin basically raised from birth."

Austin nodded, his eyes faraway. "Her mother died, and we had to give her a bottle. Patches was a wonderful cow. I miss the old girl."

Liana remembered the pictures of the cow on the walls in Austin's office. She didn't know how long cows lived but figured Patches was gone by now, given Austin's comment. "My mother loves to cook," she said.

"And you don't?" Mercedes took a bite of apple pie.

Liana smiled. "I love to eat—and that's almost the same thing. One of these days when I stop running around so much, I'm going to get nice and round. They say my mother gained weight before she died."

"Oh, I'm sorry," Mercedes said. "When you said she liked to cook, I assumed she was still living."

Too late, Liana realized her mistake. What was it about these people and this place that made her so let down her guard? "I meant my adopted mother loves to cook. I know it's a bit confusing. I was orphaned when I was four, and my aunt and uncle adopted me."

"Before that she lived in India," Austin added.

"India? How exciting! I've always wanted to travel somewhere overseas." Mercedes put down her fork. "Do you remember it well?"

Liana shook her head. "Not consciously. But sometimes when I'm dreaming . . ." She fell silent, mentally shaking herself. This was her private memory, not open for discussion. "I don't remember."

"You must want to go back." Mercedes looked at her eagerly. "I bet you'd remember if you went back. At least some of it."

"When I was a teenager, I always planned to take a trip there." Liana swirled her fork in her whipped cream. "I used to think I could learn about my parents. You know, by talking to people who knew them."

"Your aunt never talked about your birth mother?" Austin poured himself a tall glass of milk from the pitcher Mercedes had placed on the table.

"No. I asked a few times when I was really young, but it always made her upset." Liana hadn't pursued the matter, not willing to risk Christian's wrath. "I'd ask now, but . . ." Once again Liana had to stop herself from talking. *But we really aren't that close,* she finished silently.

Mercedes helped herself to another slice of pie. "Maybe going to India would be a good idea then."

"Maybe." Liana suddenly felt she was fighting for air, and the wonderful-tasting pie had turned to rubber in her mouth.

"HeartReach used to be active there," Austin said. "Grandmother switched most of our focus to Ukraine when it freed itself from the Soviets, but we still fund a literacy program in India."

"Sounds interesting." Liana was grateful to Austin for the change of topic. She had been about to excuse herself from the table so she wouldn't break down in front of them.

"Another piece?" Mercedes offered. "Come on. It won't be as good tomorrow."

Liana let Mercedes put another slice next to her half-finished one. She began to eat as the conversation drifted to the planting and the new calves they were expecting this summer. Her pie had regained its delicious savor, and she relaxed.

After much of the pie had disappeared, Mercedes washed the plates while Austin took Liana to the living room and showed her the video footage he'd taken at several orphanages in Ukraine. "I'm not sure which orphanages these are," he said at the beginning. "I filmed a lot of them, and after a while they all looked the same."

Liana saw what he meant. Cribs crowded together side by side, holding babies and young toddlers. Narrow walkways between each row allowed their caretakers access. Small children dressed in bulky layers of clothing, some smiling, but many with faces red from long bouts of crying. Peeling paint on the walls, larger cribs where toddlers played together, little tables with older children eating, tiny children sitting on many small toilets. There were mounds of stuffed animals.

"Most of those we provided," Austin said of the toys. "A good number of these orphanages exist solely on foreign help. Even orphanages subsidized by the government have inadequate conditions."

"So many children," Liana said, her eyes fixed on the screen. "Why are there so many unwanted children? It doesn't make sense."

Austin's face turned grave. "From my understanding of what happened there and in other countries like Romania during the decades of Communist rule, some of the authorities wanted the people to have many children, to raise up armies for the Soviets. Birth control was not permitted."

"But that was then. Most of those children would be grown or nearly grown by now."

"Ah, but change comes very slowly, not to mention that birth control is expensive. That means abortion often becomes the birth control of choice, frequently very late in the pregnancy so the women won't get pregnant again as soon as if they aborted earlier. Of course, that then creates a moral dilemma, and as a result, hundreds of Ukrainian women give their babies to orphanages rather than abort them. Others keep their children, but they just can't possibly fill so many hungry stomachs and are eventually forced to give them away."

Liana swallowed hard, her throat feeling full of cotton. "What about adoption? I've heard of so many couples here who want children."

"Many adoptions have taken place since the Soviets fell from power. But bureaucracy makes adoptions difficult. There are still too many children to take care of—too many to imagine." Austin motioned to the screen, which now showed a group of children with obvious deformities. "As you see there, a great number of these children are born sick or disabled because of the gross lack of prenatal care."

"Why do they make them sit on the toilets? I don't know much about it, but some look too young for potty training." The images hurt Liana's heart. A part of her wanted to cry out in rage; the other wanted to run away in denial.

Austin's mouth twisted in sympathy. "I know exactly how you're feeling, believe me. I've experienced the very same emotions. But there is a method behind the madness. As soon as they're able to sit, they put them on toilets after every meal until they go—even if it takes an hour or more. Saves on diapers. They mostly use cloth there, and when a baby pees, they seem to just stick on another layer of clothing until it's time to bathe them." He shook his head. "We sent a bunch of disposable diapers just before my grandmother died, but when I went there I found that most of them ended up on the black market. That's when I hired Olya. You'll see her here in a minute—ah, there she is."

A short-haired woman with light blue eyes, too-heavy makeup, and a thin, pinched face came on the television. She was speaking Ukrainian with a man, and Liana's eyes were riveted on her. There was something familiar about her, though she couldn't pinpoint what. Had she been in another part of the video? Or was it something about her words? Then the woman began speaking heavily accented English and the impression vanished.

"I found Olya Kovalevsky last year," Austin was saying. "When I discovered that so much of our aid went to the black market, I fired the previous director. I was angry—furious, actually—that he'd let that happen. He claimed it was how business was done and that I should be grateful that at least a little went to the orphans. But I wanted better. I found Olya, and she . . ." Austin hesitated. "Well, the truth is she had a little sister her family was forced to put in an orphanage. That orphanage later burned down, and Olya never found out what happened to her. She doesn't know if her sister died or if she was adopted. She still feels a lot of guilt, though there wasn't anything she could have done differently. That's part of why she's so dedicated to helping the children. I like to think it helps relieve her guilt—however imagined—and it helps me to know the aid is going where it should. If the orphanage directors don't use it for the children, they don't get any more. Period."

"It's good you found her, then." Liana's eyes didn't leave the screen. She couldn't believe people would cheat orphans.

There were yet more images of another Ukrainian orphanage, though they could have been repeats of the first. Liana's eyes became swollen and her heart heavy with the plight of the abandoned children.

That was not all. Another emotion had begun in her chest almost from the outset of the video—an emotion that made it hard to swallow, to breathe. Though Liana had tried to ignore it, the feeling had grown near to bursting. Now a tingling began in her arms, traveling to the very tips of her fingers. She knew the emotion now. She had felt it yesterday when her car had stopped working, causing her to swerve into oncoming traffic.

Fear.

No, it was more than simple fear. It was helpless, heart-pounding terror.

She jumped to her feet, averting her face from Austin's concerned stare. "I can't," she said, her voice sounding strange and breathless to her own ears. "I can't watch any more." She fled, stumbling blindly down the hall. She opened a door, glad to see that it led to Austin's room.

Throwing herself on the bed, she took in huge gulps of air to stop the threatening sobs. *It's just a video,* she told herself. She'd seen worse on television commercials of small children in Africa. Why did this so affect her?

A sudden, overwhelming anger flooded her body—out-of-control anger that made her want to scream and break things. An anger that blotted out the fear. *What is happening to me?*

But she knew.

"Why, Lara?" Clarissa asked. "Why did you rip the dolly's clothes and tear off her arms and head? Why did you color her all black with the marker? Tell me, sweetie. I want to help."

Liana had no answer.

"And why did you smash your new tea set?" Clarissa knelt before her to look in her eyes. Her voice took on a note of hysteria. "Please talk to me! Why don't you ever talk to me?"

"Clarissa, don't." Behind her, Travis reached down to help Clarissa up.

Crouched by the bed among the broken toys, Liana watched them warily. The light from the uncurtained window shone starkly on Clarissa's tearful face. They didn't let her have curtains anymore, not since she'd pulled them down again. They hadn't fixed the holes she'd made in the wall, either.

"I'm calling a doctor," Travis said. "This can't go on."

Liana wasn't afraid. She liked doctors. Her daddy had been a doctor.

"If I didn't know better, I'd say it's a type of detachment disorder," the doctor said the next day. "But I'm not sure how that's possible because she was not orphaned and neglected as a baby. I think it must be that she is still grieving and that these anger tantrums will pass if you continue to love and support her."

He was right. For a while clothes, toys, bedding, and walls had taken the brunt of her silent fury, but eventually the tantrums had faded, and she began to speak more and more—first to Christian and then to the others.

Liana remembered little of that black time; she didn't want to think of it now, even if it somehow related to the feelings she'd experienced while watching the video. Hands over her eyes to block out the light, she tried to make her mind go blank. To think of nothing. Or better yet, to think of Christian's eagle, flying free in the clear blue sky. The thought calmed her.

There was a tap on the door. "Liana?"

Austin.

She sat up, running her hands under her eyes to catch any stray tears. Crossing the room, she opened the door.

His brows were drawn into a tight line. "Are you all right?"

"I think I'm just tired."

"It's been a long day." He looked as though he wanted to say more. Finally, he added, "See you tomorrow then."

"Okay, goodnight." She shut the door behind her, feeling more than a little silly. The abrupt anger was gone and so was the fear. In their place came an almost overwhelming urge to eat, though after Mercedes' bounteous dinner and two pieces of apple pie she couldn't have fit in a single morsel if she tried.

Rummaging through the suitcase Austin had brought in

from his truck, she found her pajamas and toothbrush. She went to the bathroom, relieved that no one was around. She hoped Mercedes didn't think her rude for retiring to her room without saying goodnight. Tomorrow would have to be soon enough for making apologies.

But Mercedes came from her boys' room as Liana emerged from the bathroom. "Do you have everything you need?"

"Yes, thank you. Thanks a lot." Liana stifled an urge to hug the woman—odd after so many years of not wanting anyone to touch her.

"Goodnight then. Unless you want to talk."

"No, I'd better turn in. There's a lot of work waiting in that closet tomorrow."

Mercedes chuckled. "Well, if you change your mind, I'll be in the kitchen waiting for Wayne. He'll be back soon. It's nearly ten. He's rarely this late except during harvest time. Goodnight now." Liana watched her go.

In Austin's room once more, Liana checked her cell phone to see if she had any messages from the advertisement she had put in the newspaper. There was nothing. At least she had the charity job, and Austin hadn't blinked at the other bill she had given him, which she had thought quite high. Apparently, free-lancing had its advantages.

A whimper at the door drew her attention. Opening it, she found Jellybean, wagging his tail excitedly. "Come in if you want," she offered, "but I don't have any more treats." Clarissa would have never allowed dogs in the house, but Liana found she liked the idea of four-footed company. The dog rushed in and jumped on the bed.

Shaking her head, Liana snuggled under the blanket. The room was silent, but outside the window she could hear dogs barking in the distance and the yowl of an angry cat. But nothing more. There was no tapping in her mind. She couldn't hear it in the animals' voices or in the light breeze that made the tree by her window sway. Nor in the soft voices of a man and wife greeting each other after a long day apart.

No tapping of keyboards.

Liana pushed her feet under Jellybean and promptly fell asleep.

CHAPTER

11

Diary of Karyn Olsen
Saturday, April 2, 1966

Today we buried my dad. Travis was very sweet, and he got along well with Mom, who decided at the last minute to ride with us. Clari was also there, and I could tell she approves of Travis. She's a year older than he is, but they have a lot in common. They talked too much about math and engineering (yuck!).

I really can't believe Dad's dead. I think Mom's having a harder time of it than Lydia. He should never have left us. At least I have Travis. I think a July wedding would be nice. I wonder when he'll propose. Maybe then he'll finally kiss me the way I want him to.

Liana awoke, much later than usual, and stretched with the abandon of someone who had enjoyed a solid night's sleep. Her foot touched the place where Jellybean had slept, still warm, though the dog was no longer there. Strangely disappointed, she sat up, craning her neck to see out the window. Through the sheer curtains, she saw nothing but the tree outside her window and the fields beyond. Birds sang cheerily as they went about their business, as though happy to be alive.

"No nightmares or tapping," Liana mused aloud. Was it because she didn't ever have to return to the office that the tapping had finally stopped? Or was it because she was on a farm out in the middle of what seemed like nowhere? She didn't think so. The beach, the mountains—those had also been reclusive places, but neither had succeeded in silencing the tapping. The only thing really different here was Austin and his family.

She wasn't about to pursue *that* vein of thought.

Clutching her personal items, she made a dash for the bathroom, not meeting anyone on the way. A short time later, dressed in jeans and a long-sleeved cotton blouse with her hair combed back and secured in a long braid, she ventured into the kitchen. She was met by Jellybean's liquid brown eyes and Mercedes' wide smile.

"Oh, good, you're up. Sleep well?"

"Like a rock." Liana slipped into the same chair she had used at the table the night before. Jellybean shuffled over and shoved his nose into her hand. "Hey, Jellybean. What do you mean abandoning me, huh? I've never had such warm feet."

Mercedes laughed. "Heard him scratching at your door, so I cracked it a bit and let him out. He had business to do outside."

"Good thing you let him out."

"I had to bring him right back in. Likes to terrorize the chickens while Darrel's getting the eggs."

Liana rubbed Jellybean's silky red fur. "It's so quiet. Where is everyone? They can't still be sleeping."

"No, everyone's up. Austin drove off about an hour ago.

125

Said he had business in Casper. He'll try to be back tonight. My husband's off in the fields again, but he's working closer to home today, so he'll be in for lunch. Darrel's out feeding the animals and gathering the eggs before he goes to school. The other boys are still in bed—not sleeping, mind you, but watching TV in their room. Their daddy bought it for them last year when they were sick."

"Are they any better today?"

Mercedes frowned. "A little worse, I think. But that's the course of the thing. Tomorrow they'll be almost as good as new. Shouldn't have let them go out to the barn yesterday, but I never would've heard the end of it if they'd missed Buttercup's babies."

"And how are they? The little goats, I mean."

Mercedes smiled. "Beautiful. Especially that second one. Has very interesting markings on her face and the tips of her ears. I bet she'll win the county fair this year."

"I'd like to see them again, if it's okay."

"Sure, but let me get you something to eat first."

"Oh, that's okay. You don't have to."

"I want to. You're my guest." She reached for a pan and skillfully cracked two eggs into it.

Liana frowned. "I'm sorry to have barged in on you. I'd thought we'd be staying at your grandmother's place or maybe at a hotel."

"Goodness no! A hotel, when I have all the room in the world here? Austin knows better than that. And Grandmother's home is rented now. Besides, I enjoy talking to you. Heaven knows when I've had time to converse with another woman. On Sunday at church, and that's about it." As she spoke, Mercedes stirred the eggs with one hand and turned bacon with the other. Liana figured it didn't occur to Mercedes that she might not care for bacon and eggs.

Liana ate her food, watching Mercedes strain fresh milk from the cow and put it into gallon jars. "I let the cream rise to the top, and then I skim it off," Mercedes told her. "Make some into butter and some into cream for my pies."

"That cream was excellent."

"Nothing like fresh cream, sweetened with a bit of powdered sugar."

Mercedes put the jars into her refrigerator. "In an hour or so the neighbors down the road'll show up for a gallon of this and another gallon or so from last night's milking. They have ten kids and use all that I can't. They trade me for quilt scraps. The mom's a quilter. Good one, too. Her sister works at a fabric store, and that's where she gets the material for both of us. I've made a heap of quilts from those scraps. I'll show you some later."

Liana could have just as easily shot a deer, skinned it, and made a skirt from the hide as to have pieced a quilt. Though the idea had always fascinated her, she'd never had anyone to show her how, and now she was too busy making a living to worry about it.

She sighed and pushed back her chair. "I guess I'd better get to work. There's a lot of papers to go through."

"Did you forget about Buttercup and her babies? Why don't you just take a quick peek at them first? Those papers have been there for months, some of them decades. Won't hurt to let them wait a bit. Go on now. No, I'll take care of the dishes."

Practically driven from the house, Liana walked out onto the wide deck, passing the log swing set on her way to the barn. Jellybean tagged along, wagging his tail furiously.

"Go ahead and pet them, if she'll let you," Mercedes called after her.

Liana lifted her face to the morning sun, feeling the heat and marveling at how it lit up the world. Everything around her glowed with life. Buds of green forced their way through the dried brown grasses of last year, stretching toward the life-giving sun. Liana began to whistle and then laughed for the sheer joy of living. She wished the moment would last forever.

In the barn, she found Darrel carrying hay to the horses. She paused at Setzer's stall, noting how the far side of the stall also had gates that permitted him to go outside into the small corral beyond. The far gates were open, but Setzer was still inside eating.

"Good morning, Darrel," Liana called. "And good morning to you, Mr. Setzer."

"Hi." Darrel paused in his work. "You come to see the goats?"

"Is that all right?"

"Sure. She's right in there. But she doesn't like the dog around her babies. So go in and lock Jellybean out."

"Okay."

Under the child's watchful eye, Liana opened the stall and slipped inside, ignoring Jellybean's protesting whine and soulful eyes. In disgust, the dog ran toward Darrel, hoping to find someone willing to play. "Go away, Jellybean," Darrel told him. "I have to finish. The bus'll be here soon."

With a bored yawn, the dog found a mound of straw and threw himself down.

Shaking her head in amusement, Liana turned toward the goats. The mother was eating from a bucket while the babies were lying in the straw, watching as Liana approached. She crouched down beside them, and they stared at her with wide eyes. The gray one with the white and brown markings on her face and ears nibbled her outstretched hand.

"You are a beauty," Liana murmured, recalling the miracle of birth the night before. The goat's silvery gray coat was softer than she had imagined.

A butting head broke her concentration. The mother goat had left her bucket and was hitting her head repeatedly against Liana's shoulder. "Whoa, there." Liana turned to defend herself but was surprised when the goat allowed her to scratch her head. She could feel nubs where the goat's horns had been at one time. "You like that, huh? You know I'm not going to hurt your babies, don't you?"

"She's really nice for a goat," came a voice over the gate.

Liana looked up to see Darrel peering at her. "Nice?"

"Yeah. Once we had a goat I totally hated. She used to chase me around the barn when I was younger. She had horns, too, that hadn't been cut off. I had to carry a stick to keep her away. She was real ornery, I tell you. One day she butted Scott to the ground and trampled him. He was about four then. Mom got mad and gave her to a farmer. Then last year we got Buttercup. She's as sweet as honey. For a goat, anyway." He paused for breath. "Well, I gotta go catch the bus. Make sure you lock the gate when you leave."

"I will." Liana turned her attention back to the mother goat. The kids were trying to nurse again. "I'd better leave you to your business." She gave a final pat to Buttercup, not daring to touch the babies again for fear of disturbing their feeding.

Out in the barn, even Jellybean had deserted her, so Liana wandered down the stalls alone. They had four horses here, a cow with the largest brown eyes she'd ever seen, a half-grown calf, Buttercup and her babies, and a fat pig who snorted as he gobbled at a trough full of what looked like grains mixed with the remains of breakfast. Another section of the barn led to a small henhouse. Liana peered through a window cut into the wall but could only make out dim shapes, though she could hear the occasional squawking of grown chickens, echoed by the peeping of small chicks. On the far side of the barn was a door that must lead to the bunkhouse Mercedes had mentioned. Liana was curious but not curious enough to intrude upon Austin's space; she'd already stolen his room.

Liana emerged from the barn, blinking at the sudden brightness. Jellybean ran up to her, wagging his tail. Petting him, she gazed over the fertile land, bordered by the Rockies as though cradled in the hands of its Creator. In the distance, she saw Darrel waiting on the narrow paved road in front of the house with Jellybean's parents. A school bus came to a stop, and the boy disappeared inside.

Back in the house, Mercedes was nowhere to be seen. Liana figured she was either bathing or taking care of her boys. "Nothing for it but to get to work," she said. Jellybean wagged his tail. "I could get used to having you around," she told him, rubbing his ears.

In Austin's room she pulled out several boxes and began to divide papers into current or ongoing projects, past projects, and future projects. She made more piles for different types of bills, employee records, and purchase orders. These she would need to put on the computer. When the first box was emptied, she used it to store ancient records they would not need to deal with again. The second empty box she filled with more current documents. At one point, she came to a box that had been neatly labeled and organized. Unfortunately, all of it was dated ten years before.

As she sorted, Liana was drawn into the story the records told of countless supplies passed on to children and adults in need: reading materials, pens, paper, clothing, toys, diapers, baby powder. Occasionally, she ran into letters between Austin's grandmother and her employees or donors. These she saved in a separate pile but not before reading them. Her heart was gripped with individual stories of people who had directly benefited from the charity's help. Lists of past donors came to light, and these Liana also put aside. A few might have dropped out of sight for some reason, but perhaps they would be able to donate again now. Austin would know what to do with them.

Hours into her work, the smell of fresh bread permeated the room. Liana breathed in deeply and checked her watch. Not even noon yet, and already she was hungry.

"Must be the air out here," she said to Jellybean, who watched her with sad brown eyes from his place on her bed. He lowered his head on the blanket and sighed.

"Poor Jellybean," Liana said. "Want to go out?" Jellybean wagged his tail once but didn't move.

"Fine, have it your way. Be bored with me when you could be out chasing chickens and butterflies." Liana looked out the window longingly before forcing herself back to work.

When Mercedes knocked on her door much later, Liana had gone through five boxes. She was sorting more rapidly now, as she had learned what to look for. "Come in," she called.

Mercedes opened the door as far as the box near it would allow. "Some job, eh?"

"Yeah. Most of it's past stuff, though." Liana pointed to four of the boxes she'd already been through. "Those are old—some dating back fifty years. They aren't needed for anything right now. May want to keep them to someday record the totals the charity did in that year, but other than that they could be thrown away. This other box is what we'll need to put into the computer. Fortunately, it's not nearly full yet. And then I have letters from your grandmother to others—seems she always wrote letters with carbons and kept a copy for herself. You'll want those for your family history, if you're interested in that sort of thing."

"I am. I'd like to know more about her. About why my mother—" Mercedes broke off, her thick brows gathered like thunder over her black eyes that were so like Austin's.

"What happened to your mother?" Liana asked. Something about Mercedes invited the question.

Mercedes sighed. "To make a long story short, she married the wrong guy. She was unhappy, and she died of a broken heart."

"I'm sorry."

"No need." Mercedes squared her shoulders. "She could have been stronger. She could have left him. She could have lived. It was her choice. We can't always avoid trouble in our lives, but we can decide what to do with it."

"Given lemons, we make lemonade?"

Mercedes' smile was back. "Yes. We make lemonade. But come on, it's lunchtime. My husband's here waiting to meet you."

Liana stood, dusting her hands on her jeans. "I'd probably better wash up first."

"We'll be in the kitchen."

When Liana walked into the kitchen a short time later, she was surprised by the man at the table. Liana had learned that Mercedes was thirty-eight, three years older than Austin, but her husband looked old enough to be their father. His skin was wrinkled by years of exposure to the sun, and his red hair had turned an orangey white. But his body was tall and strong and brown, reminding Liana of a thick, gnarled tree trunk that could withstand even the most forceful wind.

"Nice to meet you, Mr. Johnson," she said, holding out her hand.

"Wayne. Call me Wayne." He broke into a smile that told of his easy nature, his gentleness. In that smile, Liana caught a glimpse of what Mercedes saw in him. His eyes also had a story to tell; the way they rested on Mercedes made it clear that he adored her.

They ate a warm lunch of chunky chicken stew with home-made noodles and the fresh-baked whole wheat bread Liana had smelled earlier, slathered in real butter. All the food they had grown or raised themselves. Wayne was a quiet man. He ate with silent gusto as Mercedes chattered on about the new chicks that had hatched the day before and how many months it would be before the pig and the half-grown calf would become the contents of their freezer. She spoke with a casual-ness that amazed Liana. How could you feed and care for something one moment and eat it the next? She decided she'd rather buy her food at the grocery store, never having to know it once had a name.

Liana admired Mercedes. She admired her enthusiasm, her friendliness, her hard work, the life she had created for herself. But she wondered at the fleeting glimpse of sadness in her eyes after she had kissed her husband good-bye and watched him disappear into the fields.

Something stirred in Liana's heart. "What is it, Mercedes? Is something wrong?" For a moment, Liana entertained thoughts of a cancerous tumor or another fatal disease that would tear either Wayne or Mercedes from their family.

Mercedes' sadness vanished. "Nothing. He's such a good man, my Wayne. Sometimes I don't think I deserve him at all."

Liana gathered the dirty bowls together. "He loves you. Any fool could see that. And I think you're . . . well, I really admire you, Mercedes."

Mercedes plopped into a chair, a wistful expression on her face. "If you only knew, Liana. Maybe you wouldn't admire me at all."

Liana sat opposite the woman, feeling awkward. Obviously something was bothering her, but she had no experience in getting people to open up to her. Usually, she was too busy running in the other direction.

"Darrel isn't his child," Mercedes said after a long silence. Before Liana could recover from this revelation, she plunged on. "I was twenty-five and taking psychology classes. I met this guy who was studying to be a doctor." She sighed and shook her head, a reflective smile on her lips. "We dated for a year. He was everything to me, but in the end he accepted a job in another state. He didn't ask me to go along. I was barely pregnant when he left."

"Did he know about the baby?"

She shook her head, her mouth drooping to a frown. "I thought about telling him, to make him stay or take me with him, but I didn't want a man who didn't want me. I'd seen how that had ruined my mother's life. Later I realized I should have told him. He was very young at the time and far too ambitious for his own good, but maybe we would have had a chance. My pride wouldn't let me, and now I'll never know."

Liana felt her sorrow, but before she could say anything, Mercedes continued. "It was the biggest mistake of my life— not having Darrel but having him that way. For a long time I was really lost. I thought I'd never be worthy of finding happiness again—or love. But I've discovered that God is forgiving."

God. Austin had mentioned that his sister had embraced

the religion of their grandmother, and she was glad it had helped Mercedes find peace. "How did you and Wayne get together?" Liana asked.

"He'd worked for years on the farm for my father, and it was right about this time that he took over completely. My mother had died, and my father was ill, so I used that as an excuse to come home and take care of Daddy. Actually, I was so sick and depressed that I couldn't work or pay my rent. I thought I would die. I wanted to die. But God had other plans. One day Wayne found me crying in the barn—I'd just thrown up all over. When he learned what was wrong, he scattered fresh straw over the floor and cleaned up the mess. Then he asked me to marry him. No hesitation, no recriminations, just a proposal." Mercedes' eyes filled with tears that flowed down her cheeks. "He's thirteen years older than I am, though I know he looks older. He's worked really hard all his life—physical labor—and it shows. But any success we ever had here on the farm, we owed to Wayne. I knew that. In some ways he *is* the farm, and I always felt it should go to him one day. Back then, neither Austin nor I wanted any part of the place."

Liana found that hard to believe. "But you seem so at home here."

"I do love it. More each day. I've made peace with the past and that peace has preserved me." Mercedes smiled through her tears. "But when you're young, you only think about what you don't have instead of what you do. You think of all the places you haven't been, instead of the places you have. You think of all the things you want to learn instead of what you already know. Wayne showed me how to love the land, and he gave my son the best dad a boy could have. Except for the times when he has to work late, he spends every minute with the boys and me. My biggest regret is that he isn't Darrel's

135

father. I cheated them both out of that—and that's something I will have to live with for the rest of my life."

"Does Darrel know?"

She shook her head. "No. And I don't suppose I'll ever tell him. The birth certificate lists Wayne as his father. We were married a few months before he was born. Wayne, Austin, and now you are the only ones who share my secret."

Liana wasn't sure how she felt about this deception. What if she had been younger when her parents had died? She only faintly remembered them at four. A year or so earlier and she might have had no recollection at all. Would that have been better? Would it have made her fit more smoothly into her adopted family? Or would the ache, the craving, inside her still go on and on?

Mercedes dabbed at her eyes with a dish towel. "Part of why I don't want to tell Darrel the truth is because I don't want him to wonder what might have been, like I do sometimes. I mean, if I hadn't made the mistakes, my life would certainly have been different. And I don't want him ever to question Wayne's love for him." Mercedes sighed and placed her hand on Liana's. "I'm sorry for dumping it all on you like this, us having just met and all. But sometimes when I see how much Wayne loves me, I worry that I can never give him enough. I care about him deeply; he's my best friend in the whole world, and I wouldn't trade him for any other man, but sometimes I don't think I love him as deeply as he loves me."

"It's enough," Liana said with an assurance she didn't know she possessed. "You're raising his children. You're here by his side. You're dedicated to him. That's the kind of love that lasts, the kind temporary passion cannot buy." Yes, Liana would be glad to trade any of her fleeting romantic relationships for the kind of security this couple shared. "At least that's how I see it."

Mercedes leaned over and put her arm around Liana in a brief squeeze. "Thank you for saying so. I do care for Wayne. He and my children are my life. And when it gets right down to it, past relationships are like . . ." She shrugged. "Like cattail fluff on the wind."

"Warm and fuzzy, but too easily blown away?" Liana said, allowing a small smile.

Mercedes' answering grin was genuine and full. "Exactly. Liana, I'm so glad you came. When Austin called to say he was bringing you, I thought of a plain, sharp-faced numbers lady, who wouldn't approve of me at all and who would detest the farm. Instead I found a beautiful soul sister, a woman I can really talk to. You don't know how I've needed that."

For an intense moment, Liana wished Mercedes *had* been her sister. Perhaps having a sister would have helped her cope with life. A sister might have made her relationship with her adopted mother less tense, less filled with emotional pressure to have their relationship succeed.

Liana shoved the thoughts away. "I'm glad I came."

"We'll keep in touch, of course." Mercedes stood and walked to the sink with the dishes in her hands. "I have e-mail."

"E-mail?" Liana asked. "Where, in the barn?" Too late, she realized that could be misconstrued as an insult.

Mercedes spluttered a laugh. "No, in my room, silly. I keep up on things. I have two degrees, you know, and half of several others. Some day they might even come in handy." The wounded look was gone from Mercedes' face, replaced by her usual happiness.

"You never know," Liana said. "You never know."

CHAPTER
12

Diary of Karyn Olsen
Saturday, April 9, 1966

Travis walked me to class each day this past week, though it's out of his way. And he called every night he didn't come over to make sure I was okay. I love how that makes me feel. But he rarely touches me. Sometimes I just want him to grab me and kiss me senseless!

I know he respects me and doesn't want to take advantage of me while I'm mourning, but I'm ready to move on. I tried to kiss him in my living room last night after we'd gone to a movie with a group of friends, thinking it would jump-start things, but somehow the kiss landed on his cheek instead (maybe he turned his head?). It was so embarrassing! I cried a little then—more in frustration than because of my dad. Travis held me very tight and told me it'd be okay. I believe him. Everything is all right when we're together.

Austin drove up to Walker Farm slightly before six. The

day had been grueling, but at least he had spared himself the
drive to Sheridan by asking the manager of their store to meet
him and the other store manager in Casper. The resulting meeting had helped everyone by sparking a friendly competition
between the two stores. Austin gave them the leeway to
enhance the company sales plan with the idea of sharing the
most successful plan with the entire chain.

On his way to the farm he'd almost fallen asleep at the
wheel, but now that his journey was finished, new energy
surged through him. The sun hung low in the western sky with
about an hour of light left. If he hurried, he might have time to
show Liana the old swimming hole before dinner. Too bad it
wasn't summer so they could take a swim.

He found Liana and Mercedes in the living room with the
quilt frame Wayne had made stretched out, leaving only a narrow open space around the edges of the room. In one of these
small spaces, Wayne sat on the couch reading a storybook to
Joseph and Scott, who were still in their pajamas. Darrel sat
next to them, his homework on his lap. Sitting against the far
wall, Liana was staring intently at a needle Mercedes wove
expertly through the pieced quilt. There was a camaraderie
between them that Austin recognized immediately.

"That makes sense," Liana was saying. "As long as the
stitches are uniform it looks great. But the piecing together—
that takes brains."

Mercedes laughed. "No, just a lot of measuring and
patience. It's therapeutic, really. Calms the nerves."

"After all day with those papers, I need some calming."

Mercedes laughed again, and Wayne stopped reading for a
moment to watch her.

"Hello, I'm home," Austin called from the doorway. Liana
looked up with the others, and Austin was startled to see the

change in her face. Her brows were relaxed, and her eyes signaled a peace he had not seen before. He wished he knew what
had changed.

"Finished already?" Mercedes asked.

"With Wyoming. I have a few more states to go, though.
Tomorrow I need to stop in Utah on the way home, if Liana
doesn't mind. That would save me a trip back."

"I don't mind. I have two boxes of papers to put into that
laptop you lent me. I'll be plenty busy."

"Would you like to go for a walk?" Austin asked her.
"There's something I want you to see."

Darrel looked up, eyes bright. "What is it?"

Austin smiled at his nephew's eagerness. "The swimming
hole." He couldn't explain why it was so important, and he was
glad no one asked.

"I would like to stretch my legs," Liana said.

"Can I go?" Darrel asked. "Please?"

"Is your homework done?" Mercedes looked up from the
quilt, but her fingers didn't stop stitching.

Darrel's face fell. "Not yet. But I can do it later, after dinner."

"There's still the milking."

Wayne looked up from his book. "I can do the milking
alone tonight—just this once." He smiled. "It isn't every day
Austin's here with a friend."

Mercedes face softened as she met her husband's eyes.
"Okay then, Darrel. But only 'cause your daddy said so. Just
make sure you finish your homework after dinner." She left her
needle in the fabric and stood. "Speaking of which, I'd better
go turn off the oven. Apparently, dinner's going to be a bit
delayed tonight." Her smile showed she wasn't upset at the
idea. "And no, Joseph and Scott. Don't even think about asking to go outside. You're both lucky to be allowed out of bed."

Austin, Liana, and Darrel left the house, escaping the chorus of disappointed complaints from the younger boys. They had gone only a few steps when Wayne emerged from the house. "Would you like me to saddle a few horses? It's a mite far."

"You mean for city folk," Austin countered.

Wayne's smile was slow and wide. "Exactly. Well?"

Austin looked at Liana, who had gone quite pale. "I think I'd rather walk," she said.

"Setzer would be nice," Austin said. "I promise."

Liana shook her head. "Maybe next time."

Austin refrained from reminding her that there wasn't likely to be a next time. The thought sobered him. "We'll cut through the fields."

Wayne nodded and went inside.

"I need to change first." Austin started for the barn. "I won't be long."

"Take your time. I'll visit the goats."

"I want to hurry. There's not much sunlight left."

When he was dressed in jeans and a matching denim jacket, they began their walk toward the small grove of trees that lined the river, careful to walk in the small break between the alfalfa and wheat fields. Already the alfalfa was several inches high, and the wheat not far behind. "We used to make nests in the alfalfa," Austin told Liana as Darrel ran on ahead. "My dad would be furious at us for tramping what would become the hay for the animals, but Wayne—he came to work for us when I was five and Mercedes was eight—he just laughed and told us to go right ahead. He always made sure he was the one who cut the part of the fields where we'd been playing so my father wouldn't yell at us."

"He seems like a good man."

"The best. I'm glad Mercedes finally married him. He'd been in love with her since about the time she went to college."

Liana nodded. "Anyone can see how he feels about her."

Was that envy in her voice? Austin couldn't be sure.

Darrel was far ahead of them now, jumping over the young alfalfa plants like a young goat. He seemed to know exactly where to place his feet without even looking. Skirting the field, they hurried after him.

"So, you're afraid of horses?" Austin asked.

"Just of riding them." Liana gave him a smile. "Something left over from childhood. First grade, I think."

Austin nodded. "A very impressionable age." First grade had been when he first realized that his mother loved his father more than she could ever begin to care about him.

"Not a big deal, really," she said. "I do feel like walking. My legs need it after the day I've had."

"You sorted all the boxes?"

"Mostly. It got so I could sort of skim a box and see basically what it contained. There are a few more I need to go through, but we can take them back to Nevada." They walked in silence for a minute, and then she asked, "So how did your day go?"

Austin recounted in detail the meeting and the competition he'd set up. By the time he finished, they had reached the river, and he realized he had monopolized the conversation. Besides her brief comments about the boxes of paper, she hadn't told him about her day—especially what had happened between her and Mercedes. Something had cemented their relationship, and Austin was glad for it, but a small part of him was envious.

"There it is," he said, leading her to the place where the river widened.

She stopped to catch her breath. "Did you pile up those rocks to make the dam?"

"A lot of the rocks were already here, but whether they were put here by past owners of the farm or naturally occurring, I don't know. Mercedes and I and some of our friends hauled more rocks and limbs to make it better. When the river was really low, we'd fill the cracks with smaller rocks and pieces of wood. That kept enough water here to make a good pool all summer. I learned how to swim here."

"What's that for?" She pointed to the rope that hung from a huge oak whose uppermost branches spread over the river.

"Our swing. See the big knot at the end? We'd stand or sit on that, and our buddies would push us out over the water. The braver ones would hold onto the rope and jump from that lower tree limb that stretches out over the bank. That's where Darrel's climbing up to now. It's like flying."

The smooth white of her neck was exposed as she looked up into the tree. "Sounds fun. That tree limb's awful high, though."

"Not as high as the one where the rope is tied. I actually fell into the river a couple times trying to tie it up there. But that branch where Darrel's standing is more than two feet wide and perfect for just about anything. I can't tell you how many times I fell asleep up there during lazy summer afternoons."

"Good thing you didn't roll."

He shrugged. "The ground isn't too hard. Lots of grass padding."

She laughed. "So you did fall."

"A time or two. Broke my arm once. Didn't stop me, though."

"I'll bet."

"Look, Darrel's going to try the rope!" Austin ran over to

the base of the tree with Liana close behind. Above them, Darrel stood on the wide tree limb. "Darrel, hang on tight," Austin called. "The water's too cold! And it's pretty full, too. If you fall in, your mother will kill me." As a child, Austin had swum in the river March through October—but he hadn't had a mother like Mercedes.

"I won't fall," Darrel called with the confidence of youth. His skinny hands wrapped around the rope as he pushed himself off the limb. Over the river he flew, screaming his excitement. Out once, twice, and a third time before he jumped off the rope onto the bank.

"Three times is all you can go or you can't get back without jumping into the water," Austin explained to Liana.

"Which, of course, is the best—right? In warmer weather, I mean."

"In *any* weather." He winked at her.

Darrel grabbed a long stick leaning up against the tree trunk. A metal hook at the end made it easy for him to catch the swinging rope as it neared the bank. He pulled it in. "Your turn, Uncle Austin."

"Me?" Austin put his hand to his chest in mock horror. "What if I slip?"

Darrel giggled. "Then you get wet! Come on, Uncle Austin, you never slip unless you want to."

"Okay, okay. You talked me into it. But I want to do it from above like you did—it's so much better." Holding the rope in one hand, Austin wedged his foot in the tree where it split into branches and began to climb. As a boy he had believed God had children in mind when He made this tree grow, and his opinion hadn't changed. "Too bad it's not summer!" he shouted to Liana. "Then you'd really see how it's done."

"Hey, don't yell—I'm right behind you."

He almost lost his hold at that. Liana Winn, ice princess, climbing a tree? Grinning, he covered the last few steps to the first branch, which was at least two feet wide. He was about to offer a hand to Liana but saw that she didn't need help.

Darrel followed them up, scampering past them on the tree limb like a sure-footed monkey. "Go, Uncle Austin. Go!"

Austin grabbed onto the rope and jumped. At first he had the feeling of falling, but then the rope went taut and he was flying over the swollen river. "Whoo-hoo!" he shouted. If Darrel hadn't been there, he might have let go. Yes, the water was likely freezing, but it would also be invigorating.

After landing on the bank he caught the swinging rope and climbed up the tree again. Liana was sitting on the limb, legs crossed Indian style. Wisps of hair had escaped her braid to curl gently around her face. "Nothing like it," he said, swallowing the odd lump in his throat. "Except galloping on horseback. That's like flying, too."

"I'll bet."

"Well, it's your turn," he teased.

Jumping to her feet, she took the rope from him.

"I was just joking."

She tossed her head, blue eyes gleaming. "I'm not."

"Way to go!" Darrel did a little dance that made the whole tree limb shake despite it's thickness.

Austin stepped closer to Liana. "You don't have to."

"Yes, I do." She grinned, and he grinned with her.

"Okay, then. Hold on really tight. Especially at first. There'll be a big jerk until the rope goes tight."

She adjusted her grip, took a deep breath, and jumped. Austin watched anxiously as the rope tightened and Liana sailed out over the water. "Yee-haw!" she screamed, a look of pure joy on her face.

"Yee-haw?" Austin looked at Darrel, who shrugged.

"She's pretty brave for a girl," Darrel said.

Austin nodded. "She really is." He turned his attention back to Liana. "One more pass and then jump for it. Be careful—the bank can be slippery."

Liana had her eyes closed and her face raised to the large patches of darkening sky that could be seen through the trees, as though no one else in the world existed. A stab of loneliness shot through Austin. She was . . . untouchable. Out of reach.

Then she slipped. With a cry, she plunged down, down into the dark water with a splash, disappearing into its icy depths. Darrel let out a big whoop, and Austin scrambled down the tree to the edge of the bank. "Liana?" The water was deep because of the spring runoff from the mountains, but because of the dam it wasn't particularly swift. Surely she knew how to swim. Ripples spread out from the place where she had fallen, slapping against the sides of the bank and wetting Austin's shoes.

He was debating whether he should go in after her when she broke through the water, gasping for breath. "Oooh!" she said. "It's cold."

Austin laughed. "The idea was to hold on to the rope."

She swam over to the bank, her lips already turning blue. "I know that."

There seemed to be an unfinished meaning to her words. Could she have fallen on purpose? Austin shook his head. "Need a hand?"

A brief glint of amusement shone in her eyes, and Austin wondered if she'd thought about pulling him in. Truthfully, he would have welcomed such an advance. Together in the cold water, with every nerve tingling, alive . . . He couldn't finish the thought.

She climbed up the bank without help and ran her hands down her legs to squeeze the water from her jeans. Her blouse clung to her, and she pulled out the front and then the back, loosening it from her skin. Goose bumps stood out on her arms and legs.

Austin watched her with more than a little interest, until she shivered and he remembered his jacket. "Here, take this."

She smiled. "There you go, trying to be a knight again."

"Well, if you'd rather not have the jacket . . ."

She grabbed hold of it. "No, this time I'll let you play the role. That water's like ice."

He didn't immediately release the jacket. The hands touching his were cold, but they sent heat into his body. They were close, too close. Austin didn't want to step away. There was power here, a connection. Something beyond mere attraction. Did she feel it too? The wide, surprised look in her eyes said she did.

She tugged on the jacket, and reluctantly he let it go. "We'd better hurry and get you back to the farm. Mercedes is going to kill me."

"It was my choice to go on the swing."

"Yeah, but what do you bet she won't see it that way?" Austin sighed loudly while Darrel and Liana laughed.

The sun was setting as they hurried toward the house, and a slight chill fell over the land. Liana's lower jaw occasionally quivered with the cold, but as they picked up the pace, her lips became less blue.

"What on earth!" Mercedes met them on the porch, hands on her hips. "I knew you boys would get into trouble." She clucked her tongue as she wrapped an arm around Liana's shoulders. "What'd they do to you—get you onto that rope and forget to tell you when to get off?"

"We told her, Mom." Darrel hopped excitedly from one foot to the other.

"We did," Austin agreed, knowing it was a lost cause.

"Yeah, I bet." Mercedes shook her head in disgust. "You two go wash up for dinner, and I'll get Liana a hot bath."

"But—" began Austin, feeling like a disciplined child. Mercedes had always been able to make him feel that way. Perhaps because she had practically raised him.

"No buts." Mercedes whisked Liana into the house and down the hall.

"I guess we're in the doghouse," Darrel said with a contented grin.

"No, the bunkhouse. Isn't that where dogs sleep these days?"

Darrel giggled. "Nope. The dogs sleep in the house. Last night Jellybean was in your old room."

Austin sighed. "Then I guess I'm the only one in the doghouse."

After washing up, they went to the table to wait for dinner. "Don't worry," Wayne said to Austin. "Mercedes likes to keep us on our toes. She ain't mad."

"I am too mad." Mercedes came from checking on the little boys, who were once again in bed. "They could have drowned the girl."

Liana appeared in the doorway behind her. "It was my idea." Her cheeks and lips were rosy now from the hot water. "And it was fun. I'd have done it again if I hadn't . . . fallen." To Austin's surprise, she winked at him.

Mercedes sighed. "Well, then maybe we're all crazy, because I go down there at least once a week to try it myself—but only in the summer, mind you."

Dinner consisted of tender slabs of roast beef, mashed

potatoes with gravy, green beans, and rolls. There was a peach cobbler for desert. "I could eat like this every day," Austin said with a sigh. "Of course, I'd get fat."

Mercedes passed him the plate of roast beef for a second helping. "Not if you worked from sunup to sundown. Look at Wayne."

"You work too hard, Wayne," Austin said.

Wayne paused with his fork in midair. "Got kids to put through college." Mercedes looked at her husband with gratitude. Austin knew what it meant to her for the boys to be educated. Perhaps one would choose to run the farm one day, but they would have a choice their father never had. A choice like the one Austin had made.

Dinner was comfortable, with Mercedes and Darrel doing most of the talking. After dinner, they left Darrel in the kitchen to finish his homework and retired to the living room, where Mercedes and Liana worked on the quilt while Wayne talked to Austin about the cattle venture he had started the year before. There was good money in it, if he could be successful. Austin was glad to see that Wayne's plan was stable and conservative. Unlike Austin's father, he wasn't willing to risk more than he could afford to lose.

Near nine o'clock, Austin turned to Liana. "All ready to leave tomorrow?"

"We'll have to carry out the boxes, is all. And I have to put a few things back in my suitcase."

"Let's get the boxes out tonight, if you don't mind."

She put down her needle. "Mercedes, I won't be at all offended if you take out all these stitches when I'm gone. They don't look near as even as yours. But it was fun. There really is something about quilting that takes your mind off everything else."

Mercedes nodded. "Sometimes it's really therapeutic."

Austin and Liana each carried two boxes out to the truck. Though it didn't look like rain, Austin covered them with a tarp from his tool box just in case. Then he and Liana walked back toward the house.

She covered a yawn with her hand. "I guess I'll turn in now, if we're leaving at six."

"Yeah, me too."

She stopped on the porch. "Austin, I want you to know . . . well, I had fun this evening. Thanks for showing me the swimming hole. I wish I'd had one in Nevada."

"I'm glad you liked it." Austin found himself wanting to explain further—about how that place had been his refuge from his father. How many nights he'd hidden there and dreamed about going away and making something of himself. Of becoming a man who wouldn't be afraid to face his father. The first goal he had accomplished, but the last . . . well, in some ways he was still afraid of his father.

"Goodnight." She hesitated, as though . . . as though what? Waiting for him to kiss her? Austin doubted that very much.

"Goodnight," he echoed. He let her go inside alone. Standing on the porch, he breathed in the smells of the cool night air, recalling memories of past evenings when he had stood on this exact spot. There was a deep and lasting happiness that came from the fact that he had roots somewhere, that he could always come home. He wondered if there was a place where Liana felt this connection, or if the early severing of her roots had prevented her from planting more.

Inside the house, he found that Wayne and Darrel had retired, but Mercedes was in the kitchen making butter in her blender. "We're just about out," she said. "And I want it for the pancakes tomorrow."

"You always make me pancakes when I leave."

Mercedes' eyes grew red, and she blinked hard. "They're my favorite, and it makes me feel better."

"I'll be back."

"I know."

"Well, goodnight." He leaned over and kissed her cheek.

He was halfway to the back door when her words stopped him. "You're half in love with her already. That's why you brought her here, isn't it?"

He stopped and turned around slowly. "I don't know what you're talking about."

"Yes, you do."

"We're just friends—not even that. She lost her job because of me, and I gave her another one—a temporary one. That's all. I barely know her."

"It happens like that sometimes." Mercedes' black eyes reflected her own memories. "All it takes is one meeting. A conversation. A look. A connection. And your life is never the same."

"You're talking about *him,* aren't you?" Austin felt a tightening in his chest as he approached her. He didn't want to see his sister ever hurting the way she had twelve years ago.

"Partly, yes." Mercedes blinked hard, and her eyes became wet at the corners. "Don't get me wrong, Austin. I'm grateful for my life and for Wayne, and I wouldn't change a minute of our life together, even if I could. I know that I made a terrible mistake, which I would still give anything to undo. You know how I suffered for it. I still suffer. I will always wonder what could have been. We had the beginning of something great, but we ruined everything by our selfishness."

Austin hugged her. He hadn't realized that some part of his sister had remained with her first love. Of course, she had a

daily reminder in Darrel. But he and Liana, well, their relationship didn't even begin to approach that level.

Or did it?

He recalled the emotions he had felt while watching her
drip on the grassy bank next to the river. For a moment he had
felt a connection. Or had it been purely attraction after all?
Perhaps. But certainly his concern for her lost job had not
been. Neither had his anxiousness to show her the farm and
the swimming hole. The fact was that she had not been far
from his mind since the moment he met her.

"She doesn't even like me," he muttered, almost to himself.

Mercedes drew away. "Don't make the same mistake I did,
Austin. Assume nothing. Do the right thing. Be patient. And
remember, grabbing the rose of life sometimes means getting
pricked by thorns."

CHAPTER

13

Diary of Karyn Olsen
Sunday, April 17, 1966

    Travis is acting very strangely. Distant, almost. He didn't show up in the cafeteria for lunch once this past week, and he's never home at his apartment when I call. He did stop by a few times, but even then he doesn't seem to hear me when I talk to him—like he's thinking of something else. Maybe it's because of finals. I don't know. Truthfully, I worry that it might be another girl. Last night he wasn't home when I called to remind him of our lunch plans today, and then he called me this morning and canceled. Didn't say why, and I was too mad to ask. He said he'd come over tonight, though. I'm sure it was just something related to school. I mean, if he didn't want to be with me, he wouldn't come over, right? I wish we were married already and all this dating stuff was behind us.

    The loud honking of a car drew Liana's attention away from the financial records she was typing into the laptop as she sat in

Austin's truck waiting for his return. She looked over the parking lot to the street, but the impatient driver was nowhere in sight. Her eyes lifted to the highest peaks of the Rocky Mountains that were just visible over the tops of the many buildings. From her one previous visit, she hadn't remembered Utah as such a busy place, but the capital, Salt Lake City, was apparently large and growing every day.

A wide diversity of people seemed to make their home in Salt Lake City. Liana watched people of different races and economic backgrounds pass on the sidewalk by the parking lot. An older man attracted her attention. He shuffled along slowly, stopping every few feet to wipe his forehead with a handkerchief he took from the pocket of his suit coat. When people passed, he nodded at them and smiled.

Was Austin's father like that? Liana wondered. Or was he like the old lady coming along now, not looking up at anyone but frowning at the concrete beneath her feet as though wishing it would open up and swallow everyone—including herself. Her countenance made a stark contrast to the old man's sunny disposition.

Liana's curiosity about Austin's father had begun with their departure from the farm. After hugging Liana, Mercedes had taken Austin's hand. "Go see him at the home," she said. "Before it's too late."

Austin's jaw clenched. "It was too late the day I was born."

"You have to make your peace."

"No, I don't. He killed her. You know that, don't you?"

Tears stood out in Mercedes' eyes. "He's different now."

"Are you sure that's not just your religion talking?"

"Of course it is—my religion and every other religion in the world. Forgiveness is necessary to live a happy life, and a part of you knows that, if you'd only listen."

"I'll think about it," Austin replied in a way that said most clearly he would not think about it at all. He hugged Mercedes and said good-bye civilly enough, but once on the road he had fallen into a silent black mood that accompanied them to Utah. Not even when Liana put in the Kenny Rogers CD did he recover his good humor.

Upon arriving in Utah, he offered to find an office for her in the building where he was having a meeting, but she preferred to stay in the truck. "I might need more documents from the back."

Liana closed her eyes and leaned her head back on the seat, thinking again of Mercedes and Austin. She profoundly regretted leaving the farm. There was something safe there, a connection of . . . of family? She wasn't sure.

She grinned as she remembered the swing over the river and how it really had felt like flying. Her eagle picture had come to mind, and she'd *had* to let go of the rope, just to feel what it was like. The freedom had been . . . wonderful, and the cold water hadn't changed her mind. Later on the bank there had been a look in Austin's eyes, one that had made her want to step into his arms. She shivered again at the memory.

She was glad now she had not acted on the impulse. Riding for hours with Austin in his black mood had been difficult enough without adding another aspect to their relationship.

"Catching up on beauty sleep?"

Liana's eyes flew open to see Austin leaning through her open window. "Oh, you're finished already?"

"Already? I've been in there for an hour and a half."

"Tsk, tsk. It took you *that* long to whip them into shape?" She shook her head. "You're losing it, Mr. Walker."

"Well, Miss Winn, we can't all be as talented as you." He

slapped the side of the truck and went around to the driver's side.

"Glad to see you're feeling better," Liana said as he started the engine. "I was beginning to think that black cloud was going to follow us all the way to Nevada."

He grinned. "Sorry about that. I have been a bear."

"No, just quiet—brooding. But now that you've shaken out of it . . ." Liana hesitated. If she brought it up, would he fall back into his bad mood? *What's it to me?* she thought. *After the way he's been this morning, I have a right to know.*

"What?"

"Why won't you go see your father? I know you said he was a horrible father and a drunk, but he can't be drunk now at the nursing home. He is in a nursing home, isn't he? That's what I got from what Mercedes said this morning."

Austin cut the engine and stared straight ahead, his hands resting on the steering wheel. "He's in an assisted living facility, not a nursing home. As for why I don't want to see him—well, I have no love for my father."

"You said he killed your mother."

Austin's eyes met hers, his forehead wrinkling as if plagued by a tension headache. "He left her shortly after I went away to college. Went to Texas to make his fortune in ranching. She begged him to take her with him, but he left her to take care of the farm." He shook his head as though he still didn't understand why his father had made that choice. "After all the years she'd stuck by him, he shook her off like so much manure on his shoe. He sold their best tractor and took all their savings. I believe he would have sold the farm out from under her if he hadn't already borrowed just about all it was worth from my grandmother. She was smart enough to make him sign a contract and put a lien on the title. A year later my mom took too many sleeping pills and never woke up."

"Suicide?" Liana's heart seemed to skip a beat.

Austin looked away from her and stared instead at the steering wheel. He looked lost. "The doctor was a friend of my grandmother's and ruled it accidental, but we all knew she did it on purpose. Her whole life was wrapped up in my father— much as he didn't deserve her—and she didn't want to live without him."

"But he came back?"

He looked at her. "Yeah, nearly two and a half years after her death, another business venture having failed. The only reason he came was that he was broke and sick and wanted her to take care of him. Didn't even know she was dead." Austin's lips curled in disgust. "The only good thing about her death was that she was finally free from his neglect. I confronted him then, but he never once admitted that he was the cause of her death or that he'd done anything wrong. A year or so later when Mercedes returned to the farm and married Wayne, she became our father's slave. It made me so mad, as though history would repeat itself. But Wayne wouldn't let anything touch Mercedes or the children. He made my father stay in Rock Springs. Mercedes visits him two or three times a month."

"You've never gone?"

"No."

"Why?"

"I told you why."

"It's been, what, more than ten years?"

"Seventeen."

"Why don't you go see for yourself if he's changed?"

He regarded her silently for a long moment. "Why do you care?"

Liana had been wondering that herself, and though she wasn't altogether sure it was the right reason, she had an answer prepared. "Because it means so much to Mercedes."

Austin rubbed his chin, a gesture she'd learned meant that he was thinking. He let out a long sigh. "Okay, while we're on the subject of the past, tell me why don't you talk to your adopted mother about why she and your birth mother fought? Why don't you ask her about your mother, what she was like?"

An impossibly large, painful lump formed in Liana's throat. She wanted to lash out at him, to return the hurt he'd inflicted, but she had been the one to open the door by questioning him about his father. Perhaps she'd already wounded him that same way. "Because," she said slowly, "it was all so long ago. It doesn't matter anymore."

"I think it matters to you."

"I don't want to hurt my—my mother."

"Your mother or yourself?" His eyes held hers.

Her anger at him was growing, but she felt obliged to answer. "I guess I'm afraid of what I might learn."

"Ah." He looked away and stared at the windshield. "I think you have my answer as well. What if I go and he hasn't changed? What if I hate him more? Perhaps it's better to leave the past alone."

"And yet . . . " said Liana. What about the longing inside her, the need to know her first mother?

Austin turned again toward her. "And yet," he repeated. Then he gave her a strained smile. "Tell you what, if you face your demons, I'll face mine."

She let out a long sigh. "Poor Mercedes. I guess she'll never get what she wants."

Austin snorted and shook his head. "Forget this. Let's go get something to eat. How about Chinese?"

"I love Chinese. With white rice, not fried."

He smiled, and she wondered if he was remembering the night they first met. "Ditto—I hate fried rice."

"But hold the lame fortune cookies," she said before he could get too smug about their shared taste in food. "And make it takeout. I want to get home before ten."

They arrived at Liana's condo shortly after nine-thirty. The streets were dark and empty, except for two teenagers who stood against a car, faces close together as they appeared to exchange life-altering secrets. Liana had the CD player on and was jamming to Foreigner. She liked the way the music cut out all thought, leaving only the beat and the feeling. She didn't miss Austin's look of relief when he cut the engine and the music died, nor did she feel guilty. She had spent more than half their journey listening to the croon of country music and fighting the sleep it provoked.

Austin helped her carry the boxes and put them in her small entryway. "Well, that's it. Call me if you have a question about the work."

They were standing close, so close she could reach out and touch him with little effort. She was reluctant to let him go. "I know you have to get up early for another business trip tomorrow, but do you want a quick cup of something? Maybe a bite to eat?"

"Sure." He smiled and took a step closer. "Stop me from falling asleep on the way home, I suppose."

"Wouldn't want that." Their eyes met and held, and Liana had difficulty swallowing.

The next minute his arms went about her, and they were

kissing. One hand pressed into her back and the other into her hair. Liana's arm went around his neck.

The ringing of the bell brought them apart. "Liana?" called a voice from outside. "You home?"

"It's Christian." She ran a hand through her hair, touching the spot where Austin's hand had been only a second before.

The bell rang again. "Hello," Christian said, his voice muffled by the door. "I know you have to be home. I see the light."

"He has a key," Liana told Austin.

"Better answer then."

She sighed. "I'm sorry."

"For what?"

Liana crossed the two steps to the door. "Coming." She opened the door, and Christian pulled his hand back from the knob, a key glinting in his hand.

"I was beginning to worry," he said.

"Why?"

"Because I thought you said you'd be home before now. I was here earlier, and you weren't here."

"I'm a big girl, Christian," she said dryly. "But we're late because Austin had a meeting in Utah on the way back."

"Oh." His eyes widened as Austin appeared behind her. "Hello, Austin. I thought I recognized the truck out there."

"Hi."

"We just got here," Liana said, not liking the calculating way Christian stared at her. "We were going to have a drink. Want to join us?" She stepped back so he could enter.

"Okay." Christian smiled blandly.

"You know what, guys?" Austin said. "I think I'd better cancel. I have an early flight and with such good company, I might stay longer than I should."

Liana nodded, keeping her face straight even as disappointment seeped through her.

"Thanks again for keeping me company, Liana," he said. "I'll be in touch."

"See you." She watched him saunter down the walk before shutting the door and facing her brother.

With his arms folded over his chest and his feet crossed, Christian leaned against the wall, regarding her gravely. By the set of his square jaw, Liana knew she was in for a grilling.

"What?" she asked, letting her annoyance show in her tone.

"You were going to have a drink with Austin?"

She shrugged. "Or something to eat. We've been traveling all day."

"Uh-huh." Uncrossing his legs, he took a step toward her. His hand reached out and wiped the skin above her top lip. "Your lipstick is smeared."

"Like I said, it was a long drive." She felt the muscles in her left eyelid retract several times in succession, signaling a need for sleep. "So do you want a drink or not? I'm exhausted."

"I'll let you sleep." He stepped toward the door and put his hand on the knob. "But I did find out about that supposedly minor car problem you mentioned."

"How?"

"Copy of the work order on your table."

She glared at him. "Since when did you start snooping in my house when I'm not home?"

"It's called trying to help. You should have come to me. I could have gotten you a better deal. I know people."

"So I've heard. That's what got me into Austin's accounting mess and made me lose my job, remember?"

"You're better off without it."

"That still doesn't excuse you for snooping."

"I wanted to make sure Austin wasn't putting undue pressure on you."

"I'm a big girl. You don't have to look out for me."

"I introduced you, and I feel responsible. I—look, do you think it's a good idea to get involved with him?"

Liana found it difficult to be exasperated when he had her best interest at heart. "I don't know," she said softly. "What do you think?" She could hardly believe she asked or that she was even thinking of Austin in future terms.

He shook his head. "I don't want to see you hurt again."

She knew what he wasn't saying. Her past attempts at relationships had always ended badly. Each time she'd tried to let down her guard, tried to open herself to commitment but found herself incapable of growing close to any of them. After a short while, each moved on. Worse, when the initial sting of rejection had faded, she realized that she didn't care. She had never really allowed herself to love them. Her emotions were safe, unable to escape her tight rein of control.

Like they had today with Austin.

Suddenly she was very grateful Christian had shown up. Without his interference, she might have made a mistake that could not be erased. As it stood, there was still time to distance her emotions from Austin and his family.

She stepped toward Christian. "Thanks for checking up on me."

He hugged her. "Hey, Banana, what are brothers for?"

"For painting me a picture for my birthday."

He grinned. "That, and taking you to get your car tomorrow afternoon. I called the guy, and it should be ready then."

Liana was touched. "Okay." She opened the door for him.

"Goodnight." He waved and started down the walk.

When he disappeared, she stayed on the tiny porch, lifting

her eyes to the bright stars in the sky. For a brief moment, she recalled another sky, just beginning to darken, and how she had felt flying under it.

Going to her suitcase, she withdrew the photograph of her parents from the side pouch. They were smiling for the camera, but their eyes were focused on each other over Liana's head. As a teen, she'd dreamed about how much in love they must have been that they couldn't keep their eyes off each other for even the brief snap of a photograph. Was it true? She wished she knew.

"Why did you and your sister fight?" she asked her mother's image.

Maybe Austin was right. Maybe it was time to learn the truth.

CHAPTER
14

Diary of Karyn Olsen
Friday, April 29, 1966

I want to die. I don't know how I'll go on—I really don't. My dad's dead, and my sister has made a play for my boyfriend. Worse, he let her. I still don't understand how it happened. My friends and I had a barbeque to celebrate Angie's birthday. We asked Mom if we could have it at her house because the backyard is perfect for this sort of thing. Travis was there, of course, and Clari came over as well. I should have known something was up the minute they looked at each other. But I didn't. How could I be so stupid? How could I miss the way his eyes followed her around?

When it got dark and we were all inside watching TV and eating popcorn, I noticed Travis was missing. At first I thought he'd gone to the bathroom, but he didn't come back. I found them sitting on the back porch—kissing like newlyweds! My heart seemed to fly into millions of little shards.

How could they do this to me? How? I must have yelled the

words because Clari was looking all shocked, and Travis said something about us just being friends. Friends? How could he say that? Then Mom came out and said that Travis and Clari had seen each other a couple of times since Daddy's funeral, even went on a few dates. What, I'm supposed to feel happy to know that they talked a few times before making out behind my back?

I feel so betrayed. He never kissed me that way—never. What's wrong with me that he could fall in love with Clari and not with me? I hate her. I hate them both! I left the party then without saying good-bye to anyone, and I'm never going back. I don't want to see Clari or Mom ever again.

On Friday morning, Liana checked her cell phone messages and found that she had several from people who needed help with taxes. Elated, she immediately called them back and set up a time to meet. *Maybe I won't need Austin's job much longer,* she thought. Not that she wanted to give up the job just yet—the charity's records were proving interesting—but she wanted the option to back out if necessary. Never again would she put all her eggs in one basket, especially if that basket were owned by a boss whose goal justified any means.

She dug with renewed enthusiasm into the boxes she had brought from Wyoming. Several times the phone rang, and she answered eagerly, telling herself her excitement stemmed from the possibility of another customer. Most of the calls were from telemarketers, but even when it was another tax job, she found it difficult to hide her disappointment.

Finally she recognized the truth: She was hoping to hear from Austin.

Noon came and went and still no call from him. "What am I waiting for?" she asked aloud. "If he did call, what would I say? Uh, about last night, Austin. We were both tired. It was no big deal. Let's forget it." She stopped and snapped her fingers. "Or, I made a bet with Christian, you know. Thanks for helping me win." Liana groaned and threw herself into her easy chair. As if to mock her, the phone rang again. She grabbed it.

"Lara? Hi, honey, it's Mom. You called this morning? I got your message, but I think the answering machine needs to be cleaned or something because I couldn't understand exactly what you said."

"I want to come over for a visit tonight, if you're not busy."

"Well, we do have plans for a movie and dinner. But we can go tomorrow if it's important."

Liana grimaced at the ceiling. "It can wait." Her questions had already waited for twenty-five years. One more day wouldn't matter. "What about tomorrow?"

"That'll work. About what time?"

Clarissa always did her heavy cleaning on Saturday mornings, so Liana knew later would be better. "About two—is that good?"

"Perfect. Or why don't you come a little earlier, and we can have lunch?"

"Okay, one, then."

"See you tomorrow, honey."

"Bye, Mom." Liana hung up, feeling very tired. Despite her desire to learn the truth, she was glad for a day's reprieve. She needed to plan what she would ask Clarissa. Would she have the courage to speak openly? For some reason there was a dread in her heart that terrified her.

"I hope I am not opening Pandora's box," she said to the empty room.

As Liana sat at the table in her parents' house across from her adoptive mother, her feet felt cold. *Where's a good dog when you need one?* she asked silently, thinking of Jellybean's warm fur. Strangely, she found herself missing that dog and had even bought a pound of jellybeans last night at the grocery store. Alone in her condo afterwards, she'd eaten half of them before finally putting them in the cupboard out of sight.

"Ever thought about getting a dog?" she asked Clarissa.

Clarissa shook her head as she set a plate of finger sandwiches in front of Liana. "Dogs take too much work. I've raised three children, thank you very much. It was the best thing I ever did, but I'm enjoying my freedom too much to go back to cleaning up after a dog."

She smiled as she spoke, but her answer hit Liana hard. *She'd practically raised the boys before I came to live here. Did she resent me?*

Liana had harbored this secret worry all through her growing up years, though she had never actually put a name to it before. Swallowing hard, she lifted her glass of juice to get rid of the bitterness in her throat.

"Besides, dogs shed. They destroy things." Clarissa smoothed her long red print skirt before she sat opposite Liana. "I'm afraid I'm much too set in my ways to get an animal. We did have a dog once when the boys were small. Kept him in the backyard until he ruined it with his messes and his digging. Then we put him in a pen, but that made him restless. He kept jumping on Bret and knocking him over every time we let him out. And Christian . . . well, he didn't like to get dirty unless it was with paints. So we gave the dog away." She smiled, eyes focused faraway on something Liana couldn't see. "His name was Wizard, of all things. The boys cried when we gave him away, but it was for the best. That dog was much happier with the farmer we gave him to."

"I never knew," Liana said. How much else had she missed?

"You weren't even born yet." Clarissa took a tiny bite of her sandwich and swallowed it. "The boys barely remember him. They were too small."

Liana had finished several finger sandwiches. The thin turkey meat ones had gone down easily, but her mother always put too much mayonnaise in the tuna. She took another gulp of juice to wash the taste from her mouth. "That's what I want to talk to you about, sort of. About the time before I was born. I'd like to know what happened between you and my—my—" She had been about to say "real mother," but with the constraint of long habit she couldn't. "Between you and your sister."

Clarissa's hand froze in midair. For a moment she looked like a statue, immaculately dressed, each blonde hair perfectly arranged. Only the sandwich, lifted halfway to her partially open mouth, was out of place, an incongruence that Clarissa would have intensely disliked had she been the one watching.

She recovered her poise quickly. The hand with the sandwich lowered and picked up the napkin instead, dabbing at her mouth, hardly disturbing the red lipstick. Setting the napkin on the table, she folded her hands together in front of her plate. "I knew this day would come," she said. "I always knew it. But I expected it much sooner. Perhaps when you were a teen." Clarissa's forehead creased, and her eyes took on a sadness that bit into Liana's heart.

"I don't want to hurt you," Liana felt compelled to say.

Clarissa's face immediately changed. "You aren't the one doing the hurting," she said firmly. "What happened between your—your mother and me was my doing, my fault. I wish it could have been different, but I can't change things now. It's far too late.".

Liana didn't speak, nor could she look away. Clarissa's blue eyes had locked onto hers, fixing her in place. The tiny lines around those eyes were more distinct now, too, as though preparing for heartbreak.

"You deserve to know." Clarissa shook her head, the movement barely perceptible. "I only wish there was more to tell you. I wish . . ." She closed her eyes, and Liana was free to look away. Still, she kept watching Clarissa's face, wondering at the unconcealed suffering she saw there, a feeling that seemed equal to the one rising in her own chest.

Clarissa pushed back her chair. "Come with me."

Liana met her around the table, allowing Clarissa to take her hand. Tears stung her eyes, and her heart pounded like thunder. Clarissa led her past the family room and down the hall to her own bedroom. Since Clarissa and Travis had always insisted on privacy, it was a place Liana and her brothers had not often gone. The room smelled of lilacs and the orange oil Clarissa used to clean the furniture. Sunlight slanted through the window onto the floor.

"Sit here." Clarissa indicated the bed.

With a longing glance toward the padded rocker next to the bed, Liana obliged.

Clarissa went to the closet and pulled down a small metal box from the top shelf. She sat down on the bed next to Liana, setting the box between them. Liana watched as she worked the combination lock.

"This is all I have of my sister." Clarissa lifted the lid as she spoke, her voice choking. "I loved her so much. I wish . . . I wish. . . ." Whatever her wish was would stay a mystery to Liana because Clarissa couldn't finish the sentence. She took a deep breath and drew out a paper and a passport. "These were with you when you arrived from India. Your original birth certificate and the passport the American embassy there gave you after your parents died." She handed the documents to Liana. *Lara Clari Schrader* was written clearly on both, but Liana felt no connection to the name.

"So you adopted me."

Clarissa blinked, and a single tear slid down her left cheek. "Of course we adopted you. My sister and her husband would always be your parents, but I felt very strongly that no child should ever have to grow up without someone to call Mom and Dad." Clarissa reached for another paper inside the metal box. "I also have a letter from a doctor at the hospital where your parents worked. He was the one who called to tell me what had happened. He wrote to me once after you'd come to live with us."

Liana accepted the proffered letter. A paragraph jumped out at her: *Has the child spoken yet? If you could write me a letter, I would like to know if all is well, if she is adjusting to her new life.*

Liana still felt no connection to the little girl she had been. That life seemed almost to belong to someone else.

She looked up slowly. "Was that the first you knew about me?"

Clarissa shook her head. "No. Karyn had sent me a letter before, when she was pregnant." Reaching into the box, she removed a worn envelope. Her hand trembled, and her eyes threatened more tears.

Liana reached eagerly for the letter, but Clarissa held it to her heart. "First, you need to know a few things. Your mother knew Travis first. She met him at school and fell in love. I didn't know it. I thought they were just friends." Her eyes pleaded for understanding. "He drove her to our dad's funeral, and from the moment I met him I felt something . . . different. It's hard to explain. During the next weeks, we ran into each other many times." She smiled, though her eyes glittered with tears. "He told me later that he planned those meetings—he must have found out information from Karyn about where I might be. And then we fell in love."

Still clutching the letter with one hand, Clarissa reached out to touch Liana's knees, her face earnest. "Honestly, Lara, I swear that I never knew Karyn loved him—and by the time I did, it was too late. Travis loved me, and I loved him. Not the fleeting kind of love, or the crush kind of love, but the *real* thing. It was so deep, so passionate, so . . . so right. I begged her not to make me choose between them. She refused to listen. I didn't know what to do. I knew Travis didn't love her. I knew that I'd never be happy without him. I thought I would die."

Clarissa took her hand away from Liana's knee and covered her eyes. Her head bowed, her slender shoulders shook with silent sobs. Liana watched helplessly, her own feelings numb. Karyn and Clarissa had fought over Travis? Picturing her adoptive father's face above the large belly he now sported, it hardly seemed possible.

With one hand Clarissa wiped tears from her cheeks. "Then Karyn disappeared. I didn't know where she was. She'd been careful to leave no trace. I almost broke up with Travis, but he wouldn't go away. So I married him. Oh, Lara, it was right. We were born to be together!"

That much Liana believed. She couldn't imagine either of her adoptive parents with anyone else.

"The next year I had Christian. It was a difficult pregnancy and birth, and I was a long time recovering. Mom sent a letter and a birth announcement to Karyn's old address, hoping it would get forwarded—we'd done that with cards and letters before and they hadn't been returned—but eventually that letter did come back." Clarissa reached into the metal box with her free hand and retrieved another letter. She pushed the sealed envelope into Liana's hand. The address had been crossed off and someone had scribbled *moved*. "I've kept it all these years. I don't know why. At first it was to prove to her if she came back that I'd tried to reach her. And then I just couldn't bear to part with it."

"So she never got the letter."

"Oh, she got it." Clarissa's lips pursed and she took a deep breath before continuing. "About six months after the letter came back, I ran into an old friend of hers, who said that she'd personally given it to Karyn."

"She had the letter and didn't open it?" Liana turned the letter over, searching for signs of resealing. The outside of the envelope was worn, but it didn't look like it had been opened. She let the letter fall to the bed beside the metal box.

Clarissa shrugged. "That's what it looked like. She'd obviously put it back in the mail with the address crossed off and sent it back as a way to tell us she didn't want any contact. It broke my heart. I cried a lot then—I missed her so badly. Every time I thought about her, my heart hurt. But eventually I had to let it go. Travis and Christian filled my days. Besides, I thought there was still time to make up with her in the future." She gave a bitter chuckle. "I was wrong."

"You didn't look for her after that?"

Clarissa shook her head. "I knew she wanted to remain lost. Besides, her friend had also said that Karyn was moving to Florida. In those days, with the resources we had, that was very far away."

Liana couldn't look at Clarissa's face and the pain so clearly etched on the fine skin. She stared at Karyn's letter instead, watching as Clarissa finally held it out to her. Trembling, she took the envelope in her hands and withdrew the single sheet of paper. The letter had been folded and unfolded many times over the years, and a few tiny holes had begun to show in the creases. The lower left side was stained with water—or was it tears? But whose tears? Clarissa's or Karyn's? Hearing Clarissa's story, Liana bet on the latter. The letters were small and precise, as though the author had thought out her words carefully before recording them.

July 2, 1977

Dear Clarissa:

I know you didn't expect to hear from me ever again, but here I am writing. I want you to know that I'm sorry. I see now looking back and reading my journal that what happened was my fault and that I've blamed you for too long. So much has happened here in India (can you believe me in India?) that has opened my eyes. Mostly it's because of Guenter. He's a doctor at our charity hospital, and the way he cares for the children impressed me from the very first. He swept me off my feet as Travis must have done to you. Oh, I feel so embarrassed now when I think about how I acted. I never loved Travis—not like you did. My relationship with Guenter has shown me that.

Of course it wasn't easy, shedding so many years of anger and hurt (no matter how imagined), but everything is all right now. Guenter Schrader and I were married nine months ago. And Clari, I'm going to have a baby. I'm sure it'll be a little girl. I dream for the day when I'll finally see

173

her face. I think I'll name her Lara. Or something else beginning with an L because she'll always be my little love.

Despite my joy in my work and all the babies I've helped bring into the world, I'm hoping we can somehow go to the U.S. before too long. There is so much I want to tell you face to face.

I hope you'll find it in your heart to forgive me. I'd like to be your sister again.

I love you,
Karyn

Liana's tears wet her cheeks. "She forgave you."

"Yes." Clarissa's voice was happier now. "In the years after her death, sometimes this letter was all that kept me going. But I still don't know how she got to that point—of forgiving me. I have no idea what she went through in India or before. The friend I ran into that once had said she was working as a waitress, but this letter indicates that she'd been working at a hospital. Later, after she died, I checked and found that she'd gone back to the college where she'd met Travis. She'd become a nurse. She'd never gone to Florida, or at least not for long."

"Did you write back?" Liana asked.

"Twice, but she never wrote again. Not knowing why has plagued me for a long time—I still wake up in the night and wonder."

Liana reread the paragraph that spoke of the coming baby, feeling sorry for her birth mother. To have yearned so much to have a child and then to have it all disappear in a day because of a plane accident. With reluctance, Liana returned the letter to Clarissa.

Clarissa again held the letter to her breast, closing her eyes at a fresh onslaught of pain. "Sometimes," she whispered, "I see

Karyn as she was the last time I saw her all those years ago. She was so alive, so angry. And I ask myself why I didn't do more to salvage our relationship then. I was the older sister. I should have made the effort. I will always regret that I didn't."

There was so much sadness in her tone that it stung like an accusation. "I'm sorry," Liana said in a low voice. "Having me around . . . it must not have been easy."

Clarissa's eyes flew open. "No," she said. "Don't think that! Don't *ever* think that. Oh, Lara, you are the daughter I could never have—and I wanted a daughter so very badly. I lost a baby girl once, between the boys. I was four months along. Christian was little. I was so happy to be expecting again . . . and then I lost her. It was devastating. That's why I waited so long to have Bret. I thought I'd die if I had to go through losing another baby."

"I didn't know." Liana's hand twisted in her hair, tugging the strands. One more secret festering in Clarissa's soul.

"It's not something I ever told the boys about," Clarissa said. "I mourned her alone—not even Travis understood how much the loss still haunted me. And then you came into my life." Tears once more fell down Clarissa's cheeks. "But I felt so guilty. Karyn gave me you—one of the greatest joys of my life—yet if I hadn't married Travis, maybe she would have married him and she would be alive today. Maybe if I hadn't interfered, something would have eventually blossomed between them."

"You are not responsible for her death." The words felt dry in Liana's mouth.

"I know that here." Clarissa pointed to her head, her face crumpling. "But here in my heart, I know it was my fault." She sobbed as Liana watched, not knowing what to do. They had been mother and daughter for twenty-five and a half years, but neither could comfort the other. Liana had needed only herself; Clarissa had Travis and the boys.

Hesitantly, Liana slid closer to Clarissa and put her arms around her thin body. She smelled of lilacs and makeup and something else Liana couldn't identify. She briefly saw Clarissa's eyes widen in surprise before their heads came together. Clarissa clung to Liana. "I'll never know what horrible thing happened that made her not write back," she sobbed. "I'll never know."

Liana had been thinking the same thing, but now an idea grew in her mind, an idea given seed by Mercedes. "Maybe there is a way."

Clarissa lifted her head, and Liana took the opportunity to escape the closeness that was still uncomfortable to her. "Let me see the letter again," she told Clarissa. "Look here. She mentions a journal."

Clarissa nodded. "I gave it to her when she went to college. I thought she'd get a kick later out of seeing what her life was like back then."

"Where is it now?" Liana glanced down in the metal box, but there were only a few more envelopes and papers.

"I don't know. I'd hoped it'd come back with you. But it didn't. I tried to write to the lady you stayed with before you came here, but she never replied. By now, the journal must be long gone. I'm so very sorry, Liana. It's one more thing I should have done better. But I had three children to take care of, plus my teaching. I couldn't just drop everything and go to India, could I?"

"No." Liana paused, her eyes fixed on the letter. "Not then. But you could now." There, her idea was out in the open—or rather Mercedes' idea—exposed to whatever reaction Clarissa might have.

A sharp intake of air made Liana look up. The expression on her adoptive mother's face was one she couldn't decipher. Why didn't she know enough about her own mother to recognize what she was feeling?

"We could both go," Liana continued, knowing it was something she had to do even if it cost her the rest of her savings. "You're already teaching only part time now. You could get a substitute for a week, and I don't have anyth—I mean, I can arrange to leave." Now wasn't the time to bring up her lost job, and Liana didn't think Clarissa was likely to wonder how Liana could leave work so close to the tax deadline. "Dad will be fine without you. So will Christian and Bret. Well?" She waited, trying not to show how much this meant to her. *Even if she refuses, I can still go,* she told herself.

Clarissa held very still, her tears abruptly dry. Every hair was in place, her white blouse unwrinkled, her skirt arranged becomingly on the bed. Only the streaks in her makeup and the reddened eyes showed any emotion at all.

Liana looked away, anticipating her answer. She wouldn't leave Travis. Not even her sister and her daughter meant that much.

"Yes."

Liana's head jerked up at the breathy whisper. There was excitement now in Clarissa's face, obliterating much of the previous sadness.

"We'll go to India. I should have gone when she first wrote. It's too late for that, but even if we don't find her journal, we might be able to find people where she worked who knew her." Tears once more glittered in her eyes. "At the very least I can visit my sister's grave."

"Thank you, Mom." For the first time in Liana's life, the appellation slipped easily from her tongue.

177

CHAPTER

15

Diary of Karyn Olsen
Thursday, May 5, 1966

Clarissa (I'll never call her Clari again) called five times and has left messages. I listened to them. She says she had no idea that I liked Travis in that way. She says she's really sorry. Sounded good at first, though I can't believe she didn't know how I felt since I've been talking him up for three months. But then she went on to say that she doesn't know what to do because she'd like to give him up, but she thinks they're in love. "This is for keeps," she says. "I've never felt this way before. Please don't make me choose between you."

I'm not making her do anything. I want nothing from her. Nothing. I hate her. I wish I could hate Travis, but I don't. This has to be Clarissa's fault. She couldn't be content with all her many admirers. She had to steal the one and only guy who liked me. I will never forgive her. I wish she would die.

Saturday, May 21, 1966

I quit school. What was the point? My grades were terrible, and I'd missed too much to make up. Who wants to go to school in the spring and summer anyway? Not me. To tell the truth, I don't care about school anymore. After calling me a hundred times to leave lies on our answering machine, Clarissa doesn't call me anymore. Angie said she came to our apartment last week, but luckily I wasn't home. We've worked out a way for Angie and our other roommates to signal me (red scarf in the window) if she ever comes again. If she comes when I'm home, I'll hide. Same thing for Travis, the worm, though he's never tried to contact me. I guess that shows his true feelings.

I've started working at In-N-Out. I know it's not much, but now that I'm not in school, Dad's trust fund won't pay for my rent. That stinks big time. But I don't really care, not about anything.

Mom called me and I called her back, but I hung up on her when she started talking about Clarissa. I don't want to hear it.

Monday, June 27, 1966

A knife is being twisted in my heart. Today I got an invitation to Clarissa and Travis's wedding. It'll be in July, just like I'd dreamed for my wedding. I won't go, of course. I wouldn't give either of them the satisfaction. I bet they sit and talk about me and how foolish I was. But I know Travis liked me. If it hadn't been for Clarissa, I'd be the one marrying him. I wish I were prettier. Clarissa has all the luck. Too bad her heart is as black as tar. Travis will find that out soon enough. I hope before the wedding, but I don't expect miracles anymore. Clarissa has killed everything.

Friday, July 15, 1966

Well, they're married by now (it's almost noon) and will soon be on their way to their honeymoon. I hope they get sunburned wherever they go so they'll have a lousy time. I can't believe Clarissa had her wedding without me. Growing up we dreamed about our wedding days and how we would be there for each other. But she didn't wait. She didn't even try.

I moved out of the apartment I shared with Angie to a cheaper one nearer work, not only because of money but because it's uncomfortable being there with all the students. I feel so much older than they are. Very old. But I still talk to Angie on the phone, and she said she hadn't heard any more from Clarissa. I thought about calling Mom, but I just can't. Oh, dear God, please stop this hurting. I'm so alone. I just want to die. At least I haven't gained any weight. That's the one good thing in this mess.

There is a guy who comes into work sometimes—Boyd something. He's so tall and muscular that I actually feel small around him. He keeps asking me out. I think I'll go with him tonight. I need someone, and my lousy family sure isn't here for me.

Saturday, July 16, 1966

I'm a woman now just like Clarissa. I thought it would be wonderful. I thought he would be tender and loving, but . . . Oh, I can't even think of it. It was as though he took the very most sacred parts of my soul, stomped and spit on them, and threw them away. He got what he needed, and I was left empty and alone. Unloved. I cried, and he laughed at me. Then he asked if he could come over again. I told him to get out. I desperately wish I would have listened to what my mother taught me about waiting. How could I be so utterly stupid? If she could see me now, she would die. Oh well, join the club. I've died, too. I'm someone else now. I can never go back.

CHAPTER

16

Diary of Karyn Olsen
Saturday, April 29, 1967

I haven't written in a long time, but there's been nothing really to write about. I quit my job so I'd never have to see Boyd again. Now I'm working at Denny's. I can make pretty good tips in the evenings. Sometimes a few guys ask me out, but I can't go. I'm too afraid. I will never trust another man again.

I saw Angie today—or last night, rather. (It's now about 3:00 A.M.) She came into Denny's with some of our old friends. I haven't seen her since she gave me the cards Clarissa and my mother sent me for my birthday in January. She asked me why I haven't returned her calls, and I said I'd been busy. But I realized I missed her. She looked really good. She'll be finished soon with college and start working in a hospital.

While the others were ordering, Angie got out an envelope from her purse and gave it to me. It had my mother's return address and the postmark was more than a month old. After work, I opened it and saw a letter from my mother and a birth announcement for Clarissa and Travis's baby boy. He was born a month early, according to the letter, because of Clarissa's high blood pressure. But he's healthy.

I have a nephew—it's almost unbelievable. I know I should be happy for them. I know I should forget the past and go visit them. I know I should become resigned to being "the aunt" and find joy in getting to know that little boy. I know all that. My mother took me to church every Sunday while I was little, and it seemed that forgiveness was all the pastor ever talked about. But there's just one thing that stops me. My heart cries out that it should have been my little boy in that announcement.

The letter hadn't been sealed well, so the envelope hadn't ripped when I opened it. I carefully resealed the envelope, crossed off the address, and dumped it at the post office. Maybe if I pretend I didn't open it, it won't hurt so much.

Before she left Angie told me she wanted to get together, but I said I was moving to Florida. I don't want any connection to my old life.

People rushed purposely from one place to another in the LAX International airport in Los Angeles. Every race and age group was represented—all of them in a life-and-death hurry to arrive at their destination. Loudspeakers blared out a gate departure in a woman's flat nasal tone. Following quickly came a man's all-important voice, informing Jonathan Reynolds that his party was waiting for him at the American Airlines front desk. The smell of cooking food, cigarette smoke, wine, and perfumes wafted through the air in varying strengths as Austin walked through the corridors.

He was tired with an exhaustion that went clear to the bone. He hadn't eaten yet today, and his muscles cried out at the lack of nutrition. Four different meetings in three different states in two days meant four separate flights, most lasting only an hour or two. Finally, he was on his way home, though it would be midnight before he arrived in Nevada, and then he would have to drive to his house in North Las Vegas. The company would have paid for another hotel and a flight the next day, but he preferred to do the legwork now and sleep in his own bed.

Almost numbly, he sat down outside the departure gate. Usually he enjoyed the traveling part of his job, but something kept drawing his thoughts back to Nevada. Something? No, someone—Liana.

He had purposely not called her, though his thoughts were with her constantly. He hadn't wanted to push her too hard, to force her to raise any of those walls she was so good at building. There would be time enough to talk when he returned to Nevada. But would she want to see him? He thought so. She had returned his kiss, after all.

He was unsure if he could drive her from his mind. Maybe before the trip to Wyoming that would have been possible, but now he'd glimpsed the real woman beneath the hard facade. He found her fascinating, tender, passionate—a woman who released the rope over a freezing river just for a moment of flying. Yes, he knew her better now, and he wanted to know more. Of course, it was entirely possible that she didn't share any of his feelings.

Sighing, he drew out his laptop and began to look at the e-mails he'd downloaded that morning but hadn't been able to read. The first message that wasn't spam was from Sonja, the woman he'd broken the date with little more than a week ago. Funny, he couldn't even remember what she looked like. He put the message in a file to read and answer later.

The second e-mail was from Olya Kovalevsky in Ukraine. This one he was waiting for.

Dear Mr. Walker:

I am elated to learn of the money your charity has received. God must indeed be looking His eyes out for us. You ask what is the most pressing need here. As usual, our most big need is medicine, diapers, and baby powder. Other consumables remain also important, such as shampoo, soap, toothpaste, and products for washing clothes. One director also requested simple, durable puzzles for the children, though only if there is room and enough funds. The other items are greatly more important. For to help you, I have attached a list of items and amounts the orphanages I am working with could use and how long that amount would last.

I do now have a passport, as last year you recommended, and my visa to America has been approved. So if it is needed I can go to America and accompany the supplies. I understand that at this time you cannot come and are worried about them arriving and getting through customs. I can also meet the supplies here, and this would save money. Most truthfully, I would greatly love to go to America myself as I am curious to see your beautiful country, but it would sadden me if such a pleasure took money from the orphans.

In answer to your other question, yes, I have managed to discover more about my sister. She was sent to an orphanage near Kiev after the second orphanage she was in burned down. A worker tells me she was adopted by a couple, though they have not paperwork to prove this. This lady was not certain, but she believes the couple were originally from Romania. This is unlikely since during that time the

184

Soviets did not permit foreign adoptions. Perhaps because Romania was also under Soviet rule, an exception was made. Why this couple might go to the trouble to adopt a Ukrainian baby when their own orphanages are so full, I cannot begin to discern. Perhaps they did not decide to adopt until they moved here from Romania.

While I am happy my little sister may have been adopted, I still worry about her very much. Even if this couple eventually returned to Romania, the conditions there are similar to here. Now it is as if a wall has been placed before me in my journey. I do not know where to turn. But I will pray to God. Only He can help me now. I do know people who have connections to Romania. Perhaps one of them has some knowledge that will lead me to my lost sister. I am also using the Internet to search, but as you know, it is very expensive here. In addition, my sister may not have the knowledge that she was adopted, and if she does, it is possible that she has no Internet access.

Again I apologize for burdening you with these concerns. I am very grateful for the help you give to the children. You have saved many lives and made better many more.

I send to you greetings and deep appreciation from this your friend in Ukraine.

Sincerely yours,
Olya Kovalevsky

Olya's continuing gratitude made Austin slightly uncomfortable, though he knew it was heartfelt. When they'd first met, she'd been as eager for work as the rest. Fortunately for them both, she not only had a knack for leadership but also a need for redemption that would keep her honest even under

RACHEL ANN NUNES

the most tempting circumstances. Had anyone been there to champion her little sister? He knew that she desperately hoped someone had. So did Austin.

Yet what disturbed him now was Olya's plea for puzzles, which brought to his mind the thought of a hapless Ukrainian orphan longing for a simple toy. He remembered a similar longing.

"A pair of jeans," he told his mother. "Please can't I have a new pair? Just one?"

"You have your overalls," she replied in the dull, placid way she had of speaking.

He groaned. "But, Ma, they're two years old and getting short. The kids at school tease me."

"Maybe next month."

But only a week passed before she bought the jeans. All went well until a month later in May when Austin had been at the swimming hole and hadn't arrived home to milk Patches on time. By the time he remembered and ran all the way home, his dad was out working on the tractor, using pieces of his new jeans as rags.

Austin cried. Not in front of his father but later in the tree by the river. "I hate him, I hate him," he screamed to the dark sky. "I'll run away and never come back. That's what I'll do." At twelve he was nearly a man and could do a man's work. He didn't need his father.

Mercedes found him there in the tree, and she sat next to him on the wide limb until he would let her hug him. He fell asleep with his head nestled in her lap, both of them covered with a horse blanket from the barn. He decided not to leave home because that would mean leaving Mercedes.

The next day he was at the bus stop in his old overalls, but Mercedes didn't ride the bus with him as she usually did.

"Aren't you coming to school?" he asked.

"No. I've got something else to do." She didn't remind him not to tell; she already knew he wouldn't.

After school she was waiting for him outside his last class carrying a large plastic sack. She shoved the sack at him with a smile, and he opened it to see a pair of new jeans inside. "Where'd you get them?" he asked, amazed.

Mercedes laughed, her black eyes shining. "I've been saving up. I walked to Grandma's, and she drove me to the store and then here. There's a couple shirts in there, too. They're from Grandma."

He hugged her hard. Once again, she didn't ask him to keep silent. They were both aware of their dad's opinion of their grandmother and especially of her charity—unless it was directed toward him. Austin secretly changed into those pants in the barn before school for two months before his dad finally gave his mother permission to buy him another pair.

Austin took out his cell phone and dialed a number. "Mercedes? Hi, how're the boys?"

"Good. I think they'll all be back in school on Monday."

"And Buttercup?"

"Buttercup and her kids are just fine. The boys named them Syrup and Pancake. They think it's hilarious."

Austin chuckled. "Couldn't have picked better names myself."

"Don't encourage them, Austin."

"I will so—the next time I come to visit."

"And when is that?"

"Soon. Next weekend maybe. Do you know if Fulmer is still into woodworking?"

"Yes, but only part time. Mabel made him get a job at the hardware store. She wanted insurance. Why?"

"I may have a job for him."

"Does this involve the charity?"

"Funny you'd mention that. You think you can make a few phone calls about another shipment? I'd like to get it there in two or three weeks."

Mercedes laughed. "I wondered why you called."

"Actually, I called to hear your voice."

"Oh?"

His throat had become dry, and he swallowed hard. "I was remembering the jeans, Mercedes. Did I ever say thank you?"

She was quiet a moment, and when she spoke her voice sounded choked. "Only about a hundred times."

"Well, thanks again."

"You're welcome." Mercedes let the silence last for nearly a minute and then asked, "So how's Liana?"

"I haven't talked to her. I'm still on business in LA."

"You should have called her."

"Been too hectic."

"You're calling me."

"That's different."

"You're afraid."

He sighed. "That seems to be happening a lot these days."

"So you didn't go see Dad." It wasn't a question.

"No."

"You'll have to someday."

"Maybe."

"Oh, Austin, I just hope it won't be too late when you finally get around to it. You have to forgive him. I'm not saying to forget but to forgive. It's still eating you alive."

He didn't respond to her comment. Anger burned in him at the very thought of speaking to the man. Deliberately, he typed an e-mail to Tammy, the buyer for HeartReach, directing her to purchase everything on Olya's list as soon as possible. He'd send the e-mail as soon as he had wireless access.

"Austin?" Mercedes asked.

He wasn't purposely trying to ignore his sister. He simply wasn't interested in forgiving his father under any pretense. "I'm here," he said curtly. "Will you be able to arrange the shipment?"

Mercedes sighed. "I'll get it done the first of the week. May take a few days to get everything settled. And I'll have to know how much space you'll need."

"I'll have Tammy tell you once she gets a look at the supply list." Austin was thankful the awkward moment had passed, that Mercedes was the kind of sister who continued to love him even though he didn't embrace her ideals. "Oh, and one more thing. How are you and the boys at painting wood puzzles?"

"Wood puzzles?"

Austin stopped deleting spam from his inbox, pausing at an e-mail from Christian. He grinned. "Never mind, Mercedes, I think I know just the artist for the job."

Diary of Karyn Olsen
Tuesday, February 4, 1969

    *I can't believe it's been almost two years since I last wrote. That's
because I moved into another apartment with some of the girls from
work, and I misplaced this journal. But I found it today at the back
of my closet in a box with my nursing books—but I'm jumping
ahead of my story.*

    *I had the best experience today. My day started as it usually
does—very late since I'm the night manager now at Denny's (it's so
nice not to have to put up with all the passes from the men like I did
when I was a waitress). When I awoke, I grabbed a bagel and went
to J. C. Penney's for a pair of jeans. While I was there I went to the
bathroom, and I found a woman about my age leaning over the sink
like she was going to be sick. I asked her if she was all right. She
shook her head and grabbed her stomach. It was then I realized that
she was WAY pregnant and that she wasn't leaning over the sink to
throw up but for support.*

Luckily, they've a couch there on this carpeted area, so I helped her over because she could barely walk. All the time she was moaning. I kept telling her it was going to be all right. It was obvious she was in labor, so I asked her how far along she was. She started crying and said she wasn't due for three weeks. I told her not to worry, that her baby was just fine—that hundreds of babies are born safely at three weeks early. I noticed that her contractions were still about ten minutes apart so I knew there was still time to call an ambulance. But she clung to me and begged me not to leave her alone. An older lady came in then, and I told her to get a clerk to call an ambulance.

They seemed to take a long time, but I stayed with her. I found out her name is April and that her husband was on a business trip to Texas. She doesn't have any family here in California. Her contractions were five minutes apart when the ambulance finally arrived. She wouldn't let go of my hand, so I went in the ambulance with her. I don't know much about birth, but I did read about it in school. I taught her how to breathe through the contractions so they wouldn't hurt so badly.

By the time we were almost to the hospital, she said she felt like pushing. The paramedics were nervous, but I told them to get a doctor to meet us outside. We pulled up and the doctor jumped inside the ambulance with several nurses. A few pushes later the baby—a beautiful little girl—was out. Such an incredible miracle! They let April see the baby for a minute, heaped under a mound of warmed baby blankets someone had brought, and then they took them both inside. The baby had to be checked out, and April begged me to go with the baby and to bring her news. I came back in less than ten minutes and told her the baby was fine and that they were bringing her back to nurse. April started crying when they did. While she held her little one, she thanked me again and again, telling me that I was the best nurse anyone could ever have.

I almost started crying. She'd said I was the best nurse. A nurse! That was exactly what I wanted to be. But somewhere along the way I got lost. I made up my mind in that minute. I still have my dad's trust fund, and I am going back to school. I'm going to register tomorrow. I wish I could share my news with someone, but other than my roommates there is no one. For that, perhaps I am the only one to blame.

Rays from the early morning sun splayed from the open kitchen window onto the white marble tabletop, making light patterns that varied as the curtains swayed to and fro in the gentle breeze. Liana bent over her work at the table, one hand tugging her hair and the other scribbling madly with a pencil. The pencil was always her choice for any work; she loved the feel of it in her hand and the way the dark lead marked up a stark sheet of white paper. More importantly, pencil marks could be easily erased, unlike mistakes in pen.

She let her pencil fall and rapidly punched in numbers on the squarish calculator that she preferred over the one on her computer, hearing the satisfying movement of the paper as the machine printed her numbers in a neat column. Once again it struck her how predictable the numbers were—unlike a man who whisked a woman off to Wyoming, kissed her, and then disappeared into the night. Not like sisters who fought over the same man or parents who died in plane accidents.

Scribbling in the last set of numbers, she sighed and pulled her hand from her hair, bringing several strands with it. "Done," she said. All she had left to do was to type these numbers into the forms on the computer and go over the taxes with her new clients. Then she would be free for her flight on Wednesday. *To start finding my mother.* She felt frightened and shaky at the thought. What if she wasn't able to learn anything? What if the information she obtained only made things worse?

She had a strange and unreasonable urge to talk to Mercedes. *What a stupid idea,* she thought. Mercedes was nice—more than nice—but that didn't mean they were suddenly sisters. *But I should have had a sister—would have, if Clarissa hadn't miscarried. Would having a sister make my life better? Fuller?* Liana was sure it would have. *A woman needs a sister.*

Reaching over to her computer mouse, she clicked on her e-mail program. Her arm cast shadows over the patterns of light on the tabletop. As the e-mail program connected to the Internet, she switched over to the files she had made for her clients and began typing in the final numbers. For a fleeting moment, she wished she had used the new laptop Austin had lent her for the work at Goodman's and HeartReach. *No,* she thought, *that job'll be over soon, and I have to make do with what I have.* It wouldn't be long until she could afford a better computer.

She checked the e-mail that was still downloading and was surprised at the happiness she felt to see one from Mercedes. Eagerly, she clicked on it.

Dear Liana,

It was such a pleasure to meet you last week. I sincerely hope that we can stay in touch. I know it may sound strange to you, but from the moment we met, I felt I had found a kindred soul. You must come visit again, with or without that crazy brother of mine.

Buttercup's babies are doing great. The boys named them Syrup and Pancake, which tells you where their hearts are. Joseph and Scott are feeling much better now and have been

*out to the barn to see the goats and the new baby chicks.
They drive the mother animals crazy!*

*I'm beginning another quilt. I finished the other one and put
it in Austin's room. It's much better than the old one he had
there. I left your stitches in and hope you'll come back to see
that I did.*

*Well, Wayne's calling me to come out and see something. I
think he's gone and bought that white stallion I've had my
eye on. I know I shouldn't want a new horse, but he's so
beautiful and spirited. I can't wait to ride him across our
property! Wayne is such a thoughtful man. Liana, I so wish
I could give him more. Just like you wish you could give
your adoptive mother what she needs.*

Be good!
Mercedes

Liana looked down at her precise writing on the white
papers in front of the computer, but the letters were unread-
able charcoal smudges. She blinked her eyes hard to clear
them, and the numbers came into focus. She hadn't realized
she had bared her soul so openly to Mercedes about her feelings toward Clarissa. Or had Mercedes, with her learning of
psychology, retail management, animal medicine, and building
contracting, managed to read between the lines for herself? The
words of the e-mail touched a place inside her that she hadn't
even known existed. How she longed to be able to write a letter back, full of her hopes of the upcoming trip, of her
contrasting feelings for Austin. But to do so would be to open
herself further.

I can't, she thought.

Can't or won't? said a voice in her head.

They are the same thing, she answered.

Quickly, she typed a response.

Dear Mercedes,

Thank you for writing. I did enjoy visiting your farm. It is such a peaceful place. Perhaps I will be able to come again someday. Not soon, though. I am going to India on Wednesday. That leaves only two days to get ready. Yes, I did say India. I am taking your suggestion to visit the place where I was born and hopefully meet people who knew my birth parents. I'm planning to stay a week. My (adoptive) mother is going with me. I hope it is a fruitful trip.

I think the names for the baby goats are absolutely perfect. Tell the boys I said so. Your stallion sounds very exciting. What a wonderful surprise! But you are good to Wayne as well. I think he is happy, and so are you—isn't that what's important?

Have a good day,
Liana

There was more—so much more—that she could have written. About her visit with her mother. About how afterwards, as she had been running all over Las Vegas to visit her new clients and make traveling arrangements, the bustle of the city, once so attractive to her, once so useful for blocking out other emotions, had seemed crowded and dirty, a desperate slice of humanity in a world where the tapping of keyboards blared continually for all to hear. The flat, open land beyond the tall city buildings had screamed of desert, barren of life, a clear contrast to the fertile Wyoming valley that cradled Walker Farm. The barrenness echoed the barren feeling in Liana's heart and body. Though she knew all of these emotions derived from her own inner turmoil and that there was much that was good and beautiful around her, she could not see it.

At that moment, she longed for Walker Farm, the tiny chicks like fluffy balls of new yellow dandelions, the baby goats on wobbly legs suckling at their mother's teats. She wanted to walk through fields of new growth springing from the ground and swing over a river on a rope. She wanted to sleep in a room with a quilt that held her awkward stitches, making it seem almost as though she belonged.

Tap, tap, tap.

Liana let her head fall to her hands, closing her eyes. She took deep, cleansing breaths—in and out slowly. The tapping of the keyboards gradually faded. She knew from her experience the past few days that the tapping would stay gone if she didn't think too much about India and what she might discover there.

Shutting down the computer, she grabbed her sandals and headed out the front door. She didn't have a destination, but a brisk morning walk around her neighborhood was sure to clear her mind. Intent on her thoughts, she ran into Austin before she saw him.

"Whoa! Where're you off to so fast?" His arms steadied her.

She let her eyes travel slowly up his long body to his face. "A walk."

"In your pajamas?"

Sure enough, she was in her blue plaid lounge pants and a T-shirt. "It's a casual area," she said, starkly aware that she hadn't combed her hair yet that morning.

He laughed. "I'm sure it is, but could we go inside for a moment? I'd like to talk to you."

"Okay, but only for a moment. I have work to do."

"It won't take long."

Inside, she made him wait in the living room while she changed into a fitted black suit in a stretchy rayon blend, ran a brush through her long hair, and dabbed on a bit of makeup. When she finished, she found him not in the living room where she'd left him but in the kitchen making toast.

"I didn't think you'd mind," he said. "I made enough for you, too."

"I've already eaten."

He grinned and shook his head. "I guess I can sacrifice and eat yours, too. I didn't eat much on my trip and then I slept practically all day yesterday. I ate breakfast, but I'm still hungry."

"Sounds like you need some of Mercedes' food."

"That's for sure." He took the toast to the table. "Do you have any butter? And milk?"

"In the fridge. Glasses are in that cupboard." Liana gathered the papers she'd been working on and stacked them in the corner. "How'd work go?"

"Tiring. I went to Idaho, Oregon, and two cities in California in two days." He frowned at her papers. "What's this?"

None of your business, she wanted to say, but instead she shrugged. "Taxes I've done for some people, that's all."

"Oh, good. Glad you're finding work."

She nodded, wishing she could keep her eyes from his face. "It's good to know I'll be able to build my business. I got a lot done for HeartReach as well. I'll be finished in a few weeks."

"That's good. We're putting together another shipment. I hope to have it over there by the end of this month or the first of May at the latest."

"Before you do that, I have some investment recommendations for you—might help you earn more in the long run."

"I'd love to consider any suggestions."

Silence fell, heavy with the unspoken words that lay between them. Austin drank his milk, while she watched him beneath lowered eyelashes. The breeze was gone now, and her hand felt warm where the sun came through the curtains.

Austin set down his glass. "I'm sorry I didn't call."

"You've been working." She didn't look through her lashes at him now, but at the slash of light on her hand. "I've been busy, too. I'm going to India on Wednesday. My mother and I are going."

"You talked to your mother?"

Her eyes rose to his. "Yes."

"And?" He cupped a hand around his glass, lifting it to his lips again.

"They fought over my uncle—my adoptive father. My mother did—mothers, I guess I should say. Clarissa married him, and my birth mother left. Later she married my dad. But we really don't know how it all came about."

"That's why you're going to India?"

She nodded. "My birth mother wrote a letter, but when my adoptive mother wrote back, she didn't write again. We'd like to know why."

"So would I."

"You would?"

He shrugged. "You know, I've never been to India."

There was something in his tone that hinted to be included in some way. But even if Liana could admit that she was beginning to care for him, the trip to India was hers alone to make and to plan for. Hers and Clarissa's. She wouldn't share it with him, or even with her brothers. Besides, it would complicate things to have him tagging along.

"Guess you'll have to go sometime. When you're not

working. After spending nearly a week out of the office, I'm sure you have work piled up on your desk."

"Got that right," he said with a sigh.

"Want more milk?" She stood and went to the refrigerator.

"When are you going to ask me?"

She froze with the carton above his glass. Her hand felt cold. "Ask you what?"

"When I'm going to see my dad."

She poured the milk with relief. Truthfully, she had forgotten about their agreement in all the excitement of talking to Clarissa and planning the trip to India.

"So when are you going to see him?" she asked, sitting down in her chair again.

He rubbed his jaw. "I don't know, but I'll have to do it, I suppose." Looking at his watch, he sighed again. Draining his glass in a few gulps, he stood. "I have to get to the office and that mound of work you mentioned."

"You're late already."

"Yeah, I know."

As they walked into the entryway, the vision of how he'd kissed her in this same spot made her rush to the door and open it. He paused just short of the doorway, his black eyes delving into hers. "I did come over yesterday between naps—twice actually. You weren't here."

"I was with Christian, and then we went to our parents' for dinner. We met Bret's fiancée."

"He's your other brother, right? The one with the cabin in Utah."

She'd forgotten she'd told him about the cabin on their trip to Wyoming. "Yeah, that's Bret."

"You like her?"

"The fiancée?" She shrugged. "She's beautiful."

199

He hadn't moved, but Liana was suddenly having difficulty concentrating on the conversation. It seemed so pointless when there were other more important things they should be discussing.

"No brains?" he asked.

"Brains, yes. And ambition." She stepped away from him. Maybe more space between them would clear her mind. "I guess she rubbed me the wrong way. But then, I'm not really a people person."

"You liked Mercedes."

"That's different."

"You like me."

"Yes." There, it was out. Liana held her breath at what might come next.

His eyes didn't waver from her face. She could see the thin scar on his forehead clearly, trace its path into the arch of his hair. She still didn't know how it had happened.

"There's something here, Liana. Can you feel it?"

She took another step back, shaking her head. "It's nothing."

"That's where you're wrong." His eyes didn't leave hers. "It is something. Something big. And, yes, maybe a little scary."

She was still shaking her head, willing him to stop.

"I think about you all the time," he continued. "It's driving me crazy."

He was driving her crazy. "We have nothing in common," she said. "Absolutely nothing. I drive a cute convertible, you drive an ugly brute of a truck. I work with numbers; you manage people. I like hip rock music; you like whiny country noise. I saw that cowboy hat in your closet back in Wyoming, and I bet you even have a pair of genuine cowboy boots somewhere."

"They're at my house."

"See?" She raised her hand to emphasize the point. "I simply refuse to wear cowboy boots. We have absolutely nothing in common. Nothing."

"We have steamed white rice and Chinese food."

"With lame fortune cookies," she retorted. But she was unable to prevent a smile.

"We have a rope over a river." He took several steps, closing the space between them. "We have this." He leaned forward and kissed her. At first she didn't respond, but as his arms tightened around her body, she returned his kiss.

After a moment, she broke away. "I'm not denying the attraction between us, but I can't promise anything more."

His eyes narrowed. "It's not just attraction, Liana, and I don't want to be like any other guy you've known. I think I want . . . well, your heart." He tapped her chest far above her left breast, sending tingles through her body.

She shook her head. "It's too soon." But time didn't have anything to do with her feelings, not really. To tell someone you were beginning to love them seemed difficult enough. To promise you would love them for life—that was utterly impossible. What happened if she woke up one day and decided she'd made a mistake? Love was too transitory, too potentially painful. Look at what had happened to her birth mother when she had given her heart to a man whose love had eventually gone to another. No, it was better to keep things on a level she understood.

"I don't think it's too soon," Austin said. "I know what I want."

"Do you always know what you want?"

His lips twisted into a wry smile. "Yes."

Liana wondered what such confidence would be like. The only thing she was sure about at this moment was that she was going to India, and thanks to her adoptive mother's financial generosity, it wouldn't put her in the poor house.

"I think," she said, "that you want what Mercedes has. And I'm sorry to say that you're looking in the wrong place."

There was hurt in his eyes, but Liana had only been telling the truth.

"Maybe." Austin went through the open door. "I'll talk to you when you get home."

She watched him drive away.

CHAPTER

18

Diary of Karyn Olsen
Friday, June 28, 1972

I'm packing, and I found this diary, long neglected (almost three and a half years!). Funny how I used to write in it so much. Now I don't have the time. The last entry said I was going back to school. Well, I did that, and I became a nurse—a nurse in labor and delivery. I crammed my classes in as fast as I could to make up for lost time. Now I'm leaving not only California but the whole country! I'm going to India to work in a volunteer hospital sponsored by a charity organization. I learned about this opportunity a few months ago and thought it sounded interesting and challenging, but I was reluctant to leave somehow. It was like I was waiting for something that would reconnect me with my family or tear me away forever.

That something happened two weeks ago. I went into work and found that Clarissa was in the hospital where I worked. When I read her name on the roster, I felt like someone had punched me in the gut. I wandered down to the nursery, and sure enough there was

Travis, looking in the window at a baby. He didn't notice me, but he looked just the same as when I met him. My heart wanted to burst, and at that moment I wished I could run in and grab the baby, secreting it away so that I could cause Clarissa the kind of pain she caused me.

I'm ashamed of that feeling now. I'm a nurse, and I want to care for people, not hurt them. Not even Clarissa. What kind of a person am I to feel this way toward my own sister?

Next to Travis was a little boy who was a perfect miniature of him. Must be my nephew, Christian. He stood like Travis, too, with his little hands shoved in his pockets as he stared at the baby through the window. I wondered if he knew about me. Had they shown him a picture? Or had they decided to . . . to what? Forget me? Write me out of their precious equations?

Well, I waited until Travis and his son left, and then I went to see the baby—another beautiful little boy. Didn't look a thing like Travis. I wanted to hold him, but I didn't dare. I didn't want them to catch me, and I most certainly didn't trust myself not to run away with the child. My nephew. Another baby who should have been mine.

I left work sick, knowing I had the next few days off and that Clarissa would be gone before I had to go back. As soon as I got home I called the charity and volunteered, squeezing into their program barely in time. Now two weeks have gone by, and in another two days, I'll be out of the country. I know it's the right thing to do. Maybe helping people who are too poor to help themselves will take this evil from my heart. Because I find I'm still mad at Clarissa for what she did to me. Furious, actually. With both her and Mother. Part of me wishes they had done more to reconnect with me. Mostly, though, I wish I could get over it all and forget them. It's been six years, and I've finally gone forward with my life—so why does my heart remain with the past?

Liana awoke abruptly, her heart pounding and her T-shirt soaked with sweat. The nightmare always seemed so real, but this time it was worse. The lady weeping, the child staring, her frightened eyes reflecting a pain too terrible to voice. Tears running like rain until they threatened to sweep everyone away. The piercing scream that was as sharp and jagged as the broken glass in the window behind the child who stared without speaking.

Her room was lit only by the faint moonlight radiating from behind the curtains in the window. Dark shadows made it unfamiliar to Liana, and she stumbled to the light switch, wishing she had a bedside lamp. The room sprang into familiarity with the flip of the switch, and only then did her heartbeat return to a steady thud.

She found the picture in her nightstand and looked at it for a long time. "Who are you?" she asked the woman in the picture. She looked so happy—was it only an illusion? *Perhaps I will find out in India.*

Going to the window, Liana looked out into the dark. Below she could see her tiny backyard and those of several neighbors. There was room on the patio slab for a gas barbeque grill, a table, and six chairs. A slim strip of grass exactly the size of her neighbors' strips. She loved that backyard. Easy to control, to take care of. Like her numbers, it was completely predictable and safe.

But neither did it hold the exhilaration of a swing from a tree over a river.

The moon hung low on the horizon, overshadowing the pinpricks of starlight that quilted the sky. She knew that even before the moon disappeared, the rays from the sun would light up the eastern sky and completely drown out any remaining moonlight. But for now the moon ruled the night sky that was as black as Austin's midnight eyes.

She hadn't talked to him since Monday, though she had received an impersonal e-mail about the charity. She'd replied with an update on her work. What had she expected—that he'd accept her uncertainty and reluctance with perfect understanding?

She had known Austin was different. When he had taken her to Wyoming, she had seen firsthand the life he wanted: the relationship his sister had with Wayne, never mind that a part of Mercedes' heart would always belong to someone else. What Mercedes and Wayne had was real and solid. Enough to build a life together—and to find happiness.

Could Liana ever hope for that? She didn't think so.

Most women she knew would have jumped at a chance for a relationship with a man who wanted a future, but the idea put terror into her heart. What if she began to really care about him? What if down the road it wasn't her who changed her mind, but him? What if he didn't change his mind but instead fate stepped in? A downed plane, a car accident—there were too many variations to consider.

Better to avoid the situation altogether. Austin attracted her like no man she'd ever met, but there were too many ghosts between them. Mostly hers, but his too, with his ideals and dreams that were based on his need for a relationship that didn't resemble the one that had killed his mother. Their pasts darkly colored the future.

Sighing, she turned from the window and returned to bed. Christian would be by early to take her to the airport, and she needed to get what sleep she could.

———

Both Christian and Bret arrived at Liana's door at six on
Wednesday morning. Liana let them raid her kitchen while she
put last-minute items in her carry-on. Christian was his usual
cheerful self, but Bret's silence bordered on sullenness.

"Don't mind him," Christian whispered as he carried her
suitcase to his BMW. "It's Britanni. After you left on Sunday, she
was flirting with me, and Bret was annoyed. When she told
him he ought to scrap his Accord and get a BMW like mine, he
blew a fuse somewhere. I don't think I have ever seen him so
mad since he lost that full-ride engineering scholarship back in
high school. I don't blame him, really. She's a beauty, but . . .
well. . . ." He shrugged. They were at the car now, and Bret,
opening the back door, was within hearing range.

Liana smiled at Bret as she slid into the car, silently thank-
ing him for giving her the front seat. He smiled back, but his
blue eyes were morose.

"I hope Mom's ready," Christian said as he turned onto the
freeway toward Paradise.

Liana yawned. "She will be."

Not only was Clarissa ready but both she and Travis were
waiting in the driveway when they arrived. "No, no, stay in the
front," Clarissa said when Liana tried to offer the seat to her.
Your dad and I'll sit in the back with Bret."

Bret glanced at his watch. "At this rate, you'll be too early."

"Never can be early enough for a trip out of the country."
Clarissa sat beside him and patted his hand.

Bret's stern look softened. "Are you sure you two should go
alone, Mom? If you waited another week, one of us might be
able to get off."

Clarissa's eyes briefly met Liana's. "We're sure," Clarissa
said. "This is something we have to do together."

Liana was relieved by the firmness of her voice. She knew

that Bret and Travis were protective of Clarissa, and on Sunday Travis had dropped none-too-subtle hints about waiting for a time when he could accompany them, but Clarissa had insisted they needed to go alone.

She's right, thought Liana. Not only did they need this time together but Liana didn't relish an audience as she searched for the truth. If she'd had the money, she might have been tempted to sneak off to India without even Clarissa.

But this concerns her, too, said that little voice in her head.

"All ready?" Christian asked. Without waiting for a response, he backed down the drive, whistling.

Liana frowned at him. "You're awful chipper this morning. I don't remember you ever being so happy in the morning when you have to get up before six."

"He met a girl," Bret said.

Christian shot Liana a happy grin. "I didn't meet her, exactly. She started working at our agency a few months ago, and on Monday she was transferred to my team. She's a designer. Name's Tawnia. I've been flying high ever since."

"Sounds like you really like her." Liana was excited for him but also a little envious. Christian was a bit of a playboy and could be terribly irresponsible, but he was a good man at heart.

"I do. A lot."

"What's she like?" asked Travis from the back.

"Pretty. Striking, rather." Christian glanced at Bret and then back to the cars in front of him. "Not gorgeous like Brittani, but really, really. . . ." He shrugged. "I can't describe it."

"He's speechless," Bret scoffed. "A miracle."

Christian laughed. "Well, Bret, at least my girl doesn't care what kind of a car I drive."

Bret scowled and didn't reply.

"Your car is kind of getting old," Clarissa said.

"Only five years." Bret's voice was controlled as it always was when he spoke to his mother. "It still has a lot of good miles left in it. Britanni understands that now."

"Good." Clarissa brought out her compact and checked her lipstick. "You may make good money being a civil engineer, but that doesn't mean the funds are unlimited."

"It wasn't the age of the car that concerned Britanni," Christian volunteered. "It was the model."

Clarissa pursed her lips. "There is absolutely nothing wrong with Bret's Accord, Christian. It's certainly a lot more practical than *your* car."

"Got that right." Christian gave them a wide grin. "Takes a fortune to make the payments each month. But it sure is a babe magnet. It screams success. As long as I have enough left over for macaroni and cheese, I'm a happy man."

Bret gave a disgusted chuckle, shaking his head. "Let's hope you get a good raise soon."

"I'm due for one," Christian assured him.

The conversation turned to less volatile matters as they finished the drive to the airport. Liana only listened; even if she'd had something to say, her stomach was churning so much that she doubted she could put together a solid thought if she tried.

At the airport Christian and Bret took the suitcases from the car as Travis went over the plane changes and layovers with Clarissa one last time.

"I'm surprised your boyfriend isn't here to say good-bye," Christian said to Liana.

Clarissa turned from her husband. "You have a boyfriend?"

"No." Liana shot Christian a black look. "He's not my boyfriend. He's a friend of Christian's, and I'm working for him, that's all."

"Working for him?" Clarissa's brow wrinkled in concern. "What about your job at Klassy? Did you get fired?"

"No, I quit."

"You didn't tell me." Clarissa's tone was wounded.

"It just happened. I didn't want to worry you."

"Are you sure that quitting was a wise thing to do?"

"Very sure. I want to work for myself now." She was surprised at her own confidence. "In fact, my old boss called me yesterday and offered me my job back—with a raise, I might add. I told him no." But oh, how she'd been tempted; it would have been so easy to fall into her old pattern of stability. The only thing that had saved her really was her impending trip, which she would have had to cancel.

Clarissa pursed her lips. "I wish you had told me."

"Well, all this came up." Liana waved her hands helplessly. *Please don't make a big deal of this,* she thought.

To her relief Bret came to her aid. "Well, you'd better get to the gate. Hurry up and wait, as the saying goes. And we have to get to work, right, Dad?" As he briefly hugged Liana, he whispered in her ear, "Have a good time. And take care of Mom, okay?"

"I will."

Travis was next to hug Liana. "Have a good flight, honey. Please call when you get there, and if you need anything—"

"We'll call."

He smiled. "Take care of your mother."

Liana stifled the sudden unreasonable urge to ask, "Which one?" Obviously, Travis had never looked after her birth mother.

"I will," she said.

Christian put his arms around Liana, squeezing her much tighter than the others had. "Have a really wild time, Liana

Banana," he said. "I know I'm going to. Tawnia and I need to take some photos for a design we're doing, so on Friday we're driving to Mount Charleston—we'll be alone all day. I'm going to sweep her off her feet! Of course work isn't the real reason I chose Mount Charleston. I have a really great idea for a painting I'm going to do for your birthday. The big three-oh deserves something special."

"I can't wait to see it."

"You'll have to." His expression sobered. "Of course I can't even start on the painting itself for a few weeks because of Austin. I promised him I'd paint wood puzzles for his orphans."

"That's really sweet of you."

He grinned. "Not really. It'll be fun. You should see some of the designs I'm doing—including a copy of the Mona Lisa. Tawnia's going to help. Those kids are going to have puzzles with class, even if they don't know it."

"That's great." Aware that Clarissa and the others were waiting, Liana hugged Christian one last time. "Take care of yourself while I'm gone," she said, feeling suddenly emotional. To cover up she added quickly, "And no snooping around at my condo."

"I'll miss you, too, Banana. And don't worry—I'll be here when you get back. I'm always here." He winked and strode back to the car, parked by the curb.

"Go on now, we'll be fine." Clarissa kissed her husband and pushed him toward the car. "Finally," she added when they were out of earshot. "I thought they were about to suggest stowing away in our bags."

Liana laughed, more from the surprise of Clarissa saying such a thing than from the actual words. "They are rather smothering. You'd think we'd never traveled before."

"We haven't."

"Yeah, but neither have they—except Christian. And he's the only one who doesn't mind not going with us."

Clarissa hefted her suitcase with one hand and hooked her other arm through Liana's. "Come on, daughter. Let's go find our plane."

Liana lifted her free hand to wave to Christian as he drove off. Later she would wish she had hugged him longer, had looked into his eyes and told him how much he had meant to her over the years—how much she loved him. But she had no way of knowing that things between them would soon be changed forever.

CHAPTER
19

Diary of Karyn Olsen
Tuesday, July 3, 1972

 So far India is all I expected it to be, only so much, much more. In some ways it is very backward, but then in others it surprises me with how modern it is. I feel like I am in another world entirely. The buildings, the food, the religion, the culture—everything is so differ-ent from back home, though almost everyone seems to speak English (British English!). Before now I'd only heard things about India, but seeing it firsthand is different from what I expected. I feel my eyes are open for the first time in my life—and I've only been here a few days!

 The women here are beautiful and smart. Most that I have met are small and dark and dress in exotic, flowing saris. Many are uneducated and poor, though some are in government and other high positions. Perhaps these come from the richer families. I don't know enough yet to say.

 Despite the outward differences, the pregnant women who come into the clinic are much like those back home. They are concerned about their babies, and they love them. Most really want sons and are worried about having daughters, which is really sad. The nurses here strive to help them keep the girls or place them elsewhere if their families don't want them. A lot better than the female infanticide and neglect that has been so rampant here. The thought makes me sick. Don't they understand that someone's got to have daughters? Who will all their sons marry? I'm so excited to help these women. I think many mothers and babies will live who wouldn't have otherwise. Because of me. How amazing. We don't have all the technology and conveniences here that we did back home, but we can offer them good nutrition, education, immunizations, and certain painkillers. Knowledge is the key.

Tonight I'm going to a party with the staff—over half of whom are English or American—to celebrate the Fourth of July. We even have some fireworks. It should be fun.

After a four-hour layover in New York, Liana and Clarissa flew to London for a connecting flight to India. Because of the time difference, they lost nearly an entire day. Liana spent most of the flights working on Austin's laptop, organizing more of HeartReach's finances. She desperately wished she had a novel to read instead—something entertaining that didn't require deep thought. Her heart felt caught in a death grip, and she had trouble breathing. Once she had a flash of memory of another plane that she had ridden in, of a kind flight attendant who had silently held the hand of a terrified four-year-old while the plane landed.

Liana didn't sleep during the journey. The unfamiliar and uncomfortable confines of their coach seats made it next to impossible for her to rest. Clarissa had no such difficulty. The newness of flying had worn off by their arrival in London, and she spread out the thin navy blue blanket the flight attendant provided and soon was snoring gently. She looked older in her sleep, Liana thought. Older and more frail.

On the flight from London while Clarissa slept, Liana struck up a conversation across the aisle with a white-haired Englishman who had apparently been to India many times. When he learned where they were staying, he clicked his tongue.

"What?" Liana asked.

He shook his head. "Nothing, really. Just that street where you're staying, Suddar Street, is crammed with economy hotels. Many, many tourists end up there. Mind you, it's a good place to stay if finances are a concern, and it's close to many things. But I am afraid you will find the streets also crammed with many poor people, children mostly, begging. If you give to them, be sure you don't do it close to your hotel, or they'll begin to recognize you and will lie in wait for you to leave your hotel and then follow you around. You will not have any peace at all."

"Oh," Liana said faintly. She didn't know much about Calcutta, but she had figured that such a large city was likely to have resources to help the poor.

The man smiled. "Don't be too concerned. There do seem to be fewer beggars each time I go to Calcutta, and it is a truly wonderful place. I've been a dozen times, and still the city overwhelms me. It is a city ready to burst at the seams— over ten million people now. People who love football and cricket . . . and music. There is a plethora of musical and cultural events. Much to see and do. You will enjoy yourself greatly. Don't miss the Botanical Gardens and the banyan tree. That you simply must see. It's two hundred years old! The largest in the world."

The Englishman assumed she and Clarissa were going to India solely for pleasure, and with her natural reticence, Liana didn't correct his assumption. She encouraged him to continue his discourse; listening to him extol India's virtues at least broke up the monotony of the flight.

By the time they arrived in the airport in Calcutta early Friday morning, she had been awake for thirty-six hours straight. They hired a taxi that took them directly to their hotel. There was a lot of traffic on the streets, and already more than a few pedestrians—most of whom seemed to be women carrying large wicker baskets or cloth bags full of groceries.

The hotel lobby was well kept, and the Indian clerk greeted them with a smile. Clarissa exchanged pleasantries with him in English as they checked in. Once inside their room, Liana let her purse slide to the floor and lay down on a single bed with a sigh of relief.

"Well, at least the beds are firm," Clarissa said, "and the room looks clean. You're not upset, are you, dear? Your father wanted to find a five-star hotel, but I wanted to really experience this trip. You know?" She looked around the room, her face vibrant. For an instant Liana could see the passion that had caused her to choose a man over her the welfare of her sister.

"It's fine," Liana said, shutting her eyes to block out Clarissa's exhilaration.

"And cheap. Just forty bucks a night."

"I'm surprised they threw in a bathroom for that price," Liana replied. "And a refrigerator."

"Yes. We'll have to go food shopping as soon as we've rested a bit."

Liana mumbled something from the bed and let herself drift off. Truthfully, she could be in the most rat-infested hotel in the world and she wouldn't care.

When Liana awoke, feeling much better, the air was alive with spicy smells that made her mouth water. Her stomach rumbled a demand for food. Clarissa looked up from the magazine she was reading at the small square table. "Good, you're awake. I was wondering if maybe I should brave the streets alone in search of something to eat."

Liana yawned. "What time is it?"

"Twelve-thirty, local time. We lost about twelve hours crossing time zones. You've slept about five hours."

"I needed it." Liana sat up and stretched, yawning again. She could take in the room now with its two single beds, table, refrigerator, and telephone. There were dressers for their clothes and colorful Indian paintings on the walls. A vase on the table held fake flowers. Except for the exotic print of the bedding, the vibrant paintings, and the rounded tops of the windows, she could be in a motel in America. And the smells, of course. Each breath brought in an image of spicy, delicious foods.

"We can get something to eat and then go to Charity Medical," Clarissa said, reaching for her purse. "I think we'll have to take a taxi there, though. I can't find it on the map."

"Here, let me see the map. A man on the plane showed me where it was while you were sleeping. But you're right about the taxi. It's too far to walk. Or we could try the subway. I bet we'd find it that way. Plus we'd be experiencing Indian life, like you wanted."

Clarissa wasn't convinced. "I think the first time we should go by taxi. Maybe we can come home on the subway. At any rate, you'd better change. It's warm out there. Mid-eighties, at best. I had to turn up the air conditioning while you were asleep."

"At least they *have* air conditioning."

Clarissa frowned. "Are you sure you're okay with staying here?"

"Perfectly. I was kidding. It's nice."

Clarissa smiled hesitantly. "We can always move later."

"We're not really here for a vacation." Liana hefted her suitcase onto the bed and opened it. "We're here to find out . . . you know."

Clarissa came to stand beside her. "I think we should have some fun, too. We should enjoy being . . . well, together." She stared at the gauzy flowered skirt in Liana's hands, not meeting her eyes.

Liana searched the planes of her face. How different Clarissa seemed away from home and without the rest of the family—unsure of herself, fragile, easily hurt. "Okay. We can try. But now that we're here, I'm anxious to find out what happened."

"I'm sure we will." Clarissa's smile was back. She went to the bathroom, and Liana could see her combing her blonde hair in front of the mirror.

Choosing a silky mauve blouse with cap sleeves to go with her skirt, Liana quickly changed. She wrapped her hair up loosely and secured it with a clip. That would keep her neck cool.

They took the back way out of the hotel, walking down the quaint red cobblestones to Suddar Street. As soon as they were spotted, a half dozen dark-skinned children ran up to them, brown eyes soulful, their small hands held out. "Please," they chorused. "Please."

"Look at those colorful clothes they're wearing." Clarissa

reached for her purse. "They're adorable. What amazing dark hair and wonderful skin."

Remembering the advice of the Englishman, Liana put a hand on Clarissa's. "Wait," she said.

When they had gone a short distance, the first children fell away, looking for more sympathetic tourists. More children lurking in front of other hotels took their places. Clarissa gave these some of the Indian rupees they had exchanged for American dollars at the airport.

Liana scanned the area with interest. There was an abundance of hotels and places to eat, many with their huge signs in English. In fact, she was hearing on the street as much English—British English—as Hindi. The man on the plane had told Liana that about thirty percent of the people in India spoke Hindi but there were fourteen other official languages. English was also widely used for national, political, and commercial communication. Though the English words were sometimes heavily accented, Liana didn't have any trouble understanding their meaning. A good thing, since neither she nor Clarissa had much affinity for learning languages.

"You know, I can just imagine Karyn here," Clarissa said, waving an arm that took in a beggar woman and her three small children. "This is so her. She'd want to be with these people. I mean, she was really shy, but when someone got hurt on the playground or something, she was right there with a kind word and a Band-Aid. I can imagine her here, rolling up her sleeves and going to work." Her eyes took on a sad look. "Oh, I wish I had come to visit when she was alive. I can't believe how much I still miss her!"

Liana put her arm around Clarissa, who looked at her in surprise. She patted Liana's hand where it rested on her shoulder. "I'm glad we could do this together."

They found a clean-looking restaurant with smells so enticing they had to go in. Liana ordered chicken curry with a drink called lassi that tasted like liquid yogurt with a hint of roses. Clarissa had rice with a bread called chappatis, served with vegetables. "This is wonderful," Liana said. She had always loved spicy foods, and this was the best she'd ever eaten.

"It's a little on the hot side." Clarissa choked and reached for a second glass of water.

After lunch, they found a taxi and gave the driver the address of the hospital, which turned out to be nearly twenty minutes away. "I'm glad we didn't hire that man pulling his cart to take us," Clarissa whispered. Liana smiled but didn't reply. Her stomach was doing flips, though she wasn't sure if that was because of the curry at lunch or her nervousness.

Wedged between a high-rise apartment building and other offices, Charity Medical, constructed of white-painted brick, was not very impressive, but it did have a nice-sized courtyard where a few flowers were planted in spacious wooden boxes. Inside a large reception room, many Indians waited to be seen—old people with the weight of the world in their eyes, sick youngsters moaning as they clung to their mothers, more children running after each other and giggling. As they entered, the running children stopped and stared up at them with curious brown eyes.

"Hello," Liana said to the receptionist when Clarissa remained silent. "Do you speak English?"

"Yes, I do," came the reply in only slightly accented English.

Liana glanced at Clarissa, whose eyes had fallen on a very pregnant woman sitting alone near the door. As they watched, a white nurse came out of a large door and ushered her inside. With a flash, Liana understood that Clarissa was imagining her sister here, trying to see this place as it had been twenty-five years ago. How had Karyn felt upon seeing it for the first time? Had she helped any of these people here, or perhaps their relatives? Had she been happy?

With difficulty, Liana dragged her attention back to the receptionist. "We need to see Dr. Mehul Raji. Here's the spelling. I'm not sure I'm saying it right."

The woman took the paper. "Ah, Dr. Raji, yes. But he is very busy. Could I perhaps help you?"

Liana met the large, friendly black eyes, made to look even blacker by the generous dark makeup around them. The sleek black hair, pulled back to a severe ponytail under her white cap, was unmarred by streaks of white. Her face was unlined, and her figure short and slim, yet she didn't give the impression of being very young. Could she have known Liana's mother? Perhaps worked with her?

"I really need to see him," Liana said. "My—my mother used to work here. She and my father died in a plane crash. It's been more than twenty-five years, but Dr. Raji knew them."

"Oh, you must be talking about Dr. Raji's father. He is retired. I will call him."

"I don't want to be any trouble. Could you just give me his address? We can go there."

"No trouble," the receptionist said with a smile. "He lives upstairs. Third floor. He has an apartment. So do many of the employees here." She reached for the phone before adding conspiratorially, "This job does not pay enough for an outside apartment, unless there are several to share. Many volunteers live here or with families nearby."

"Oh. Thank you." Liana's hand gripped the counter as another vision arose from her past: Mamata. She and her parents had lived with this lady. Was the house close by? Would she recognize it if she saw it? Would she remember where she had slept?

The receptionist was speaking rapidly into the phone in a language Liana assumed was Hindi. Her lyrical voice had a soothing effect on Liana, though she didn't understand the words. She took a deep breath.

"He is able to see you," the woman said. "I will show you the way."

An older Indian woman with graying black hair had arrived at the desk, and the two spoke briefly in Hindi before the newcomer turned to Liana and said in very poor English, "You mother saved my babe. I feel her this." She held two small fists tightly together in front of her sunken chest. "Good woman. Good, good woman."

"Thank you," Liana whispered. She put a hand on Clarissa's shoulder. "This is her sister from America."

The older woman turned to the younger one, who translated quickly. Smiling in understanding, she took Clarissa's hand in hers and held it without speaking. Tears sprang from her eyes.

"Thank you," Clarissa whispered at the silent tribute.

"Come this way." The first receptionist motioned with her hand.

She led them through the halls of the hospital, where a mixture of English and other languages came from the employees. The entire hospital was clean, though badly in need of paint. Everywhere they looked, friendly faces—both light-skinned and dark—met them with wide, though often tired, smiles.

A small door at the back of the hospital took them to a flight of stairs. "He lives at the top," the receptionist said. "Second door. Knock. He is waiting."

"Thank you." Liana began to climb the stairs.

"I'm so nervous," Clarissa said after the receptionist had disappeared.

"That's just the Indian food we ate."

Clarissa laughed as Liana had intended. "Maybe."

At the appointed door in the dark and narrow corridor, Liana knocked. Clarissa held a hand over her heart as she caught her breath. A gnarled Indian man opened the door. He was shorter than Liana and thin to the point of emaciation. His hair was stark white against the dark color of his skin. He held out a hand in welcome. "Come in, please," he said in cultured British English.

"Thank you for seeing us," Clarissa said.

"You must be Karyn's sister. I see a resemblance. But she was bigger, taller. And you"—he turned to Liana—"you are her daughter. I am very happy to meet you again after all these years." He took Liana's hand and held it as the woman below had done with Clarissa. "Oh, but I am forgetting my manners. Come, let us sit down and talk."

He led them further into the small, windowless room where an L-shaped couch and a wide coffee table took up most of the available space. There was also a bookcase, crammed with thick, musty-smelling volumes, and a small TV on a narrow wooden stand. On the floor lay a rug woven with bright colors.

"It is very beautiful, is it not?" he asked, seeing Liana's interest. "Perhaps you might like to buy one of our Indian rugs and take it home with you. I can give you the name of the man who sells the most beautiful ones."

"I'd like that." Liana stared at the rug a minute more before raising her eyes to his. Questions rushed to her lips, but she forced herself to speak slowly. "I suppose you wonder why we're here."

"To learn about your parents."

"Yes, I'd like to know everything you can remember about them. And I also want to know if they might have left anything behind. A journal, maybe?"

"My sister liked to write in her journal," Clarissa added.

Dr. Raji opened his mouth to speak but was distracted by a movement in the hallway. "Ah," he said as a tiny dark woman appeared. "This is my granddaughter, Mridula, bringing us tea and a few small cakes. Thank you, my dear."

Setting her tray on the table, Mridula smiled lovingly at Dr. Raji. "Tea?" she asked before pouring a cup for each of them. Liana's stomach was still full from lunch, but not wanting to appear rude, she accepted.

"Mridula is studying to be a doctor," Raji said. "She is— how do you say it in your language?—following in the foot-steps of her father and grandfather."

With her long black hair and innocent face, Mridula looked too young to be studying medicine. She took a cup of tea her-self and settled on the arm of the couch next to her grandfather. He put a hand on hers, and a look of affection passed between the two.

"But right now what seems to occupy most of her time is taking care of me," Dr. Raji said. "Fine thing for a young woman to have to do."

Mridula's kohl-lined eyes flashed amusement. Obviously, this was a common thread of discussion between the two. "Oh, Grandfather, you know I enjoy staying with you."

Dr. Raji's wrinkled face beamed. "No more than I enjoy having you. Now what were we talking about?"

"My parents." Liana took a sip of the hot tea without sugar, savoring the blend of unfamiliar spices.

"Your parents?" Dr. Raji's brows drew together. In apparent confusion, he turned to his granddaughter. "Who are her parents, Mridula?"

"They used to work for Charity Medical," Mridula supplied gently, casting Liana and Clarissa an apologetic look. "Guenter and Karyn Schrader."

Liana glanced helplessly at Clarissa, who had frozen with the sugar spoon in her hand. By the look Mridula had given them, she guessed this wandering was a frequent occurrence.

"Schrader?" The lost look vanished. "Schrader—yes, I knew them well. Wonderful people. Very dedicated."

"Their daughter is here to learn about them."

Dr. Raji turned back to Liana and Clarissa. "Oh yes, I'm sorry. Sometimes I . . . my mind wanders a bit."

"Do you know if my parents left any belongings?" Liana asked, anxious now to learn something—anything—before his mind wandered again. "Belongings someone might have saved all these years?"

Dr. Raji started shaking his head but stopped midway. "Wait. I remember Mamata said something about a box she wanted me to send to the United States. I told her to bring it here, but she didn't." He looked up at the ceiling, trying to remember. "Ah, yes, she became ill. Some sort of numbness in her left side. Her doctor eventually discovered a tumor. They could not operate, and she died quickly. Maybe a year or two after your parents."

Liana bit back tears of disappointment. Any belongings her parents might have left in Mamata's house would have been disposed of long ago by the new owners.

Dr. Raji smiled at a memory he alone could see. "Guenter

and Karyn—they were two of a kind. I knew the first night they met that they would marry. Guenter was enamored of her from the first, but he had to do some convincing." He laughed and leaned forward to lift his cup of tea from the table. "Karyn led him on a long chase. Yes, both extremely dedicated. Helped a lot of people. No one could operate as Guenter could, and Karyn delivered more babies in her first year here than any of the doctors. The women liked her very much."

"She wrote to me," Clarissa said, "and I wrote back—twice. But I never heard from her again. It was just before she had Lara. Do you know why she never wrote? Did something happen?"

"Lara." Dr. Raji held his teacup in both gnarled hands, as though warming them. "Yes, that was a dark time. Very difficult for them." He paused, staring at his tea. "When I remember, I take flowers to their graves. I'm the only one who remembers them, except for Arun. Everyone else is too young, or they've moved on." He gave a deep sigh. "There are too many graves. My wife, my daughter."

Liana exchanged a look with Clarissa. She suspected the old man had begun to wander again. "What happened?" Liana made another attempt.

"Happened?" His eyes lifted to hers without recognition. "I don't know." He turned to his granddaughter and said something in Hindi.

Mridula took his tea from him and set it on the table. "Excuse me, please. He must lie down now. I will return shortly." Like a small child he put his hand in hers, and she led him gently from the room. The seconds ticked into several minutes before she returned. "I am very sorry," she said. "He is getting much worse. It will be a disappointment when he comes to himself and realizes that he has missed your visit."

Swallowing her own bitter disappointment, Liana set down her cup and arose. "We shouldn't take any more of your time."

"Perhaps you could leave the number where you are staying," Mridula offered. "If he becomes better, I will call."

"Thank you." Liana wondered how long such a visit would last, and if he ever remained lucid for any length of time.

"What about this Arun?" Clarissa asked at the door. "Did he or she really know my sister?"

Mridula nodded. "Arun is actually her last name. She is one of the receptionists downstairs—the older one. She speaks only a little English."

"I think we met her," Liana said.

"Your mother delivered her last baby, oh, maybe twenty-six years ago, after they came back to work at the hospital again. Arun didn't work for the hospital at that time, though, so she did not know your parents well."

"Came back?" Liana was confused. "You said my mother delivered Arun's baby when she came back. From where?"

"I am not sure. I was a baby then. Grandfather would know, but he—" Mridula shrugged. "Arun told me once that they had been abroad for a year at another hospital."

Clarissa arched an eyebrow. "Maybe that's why she didn't answer my letters. Maybe she didn't receive them."

Her face was so hopeful that Liana felt she had to say, "I bet you're right."

They both stood and thanked Mridula. "You might go to the house where your parents lived," she said as they turned to leave. "Mamata left her house to the hospital, and there have been two couples living there recently. They are both leaving soon, and Charity Medical has decided to turn the house into a ward for sick children. It is not certain, but perhaps you may find something still there in the house."

That the house belonged to the hospital was more than Liana had hoped. "Do you know the address?"

"I will write it down for you." Mridula disappeared into the small apartment.

Clarissa touched Liana's arm. "Don't worry. We'll try to come to see him later, and maybe we'll be able to talk to the receptionist downstairs. Something will turn up."

Liana's attempt at a smile failed. She didn't know exactly what she had expected to find in India but certainly not that the only keeper of her parents' memories was a frail old man with frequent bouts of senility.

"There you are." Mridula handed them a paper with two addresses written in neat letters. "You can't miss it," she said. "It's the only white house on the next street. Very old and tall. It was an English house once. I have also written the address of the cemetery my grandfather mentioned."

"Thank you so much," Clarissa said. Liana nodded.

They went down the stairs, their hollow footsteps loud in their ears. As they entered the hospital, a team of medical personnel bustled toward them with a gurney that held a patient writhing in pain, and Liana and Clarissa stepped back to allow them to pass. Retracing their steps to the front desk, they asked for the older receptionist, but she had gone on an errand.

"Does she work tomorrow?" Clarissa asked. After learning what time the woman would be there the next day, they left the hospital.

CHAPTER

20

Diary of Karyn Olsen
Wednesday, July 4, 1972

What a party! Not only was practically the entire staff at
Charity Medical there but also the American representatives for several other charities and many Americans who live and work in
India. It was really fun. The only time I felt awkward or out of place
was when the representative of a charity asked me if I would help
teach reading to some of the poor people. I said I couldn't possibly
teach anyone to read, but she said that we would really be teaching
hygiene and that sort of thing. The promise of reading was to entice
people to come. I thought that was a little dishonest, but she said
teaching them to read was easy enough, as most of them have
already been exposed to many other languages, which has increased
their cognitive abilities—whatever that means. I agreed to go once
a week to help.

Not all members of our staff are English or American. We have
Germans, French, and Chinese, with a few Indians (from India, not

American Indians—such a change for me!) thrown in. One doctor was really nice to me. His name is Guenter Schrader. He asked me to dance, and I did. He's not much taller than I am, but he's definitely muscular. Reminds me of Travis a bit in build, though he's very blond and his face is oval instead of square. He has long white eyelashes and blue eyes. He looks German to me (as if I know how a German is supposed to look!). One of the nurses said we were made for each other with our matching hair. After that I didn't dance with him anymore. I don't want anyone but Travis, and Clarissa stole that dream.

As Mridula promised, the white clapboard house was easy to find. It was tall and thin, squeezed between a bakery and another house as though it were an afterthought to use up the space. The windows were small and square, set evenly along the stretches of peeling paint. There was a narrow balcony on the second floor, and they could just see parts of the red tiled roof. Several feet out from the house was a cast-iron fence that Liana did not recognize. However, the balcony looked familiar. Her eyes returned to the second floor.

"What is it, honey?" Clarissa asked.

Goose bumps rose on Liana's neck and arms. "I remember that balcony. I remember seeing people below. It was off my parents' room—I think." She took a deep breath and rubbed her chilled arms. "It's so hard to remember."

"You were only four. That's as early a memory as anyone has." Clarissa reached out to the cast-iron gate. "Come on. It's open."

"I don't think there was a fence or a gate here before."

"It's been twenty-five years."

Of course. Things never stay the same. Liana's heart worked overtime as they approached the door. The chills were replaced by a heat that was more in keeping with the weather.

Someone had attempted to plant grass in the two feet of space on either side of the walk, but the yellowed and wilting blades were sparse. Several brightly colored toys lay on the grass, signaling the presence of a child or children somewhere in the house. Liana was glad.

A young woman with short red hair and a thickly freckled face answered their knock. Clarissa explained their mission, while Liana stared past her. The door opened up into a room with a piano and several chairs perched on an exotic rug. It seemed familiar, but in a dollhouse way, as though everything had shrunk in the intervening years. There were stairs leading to the second floor, and Liana imagined herself climbing them as a child. The image superimposed itself with the reality, disorienting her, and she reached out to steady herself on Clarissa's arm. Clarissa placed her hand over Liana's.

"You're very welcome to come in," said the woman with a British accent. "Of course, there aren't any boxes of things lying around, but there is an attic—with a lot of junk crammed inside. I've only been up there a few times myself to store some of my son's baby things. In fact, I might as well take the opportunity to get those boxes now. I don't know if Dr. Raji told you, but our time here is up and we're going back to England. My brother and his wife, too. They share the house with us."

"I hear they're going to make it into a children's ward," Clarissa said.

She nodded. "Good thing, too. We need one." She held out her hand as they entered. "I'm Jane DeCamp, by the way."

"Nice to meet you, Jane." Clarissa shook her hand warmly. "As I said before, I'm Clarissa Winn, and this is my daughter, Lara."

Liana didn't even flinch at the name or make a correction. She was Lara, especially here. Maybe it was time to accept the name. She shook Jane's hand absently, her attention on the black railing by the stairs.

"It's up there," Jane said, seeing Liana's stare. "Come on. I'll show you." She led the way up the steep staircase.

Liana followed last, fingering the black wood of the banister, brought to a dull shine from the oily touch of many hands. Strange that this house was all so new yet somehow deeply familiar, as though she had dreamed about it, not actually lived here. Ahead on the landing, Jane and Clarissa were talking, but Liana couldn't concentrate on the words. They began climbing another flight of stairs, and this time she didn't follow.

Jane and Clarissa paused halfway up the stairs. "Lara?" Clarissa said.

"I—that used to be my room, I think." Liana pointed to an open door in the middle of the hall. "The other was Mom and Dad's. That one was our sitting room. And that end one is the bathroom."

"Are you sure?" Clarissa asked gently, coming to stand beside her.

"Not really. But I think Mamata slept downstairs. And upstairs was someone else—two nurses, maybe. I used to play with my doll here in the hall." Liana looked down at the dark green carpet. "I don't remember carpet. I think it was wood."

Jane descended the stairs. "Would you like to see the rooms? They're a little messy because I've been packing—my husband and I have this floor. My brother and his wife are downstairs. Until recently, we had some nurses staying upstairs, but they moved to a new apartment complex a few streets over." She grinned and added, "It's a box, but they have air conditioning, and we don't."

Liana was feeling rather warm but knew it had nothing to do with the temperature. She moved as if in a dream. "I would like to see the rooms," she said.

"Go right ahead. They're empty anyway. My son is with his dad." Jane took a step forward and then stopped. She glanced at Clarissa and then back at Liana. "Why don't we wait here for you?"

Not wanting to be troubled by idle chatter that would block out any impressions or memories, Liana was desperately glad the other women stayed behind. She went into the sitting room first, but either it was so changed that she didn't recognize it or the room had not made an impression upon her as a child. The room that was her parents was also unfamiliar, except the balcony. Quickly, she crossed to the double glass doors and opened them.

"*Be careful, dear. Don't climb on the railing. You don't want to fall.*"

"*I won't, Mommy. I just want to sit here with my doll.*"

"*Why don't I come out with you? We can watch the people passing.*"

"*Oh, can you, Mommy? Oh, wait! There's Daddy. Let's run down to him. Do you think he'll take me to see the horses again? He said maybe one time we could ride them.*"

"*Maybe tomorrow. You do remember what tomorrow is, don't you?*"

"*My birthday!*"

Liana shut the door as the memory faded. Horses? She hadn't remembered any horses in India—not until that moment. The memory was clouded and very distant, but now she did believe they had gone to see horses for her fourth birthday. Did they ride them or just pet them? She didn't know.

Liana walked with steps slowed by dread to the room she

had saved for last. Would she recognize any of it? Would it bring out another forgotten memory? Or would it be completely foreign to her?

As in the other rooms, brown cardboard packing boxes littered the floor. A brown crib stood where her bed had once been, and the walls were now blue with a midway border of colorful stenciled trains. There had been flowers before, she remembered. All colors of flowers against a background of the palest pink. Disappointed, Liana walked to the freestanding closet that was made of the same black wood as the banister on the stairs. This she remembered. She had put her clothes inside. Liana opened the double doors, feeling excitement. Yes, she had used the little shelves on the left side for her pants and shirts and the rod on the right for her dresses. In the wider drawer below she had put her shoes. There were several shelves above the cupboards and a rod that she didn't remember but couldn't possibly have reached anyway at age three or four. Her mother must have used it for other things. The closet now held clothes and memorabilia from another child. But Liana remembered something more.

Shutting the doors, she went around to the side of the closet. Sure enough, scratched into the wood was her name in messy letters. L-I-A-N-A. Or was it L-A-R-A? The letters were so wobbly and malformed that she couldn't be certain. Had her insistence at being called Liana resulted from her own poor handwriting? Whatever the conclusion, she had left a permanent mark in the house, something that told her she had once belonged here.

"What have you done?"

She held the bent hanger behind her back. "I was practicing."

Mamata looked at the scratches on the side of the closet. "So I see. Indeed. You wrote it just as I taught you. Very good. I'm proud that you remembered. What a good learner you are!"

Liana smiled, dropping the hanger and putting her arms around Mamata's neck. She had been so excited to write her name on something that was hers. But when she'd seen how the scratches wobbled, she worried someone would get mad. But Mamata wasn't angry, and she would talk to Mommy and Daddy, and then they wouldn't be angry, either.

"Come now, dear. Let's get you something to eat. I made rasgullas for you."

Liana kissed the wrinkled brown cheek. "I love rasgullas! They're so sweet. Mmmm. We have to save some for Daddy. He likes them, too. They're coming home today, right? Let's hurry, my stomach's talking—it wants to eat!"

Mamata laughed, but her eyes were strangely sad.

Liana slumped down next to the closet, her arms clutching her knees. It wasn't until the next day that Mamata had finally told Liana why her parents hadn't come home, why they would never come home again. Now she knew why the old woman hadn't been angry at her mistake. As for her parents, they never had the opportunity see her literary endeavor. Tears leaked from her eyes as Liana sobbed, unable to hold back the emotions.

She was glad she had come to India—fiercely glad. The memories brought pain, yes, but they also reminded her how much she had been loved. She hadn't always been the one on the outside looking in; once she had been in the center of a family.

Until it was gone.

The tears slowed, and Liana opened her purse, rummaging for her compact. She wiped the mascara from under her eyes and dabbed on a bit of powder. She knew she couldn't completely hide the fact that she'd been crying, but at least she could minimize the damage.

"Thanks," Liana told Jane when she emerged from the room. "I was so young, but I remember more now."

Yet one thing certainly had not become clear, and that was the scene from her nightmare. Was that the day Mamata told her about the crash? She seemed to remember that, though. The disbelief, the crying that welled up from the empty place inside, and holding onto Mamata, begging not to be sent to America to the aunt and uncle she didn't know—didn't care to know. The memory did not match the nightmare.

"You're quite welcome," Jane said gently in her British lilt. The woman couldn't have missed Liana's reddened eyes, but neither she nor Clarissa commented.

"Could I see my sister's old room?" Clarissa asked.

"Of course." This time Jane led the way, and Liana lingered in the hall as Clarissa walked inside and opened the doors to the balcony.

"Wake up, sweetie. It's okay. It was just a dream."

"Don't leave me, Mommy. Please don't leave."

"I won't. I'm here."

"Sleep with me. Don't leave. Please, Mommy?"

"I said I'd stay. Of course, I will. I'll always be here for you, sweetie. Move over. I'll put my arm around you. Is that better? Hush now and sleep."

Liana was puzzled at this new memory. The voice was her mother's, and she was comforting her after the nightmare. *The nightmare* or *a nightmare?* Liana couldn't remember.

"I think my sister would have loved that balcony," Clarissa came from the room saying. "She loved watching people, even as a little girl."

"I must confess that I do, too." Jane shut the door behind them and resumed her course up the stairs.

On the third floor, Liana followed Jane to a small closet that held a pull-down ladder leading into the attic. While Jane occupied herself carrying boxes of baby clothes down to the third floor, Liana and Clarissa checked dozens of other boxes and the two large trunks. The attic space was short, and they had to crouch near the boxes so they didn't hit their heads on the support boards that made up the ceiling. Everything was covered in a thick layer of dust, and it wasn't long before they began sneezing.

"Nothing here but a bunch of old clothes," Clarissa said, shutting the lid to one trunk.

Liana sighed. "Same with these boxes. Clothes and some knickknacks." Holding up her skirt, she duck-walked past an old metal highchair to another slew of boxes, wondering if the chair had been hers. Probably. Or did Mamata have children? She asked Jane if she knew.

"I think she had a daughter," Jane said. "But she would have already come and taken anything of value."

Clarissa rubbed her nose, leaving a streak of dust. "That would explain why there are no pictures or jewelry or nice furniture."

"I bet those trunks are worth something." Liana shut the boxes she was searching in disgust. Broken dishes, old menus, catalogues—why had Mamata kept them?

"Lara, come here, quick!" Clarissa's voice was excited. "I might have found something. Baby clothes—a few tiny ones. More that are bigger."

Liana hurried to the second trunk where Clarissa crouched, trying fruitlessly to keep her pale blue skirt off the dusty wood floor and search at the same time. She moved over as Liana approached. Inside the trunk on one side sat a large cardboard box that had seen better days. The box was full of baby clothes, a jumble of lace and pink ruffles. She held the newborn outfits up one by one to see them better. The material had been protected in the trunk, but the lace was yellowed and slightly brittle.

Carefully, Liana laid the tiny dresses on top of the books and magazines that filled the other half of the trunk. Right below these outfits were much larger ones, belonging to a toddler at least. There were stains on them, and some bore the result of many washings. As she dug deeper, the outfits increased in size until at last her hand fell on one she remembered. A blue polka-dotted dress, with yellow lace that had once been white. She held the dress close to her face, but the only smell remaining was of mothballs and dust.

An arm of a doll caught her attention. Quickly removing the few remaining outfits, she grabbed the doll. "This was mine," she said. "Oh, Mother."

With tears in her eyes, Clarissa patted her daughter's arm, though the mother Liana called for was not her. "Look," Liana said, pointing to several letters, still in their envelopes. With a brief glimpse at the return address on the first one, she handed them to Clarissa.

"My letters," Clarissa whispered. "She saved them all these years."

Liana saw the journal then—a small blue book with a puffy cover. Her breath caught in her throat and her heart lurched. She had braced herself for not finding anything after her disappointing visit with Dr. Raji, so this discovery was far more than she'd hoped for. Reaching for the journal, she saw pages and pages of neat handwriting. *My mother,* she thought. *In here is my mother.* It was all she could do not to sit down and begin reading right then. But it would be better if she waited. Then she could savor it in more comfortable circumstances, without watching eyes.

There wasn't much more in the box, except some papers in a language none of the women recognized. "My father was from Romania," Liana reminded Clarissa. "It could be Romanian or Russian."

"Maybe Jane knows."

"I think it's probably Russian," Jane said when they asked her. "It's certainly not Hindi or German. I'm very glad you found what you came for."

"Thank you so much." Liana was still clutching the journal and her doll—a soft-bodied thing with a white plastic face, dark curly hair, and bright blue eyes framed with long black lashes. Its long white dress, trimmed by once-white lace, and the soft white leather slippers brought a feeling of nostalgia. *I once had a matching outfit,* she remembered. The doll had obviously been well loved but also well cared for. Reluctantly, she repacked the box, setting the journal and the doll on top and closing the lid.

"We should check the rest of the boxes, just to be sure," Clarissa said.

They began another search, but the only thing they uncovered were some dresses that may or may not have belonged to Liana's mother and a moth-eaten suit that could only have belonged to Mamata's husband, who had preceded her in death long before the Schraders had come to live with her.

After leaving the attic, they used the bathroom on the second floor to clean the dust from their hands, faces, and clothes. "We'll have to change," Clarissa said, wrinkling her nose at a stain on her skirt.

"I'm ready to call it a day, anyway," Liana replied. "I'm exhausted."

"Jet lag. Our bodies think we've been up all night. It's almost seven in the morning back home. Maybe we should visit the store for a few things to eat tonight and tomorrow morning."

Liana nodded. "Good idea. I'm too exhausted to eat out. Even my mind feels numb."

"Let's ask Jane if she knows where a nice grocery store is."

Jane not only knew but offered to drive them there. "I need a few items myself. On the way back, I'll drop you off at your hotel. You said Suddar Street, didn't you?"

"Yes, but we'll accept only if it's not out of your way." Clarissa's hopeful look made Liana remember with amusement her assertion of wanting to experience India. Apparently she was already willing to abandon the local transport and restaurants.

Jane's smile caused her many freckles to merge into one another. "It is out of the way, but I have nothing planned for tonight. My husband is in England to see about arrangements, and he took our son so I could pack up here. I'm missing them dreadfully, but since my brother and his wife will be at Charity Medical until late, it's just me and boxes to fill. A little break will cheer me up."

"Thank you," Liana said, liking Jane more and more. Not in the soul-bonding way she had liked Mercedes, but Jane was so open and honest, and so young—it was hard not to like her.

Out in the street, they piled into a battered old car that had long ago lost any obvious color. It was so tiny Liana doubted for a minute they could fit. *Austin wouldn't be able to,* she mused. Christian and Bret wouldn't have found it comfortable, either. But the women fit inside, and Liana discovered the tin can wasn't as uncomfortable as she had assumed.

From the backseat, she watched Calcutta fly by. The city

teemed with vibrant life, and Liana was fascinated by what she saw. Calcutta appeared to be a city of contrasts. From its poor hovels to the elegant marble buildings, a medley of Occidental and Oriental styles. From the beggars on Suddar Street to the striking gold jewelry so many inhabitants wore. From the many roadside shops featuring Indian handicrafts to larger stores with automatic doors and security guards. Everything beckoned to be discovered. Now that Liana had found what she had come for, she hoped to take time to experience India.

After buying a few staples and other items at the store, Jane drove to their hotel. Only when she had arranged to take them sightseeing the next morning did she let them out of the car and drive away. They were immediately accosted by four children with their little hands extended. Clarissa gave them a large chocolate bar from a shopping bag, and they eagerly unwrapped the paper and began divvying up their treasure. Almost immediately they were interrupted by a hotel employee who appeared and shooed the children away.

"So do you want to sleep or eat first?" Clarissa asked Liana. She carried the two bags of groceries, while Liana held onto the precious box containing her childhood memories and her mother's journal.

What Liana really craved was to open that journal, and for that she wanted to be alone. Clarissa would also want to read it, but by unspoken consent the first read was Liana's. "Eat, I guess," she said. "Maybe a yogurt and a slice of bread."

Later, when regular soft snores came from the next bed, Liana turned on her lamp and began to read:

Diary of Karyn Olsen. . . .

CHAPTER

21

Diary of Karyn Olsen
Thursday, July 20, 1972

I am feeling more and more comfortable here. I love it! Already
I've delivered five babies. Not assisted but delivered all by myself.
Apparently, if you can do something here, you do it. Never mind
your college degree. The doctors are kept too busy with surgeries and
serious illnesses to worry about pregnant women. Birth is viewed as
natural—at least for the poor women—and is something a nurse is
equipped to take care of. I hold their hands, teach them to breathe,
and tell them when to push. I labor with them, sometimes for days.
So far everything has gone well.

Dr. Schrader asked me out. There I was, sweaty from being in
the labor room for twenty-nine hours straight, my hair pulled back
in a ponytail and blood on my white coat, and he asks me out! I told
him I wasn't interested. He didn't seem at all fazed by the rejection
and next asked me to fly to a remote village with his team. There
were some women who were expecting that he thought I would like

to help. I'd heard good things about his team and their adventures, and of course I immediately agreed to go. I can't wait!

Sunday, August 6, 1972

I'm crying as I write this. I don't know if I can stay in India after all. I don't want to see death or poverty this close! Yet if I leave, that would mean one less person to help these women. Oh, I wish Dr. Schrader had never asked me to fly to the villages. Some of these people are literally starving, something I never dreamed I would see so close up, and the way they live is terrible. No clean water, hovels to sleep in, clothes that should have been thrown out a lifetime ago.

I lost my first mother after she gave birth to a baby that will likely starve to death itself (though I gave it to a neighbor to nurse). The mother was just too weak and the labor too long. In a modern hospital, we might have been able to save her. I cried all day. I must find them food somehow. There is no reason not to bring food when we come. I'm going to contact some charities to see what aid they can give.

Dr. Schrader is tireless. I have seen him sit by a patient all night. I have seen him weep with the survivors when there is a death. He is gentle with the children. He is gentle with me as well. He held me yesterday after my patient died. I didn't have to say anything. He knew.

Friday, August 25, 1972

Guenter Schrader keeps asking me out. He is adorable the way he talks to me in his accented English. He knows five languages in all—English, German, Russian, Hindi, and Romanian. He is the son of a German soldier and a Romanian woman. Their story is incredibly romantic. Guenter's father was serving in the German army in Romania and fell in love with Guenter's mother. When his service was up, he refused to return to Germany but married her and stayed with her and their son until he died when Guenter was fifteen years old. Guenter spent his early years in Romania, where he learned Romanian and Russian, but later he went to live with relatives in Germany where he was educated.

Guenter said he feels very lucky that his father stayed with his mother. He has an uncle who was in the German army in Ukraine about the same time Guenter's father was serving in Romania. But this uncle left a child behind and never looked back. For many years, Guenter's father sent the child and his mother money when he could, and Guenter still keeps in touch with his cousin.

Anyway, I finally said that I would go out with him. (How could I say no when he asked me in all five of his languages?) So tonight he took me to dinner at a beautiful little restaurant here in Calcutta by the water. It was so nice to be away from Charity Medical where I spend almost every second. We weren't battling for life and death, but just two people out on a date. He was kind and courteous to me. He didn't try to kiss me at my apartment door, though. I didn't think I was interested in him that way, but to my surprise I was disappointed.

Tomorrow we're flying out to the villages again, as we do almost every weekend. This time I have food to bring, bought with my own small savings. I hope to arrange more in the near future. A few weeks ago, I made some calls to America and found Angie. She promised to get together some help, and I'm waiting to see what she will send. And praying. I hope the little boy I delivered is well.

Saturday, September 16, 1972

We have just finished watching an Indian sunset. Out here away from all the lights of the big city, it's so beautiful. Of course, every-thing is beautiful when I am with Guenter. I've been so worried these past weeks. I could see myself falling for him, and I never thought I could feel this way again.

244

*This trip to the villages we brought with us a sizeable food sup-
ply that came from America last week on a plane. Angie was true to
her word, and she's promised there will be more to come. I'm so
grateful. But there was one thing in the shipment that she meant for
me. "I know how much you love chocolate," she said in her letter.
Well, it was one of those packages of Hershey kisses. I've only been
here two and a half months, but it felt like a year since I'd seen those
little chocolates wrapped in that silver foil. I brought them with me
on this trip, thinking to share with the children. But then I found
myself watching the sunset with Guenter and it was him I wanted to
give them to. I ran to the tent to get them.*

*"A kiss?" he said when I handed him the package. He was very
puzzled because he's never seen any before. Then he leaned over and
kissed me, without touching me or holding my hand. I kissed him
back, not real hard, but soft and tentative. I was so nervous! Then
his arms went around me and all the awkwardness vanished. We
watched the rest of the sunset together, holding hands and kissing. It
was the most beautiful in the history of the world.*

*Oh, I wanted to make sure and record that the little boy I deliv-
ered whose mother died is growing strong. I hope my other patients
do as well.*

Sunday, October 1, 1972

*Guenter asked me to marry him this morning. He sneaked into
the tent that I share with the other two nurses, and when I awoke he
was sitting on the edge of my sleeping bag. The others were still
asleep. "What are you doing here?" I whispered. "They'll never let
us live it down if they find you here." He shrugged and took my
hands, holding me at arm's length. When he spoke his accent was
more noticeable, as it is when he is deeply emotional. "I want to be
with you for the rest of my life, Karyn," he said. "I want to help*

people, I want to be a doctor, but without you by my side, it has all become meaningless. I want you to bear my children. I want to grow old with you. I want to die with you by my side. Please, will you become my wife?"

I started to cry. Why is it that you cry when you are happy? Since I lost Travis I've wondered if I would ever have the chance to be married to a man I loved, and here my dream is coming true. I love Guenter with a fierceness I do not recognize in myself. It is a focused, urgent feeling, and yet tender and all-compassing. The feelings I had for Travis were but a child's first crush compared to my love for Guenter. That we enjoy the same things and share the same life goals is but the silver lining wrapping our Hershey's chocolate kiss. Or perhaps it is the very core. Who is to say? It really doesn't matter.

Of course I told him yes. Then my friends woke up and kicked him out. I didn't even mind their teasing.

Monday, October 30, 1972

It is the happiest day of my life. Today Guenter and I were married.

Tuesday, October 30, 1973

It has been exactly one year since our wedding, and I have still been unable to conceive. That is the only thing that keeps me from complete happiness. Guenter is everything a husband should be, and I love him more each day. Though we often go for days without a minute to ourselves, we are very happy. Guenter is sure we'll have a child soon, and I pray that he's right.

How ironic that earlier this year in America the Supreme Court ruled in Roe v. Wade that women have the right to obtain abortions. Given my desire to have a child, the ruling seems horribly cruel. Even worse, some of the women here continue killing their newborn daughters. *So many don't accept the help we offer, preferring to hide the fact that they ever had a child rather than let us place their babies with others. I sometimes ask God why these women are allowed to become pregnant when they will only kill their babies. Why not me instead? I'd have as many babies as He'd give me—a dozen or more—in a heartbeat.*

Wednesday, January 7, 1976

Today I am thirty years old. I can't believe how quickly the years are passing—like fleeting moments of a beautiful Indian sunset. In October Guenter and I will have been married four years. We are still working at Charity Medical in the never-ending quest to save and better lives. I have delivered exactly six hundred and three babies, assisted in thirty-five caesarian deliveries, and taught forty-three people to read (and to practice proper hygiene!). I love my work with a passion that is surpassed only by the passion I have for my husband.

Oh, that I could give him a child! We've done some tests, but there doesn't seem to be any reason why we haven't conceived. I hoped I might be pregnant this month, and that I might have a wonderful surprise for him tomorrow, but my period arrived late last night. I cried for hours in the bathroom. Fortunately, Guenter was at Charity Medical for an emergency. He gets so protective when I'm upset. I sometimes wonder if that terrible night I spent with Boyd back in America resulted in some disease that has caused me to be infertile. While I feel I have paid for that terrible mistake, sometimes I fear I deserve to keep paying. But what about the good I have done since that horrible night? And what about Guenter? He doesn't deserve any of it. The possibility of such a permanent consequence gives me no end of agony.

I think of Clarissa and her two babies (could she have another one by now?) and wonder how they are. Strange, but the love I have for Guenter seems to have rid me of any bitterness I experienced in my old life. I know now that I was wrong. Back then I couldn't see that much of what happened between Clarissa and me was my doing, not hers. Or Travis's. Now that I look back on it, he never offered more than friendship to me. I was angry at how he could fall so quickly for my sister, but when I met Guenter, I finally understood how that could happen. When it's right, you know it's right. I was too young to see that then. In my defense, I believe my father's abandonment of our family when I was so young and then his death when I was twenty had a lot to do with how desperately I clung to Travis. That he and Clarissa could fall in love and leave me behind was another form of abandonment. Even so, I wasted too many years wallowing in my hurt.

I wish I could talk to Clarissa or to Mother now. I regret how horribly I acted toward them both. I need to tell them—to ask forgiveness. I did send a letter to Mom's old address, but there was no response. She must have moved too long ago for my letter to be forwarded. Maybe I'll ask Angie to help me find them.

Please, God, give me a child.

Friday, December 3, 1976

I'm going to have a baby! That's right! A baby! I found out only yesterday. I'm a week late on my period, but that's happened so many times before I didn't really even think about it. Then I decided to do a test at Charity Medical. I almost couldn't believe it when it was positive. Guenter is in seventh heaven, though he says there's no way I'm going to be allowed to fly with him to the villages until the baby is here. I hate to say that I agree. There is too much work there, and I won't risk my baby's life. Oh, I hope it's a girl. I want to name her Lara.

CHAPTER
22

Diary of Karyn Olsen Schrader
Thursday, August 4, 1977

    I thought when I married Guenter it was the happiest day of my life. I was wrong. Today when I held my little daughter, with Guenter by my side, I knew true happiness. This is a little person we created together. She is all ours. I pray the days will go by slowly because I don't want to go back to work and be apart from her for one second. Luckily, Guenter is urging me to take all the time I want. When I do go back, if I do, Mamata, our landlady who is renting us her second floor and who cooks for us, has agreed to be her nanny. Mamata is exactly what her name implies: love and affection. Plus she speaks excellent British English and will be able to read to my little Lara. But I will not think of that now. This precious baby is all mine, and I am going to enjoy every minute with her.

    Angie found Clarissa's address, though I'm not sure how she did

*that because Clarissa lives in Nevada now. I wrote to Clarissa last
month. She hasn't written back yet, but the mail here is slow.*

I am the luckiest woman alive.

Liana had read for hours before falling asleep with her
mother's journal in her hand. At first the entries were nothing
special, except that her mother had written them, until she
made the first mention of Travis Winn on her twentieth birthday. Then Liana had read with fascination the journey that had
taken Karyn away from her family. Liana's tears flowed freely.
She finally gave in to her exhaustion only after reading that her
mother had finally given birth to the baby she had longed for.

Me, she thought, and smiled.

Liana could hear Clarissa in the bathroom showering. She
fingered the journal longingly, eager to read about her early
years, but her wristwatch showed nearly eight-thirty and Jane
would be arriving at nine for their sightseeing plans.

She put the journal in her suitcase, which she hadn't yet
fully unpacked, and found a tan pair of slacks and a matching
short-sleeved blouse that should be light enough to stay cool
but dressy enough for any museum.

"Oh, you're awake." Clarissa smiled as she came from the
bathroom. "I woke up so early—about three or four—and
couldn't go back to sleep until seven. Then when my alarm
rang at eight, I didn't want to get up." She sighed and flopped
onto the chair and toweled her wet hair. "I think by the time I
finally adjust to being twelve hours ahead, the week will be up
and it'll be time to go home."

Liana stretched muscles that were sore from crouching in
the attic. "I actually slept pretty well." *For a change,* she added
silently.

"I'm glad someone did," Clarissa said. "We should probably
call Dr. Raji this afternoon. See if he's up to visiting again."

Liana agreed, though she didn't hold out much hope of his being lucid. *Besides,* she thought, *the journal is what I came here for.*

Jane was waiting outside as they left the hotel. There were no beggar children in front today, probably because of the burly hotel employee who was smoking by the door.

"First we'll go to the India Museum," Jane said. "Then we'll hit a few more nearby places before visiting the Armenian Church and the Nakhoda Mosque. You will like those. And of course, we can't miss the Botanical Garden."

Clarissa laughed. "Sounds like a lot for one day."

"You're right." Jane grinned. "We'll probably only get in a few, but I like to be optimistic. I guess you'll have to go to whatever we miss another day. You could spend several weeks at least, just going to the museums here. They have a great many of them."

Liana enjoyed the India Museum with its relics of ancient civilizations, but her favorite place was the Nakhoda Mosque, which Jane told them could accommodate ten thousand people at once. By the time they had finished at the mosque, it was after one, and they were all ravenous. Jane took them to a restaurant where they ate rice, lentils, vegetables, and savory fish curry. Fortunately for Clarissa, this restaurant offered a mild version of their curry dishes. For dessert Liana ordered the rasgullas from her memory of the day before—little balls of rose-flavored cream cheese. She hadn't remembered what they looked like, but when the waiter brought the sweet white balls, she dug into them with excitement, her tongue remembering what her mind had not.

Often throughout the day, Liana thought of her parents, especially her mother. Had she eaten here? Had she loved rasgullas as much as Liana did? Or had that sweet tooth been something Liana shared only with her father? There were so many questions, and each answer she had found in the journal so far had only brought more questions. She hoped the journal would resolve them soon. There were also the documents in the unknown language. Could one of the many tourists who were visiting Calcutta even this early in the year translate them?

"Well, how about going to one more place?" Jane asked after lunch.

"Oh, I couldn't." Clarissa touched the side of her head. "Though I am grateful for the offer. I need to lie down for a bit. And besides, you're supposed to be packing."

Jane laughed. "Okay, home it is."

"Thank you, Jane," Liana said. "This has been a perfect day."

The children were waiting outside their hotel again, and when they recognized Liana and Clarissa, they came running. While Liana balanced two Indian rugs and three large bags of Indian tea, Clarissa gave them the light tan squares of Indian fudge called *mysore pak* that she had in her purse. "Good thing I bought these at the restaurant."

Inside, the manager of the hotel saw them and motioned them over. Not satisfied to wait for their approach, he met them halfway across the entryway. "I have been wishing to reach you," he said. "You have a call—many calls—from America. It is your husband. He called once and then again and again. He says it is very urgent. You must call him."

"Thank you." Worry instantly lined Clarissa's face.

Liana felt a twinge of dread as the meaning sank in. Why would Travis call in what was for him the middle of the night? What could have happened?

They hurried to their room, where Clarissa immediately placed a call. "It's probably nothing," she assured Liana. "Maybe he just got lonely and then became worried when we didn't call him back."

Liana said nothing. The dread in her heart was more pronounced now.

"Travis?" Clarissa said into the phone. "We got your message. What is it?" She paused, listening. "What? No! Oh, dear Lord, please, no!"

Liana knew something was very wrong; Clarissa didn't often pray aloud. "What?" Liana asked.

Clarissa held up her hand, still listening. "Okay, I'll calm down." She took a deep breath. "I'm fine. How are you holding up? Is Bret with you? Yes. I'll call the airlines now to change our tickets. You did? Good. When? We'll be there. What time will we arrive? Okay, see you tomorrow."

Liana sat on the bed, her fists clenched tight. She stared at Clarissa, whose face was pale and frightened. "It's Christian," Clarissa said, standing by the phone, a lost expression on her face. "He's had an accident."

Liana gasped. "In his car?"

Clarissa shook her head. "He fell out of a tree at Mount Charleston. The girl he was with had to leave him and hike out for help. Her cell phone didn't have service there, and he hadn't taken his. The rescuers barely made it back to him before dark. She called your father from the hospital."

"Is he going to be okay?" Liana could barely voice the words.

"They don't know. He's just got out of surgery. They can only wait now. Your father thinks—" She broke off with a little cry, holding out her arms. Rising, Liana stepped into them, feeling stunned and nauseated. "Your father thinks we should hurry home, just in case. He changed our return flight. Our plane takes off tonight at a little after seven, and we should get home at ten or so tomorrow night."

What if that's too late? Liana didn't say the words aloud. Instead she said, "I'll start packing." She drew back from Clarissa, holding in the tumult of emotions that threatened to sweep her away.

"Good idea." But Clarissa grabbed her hands before Liana could turn away. She looked deeply into her eyes. "Don't lose hope. He has to be okay."

Nodding tearfully, Liana turned toward her suitcase on the bed and began to make room for the items they had found in Mamata's attic.

"Lara?"

Liana turned to look at Clarissa, who was staring out the window. "Yes?"

"It's only three. There's time to go to the cemetery before our flight. I mean, if you would like to go."

"I would." Despite her worry about Christian, Liana didn't want to leave India without at least seeing her parents' graves.

"Okay, then. After we pack, we'll call a taxi to take us there and then to the airport."

———•◦•———

Clarissa gave Mridula's paper to the taxi driver. "It's the second address."

"Did you remember to call Jane and Mridula to tell them we were leaving?" Liana asked. The hour they'd spent packing had gone by in a blur, and she didn't want to leave anything undone. Yet all she could think about was Christian and how at the airport in Nevada he had told her that the real reason he was going to Mount Charleston was for her birthday painting.

"Yes, I called them." Clarissa had been calm and efficient since the phone call, but Liana wonder if she felt that way inside. Perhaps she had let the teacher in her take over.

Liana spent the taxi ride wishing she was still in Wyoming with Austin and Mercedes. Wishing she could curl up in the quilt she had helped stitch. Wishing she had never told Christian she wanted a painting for her birthday.

"We're here," Clarissa said needlessly as they pulled up at a cemetery surrounded by a short white wall. "We'd better ask the caretaker where it is, though. We could be a long time searching."

Liana came from her thoughts with a start. While Clarissa made sure the taxi driver would wait, she looked out over the long stretch of graves.

"Jane told me this is mostly a foreigner's cemetery," Clarissa said, steering her toward a small white building next to the graveyard. "The hospital actually owns a section that they make available for their employees when necessary. A nurse died last year, and Jane went to the funeral. She said the hospital's section was in the back on the right, but we'd better make sure."

The caretaker in the office did not speak English, unlike most of the other Indians they had met. Clarissa wrote out the names on a piece of paper and the caretaker smiled, his teeth very white against his dark skin, except for the gap on the bottom where two teeth were missing. He gave them a map of the cemetery and highlighted the area where they needed to go.

"Thank you," Clarissa said. The man answered with a bow and a stream of words Liana didn't understand.

A few minutes later, Liana came across her parents' graves, marked by a single rectangular stone, lying flat on the ground. She crouched down, feeling the muscles in her legs rebel from her time in the attic the day before and all the walking that morning.

"I'm decades too late, I know," whispered Clarissa, kneeling beside Liana. "But I'm here, Karyn. Your Clari's here. And I've brought Lara." Clarissa touched Liana's hand and squeezed. Liana squeezed back, feeling a rush of love for both Clarissa and her birth mother. Tears gathered in her eyes but did not fall.

Liana traced the carving of her parents' names with her fingertips, letting the tears fall. These were her parents, the people who had given her life. They had loved her, perhaps more than anyone ever would—besides Clarissa and Travis. Liana had realized these past few days how much Clarissa did love her.

"We should go," Clarissa said after a long while.

Liana began to rise, looking sadly at the rows and rows of headstones that marked the final resting places of people she would never know. She was glad she had come to pay her respects. As she gave a last pat to her parents' stone, her eyes fell on the adjacent grave. She blinked away her tears, struggling to see if she had read the name right, or if her grief had caused her to see something that wasn't there—something that couldn't possibly be there. Crawling over to the stone, she brushed away a few dead leaves and grass clippings to see it better.

Our precious daughter
Lara Clari Schrader
Born August 3, 1977
Died January 5, 1978

The five months you gave us were
the best we have ever known.
We will love you forever.
Your parents,
Guenter and Karyn Schrader

Liana stared at her legal name on the stone. Time slowed, and small details called her attention: a curled leaf blowing across the engraving, a gnarled twig wedged between the grass and the stone, the last *R* in *Schrader* filled with sand, Clarissa down on her knees, holding her breath, her hands clenched in the grass.

The same name, the same birthday, the same parents. But this baby girl had lived for only five months. Five months. Gravestones didn't lie, did they?

Beside her Clarissa gave a small cry. "It can't be!"

Liana's feeling exactly. If the baby buried here was Lara Clari Schrader, who was she?

CHAPTER

23

Diary of Karyn Olsen Schrader
Wednesday, November 23, 1977

I am in Germany, holding Lara. She is dying. We have done
everything we can, but her heart continues to fail. We scraped
together every last bit of money we had to come here so she could
see some of the best cardiologists in the world, but they can't do anything for her. I sit here in the home of Guenter's old uncle, the one
who fathered a son in Ukraine and then abandoned him. He lives
alone and is very ill himself. He still wants no contact with his son in
Ukraine, though Guenter told him we have his address.

I watch Lara every second. She rarely cries now as her heart
grows weaker. She has trouble even nursing, and I have to feed her
my breast milk with a spoon. It's an all-day process, but what else is
there for me to do? I won't leave her for an instant. Guenter stays
with us. He feels terrible that he can't help her, even though he's a
doctor. All we do now is pray for a miracle. Why us? I ask. Why my
precious Lara? There is no answer.

Liana looked up from her mother's journal as the captain of the airplane put on the seatbelt sign for landing in Nevada. How ironic that her birth father had fulfilled most of his wishes—he had lived with Karyn and loved her, she had borne his child, and they had died together.

Borne his child.

Yes, and that child was buried next to them. So who was Liana? So far, not even the journal had shed light on the matter.

She looked over at Clarissa, who had woken up at the captain's announcement and was staring out the window. There were new lines on the fine pale skin, or perhaps old lines grown deeper from her worry over Christian. They had talked to both Travis and Bret when the plane landed in New York and then again in St. Louis, but there had been nothing new. Christian had not awakened after his surgery, and the doctors didn't know if he ever would.

Liana and Clarissa hadn't talked about what they had found at the cemetery, but it was all Liana could think about besides Christian. She felt lost. Who was she? Some orphan child Mamata had sent to America to give her a better life? But no, she remembered living with her parents—with Karyn and Guenter Schrader. She remembered calling them Mom and Dad. She remembered . . . but was her memory accurate? Or was it all imagination? She felt more intensely than ever that she didn't belong—had never belonged anywhere.

In only one small thing she did find satisfaction. Her name wasn't Lara and never had been. She was Liana, though whether she had a birth certificate that stated her name was quite another matter.

Her questions and conjectures surrounding the circumstances of her birth were not all filled with worry and fear. Perhaps her mother had conceived again quickly and given birth to another daughter. Maybe Lara's birth certificate had been sent with Liana to America by mistake. That meant maybe Liana wasn't nearly thirty after all.

If only Liana had known the right questions to ask Dr. Raji before he had grown confused. *It's not too late,* she thought. *I can call and talk to Mridula. There have to be records somewhere. And there's still my mother's journal and the documents.* She wished she had been able to read more, but she hadn't with Clarissa awake most of the flight and worrying aloud about Christian. The closer to Nevada they came, the further Clarissa's veneer of calmness slipped.

"We're here—finally." The unhappiness in her adoptive mother's voice made Liana feel guilty. She was spending too much time worrying about her own life when Christian was fighting for his.

Clarissa put her hand on Liana's shoulder and spoke, showing that she wasn't oblivious to Liana's turmoil. "It doesn't matter what happened or how you got to us. You are part of our family, and we love you."

A warmth spread through Liana. She nodded, unable to speak through her threatening tears. "You go on ahead. I'll get our carry-ons."

"We'll do it together." Clarissa smiled and pushed her way into the aisle where other passengers were crowding in their eagerness to leave the plane.

When they finally arrived at the baggage carrousel, Liana was surprised to see Austin waiting for them. Dressed in blue jeans and a black leather jacket, he looked very different from the professional Austin she knew—more like the man who had taken her to the swing over the river. He shrugged at her inquiring stare. "Neither Bret or your dad wanted to leave your brother at the hospital."

"Has there been any change?" asked Clarissa eagerly.

Austin shook his head, his eyes somber. "I'm sorry."

"Are you going to introduce me?" Clarissa looked at Liana.

"Oh, sorry," Liana said. "This is Austin Walker, Christian's friend." Liana glanced at Austin. "How did you find out?"

"I saw it on the news last night, and I went to the hospital. When I heard you were flying in tonight, I volunteered to pick you up."

"Thank you." Liana was glad he was here. With the discoveries she had made during her two days in India, she hadn't thought much about him, but now his solid presence made her feel more secure. He, at least, was real, and perhaps his feelings toward her were as well.

"How was your flight?" Austin picked up her suitcase in one hand and Clarissa's in the other. It was plain he was trying to steer the conversation to a semblance of normalcy.

She grimaced. "Long. But at least we regained the day we lost on the way over."

He grinned without real joy. "That always helps."

They fell into an expectant silence that lasted throughout their journey to the hospital. The fear in Liana's heart grew with each passing mile. She prayed desperately that Christian would be awake when they arrived. *He has to be all right,* she said in a continuous silent litany. *He just has to be all right.*

When they arrived at the hospital, Travis and Bret met them at the nurses' station. Travis's square face was haggard and gray above his brown polo shirt, and he appeared to have lost weight. *He looks so old,* Liana thought. She couldn't remember ever seeing her good-natured adoptive father cry, but as he hugged Clarissa he began to sob, his big shoulders shaking convulsively.

Liana stared, rooted to the spot. She tore her eyes from

Travis and Clarissa and focused on Bret. His eyes were red, and his face stark white. His pale blue button-down shirt and dark blue slacks were wrinkled. His eyes held an agony Liana didn't recognize. Or did she?

"I'm so sorry, my little one. They are not coming home. There has been an accident."

"What do you mean, Mamata? Where is my mommy? My daddy?"

Mamata took her in her big arms, her brown eyes sorrowful. "Oh, my little dear, the plane, it crashed. Your mommy and daddy cannot come home to you. They are in heaven now."

"No! No!" Liana's little fists hit against Mamata's solid body. "I don't believe you! They're not in heaven! They're not! I hate heaven!" She pulled from Mamata and ran to her room, hiding under her bedcovers as violent tears wracked her small body.

Clarissa pulled back slightly from her husband and voiced the question Liana could not. "How is he?" Travis swallowed hard and opened his mouth, but nothing came out. "Oh no," Clarissa whispered. "He's—he's gone, isn't he?"

Travis nodded. He pulled Clarissa to him again, and together they wept.

Liana's eyes filled with tears. She held her eyes open wide so the tears wouldn't spill out, as if not crying would make it all untrue. *No!* her heart screamed. *No!* She wanted to run fast and far. She wanted to hide from all of them.

At that moment, Travis and Clarissa parted. Clarissa reached for Bret, who was standing nearby, looking as lost and miserable as Liana felt, and grasped his hand. Liana felt her own hand being pulled by Travis, and into the circle of his arms she went. Clarissa and Bret were also in that circle, and they clung to each other as a family, crying and consoling one another.

All thoughts of India and her questionable parentage were for the moment far from Liana's mind. She was right where she belonged.

Except.

Except one thing was missing. Something vital. Something she could never replace.

Her big brother Christian.

They went in as a family to say good-bye. He was lying on the bed, his head swathed in heavy bandages.

Please don't be dead, Liana silently begged.

People who fall out of trees have every right to be dead, he seemed to argue back.

Then, still in her mind, she told him all about India. He didn't answer, and she wondered if she was going insane to expect him to. For a brief moment she wanted to be alone with him, to shake him and make him wake up. Or at the very least hug him and throw herself weeping onto his too-still body.

She did none of that. She clung to Bret's hand, or Clarissa's, or Travis's, and wept softly, decorously with them. When the time came to let Christian go, she kissed his wan cheek once and let them lead her from the room.

CHAPTER

24

Diary of Karyn Olsen Schrader
Thursday, January 12, 1978

Lara died a week ago, just after turning five months old. We are back in India. I insisted on bringing Lara's body in the little coffin so that I can bury her near us. India is my home now. I will never leave it or Lara. My heart is empty. There is no life, no love—not even for Guenter who is my only partner in this unending grief. Our Lara will never sit up, take her first step, or go to school. How can I go on without her? Nothing in my life has prepared me for such pain. I pray for the sweet release that can only come with death.

There was a comforting moment when we returned and found not one but two letters from Clari waiting for us. She says she forgives me and wants to see me again. She says she's sorry. Her letters are bittersweet for me—sweet because of her love and forgiveness, which I so desperately crave, but bitter because they tell of my mother's death more than two years ago. No wonder Mother didn't answer my letter! Clarissa's letters are also bitter because now I will have to tell her of my loss. I can't do it yet. I simply can't. She didn't know or love Lara—how could she possibly understand? I'll put her letters away to answer later.

Christian's viewing and funeral were held late Wednesday morning. Liana stood numbly by his casket with the others as people offered their sympathies. She wasn't surprised to see Austin. He had stayed at the hospital until she had left with her parents, and though she hadn't seen him since, she had known he would come. He smiled at her, hugged her briefly.

"Are you all right?"

"Fine," she whispered. "Thank you for coming."

"I called your cell."

She didn't know that. "It needs to be recharged."

"I stopped by."

"I've been staying at my parents'."

He looked as though he wanted to say more, but there was a line of people behind him and he had to move on.

At the funeral Liana listened in a haze as people talked about Christian, painting his life as a saint. Several times Liana felt an overwhelming urge to remind everyone how hopeless he was with money, how he had sometimes teased with malice, and how he'd never had enough courage to pursue his dream of being an artist. That at least would have evened out all the sickly sweet stories. It would have made Christian *real*.

Of course she didn't say any of these things because he had done all of those good things, too—especially befriending a young orphan cousin. Who was she to bring to light Christian's flaws when she had so many more? Most of all he had openly acknowledged his failures, while she hadn't found it within herself even to admit what it was she wanted in life, much less take the risk of trying for it.

After the funeral, the family went home, where well-wishers crowded, bringing more sympathy and food. Austin was there, too—sitting quietly, helping when needed, talking with Christian's friends. Through the afternoon Liana and Bret and their parents stayed close. Liana found it ironic that she felt more a part of the family through Christian's death than she ever had during his life.

How can I go on without him? This thought kept recurring in her mind. Once she had thought she didn't need him, didn't need anyone, but now she knew that was a lie. She did need Christian and the others as well. It wasn't only gratitude she'd felt toward them all these years but love. The realization frightened her. Love was beyond her control. It could not stop death; it left the survivors aching and empty. She detested that weakness. She had cried plenty under her blankets these past nights in her old room at her parents' house, but most of her grief had been openly shared with her family.

Her family? The very idea mocked her. She had read far enough in her mother's journal to know that Karyn hadn't quickly become pregnant again, that the tiny baby dresses she had found in India hadn't belonged to her, only the larger outfits. The mystery around her origins was even deeper than before. She desperately hoped the journal held the answer and that soon she would feel up to reading more; each reading so far just further drained her grief-depleted strength.

All their visitors had finally left, except Austin. He was in the kitchen with Clarissa and Travis, finding room for all the casseroles and desserts that rained on them from their caring neighbors and members of Clarissa's church.

With her parents and Austin in the kitchen and Bret somewhere with his fiancée, Liana found herself alone in her parents' sitting room. It was one of the few times she had been alone since the accident. Rising quietly from the couch, she headed for the back door, which led out onto the patio next to the pool. The night was warm and cloudless, and the moon reflected in the still water where she had spent so much time in her youth.

With Christian.

She took a deep breath and held it, walking around the pool, remembering. *"Catch me, Christian!"* *"Will you show me how?"* *"Come up! Come up! Don't stay under so long. You're scaring me!"* *"You'll come back home soon, won't you? You won't leave forever?"* *"Stop tickling me!"* Giggles rose and died on the wave of her memories, leaving a sorrow that cut through her with crystalline intensity.

She slumped into a lawn chair. *He died because of my picture,* she thought, knowing that was ludicrous. Still, it made her feel better to take responsibility, as though to do so meant she maintained some control. Control over that which no one had ever succeeded in controlling.

Voices came from the side of the house, the words indecipherable, but the angry tones were apparent. Britanni's normally dulcet voice sharply answered Bret's accusing one. The sounds grew louder.

"You'll regret this," Britanni nearly screamed, full of venom. "Tomorrow or the day after you'll be calling, begging me to come back."

"Maybe." Bret's deep voice was firm, unyielding. "But for now I think you should go."

Britanni uttered something that sounded like a curse. A few seconds later a car door slammed, the engine roared, and the wheels squealed into the night.

Bret rounded the house and saw Liana sitting by the pool. "I guess you heard that," he said, sitting in the chair next to her.

Tears on his cheeks glistened in the moonlight like the water in the pool.

She shrugged. "Some. I take it Britanni's not too happy." She waited a couple heartbeats before asking, "What happened?"

Bret stared out over the water and was quiet for a long moment. The tears dried on his cheeks. "He wanted me to go with him," he said finally.

"He what?"

"He asked if Britanni and I wanted to go with him and that girl from work. Sounded like a lot of fun, and I could have gotten off work—even at such short notice. We haven't been very busy."

"But you didn't."

"No." He bent over and picked up a small pebble lying at the foot of his chair, rolling it between his fingers. "I was upset at him for how Britanni acted that Sunday. You know, the jabs about my car and her flirting with him. I blamed him for being so charming. I didn't want them together again."

Wallowing in her own guilt, Liana recognized where Bret was going with this admission. "It's not your fault," she said.

He threw the pebble into the pool and watched the ripples spread over the water, making the moon dance. When he spoke, his voice was painful for Liana to hear. "I should have gone. I wanted to. And maybe if I had, I could have prevented it, or helped—something. At least I would have been there for him."

"He was getting pictures for *me*," Liana said. "For a painting he was going to do for my birthday. Without me, he wouldn't have been in those mountains at all. He would have picked some other place for the photographs he needed to paint from."

Bret's eyes, black in the moonlight, glittered with new tears.

"He loved painting and taking pictures. He would have been there anyway. If not last week, then next."

Liana had been telling herself the same thing, but hearing Bret say it aloud made her feel better. He didn't blame her, an interloper into the family, for the death of his only blood sibling.

Bret reached out suddenly and put his hand on hers where it lay on the armrest. "I know you and Christian were really close, and I never begrudged you that. He was everything a big brother should be—to both of us. But it's just us now, Liana. Do you think . . ." He fought tears. "Do you think maybe we can be closer? I'd like to be the big brother now, your big brother."

Liana swallowed a cry in her throat, yet it still emerged as a whimper. "What we found out in India—I'm not really related."

"It doesn't matter." His hand tightened over hers. "You're my sister and were from the moment you stepped off that plane sucking your thumb. And even if that wasn't true, you really became ours when you were adopted. What difference does it make who your birth parents were?"

It made a difference to Liana—a big difference. All her life she'd at least had the knowledge of her roots to cling to when she hadn't felt a part of the family. Now she had nothing. Yet she couldn't tell that to Bret, not when he was looking so seriously at her, not when he was offering to be her big brother. She couldn't have told even Christian.

"The way I see it is that we need each other," Bret continued. "The days ahead aren't going to be easy. Only you and I know what it was like being raised by our parents. Only you and I know Christian the way siblings do. Only you and I are left to remember. We can keep it alive, be there for each other."

Warmth spread through Liana's heart. Maybe she was wrong. Maybe she still had something to cling to. She turned her hand into his and held on. After a long comfortable moment when the rawness of her emotions had abated, she said lightly, "You have a deal. But I do believe you're just trying to distract yourself from losing your fiancée."

"I didn't lose her. I sent her packing." Bret gave a long sigh. "She was at it again earlier with your boyfriend—flirting, I mean. At least he doesn't lead her on like Christian did or goad me about it."

"He's not my boyfriend."

Bret met her gaze steadily. "Then why is he here?"

"He was Christian's friend."

"Christian had a lot of friends, and they've all headed home. I think he's here because of you."

"Well, he's probably gone by now."

"I doubt it."

Liana let the subject drop because she suspected he was right, and she was glad when Bret—dependable Bret—let it go as well. Christian would have dug at the wound until it bled. Oh, how desperately she wished he was here to do that now!

"We should go inside and see how they're doing." Bret stood, taking her with him. "It's been a real shock for them." Travis and Clarissa had aged ten years in the past few days, and Liana hoped that now with the funeral behind them they could begin to recover.

They found their parents with Austin in the family room, an array of snacks and drinks on the coffee table. Austin sat in the easy chair, and Clarissa and Travis on the couch. When Austin saw Liana, he moved from the chair and let her have it, sitting on the floor next to her legs. Bret sat in one of the straight-backed chairs they'd brought from the table for the many visitors.

Travis looked toward the back door. "Where's Britanni?"

Bret grimaced. "She went home. Uh, this may not be the right time to tell you, but I'm not getting married after all."

"Thank heavens!" Clarissa colored and added quickly, "I mean, I just don't think she's right for you, son."

Bret nodded. "I have to agree."

No one spoke for a long moment. Liana felt Austin's presence acutely, as though electricity leapt the small space between his arm and her legs, joining them together.

"That girl Christian worked with was sure nice," Travis said into the silence. "What was her name?"

"Tawnia," Bret answered. "She was very nice. Pretty, too." He frowned and shook his head. "Not that it matters. But Christian would have pointed it out."

Liana was amazed to feel her lips curving in the slightest of smiles.

Clarissa set down her cup. "I'm glad she was with him in the ambulance before he lost consciousness." She sniffed hard as her eyes threatened tears. "She told me at the funeral that Christian told her to tell us how much he loved us." She turned to Travis, her face ashen and etched with pain. "Dear, I'm suddenly very tired. Let's call it a night, okay?"

Travis put his arm around her and kissed her cheek. "That's a good idea. Bret, Liana, if you're staying, would you lock the doors when you're ready?"

"Actually, I was going home tonight," Liana said. "I need some clothes and things. But I just realized I don't have my car."

"I'll drive you," Austin offered, as she had known he would.

"Thank you."

"I'll lock up, Dad," Bret said. "I'll be staying over."

Keenly feeling Christian's absence, Liana hugged her parents and brother goodnight and went outside with Austin, who was carrying the suitcase she had taken to India. Had Christian been here, he would have made them laugh—perhaps after making them angry, but in the end they would have been happy. Liana wouldn't have felt such a huge part of herself missing.

"How can I go on without him?" She didn't know she'd said the words aloud until Austin replied.

"Just one day at a time."

She whirled on him. "What do you know about it?"

"I know that you loved your brother."

"He wasn't my brother!" Anger drove the words. "Or even my cousin."

He blinked. "What?"

"You want to know what I found out in India? Well, I'll tell you. I wasn't born Lara Clari Schrader. Lara is buried in India next to the people I thought were my parents. She was only five months old." Liana held up a hand. "And before you ask, no, she wasn't a twin or an older sister. The ages are all wrong. I have absolutely no idea who I am or where I came from."

Austin glanced over to the neighbor's house where a man stood smoking on his front porch, watching them with undisguised interest. "Let's get in the truck and talk about it."

"You drive, I'll talk." Liana was suddenly anxious to get home. She wanted to light scented candles and soak in a nice hot bath and pretend the past week had never happened. Had it only been a week since she'd flown to India with hope in her heart? Now all hope was dead.

Except for Bret and Clarissa and Travis. She couldn't pretend they didn't exist, not now that she knew she loved them, and they loved her—no matter that she wasn't who they'd thought she was.

On the drive to her condominium, Liana explained to Austin what she had read in Karyn's journal, finishing as they pulled up at her place. Austin turned off the engine and faced her. "That's amazing they would dedicate their lives like that to helping others. I'm sorry I never got to meet them."

Liana was silent. She felt the same, but her emotions were mixed. Their whole lives seemed to be a lie. What had she been to them? *I did live with them,* she thought. *I did call them Mom and Dad. But how?*

"There has to be an answer, of course," Austin said to her unspoken question. He placed his hand on her leg, and she could feel the warmth of him through the black silk dress Clarissa had somehow arranged for her.

"Didn't you tell me your birth father was Romanian?" he asked, looking thoughtful.

"Half. His father was German. According to my mother's—" No, it wasn't really her mother's journal. "According to the journal we found in India, he spoke several languages quite well."

"I know people in Ukraine who speak Russian."

Recalling the orphanages in his video, she shuddered. "I'm going to finish the journal soon. There aren't a lot of entries left, but I have to read each one carefully so I don't miss what I'm looking for—if the information is there at all." She reached for the door.

His hand tightened on her leg briefly before withdrawing. "I'll stay if you want. I mean, if you don't want to be alone."

For a moment Liana was tempted to accept, to subdue her sorrow and uncertainty in his company. Maybe for a while she could pretend that everything was normal. They could watch a movie and fall asleep in front of the TV, or maybe they could sit out on her patio and stare at the stars. She didn't want to be alone. She wanted to feel anything but this all-consuming grief. Who cared if that was unfair to Austin? Yes, she would let him stay and make her forget.

While Christian slept in the cold earth. Alone.

"I think that's exactly what I need—to be alone," she said. "I've been with someone constantly since it happened."

"Liana," Austin's voice was low, "I want you to know how very sorry I am. Christian was a good man, a good friend. I will miss him. If you ever need anything—to talk, whatever, I'll be here."

She looked at him with tears in her eyes, thinking again how Christian had died finding a picture to paint for her birthday. The film from his camera now lay deep in her bag next to Karyn's journal, a constant reminder of her guilt. Why she had asked for it was beyond her comprehension. Its presence only made her grief more intense.

"Thanks for the ride," she said, and before he could reply, she jumped from the truck, banging her arm painfully on the door in the process.

"I'll call you!" Austin shouted after her.

She waved without slowing, and with a sigh opened her door, shutting it firmly behind her.

Diary of Karyn Olsen Schrader
Monday, March 27, 1978

Guenter is making me go with him to Ukraine. He's worried about me because I've lost weight and been sickly. He thinks we need a change of scenery. I'm furious at him for making me leave Lara's grave, but some part of me agrees that something must be done. There is no joy in the world. I love Guenter, but even in him I can't find peace. I still have not written Clari. I hope she somehow understands.

We will be in Ukraine for one year, working at a hospital there. Guenter has been in contact with his cousin, Pavlo, and he has secured these volunteer positions for us. Basically, we will receive room and board, a bit of spending money, nothing more. Pretty much the same situation we have here. I have not worked since Lara's birth, but I guess I will now. Pavlo said they need volunteers. It is difficult because Ukraine is under Soviet rule, and foreigners, especially Americans, are not welcome. But since Guenter is officially a

Romanian citizen through his mother, and Pavlo is his cousin, we are allowed there.

I am leaving everything here except a few of my documents and my clothes. I will return very soon. I must come back to Lara.

The phone rang insistently late Friday afternoon, blotting out the tapping noise Liana was hearing even when she wasn't working on her computer or thinking about her uncertain parentage. Wearily, she let the doll she had brought home from India slide to her lap. Reaching for the phone sitting on the end table next to her easy chair, she wondered if it was Bret asking for the fourth time if she was out of bed yet. Or maybe Austin wanting to go out, or Clarissa asking her to come over. She didn't want to see any of them.

"Liana?" It was Clarissa.

That her adoptive mother used Liana instead of Lara didn't escape her. Was it the first time she'd used the name? "Yes, it's me. How are you?" With one hand she toyed with the doll.

"That's what I called to ask. I thought you were going to come over for dinner today. I expected you here already. It's after five."

Liana sighed. "I'm just too tired."

"You said that yesterday. I'm worried about you."

"I'm fine, really. In fact, I'm about to do some work."

There was a short silence and then, "Did you read the rest of the journal?"

"A little. But mostly I've been catching up on sleep." In fact all she wanted to do was sleep, to slip forever into oblivion that did not hold any pain.

"He's not coming back, Liana." Clarissa's voice was firm, though it held an underlying sadness that bit into Liana's heart. "We have to go on."

What was it about Clarissa that she could find a way to go on? Was it because she was a mother to other children who needed her? Karyn hadn't seemed able to do much of anything after the death of her baby. Her continuing misery was all too apparent in the pages of the journal, a misery Liana now shared. Surely this was a devastation from which no mother— or sister—could ever recover. And yet . . .

"Liana?"

"I know. But I just—" *I just can't seem to function.*

"It's normal to feel depressed, honey. We all feel it—we all miss him so much. It's better that we face it together."

"I know." Liana did feel better when she was with them, and that was precisely why she stayed at her condo. She didn't *want* to feel better. She wanted Christian. She wanted to be Lara. She wanted her life back. Though far from perfect, it was much better than what she had now. If only she had been able to appreciate that before.

"I do have some good news," Clarissa said. "I don't know if he told you, but your young man came by yesterday morning and took a look at those papers we brought back. He's pretty sure they're written in Russian. He may be able to find out something."

"He's not my young man."

"Well, his charity does a lot of work in Ukraine, and he said some of the older documents they deal with are in Russian. So I made a copy for him, and he e-mailed it to an employee of his in Ukraine to see if he's right. And I sent another copy to a friend of mine who works at a university in California. We'll have word back soon if the papers contain anything useful."

Liana swallowed hard. "That's good."

"But Lar—Liana, it doesn't matter."

"I know," Liana whispered, though it *did* matter. When she

and Clarissa were finally becoming mother and daughter, why did Liana feel it was all about to end? Could she save either of them from further anguish?

"Are you sure you don't want to come over? Or I can come there."

"I'll come tomorrow, M—Mom. I need to get a little work done. I haven't worked at all since—" *Oh, dear God,* she thought, lifting her face toward the ceiling, *will I always measure time by Christian's death?*

"You should take some time off. Your dad and I are thinking about going to Bret's cabin for a week or so. We'd love it if you'd come."

"We'll see."

Liana hung up, wondering why she couldn't accept Clarissa's love. They had been so close the past week—a closeness Liana had long craved. Why was she pushing her away now? Was it the same reason she was pushing Austin away?

"Because I need to know who I am." With a sense of desperation, she opened the pages of Karyn's journal, and her mind was immediately absorbed into the life of the woman she had so long believed was her mother.

Before she had finished even one entry, a banging at her front door jolted her from Karyn's life. "All right, all right. I'm coming." She figured it was Bret again; he'd been over three times in the past two days, playing big brother.

She was wrong. Austin stood on her small porch, his black hair looking as though he'd been riding in her convertible. "What do you want?" she asked, without expression.

"Come on," he said. "We're leaving."

"Leaving?"

"I have a surprise for you."

Liana looked down at her blue plaid lounge pants and T-shirt. "I'm not dressed."

"You look fine."

"I have work to do."

"It can wait." He lifted his chin in a way that told her he wouldn't take no for an answer. "What you need is to get away from here."

"You sound like my mother."

"Smart woman. Come on, it's just a drive." He grinned and added, "Please?"

The idea was beginning to appeal to her. "Will I need anything?"

"Well, if you do, I still have your suitcase in the back of my truck."

"Oh, that's where it went." She rubbed absently at a place on her inner left arm above her wrist, wincing when she realized she had a long ugly bruise there, though she couldn't for the life of her remember how she'd done it. "Well, let me at least change into some jeans and grab my purse."

A few minutes later, dressed in black jeans and long-sleeved white T-shirt, she was in his truck, heading for her surprise. They talked easily, and Liana admitted to herself that she had missed him these past two days. Strange that he had become an important part of her life in such a short time. She didn't even want to think what that might mean.

After an hour on the freeway she became suspicious. "How much longer for this surprise?"

"Well, quite a bit actually."

She stared at him. "What?"

"We're going to the farm. Mercedes is expecting us."

Suppressing the brief surge of joy at the idea of seeing

Mercedes and the farm, Liana let herself grow angry. "Who do you think you are?"

He glanced up from the road uncertainly. "Austin?" he ventured, and then, "Hey, your mom wanted you to get away. You said so."

"My brother just died. I should be with my family."

"Then why weren't you?" When she didn't answer, he continued, "Look, I know this is a hard time for you. I was Christian's friend, and I miss him, too. And I care about you. Please let me help."

"You aren't my knight in shining armor, as I keep telling you. I'm a big girl, and I certainly don't need you swooping in on your white horse and whisking me off into the sunset to live happily ever after."

She watched his Adam's apple go up and down his throat as he swallowed. "Not a white horse," he said, shaking his head with mock dejection. "A white truck. And it's not off into the sunset. It's only Wyoming."

Her lips twitched, and she had to struggle to keep a serious face.

He brightened. "I did buy you something, though." Reaching under the seat, he pulled out a sack. "I hope they're the right size."

A large shoe box tumbled from the proffered sack, falling open to reveal a pair of brown leather cowboy boots. She groaned.

"Well, try them on."

"I am *not* wearing cowboy boots. No way, no how."

"Yes, you will. It'll be better when we're riding the horses."

"Horses?"

"I thought it would be fun. What do you think?"

She stared at the boots.

"What if I fall, Daddy?" Liana gripped the horse's mane tightly.

"Daddy's got you. I'd never let you fall." His arms went around her, making her feel secure. She was on top of the world!

She giggled. "This is fun! Can we come again?"

"Sure. When I come back from the villages."

"We planned to go riding the day after they came back," she said to Austin, "but they never came back." Now she finally understood her fear of horses.

"I came back." He met her eyes briefly before returning his gaze to the freeway. "I'll always come back, if you want me to."

She stared at her hands. His words reminded her of Christian and how at the airport he'd promised always to be around. "You may not always be able to keep your promises. Sometimes it's beyond your control."

Austin seemed to understand that she was speaking about something different now, something entirely unrelated to horses. "I guess, then, you just do your best. Now how about a little Kenny Rogers?" He tossed her the CD, and the tension building between them vanished.

"You've got to be kidding. You just played one of your country songs three times in a row. I'll admit Kenny grows on you, but some rock music would go a long way toward a little sanity right now. Remember you could get five to ten for kidnapping if I called the police. I have my cell."

"Did you bring some CDs?"

"You know I didn't."

"Sorry, then."

"Sorry, nothing. We'll listen to the radio." She tried to turn the channel but received only static.

He gave an apologetic half shrug with his left shoulder. "It's broken. Not sure what happened. It'll only play CDs now."

Liana groaned. "Next time we take my car. Not only is it a

lot cooler car—and I don't mean colder—but the radio works *and* it has some good CDs."

"So, there's going to be a next time?" Austin grinned at her.

Liana rolled her eyes and folded her arms across her stomach. "I can tell this is going to be a very long trip."

CHAPTER
26

Diary of Karyn Olsen Schrader
Friday, January 5, 1979

It has been a year since I lost my precious Lara. And still I go on. I don't know how I do it. Guenter has been understanding. I know that he still feels a deep pain regarding our beloved daughter's death, but he is a man and can never know how a woman's heart clings to her child, how all her hopes and dreams revolve around a tiny smile, a sigh, a soft groan in the night as her baby searches for her breast. All that is gone. I keep thinking of my poor baby all alone in that cold grave. Sometimes I feel I'm a walking corpse, lifeless like the still forms of the poor that Guenter and I and the other volunteers have to send to the morgue each week—those that could not survive despite our best efforts. Like Lara. Oh, how much I miss my baby!

The only comfort I find at all is when we visit the orphanages here in town. These are unwanted children, especially those who have been born with diseases. What did they do to deserve *abandonment? Why don't their parents understand that they are gifts from God? I hold them and rock them as we care for them. I thought it would hurt too much when Guenter first suggested that I accompany him, and it does hurt—terribly—but strangely there is comfort, too. I like the baby orphanage the most, where the children up to four years old are housed. When I care for them, it's almost as though I can see beyond the veil of this earthly life into heaven where I must believe my Lara is now. Must believe or lose my sanity altogether.*

I'm not supposed to be allowed in the orphanages at all. The Soviets are afraid that the truth about the poverty and neglect these children endure will make it to the outside and turn world opinion further against them. It's a sad thing to see a country with so many orphans. Don't they understand that children are the future? I know it's simply that the people can't care for so many children, and birth control is expensive, but still I can't understand.

I have not yet conceived. I don't believe I ever will. Lara was my one and only chance at motherhood. I don't even like Guenter to touch me, though I haven't told him so, and I continue to accept his advances. What once was so precious between us now only reminds me of failure.

Austin looked over at Liana, who had curled up on the seat and fallen asleep, her long hair splayed everywhere. Every now and then a lone passing car would light up the cab, revealing her features. She looked much younger now that her brow was relaxed and the sadness in her blue eyes hidden. He hoped he was doing the right thing, taking her to Wyoming. But at least Mercedes could pick up the pieces if it was a failure.

He was so tired he could barely keep his eyes open. He wished for the fourth time since midnight that he had stopped at a hotel. But he had been in a hurry to get Liana to the farm, to have some time with her in case she decided to end their relationship before it really began.

One other thing besides the woman next to him kept him driving. He would have to keep his promise to her, and that meant it was time to go see his father. This trip would help determine not only the direction Liana's future might take but also his own.

A soft moan drew his attention from the road back to Liana. He reached out to smooth her hair, enjoying the soft feel of it against his skin. At his touch, she gave a startled cry.

"Liana? Are you all right?" She didn't answer, and he realized she was dreaming. "It's okay," he murmured. He pulled to the side of the road just as Liana sat up with a sudden jerk. "It's okay. You were dreaming." He flipped on the cab light.

She looked at him, her eyes wide and frightened, hand against her chest. Her breath came in rapid gulps, and he could see her pulse beating furiously in her white throat. He tried to hold her, but she pushed him away.

Then slowly, the confusion left her face. "I—I'm sorry. It's the dream. It's always the same dream."

"What dream?"

"I used to think it came from the time after my parents died, but now I think it was much earlier." She shook her head. "I guess I'll never know."

"Do you remember it?"

"There's a child. She's crying—silently, though—and a woman is consoling her, but she won't stop crying. There's another woman, too, and she's also crying. Then there's this hideous scream that goes on and on." Liana shuddered.

Austin reached out to her, and this time she accepted his embrace. After a long moment, she drew away. They stared at each other, and Austin felt her eyes travel over his face, pausing over his left eye.

"You never told me how you got that scar," she said.

Instinctively, he reached up and felt the old wound that disappeared into the high arch of his black hair.

"I tried to get them rows straight, Father. I did. I can do them over."

"Get out of the way. I'll do it myself."

Not satisfied with Austin's slow descent from the tractor, his father pulled him down by the back of his shirt, letting go before his feet were on the ground. He toppled forward, his head cracking against the side of the machine. Pain shot through his skull. He held his hand against his head, already slick with blood that seeped under his fingers and ran down his face.

His father gave a snort. "Get yourself up to the house. See your ma."

Austin obeyed. Near the barn, dizzy with pain and loss of blood, he'd fainted.

"Austin! Austin! What happened?" Mercedes' anxious voice drove him to consciousness. He was lying on the ground near the barn, his sister kneeling next to him.

"I hit my head on the tractor. Dad. . . ." He couldn't tell her more; his thoughts were all muddled.

Her expression darkening, she took the cloth from the egg basket she was carrying and pressed it over his wound. Austin felt as though all his brains were leaking into that cloth.

"Am I dying, Mercedes?"

"No. You'll be okay." But her voice was scared. "Come on. Let's get to the house. Lean on me." Pain knifed through his skull as he climbed to his feet, feeling as weak as a newborn calf.

Mercedes half carried him in to Mother, who turned pale and took him to her own bed. There, she bathed the wound and made the bleeding stop. Ever so gently, she wiped the blood from his face and hands with a wet cloth. The cloth was rough, reminding him of his puppy's wet tongue, but her touch was much softer, lulling him almost to sleep. Then she set aside the cloth and stroked his cheek with her fingers. He could see through his lashes that her eyes were filled with tears.

When Father came for lunch, Mother was wearing her town dress, her face firm. "You're takin' us in to see the doctor. The boy needs stitches."

"I got work to do."

Mother didn't back down. "I can't drive that old truck of yours, so you're gonna take us now, or I'll find a way to drive it, and I won't be comin' back." It was the first and only time his mother had stood up to his father, and that almost made it worth the pain.

Grandmother arrived at the hospital as they were leaving. Even Austin could see that her eyes glinted with anger as she glared at his father. "If you ever lay a hand on this boy again, I'll sell the farm right out from under you—you do remember who owns it now, don't you? You'll lose it all. I swear to the Lord above that I mean every single word. You may treat my daughter like a piece of manure—she's a grown woman and makes her own choices—but I'll be hanged if I let you hurt my grandchildren."

Austin sighed, pushing aside the memory. His father had never touched him again, but he continued to strike fear into Austin's heart every time he raised his voice.

"Austin, are you all right?" Liana's brow creased with concern.

Austin was tempted to tell her the scar had been the result of an accident, but it hadn't really been an accident. His father had wanted to hurt him that day, perhaps not as badly as he had been hurt, but the intent had been there. Austin now believed that his father might have grown more physically abusive after that day, if not for the threat of losing his farm. That painful, ten-stitch gash in Austin's head might just have saved his life.

"My father pulled me off a tractor," he said. "I hadn't made the planting rows straight enough."

"I'm sorry."

Austin remembered his mother and the way she had cleaned his face. "You don't have to be."

"How old were you?"

"Ten or eleven—I think."

There was a flash of pity in her eyes. "We both have a lot of ghosts to deal with, Austin." She laid her hand on his arm, squeezing briefly. "It's not easy."

"No, it's not." He restarted the engine.

To his surprise, she turned on the Kenny Rogers CD. "I'll never be able to sleep with this racket," she explained, "much less have a nightmare."

"I thought you said it put you to sleep."

"Not anymore."

"I see." For all her protestations to the contrary, he suspected she was beginning to like country music.

"How much longer?" She stared at the horizon, where a hint of light signaled the coming of the sun.

"A few more hours," he said, feeling suddenly wide awake. "But do you mind if we stop for a minute in Rock Springs? There's someone I need to see."

———•———

They had to wait half an hour outside the assisted living facility before the doors opened for the day and they were let into the lobby. When a short, round-faced receptionist with close-cropped hair finally unlocked the door, both Austin and Liana were shaking with cold, unused to such early morning temperatures in Nevada. Neither had brought a jacket.

The receptionist smiled at them, her happy face making up for the lack of warmth outside. "Sorry, I didn't realize anyone was out there. We don't usually get visitors so early."

"I've never been here before," Austin said. "How does it work?"

"Who are you here to see?"

"My father, Jed Walker."

She smiled again. "Come over to the desk, and we'll look up his name. Then I'll show you on the map where his apartment is located. If you want, I could call ahead to let him know you're coming."

"I'd appreciate that." Better not to surprise the old man.

"It is rather early."

"He'll be up. He's used to rising with the sun."

Austin glanced over at Liana as the receptionist looked up the name. "I'll wait here for you," she said. "Unless you want me to come."

Austin was tempted to accept her offer. With her presence, neither man would bring up the past, and Austin really didn't want to go there. But wasn't that precisely why he'd come? To bring up the past and somehow come to terms with it? Still, he wavered—until noticing the deep shadows under her eyes that warned him she'd had enough to deal with recently. "You'd better stay here and rest. I'm not sure how he'll react." He'd heard of men becoming meaner as they grew older, and his father had started out mean. Austin certainly wouldn't put Liana within the man's reach, not in her present condition.

She nodded, stifling a yawn. "Okay."

"Here we are." The receptionist placed a photocopy of a

map on the long desk in front of them. "Just go down this corridor here, turn right, go up one floor in the elevator, and left to room twenty-six. You can keep this map if you like."

"Thanks." Austin moved from the desk.

"Good luck." Liana walked toward a set of couches gathered around a coffee table filled with magazines.

Outside his father's room, he knocked, and the door was immediately opened. A wrinkled old man Austin barely recognized stared at him. He was dressed in a flannel shirt and denim overalls, the uniform he had worn his entire life, though this particular outfit was much cleaner, less worn. The black hair Jed had given to both his children had faded to a dull gray, and his lean figure was bent and stooped. He was shorter than Austin remembered, a full head shorter than Austin, and his pallor was that of a man who spent most of his days in bed. Only the eyes were the same fathomless black—and yet they were not.

"Hello, Father." Austin dipped his head with the barest of movements. Though he knew his father was in his late seventies and had long been in failing health, he was surprised to see him so old and sickly.

"Hello, Son." Jed stepped back. "Come on in."

The studio apartment was a comfortable size, and Austin was glad to see the money he and Mercedes spent each month for his care had not been wasted. The furniture was no longer new, as it had been when Mercedes purchased it over a decade ago, but it was well cared for and clean. There were a few dirty dishes on the counter and a skillet on the stovetop, but those appeared to be from today's breakfast.

"Have a seat." Jed sat in an oversized brown leather recliner, pulling out the footrest. Austin looked at the thin bare feet for a moment, seeming so helpless and frail against the dark leather. These feet did not belong to a man who would pull his son roughly from a tractor or threaten to kick him to kingdom come. Austin's eyes traveled up to his father's face. He didn't sit.

"So you've finally come," the old man said, his voice gruff and hard.

"Yes."

"Why?"

Austin wanted to say that he was forced to come, first by Mercedes and then by his agreement with Liana, but neither was really true. "I want to know why."

"Why what?"

Hurt welled up inside Austin, so deep and wide that he couldn't have stopped his words if he had tried. "Why you were so mean. Why you hated me so badly. Why you left Mother."

Jed's jaw worked several times, as though chewing a wad of tobacco. He started to talk, stopped, and started again. "I don't know."

That made Austin angry. "You don't know?" he sneered. "Then you admit it, at least. That you were a horrible father and you killed my mother."

The old man's jaw worked again. "I *was* a horrible father. Still am. I know I don't deserve you or Mercedes. But I didn't kill your mother."

"Yes, you did!" Austin was not about to back down on this point. "She loved you—you were her whole life—but you left."

Jed came to his feet, fists clenched, but he was still only a shadow of his former self. "I left, that's true. But I did it for her as much as me. I thought with me out of the way, your grand-mother would take care of her. I didn't know she'd go and kill herself."

"You didn't know anything about her!" Austin accused. "You didn't care. You cared only about yourself."

To his surprise, tears glittered in the old man's eyes. "I did your mom wrong. And you." He lifted his head in supplication. "I can't take it back. I would if I could, but I can't." He slumped again onto his chair, his black eyes never leaving Austin's face.

Austin knew then what was different about his father's eyes. They weren't as hard and unyielding as they had once been. They held a deep sorrow.

"I've hated you," Austin said slowly. "All my life I hated you, and I swore I would never be like you."

Jed dropped his eyes to the shag carpet. "Can't say as I blame you."

A part of Austin felt a twinge of pity for him, here all alone, a bitter old man without hope for the future, but the other part wanted to hurt his father as he'd been hurt. Hurt so many times. "I stayed away from drink, found another career— anything not to be like you," Austin continued. "But I haven't been able to move on, either. I haven't married, had a family— I can't tell you how afraid I am that I might someday treat my son like you treated me." Austin's eyes stung with unshed tears. He would not let them fall in front of this man. "I wanted to die too many times to count. Did you know that? Do you even care?"

Jed's gaze rose again to meet his. "I thought I would make you a man. I didn't know that it took one to make one." He shook his head and grunted. "I never was no father to you."

Neither spoke for a long time, and finally Austin sat stiffly on the couch opposite the recliner.

"Thank you for payin' for this place," Jed said, seeming relieved, as though the act of Austin's sitting had partially redeemed him.

"I do it for Mercedes." Austin had been willing to do anything to keep his father away from his sister and her children. Though Wayne had been originally responsible for finding this place for Jed, things had been tough on the farm in the past few years, and Austin had recently taken over the payments completely.

"I know why you done it. I'm still grateful. They have nurses here, and a doctor. A pool and recreation room, too, for those who can use them. And they fix my food if I need them to. I even have a friend or two."

Austin felt a pain in his chest. His father had friends. He was glad—he was—but the memory of his mother in her casket made it hard to feel anything but resentment . . . and regret. He stood as stiffly as he had sat. "I have to go now. I've a friend waiting for me downstairs. We're on our way to the farm."

Jed nodded and came to his feet, this time very slowly, as though his body ached. He shuffled to the door to see Austin out. "Thanks for comin', son." A skeletal hand touched the sleeve of Austin's T-shirt, stroking the material. The hand bore no resemblance to the strong ones that Austin had so feared in his youth. Only the knuckles were as big as before, connected to each other by thin sticks under the sagging, wrinkled skin.

"I meant what I said," Jed continued gruffly. "I can't never make it up to you or Mercedes, but if I could take it back, I would. Somethin' inside me broke when your mother died. I ain't the same. You may not believe me, but it's true. I swear on my own grave, I'd take it all back."

As an apology for years of abuse, it wasn't much, it certainly wasn't enough, but Austin figured that was all he'd ever get. And somehow, it was at least a beginning.

"Maybe I'll come another time," Austin said, though the

very idea made him sad and angry . . . and afraid, but he'd still come.

"Thanks," came the gruff reply. The bony hand slipped from Austin's arm. "And next time bring your young lady the receptionist told me you come with. I promise not to bite."

CHAPTER

27

Diary of Karyn Olsen Schrader
Friday, February 16, 1979

There was a new child at the baby orphanage today—Meka. She came from another orphanage that closed down for lack of funds. I have no idea how long she was there. At least six months, though, according to the director here. Of course, they put her in quarantine as they always do when they get a new child. She didn't even cry at being left all alone but just curled in a miserable ball and sucked her thumb. When I took her out of the crib and held her there was a glimmer of happiness in my heart, as though for that moment I was alive again. She is perfect in every way and beautiful like many of the children here. She is sixteen months old, but she looks much younger. Guenter says she's undernourished, so I gave her some of the lunch I brought for myself. She devoured everything I gave her.

Unlike many of the others who are also kept in cribs all day, Meka has learned to crawl. But not to walk. I doubt she will learn

295

for a long time, being stuck in a crib all day. The fact that she can crawl indicates to me that she may not have been given up by her family as early as many of the others.

I wish a family would adopt her soon, before she is too neglected here, though I'm not sure how likely that is. A boy would have a better chance. Too many Ukrainians remember the famine of 1932–33, when Stalin forced export of grain, leaving between seven and ten million people here to die of starvation. The horror of that cruelty is not lost on me, but the worst of it is that now people are afraid of taking on any added burden—especially a girl who might not be able to pull her weight. If only the Soviets would allow foreign adoptions. I know many Americans would love to take one of these babies home to love.

Liana eyed the horse with mistrust. Up close it was even bigger than she remembered, and she wasn't sure she was up for this venture of Austin's. The sun was high in the sky and the day was bright and beautiful, edged with new green everywhere. Even the mud in the yard outside the barn, caused by rain the previous day, seemed but a cradle for baby plants.

"Maybe we should do this tomorrow," she said. They had arrived at Mercedes' in time for a late breakfast, and afterwards both had grabbed a quick shower and slept a few hours. Then Austin had taken her out to the barn and saddled Setzer for her. When she'd seen the muck in the yard she recanted her vow not to wear the boots he'd purchased for her. Her leather clogs simply weren't practical, and she was afraid they'd fall off. No way would she let pride stand in the way of comfort—and to her surprise the boots were comfortable, much more so than she'd expected from pointed toes.

"But Setzer's dying for a ride," Austin said.

Liana petted the horse's soft brown coat that someone had combed to a glossy sheen. "Setzer can find another rider."

"That's Mr. Setzer to you," Austin said, reminding her of the day she had first met the horse.

Liana tossed her head at Austin, feeling the heavy braid down her back. "That's what I used to call him. If I'm going to ride, I'm the boss, right? That entitles me to be on a first name basis."

"That depends."

"On what?"

"If you really are the boss." Austin's arm went up as Setzer lifted his head high and down again as though nodding in agreement.

Liana grimaced. "Down, Jellybean," she told the dog that had put his paws on her jeans. "Okay, how do I get on?" She stepped closer to Setzer, and his scent filled her nose.

"Hold onto the saddle horn, put your left foot on the stirrup, and pull yourself up, lifting your right leg up and over the horse. Normally, you'd have put the reins up around the horn, but I'll hold them this time just in case."

"Just in case what?"

"Nothing. Are you going to get on? I can get on first, if you want, and ride with you."

"I can do it," Liana said, lifting her chin. She most certainly didn't need him to ride with her. Things were awkward enough between them without allowing his nearness to cloud her judgment. Adjusting the fanny pack Mercedes had lent her, she grabbed onto the horn and lifted herself onto the horse. "Hey, that was easy." Setzer looked around at her briefly but held steady.

Austin handed her the reins, making sure they were knotted together so one wouldn't accidentally slip. "Basically, if you want to go right, pull right, letting the left rein fall against the side of his neck. Do the opposite to go left. Gently, though. He'll know what you want. Pull back to stop. When you want him to gallop, relax the rein a bit and sort of kick him in the sides."

"Kick him?"

"Not enough to hurt, but enough to let him know what you want. Think of it as a tap. Mercedes says Windwalker over there doesn't need much urging—" He motioned to the new white stallion Wayne had bought Mercedes. "But I know from experience that Setzer likes to be sure."

Liana nodded her understanding, though it really didn't matter. There was no way she was going to be kicking *any* horse; she had no intention of galloping.

"Hold steady now while I mount." Austin walked to a post where he had left Windwalker and swung easily into the saddle. "Ready?" He started off in the direction of the road, followed by an excited Jellybean, whose red tail flipped madly back and forth behind him.

"Setzer," Liana said, slapping his neck gently. "Anytime now would be good. Come on, boy." Setzer didn't move. Liana found herself grateful that Mercedes and her boys had gone into town for groceries. Only Austin would see her disgrace. Austin and Jellybean.

Several yards ahead, Austin stopped and glanced over his shoulder. "Coming?"

Jellybean looked at her quizzically, as though wondering what kept her.

"Yeah, I'm coming," Liana called. She lowered her voice. "Setzer, I'm the boss. You know how to tell? I'm not calling you Mr. anymore. So get going." Still nothing. Gingerly she tapped his sides with her new boots. Setzer began walking, and Liana breathed a sigh of relief.

They rode side by side down to the narrow paved road that ran in front of the farm. Austin turned right onto the pavement and after another ten minutes started up a dirt road into some hills covered with trees. "Best place to ride around here," he explained.

Liana was too busy trying to find out how not to jerk up and down so uncomfortably as Setzer walked. Already her bottom was growing sore. Finally, she relaxed and let herself sway slightly forward and up with each step. "I get it," she muttered. "You have to be a boneless fish."

"Huh?" asked Austin, looking as though he'd been born on a horse.

"Nothing."

"This is one great horse Mercedes has here," Austin said. "I can understand why she wanted him."

"You ride a lot?"

"Used to. Riding was one of my greatest joys when I was a child. It was the one place I felt big—taller than my father— and safe." Austin shook his head, frowning. "Sorry, that slipped out. I wanted to leave it behind this afternoon, but sometimes the thoughts are hard to put aside."

She knew exactly what he meant. Christian and that grave in India were never far from her mind. "Thank you for bringing me."

"You're welcome." He glanced ahead at the base of the trees. "This'll be the last chance to run for a while. We can race to those trees. You up to it?"

"Sure." She gripped the horn of her saddle.

"Giddy-up!" called Austin, clicking his tongue. Windwalker

leapt ahead, a streak of white against a background of green. A barking blur of red shot after him.

Liana pressed her heels gently into Setzer's sides. "Come on, after them." Fortunately, Setzer didn't need further encouragement. His stride lengthened, and all at once he was running. At first Liana bobbed up and down like a piece of meat tied to the saddle.

"Go with the horse," her daddy said. *"Like you're a part of it. Lean forward, and lower your head."*

Liana leaned forward and experimented until her backside didn't slam so hard against the saddle. She tried holding her knees more firmly against Setzer's sides. And then suddenly it didn't hurt anymore.

They were flying.

———•———

At the top of the fourth rise, Austin reined in Windwalker, who snorted and tossed his head spiritedly as though begging for another hill to climb. Liana was glad when Setzer stopped walking of his own accord, sides heaving. She was afraid that pulling back on the reins might make even this gentle horse rise into the air and dump her off.

"Look like a good place for a quick picnic?" Austin dismounted.

Still on Setzer, Liana surveyed the soft-looking grasses that covered the clearing. Overhead the tree branches didn't quite meet, allowing the sun in the cloudless sky to filter down and warm them. A few birds sang from the trees, and she saw a little animal scurry over an old tree that had fallen onto a large boulder. Leaves at the top of the trees whispered softly in a high breeze that did not reach them below in the clearing. The smell of the air was sweet and fresh and earthy.

"It's perfect," she said. "But how do I get down?"

"Hold onto the horn and swing your right leg down—the opposite of getting on."

"Oh, I see. Really quite easy." She waited for Jellybean to jump up on her, but the dog had vanished. Liana wasn't surprised; the lazy dog's interest had waned with each mile. "What about the horses? Do we take off their saddles?"

"If we were going to be long, I would. But I promised Mercedes we'd be back by dinner." He tossed her the denim jacket he'd taken from his saddlebag. "Might get a little cold now that we've stopped moving. Good thing I left it at the farm—freshly washed thanks to Mercedes."

She gratefully slipped it on over her T-shirt, rolling up the sleeves, remembering the last time she had borrowed this jacket.

"What's so funny?" he asked.

"I was thinking of the swimming hole. I'd like to go there again before we go home."

He grinned. "So you can let go of the rope again?"

"Hey, it was slippery."

"Yeah, right. Let's see what Mercedes packed for us." He brought out a thin quilt, green on one side and watermelon red with black seeds on the other, and laid it on the grass, followed by several plastic containers and a loaf of bread. Liana, who hadn't felt like eating since that fateful phone call in India, was suddenly ravenous.

"Any chocolate cake in there?" she asked.

"Nope. There's apple pie, though. And fried chicken and potato salad. Oh, wait. Here's your chocolate." He threw her a large milk chocolate candy bar.

301

Liana caught it. Leave it to Mercedes to understand that a woman in mourning needed chocolate.

She settled onto the edge of the blanket opposite Austin. For a while they were busy eating, and only after her second helping of chicken and her third of potato salad did Liana sit back, content. Remembering the chocolate bar, she brought it out and opened the wrapping. "Mmmm," she said, savoring the taste. "A food of the gods. Want some?"

"You still have room?" he groaned, lying on his side next to her, head propped up on his elbow. "I must have eaten enough for a week." But he accepted a piece.

A robin landed on a branch above his head, chirping her song of the day. A butterfly landed near the edge of the blanket and was off again, floating aimlessly like a feather in the wind. "An ant has joined our picnic." Liana flicked it off the blanket.

Austin grabbed her hand and brought it closer, lifting the sleeve of the jacket. Silently, he traced the bruise above her wrist.

"Must have hit it somewhere," she said.

"Looks like one you'd remember."

She shrugged and pulled back her hand. "There's been a lot going on. There's a lot I'd like to forget."

He nodded and didn't pursue the matter. "So did you like the ride?"

She couldn't help smiling. "When we were running, it was like flying, just like you said. Like the swing over your river. Like the picture—" *Oh, Christian's eagle picture!* Why did she have to remember that now?

"What picture?" he asked.

She picked at a few crumbs on the blanket, not looking at him. "One Christian painted for me. It was an eagle."

"I'm sorry."

She looked up at him. "Will it always be like this?" she asked. "When your mother died, did you constantly remember things that reminded you of her?"

He nodded. "Yes, but it gets easier. Time does help— believe it or not."

"He was taking pictures, you know. That last day."

"So I heard."

"They were for me. He was going to paint another picture for my birthday."

Austin sat up and took her hand. "Christian was a grown man, and he should have known better than to climb onto a limb that wasn't safe. It's not your fault."

"I know."

"Do you really?"

She breathed shallowly to stop the ache in her chest. "Yes, but now I wish he'd gone into engineering like Bret. I wish he'd never seen a paintbrush. I wish. . . ." She shook her head and gazed into the trees.

"The pain will go away," he said, his voice scarcely above a whisper. "Not today, not next week, or even next month, but it will fade."

"I know. That's what I'm afraid of."

"Exactly." His longing sigh told her he understood.

She reached for her fanny pack, unclasping it from her waist. "I have the pictures." Developing them was the one reason she had left the house yesterday—that and to pick up milk for the cereal that had been her only food since she arrived at her condo. She'd brought the pictures on Austin's surprise "drive" to maybe show him, as though doing so might some-how help her make sense of them, but she hadn't found the right opportunity. Now she almost wished she had left them back at the farmhouse. There had been only twenty pictures on the unfinished roll—close-up pictures of a bird on a tree branch, a delicate flower, a squirrel carrying something in his cheeks, and even a bee in mid flight. There were four of the Las Vegas valley at sunset, each from a different vantage point. The last two pictures were of a squirrel on a tree branch high above the ground, one with the animal crouching, the other with it leaping across to another tree as though flying. Liana wondered if this last picture was the one he had planned to use for her painting, the one he'd snapped before his fall.

"He was a good photographer." Austin studied each picture. "They feel alive."

The ache in Liana's chest grew larger, too large to be contained, whether in her body or in the entire world. She swallowed hard and returned the pictures to her pack, next to the one of Karyn and Guenter Schrader and the child she had once been. This family photograph now seemed a lie, but she couldn't leave it behind, anymore than she could forget Christian.

"About us," she said.

Austin met her eyes. "Yes?"

"I don't think . . . I mean, I really like you. I like who I am when I'm with you. But . . ." She trailed off, not knowing exactly what she wanted to say.

He shook his head. "No buts. That's where we begin. I know what I want, and I know you can't promise me everything I'd like right now, but I need to know if there's room for me. I need to know if you are going to let the past stand in the way of our future."

Liana thought about that for a moment. "I don't even know who I am. How can I begin a relationship like that?"

"Don't you mean that you don't know who you were?" He

pulled her closer. She could feel his breath on her cheek and wanted more than anything to allow herself to love him. "Whatever you were," he continued, "wherever you came from, you are who you are now." Austin's hand stroked her hair. "Every experience you've had has made you the woman I see right here."

His face was so close she could see every tiny line around his eyes, the beginning of his beard, the scar on his forehead. *I am who I am now,* she thought. That much was true. And maybe that was all she needed to know. Maybe she didn't have to be sure.

Her hands went around his neck, linking at the back. She pulled him close.

CHAPTER

28

Diary of Karyn Olsen Schrader
Tuesday, March 13, 1979

At the baby orphanage today, Meka, the new child I wrote about
before, was just sitting there, looking so sad. Her blue eyes were
focused on the tiny, dirty window, and I wondered how she must feel,
having been raised for a year or so by her family and then left one
day with strangers. The orphanage workers tell me she cries out a
name at night, always the same one—Halyna. I can't imagine her
confusion and fear. I was abandoned by my father, but my mother
and Clari were always there—until I walked away.

I asked if I could take Meka outside (yes, I have learned quite a
bit of Russian now—and Ukranian as well, though use of that language is basically prohibited by the Soviets). The director agreed,
and because I don't really like to be out walking the streets alone, we
arranged for me to take her home for the evening. She was bundled
in so many pieces of clothing that she looked like a little ball. Here
they don't seem to change the babies that often but add another layer

of clothing if they wet. It's one thing I don't understand—that and how they make the babies sit on the toilet for hours after they eat, until their little legs turn purple, in the hopes of toilet training them. Isn't that abuse? Yet I recognize how few the workers and how many the children.

Guenter wasn't with me when I took Meka from the orphanage, having had an emergency surgery at the hospital, and I wondered what he'd say when he came home. But he smiled and played with her. We went out for a walk later, and Meka suddenly froze, staring at a lady. Then she relaxed as the lady passed. I wish I could see her thoughts. Did that lady look like her mother, the woman who had given her away? Was it perhaps her mother, who no longer recognized her own child after so little time away?

After that Meka wouldn't smile or laugh, and she held herself stiff as I carried her, as though she didn't want to get too close. It broke my heart. I wish I could give her what she needs. Maybe a nice family will come and adopt her.

Wednesday, April 11, 1979

I visit the baby orphanage a short time each day now. It takes away from my work at the hospital, but I must make sure Meka is all right. I take her food, and she eats it with an enjoyment that I love to see. But no matter how much I give her, she is still too thin. Since I let her out of the crib during my visits, she's learning to walk now and can take a few steps by herself. On my days off from the hospital, I keep her with me all day and night.

I must confess, I want her. I told Guenter, and he seems happy that I have found something to live for. He has extended our stay a few weeks in Ukraine so that we can try to adopt her. I don't know how it will happen since foreign adoptions are not allowed, but somehow it must. I cannot lose her as I did Lara. The orphanage director has promised to help. If only I had brought Lara's birth certificate. Meka is a few months younger (the records say she was born on October 20th), but perhaps we could pass her off as Lara to get her out of the country. I know that with her dark hair and fine bones she doesn't look much like us, but it might work. At least we have the same color eyes. Whatever, I can't leave her behind. She has brought me back to life, and we are her only chance at a real future.

Friday, June 8, 1979

The director let me take Meka home for good, and she has been with me all week. I love her so much already. I'm so afraid that her birth mother will come back for her, though the director assures me that the mother signed a paper and likely has another child, or more, to care for. I'm working the night shift at the hospital now so that I can stay with Meka during the day. Guenter is with her in the evenings. I can see that he loves her as much as I do.

We have had no luck with the adoption through regular channels, but Guenter says his cousin knows someone who may be able to help get us papers. I am so happy. I know Meka is not my Lara, but she has filled every empty part of my heart. I still mourn Lara, but now I know I can live without her and be happy. Meka has taught me this.

Of course, everything is not easy with my new daughter. She was abandoned, and I think that is what causes her to have such scary bouts of anger sometimes. She has broken every breakable dish we have—she throws them when she doesn't get exactly what she wants. Everything has to be just so with her—her stuffed animals, her blankets, her socks, and even her dish at dinner must be the one she always uses. Sometimes I feel she's testing me. But she is beginning to open her heart to us. Together we will all learn to love again.

Thursday, August 16, 1979

*My heart is pounding with terror and my hand shakes so badly
I almost can't write. At the airport the passport guard did not accept
the letter we had for Meka. He said we could not leave the country
with her because our documents were not entirely valid. Guenter
argued with him in Russian, but the guard was right, and we knew
it. Still, I was not about to leave Meka. She began crying and fussing
as we stood there wondering what to do. Nothing I could do would
calm her—probably because I was crying myself.*

*Suddenly, Guenter plucked her out of my arms and gave her to
the guard. "Fine," he said calmly. "You keep her. We have a plane to
catch." Then he gathered up our documents, took my hand, and
started to walk away. I was pulling against him, unable to believe
his callousness. She was our daughter in spirit, if not biologically.
How could he abandon her? His grip on my arm was like iron, and
I could not break free.*

*Meka was screaming really loud, as though she knew exactly what
was happening. I was ready to start screaming myself when the guard
came around the desk and gave her back to me. "Get on the plane," he
said shortly in Ukrainian (not Russian!). "Do not come back."*

*I held Meka to me and ran. When we got to the gate I saw that
Guenter had tears sliding down both cheeks. On the plane he took
Meka from me and held her tight. "I was so afraid," he said. Then I
understood that it had all been a ploy. He would not have left her
either, but he had hoped the threat would work. Fortunately, it did.*

*We are in the air now, and Guenter is still holding Meka, who
sleeps in his arms. I think it will be some time before he lets go. I
have never loved him more than I do at this moment. Regardless, I
will not feel completely safe until we are back in India.*

Monday, October 3, 1979

I have never been happier. At last we can be a family. We have named our precious little girl Liana Meka Schrader. She seems content with us, except for occasional bouts of anger. The child psychologist that I took her to confirmed my suspicions. He said her behavior likely stems from issues of trust, having been abandoned by her family, cared for by overworked orphanage employees, and then finally coming to us. He said if we continue to give her a secure and loving environment, she will learn to trust us and the episodes should disappear completely. He said it might take longer, though, to get her to stop sucking her thumb! I say, let her have it if it comforts her. She has already endured so much for a small child. If need be, we can scrape money together for braces later.

Guenter is back at Charity Medical, and we are again living with Mamata. She is such a sweet person—a perfect grandmother for Liana. Eventually, when I return to work, she will look after Liana.

I found a letter from Liana's birth family—from a sister. It was with the documents given us by the orphanage. It was received some months after Liana was put into the first orphanage, and it was the last letter or contact from her family. Guenter has made a translation, and I'm including it here because I know someday Liana will want to know what happened.

To my sister, Meka:

Dear little sister, my fifteen years of life has been a tenuous existence, and I earnestly hope that yours will not be the same. If we ever meet again in this life, which will happen only through the will of God, I will have all that I could desire. However, I must admit that I fear the questions you will ask, and if I will be brave enough to tell you the truth about why we gave you up. I write it all down now in the hope that someday you may read it and forgive me.

My father died when I was five, leaving our mother a widow who was very poor. She worked at a packaging plant. Several times she lived with men, searching, I believe, for a husband to take care of us. But always they would leave. She was a hard worker but not very wise when it came to men. She had many miscarriages before you, but when I was fourteen her belly began to swell with new life. I remember my great excitement, thinking I would finally have a brother or sister. There was fear, too, I admit. Mother cried with despair almost daily, wondering how she would feed another mouth.

You were born on a cold day in October. The wind that day was one that penetrated your coat and all your clothing no matter how many layers you wore. Mother was taken with birthing pains during the night, and I was very frightened because there was so much blood. I took her to the hospital, spending all of our savings on a cab. You came before the doctor arrived, but the nurses were prepared. Mother was weak and barely conscious, so I took you in my arms. So tiny, so very, very tiny. But perfect—a miracle. I loved you intensely from the minute I held you. Mother was disappointed that she did not have a boy, for she was certain he would be able to grow up and support us, but she also loved you deeply. Never doubt that. Though use of our language is forbidden by the Soviets, she later spent hours holding you and singing old Ukrainian lullabies. I loved those nights, and I would sit by her feet and listen.

A few days after your birth, Mother went back to work at the factory. I stayed with you, taking you to her for feedings. This went on for about ten months until Mother *became sick and had no milk. Soon she could not work at all, and I began to clean houses to earn money. I would take you with me sometimes. I would worry when I left you with Mother because she was so sick and couldn't take care of you. Sometimes we wouldn't have anything to eat all day. Many times you cried yourself to sleep in our arms for want of food. I could not give you anything because I had nothing to give. On these days my heart broke. I would beg from the neighbors, from restaurants, from strangers in the street—anything to stop your pitiful cries.*

Then we took you to the orphanage. Mother said it was the only way and I believed her. It was a terrible, snowy day in the middle of winter, and we traveled a long way because Mother said she had heard it was the best orphanage. That day the cold lodged in my heart, and it has never left since; a part of me died when I handed you over to the orphanage workers. I cried and you screamed—a scream I will remember forever. I had prayed all the way there that you would get a better life, that you would find a family to adopt you. Then I went home and prayed to die. Without you there was no love or life left in our tiny apartment. But it was Mother who died, and I was left alone in the world. I have lived with our neighbor ever since. She is a stern, unsmiling woman, but she has taught me many things. She has books that she lets me read after I come home from my new job at the factory. I work very hard. I want you to know that I am trying to put away money for school. If I survive, I will come looking for you one day. I will never stop until I die or until I learn that you have died.

I do not excuse what we did. We should not have given you up, but please understand that there was no other choice. You were so tiny—we could not stand to see you die

*for want of food, die before our very eyes. We wanted you
to have a better life—I believe that you will. I have since
heard that many children in the orphanages also die, alone
and afraid, but I pray every day that this will not happen
to you. Mother said it was the best orphanage, and I must
believe her. She loved you as much as I did.*

*Oh, Meka! Please stay alive and be happy. Only then
will my soul finally obtain rest from the guilt that tortures
me. Only then will my broken heart be mended.*

Your loving sister,
Halyna Shevchenko

CHAPTER
29

Diary of Karyn Olsen Schrader
Monday, March 10, 1980

After months of having no luck officially adopting Liana through the U.S. Embassy, we have decided to let authorities think she is Lara. Since Lara died in Germany, not many outside our close circle of friends are aware of her death. I know it's dishonest, but I don't know what else to do. I don't know how an official in his right mind could send her back to Ukraine, but the fear remains like a lump of rock in my stomach. I simply can't lose another precious daughter! Most people we haven't seen in a while honestly believe Liana is Lara anyway, and we don't tell them any differently.

The problem is that we have been calling her Liana (my best friend in grade school was Juliana, and I've always loved the name). I simply can't bring myself to call her Lara, though I love her every bit as much as I did Lara, maybe more. That name belongs to my first child and is hers alone. I guess for now we'll say Liana is her nickname. I'm not sure how we'll explain this to Liana later.

Hopefully, she will be able to understand why we did what we did, or perhaps it will be possible in the future to correct her name officially.

I showed Mamata where I keep my sister's address and Lara's birth certificate. I told her if something ever happened to us that she was to send Liana to Clarissa in the States with Lara's birth certificate. I also told Dr. Raji at Charity Medical to make sure Liana was sent to Clarissa, but I did not tell him about the birth certificate. Strange how the love of a child can change you. I never thought much about my own death before, but now I have someone who depends on me for her care. It is only responsible to have a backup plan.

Of course nothing bad is going to happen. We are going to have a long life together, Guenter, Liana, and me. I've even thought about adopting more children in a year or so. There are many available here, and Liana could use a brother or sister.

A sound behind her came from the back door of the house, and Liana lifted her eyes from Karyn's journal, her eyes and cheeks wet with tears. As she had suspected since seeing the grave in India, Guenter and Karyn Schrader had not been her birth parents, but they had loved her deeply all the same. Deeply enough to risk imprisonment for smuggling her out of a Soviet-ruled country, deeply enough to let her use their beloved birth daughter's name to come to America. Reading of their love made the wound in her heart less painful, if not smaller. *Christian would have loved to know this,* she thought, and the now-familiar agony of missing him rose up within her breast. But this time other memories—of her first adoptive parents, of growing up with Christian and Bret—began to fill the void Christian had left.

"Like some lemon tea?" Mercedes touched Liana's shoulder.

Liana nodded and tried to wipe away the tears. Mercedes

set the tea tray down on the metal and glass patio table and handed her a napkin. "Thanks," Liana said, mopping her face. Beneath the chair, Jellybean shifted his weight against her feet, eyeing her hopefully for a treat. He had been her almost constant companion since she arrived at the farm the day before, and Liana was grateful for his silent presence.

Mercedes sat in the chair next to Liana, surveying the dark clouds billowing in the sky above the barn and the fields. "Good thing Wayne and Austin put a roof on this deck," she said. "I'm not fond of getting too wet, but I love the rain. Especially the smell. Can you smell it—the coming rain? Can you feel the heaviness in the air?"

Liana sniffed and found Mercedes was right. There was a different smell, and the air around them did seem to be moist and heavy.

"My favorite place to be in the rain is out by the swimming hole," Mercedes continued. "Suddenly all the birds and other animals go silent as they hide in their homes. Then come the drops, beating down on the earth and the water. Yet that old tree is so big and the leaves so thick that you can sit on that wide limb and never get wet. Then I take a deep breath. I love the rich smell of the earth as it soaks up the rain."

Liana looked at Mercedes, whose face was tilted toward the dark sky, her eyes closed.

Slowly, Mercedes opened her eyes and turned toward Liana. She motioned to the journal. "Are you okay?"

Liana realized then that Mercedes had been giving her time to recover from her tears. "I discovered that I'm adopted. Not only the once I knew about but twice." She shook her head. "It's a very odd story."

Mercedes smiled. "This is an odd world. But the really strange thing is that sometimes the world's very oddness is what makes it so beautiful." She pointed at a rainbow that showed in the distance behind the clouds.

"It's raining over there?" Liana asked.

Mercedes nodded. "It'll be here soon."

"Have you seen Austin? When I woke up, everyone was gone."

Mercedes grinned. "I made him go to church with us—you were out pretty heavily, so we didn't wake you. On the way home Austin and Wayne stopped off with the boys to make sure the cattle had enough water. Not that they'll need it now."

The rain began to fall, softly hitting the roof of the deck and running off the sides. A mild breeze blew toward them, making Liana glad for the jacket Austin had lent her. She sipped the hot tea Mercedes had brought and nibbled on a piece of delicious banana bread.

"I'm glad we have this moment," Mercedes said. "Austin and I've been talking, and we'd like you to work full-time for HeartReach. We think you could take over some of our part-time employee positions as well as the finances, fundraising, and so forth. Your ideas could really breathe new life into the whole charity. Of course, it wouldn't only be accounting. That's the catch. You'd have to work with all aspects of the charity until we grow enough to hire others. That would require a lot of working with people and organizing. Do you think that's something you'd like to try? We wouldn't want you to feel uncomfortable."

Liana was stunned. She could see that it made perfect sense from their point of view—she was good at finances, where they seriously needed help, and the fact that she needed a job would make hiring her a logical proposition. But it wasn't an option she'd ever considered. She would have to work with people, maybe even visit orphanages. The irony of working with Ukrainian orphans did not escape her.

"I've shocked you, haven't I?" Mercedes made a sound in her throat. "Sorry. I should have led up to it, I guess. But it just seems the perfect solution. You have a lot of talents besides numbers—anyone can see that."

"I just didn't expect . . ." Liana blinked. They could have no idea, of course, of her true heritage. Austin believed the documents she'd brought from India were in Russian, but he couldn't know that the job he offered would be so close to home. Was that fate? Or was it a signal for her to run fast and far?

"I think Austin was afraid you'd say no," Mercedes went on, ignoring her silence.

"And you're not?"

Mercedes grinned. "Not really. I think it's a great opportunity. You need a challenge." She said it in a way that was not condescending or arrogant. Just one friend speaking to another.

How could Liana say no? The urge to refuse weighed heavily upon her, and yet at the same time, she understood this was a chance to change lives. Lives that like her own had been devastated by poverty and neglect. A chance to give back. To make a difference. She could accept and reach out . . . or walk away.

"Austin's great to work for," Mercedes was saying. "You can trust him." The words held an unspoken double meaning.

"There's no telling the future," Liana said. "A person can want to always be there, to do what they've promised, but something can stop them. Look at my parents—my first adoptive parents. And my brother. They're gone, yet they wouldn't have chosen to die." She tucked her feet tighter against Jellybean.

"I can't imagine losing a brother." Mercedes held her hand to her heart. "Growing up, Austin was all I had. If I had lost him then, my world would have ended."

"That's how I feel," Liana admitted. Yet it wasn't quite true. She still had Bret and Travis and Clarissa. And the memory of Karyn and Guenter. Both sets of adoptive parents had given her a good home, full of security and love—though until now she had not recognized it as such. There had been no abuse in her life that she could remember, no indifferent caretakers since the orphanage. And now she had Austin . . . and Mercedes as well. Or could have.

"I do know what it is like to lose someone you love." Mercedes' black eyes were grave. "I wonder, would you rather not have loved him at all? I mean, to save yourself the pain."

"No." Liana blinked back tears, but it was hopeless. They came as though of their own will. She refused to give up loving Christian, just as she would not give up the chance of loving Austin.

"My mother was not a good mom," Mercedes said, "and yet I find I would not trade her for any other." She twisted her lips in a wry smile. "That's what love is, I guess. A risk. Not a guarantee of happily ever after. But it is worth it—even when it's followed by tragedy." Mercedes was gazing out again past the barn in the direction of the trees and the small family cemetery Liana had only seen from a distance. Liana wondered how many others Mercedes had lost besides her mother and grandmother. Suddenly she wanted to know everything; she wanted to be as close to Mercedes as a real sister should be.

"Austin and I," Liana began and stopped. She tried again. "I care for him—more than I want to. The truth is I've never had a relationship that lasted longer than a month. But Austin's different. He wouldn't be satisfied with a month. I knew that when he brought me here."

"That's why he did it, I think."

"Maybe." Liana gave a short laugh that surprised her. How could she laugh without Christian?

"This farm brings out a side of him he doesn't ordinarily show people," Mercedes said. "You're the first woman he's ever brought to meet me. That's how I knew it was serious."

Liana cupped her hand around her tea, letting the ceramic mug warm her fingers. "I didn't know."

"I don't think he did, either." Mercedes leaned over and put her arm around Liana's shoulders in a brief hug. "I'm glad he brought you. I really am."

"So am I."

"Hello, M—Mom?" Liana gripped the receiver tightly.

"Liana!" came the rushed response. "Are you all right?"

Mercedes nodded at her encouragingly before leaving the kitchen. "Yes," Liana said, "but I'm in Wyoming."

"I know. Austin called yesterday."

"Good. I'm glad you're not worrying."

"When are you coming back?"

"In a few days. I'll call."

"Is everything—can I do anything?"

"No." Liana fought tears. "I just wanted to say thank you."

"Thank you? For what?"

"For taking me in. For loving me. And I'm sorry we haven't been as close as we should have been. It's my fault. I guess I was so afraid it would be over again, that I'd lose you, too."

Clarissa was silent for a long moment. "I think I knew that. I was glad you always had Christian."

"He promised never to leave me." Liana was sobbing hard now. It hurt so badly.

"He didn't want to leave. He loved you very much! Like I love you."

The words spread warmth tingling through Liana's heart. "I know. I really do. Look, I'm sending you a copy of the journal tomorrow. I should have given you one before, but I just . . . I needed to find out first."

"But it's okay now?"

"Yes." Liana wished she could hug her mother. "I'll come over the minute I get home," she promised. "But I won't be alone."

"Austin?"

"Well, yeah, but that's not who I was talking about. The name's Jellybean. Mercedes is letting me keep him for a while— maybe permanently, if I can find a place where he'll be happy."

"Who is he?"

"You'll see. It's a surprise." Liana smiled through her tears. There was no way Clarissa could help falling in love with Jellybean once she met him. "I'll see you soon, Mom. I love you."

"I love you, too, Liana."

And Liana knew she did.

———·•·———

Liana looked up from the translation that had come through on Austin's computer. It was from Olya Kovalevsky, the employee she had seen in the orphanage video. Her face came clearly to mind—the blue eyes, heavy makeup, pinched face that bore the mark of hardship. Her translations confirmed Liana's discovery in the journal that she had been born Meka Shevchenko, placed in an orphanage by her single mother. One of the pages turned out to be the original letter from Liana's sister, and the contents had shaken Olya to the point where Austin was concerned.

"I think you should read what she says about the letter," he said, arrowing down to another e-mail.

Liana felt reluctant to read his personal e-mail from the woman, but if she accepted his offer to run HeartReach, she would probably have to get used to doing so. Then again, she hadn't accepted yet. She could still say no.

"It's about her sister." Austin's eyes were on her, kind and warm. "I know this is difficult for you."

"I'm fine." She looked away before he could read the fear in her eyes.

Dear Mr. Walker:

I have been touched to a great degree by the copy of the letter in the e-mail attachment that you sent to me last week. Though circumstances with my sister were somewhat different, so much is similar that this letter could have been written from my own heart. My tears at the orphanage were unending, and my father had to carry me from the place. I ache with this woman who wrote the letter and wonder where she is now. I have found no leads to her. So many died during those years, and I suspect your friend's sister did not make it into adulthood as I did. I hope that my Sveta was as fortunate as your friend to be adopted by a loving family. I have come to realize that it is possible I will never discover the truth about her. I must go on in my life without knowing. I have only the wish that I could believe she forgives me.

Please do not judge me unfit because of this emotion. I am pleased more than I can express for the opportunity to help the children, and I will do my best for as long as you permit.

Sincerely,
Olya Kovalevsky

As Liana read, her fear vanished, replaced by the sorrow Olya expressed. *But it's okay,* Liana thought. *It isn't her fault.*

A flash of memory came: the child crying silent tears in her dream while a woman consoled her, the other woman also crying, the unending scream. All along she had assumed the child in the dream was herself, but now she understood the child had been Halyna, who like Olya had mourned the loss of a baby sister. Halyna who had not wanted to give Liana up. Halyna who had tended her and loved her. And the crying, saddened woman had been her mother. Only the scream had been Liana's, as the orphanage workers had taken her away.

How comforting it had been for Liana to read the letter from her sister in Karyn's journal, to know that she had been loved but that like so many other women at the time, her birth mother had had no other choice. She didn't blame her—how could she? She was alive and well and happy. Even without Christian, the future stretched out before her with more promise than she'd ever thought possible. Too bad she couldn't give some of that comfort to Olya.

Or maybe she could.

With her heart thumping, she copied the e-mail address and began a new e-mail.

Dear Olya:

You don't know me, but I am Liana (or Meka Shevchenko in the documents Austin Walker sent you). I have been offered a job with HeartReach, and I have decided to accept. Likely we will be working together in the future—at least through e-mail. But this is not why I am writing you today. The real reason is that Austin has told me about your search for your sister. I want you to know that your family did the right thing. If my sister and mother had not taken me to the orphanage, I would have died of starvation. I would never have had the opportunity to be where I am today, to have had parents who took care of me as every child should have. It is difficult for me to tell you this, as I am not accustomed to talking about personal matters, but I hope some day we will meet so I can put my arms around you and tell you that your sister was grateful for your love, as I am for that of my sister. Your love went deep into her heart and never, ever left, regardless of what happened around her. There is no blame; there is only where we go from here. I am pleased to be able to work with you and hope that together we can make many lives better.

Sincerely,
Liana Winn

Liana sent the e-mail without pausing to analyze it. Her hands were trembling, and she didn't dare look up at Austin, who had most likely read what she had written, though in her rush to comfort Olya, she had not considered his presence. Finally, she dared raise her eyes to the man that she was beginning to love.

He was smiling as if nothing had happened, though when

he spoke his first words came out suspiciously hoarse. "So, you accept?" He stopped to clear his throat, his eyes saying far, far more. "Really?"

Liana nodded. "I guess I am."

"I'm glad, Liana. For more reasons than one." He pulled her to her feet and into his embrace.

She understood what he meant. At least she'd committed to something—and who knows where that might lead her.

Christian, she thought. *Look at me. I have a boyfriend. And three families who've loved me.*

Of course they loved you, Banana, she could almost hear him reply. *Why wouldn't they?*

Why indeed? As she'd told Olya, the love was inside her heart so deeply that nothing could ever take it away.

Diary of Karyn Olsen Schrader
Sunday, July 27, 1981

My darling Liana will be four in October. Each day she grows more beautiful. I have finally managed to get some fat on her tiny bones, but she will never be as big as her mother. (I confess, I've gained a few pounds—all those delicious balls of rasgulla!). Emotionally, she is doing well. We have not had a tantrum in some months now. When she is awake she doesn't seem to remember the orphanage at all. But sometimes she has bad dreams and calls out that same name. I comfort her and hold her the rest of the night.

Earlier this year I went back to work at Charity Medical. I don't work often or long but enough to pitch in. The women here need me, and Liana has fun with Mamata, who is like a grandmother to her, as I had hoped. Even so, I don't like to be away too much, especially not overnight, and because of this I have cut down my flights to the villages. I go only once a month now.

One big thing remains undone. I need to contact my sister. I ran across her letters this week, tucked in among Lara's baby things. I was going to write last night, but as we watched the sunset on the beach with little Liana between us, Guenter told me that we should visit instead. Maybe for Christmas. It would take all our savings and then some, but after so many years perhaps only a visit will do.

Life is perfect and beautiful, and I am so grateful for every single thing. Strange, but I am even grateful for the trials, because without them I could not possibly understand how precious happiness is. If I died today, I would die content.

ABOUT THE AUTHOR

Rachel Ann Nunes (pronounced noon-esh) learned to read when she was four, beginning a lifetime fascination with the written word. She began writing in the seventh grade and is now the author of more than two dozen published books, including the popular *Ariana* series and the picture book *Daughter of a King,* voted best children's book of the year in 2003 by the Association of Independent LDS Booksellers. Her newest picture book, *The Secret of the King,* was chosen by the Governor's Commission on Literacy to be awarded to all Utah grade schools as part of the "Read with a Child for 20 Minutes per Day" program.

Rachel and her husband, TJ, have six children. She loves camping with her family, traveling, meeting new people, and, of course, writing. She writes Monday through Friday in her home office, often with a child on her lap, taking frequent breaks to build Lego towers, practice phonics, or jump on the trampoline with the kids.

Rachel loves hearing from her readers. Write to her at Rachel@RachelAnnNunes.com or P. O. Box 353, American Fork, UT 84003–0353. You can also visit her website, www.RachelAnnNunes.com, to enjoy her monthly newsletter or sign up to hear about new releases.